THE
GODDESS OF
NOTHING
AT ALL

CAT RECTOR

First printing October 2021

Edited by Charlie Knight
Cover Art by Grace Zhu
Cover Text Design by Cat Rector
Interior Formatting and Design by Cat Rector
Viking Era Ornaments by Jonas Lau Markussen

Further contact information for contributors can
be found at the back of the book.

ISBN 978-1-988931-08-1 (paperback)
ISBN 978-1-988931-10-4 (hardcover)
ISBN 978-1-988931-09-8 (ebook)

www.catrector.com

To the people who wouldn't let me quit.
I tried to tell you I wasn't a real writer. You didn't believe me.

Thank you.

"Because you don't notice the light without a bit of shadow. Everything has both dark and light. You have to play with it till you get it exactly right."

— Libba Bray, *A Great and Terrible Beauty*

TRIGGER WARNINGS

Don't let the beginning fool you. This is not a soft book. I don't shy away from challenging topics, and many of my characters will be pushed to their emotional limits.

This book may not be for you.

The book features scenes of:
Vulgar language
Gratuitous violence and torture
Mental, emotional, and verbal abuse
Unhappy situations for LGBTQA+ characters
Mentions of sexual coercion and rape
Death and violence involving animals
Discrimination and fantasy slurs
Death

An extensive list of warnings, tropes, and representation can be found on my website, CatRector.com

Don't forget to hydrate.

PREFACE

At the time of publication, we have no real record of who Sigyn was or what role she played in Norse Mythology, except for a single story in the Eddas that barely acknowledges her existence. This work of fiction is inspired by the few facts that we have. I've done my best to be accurate and respectful to the subject matter by doing countless hours of research, but I'm no scholar and this is no historical text. In order to make the story flow, I've had to add, subtract, and fudge the numbers, but I've done so in a way I hope is forgivable and enjoyable. Nearly every god portrayed here comes out tarnished, but this is, after all, a story of moral ambiguity.

More than anything, I've strived to claim a spot for Sigyn that doesn't relegate her to the role of battered woman, child bride, or some of the other...less kind narratives.

If you're new to the Norse myths and would like more resources, I've included a list of research materials in the back. You can also find recommendations for other works of Norse fiction on my blog via my website, CatRector.com.

Also, this book has been written and edited in British English. Don't worry, I can spell.

Usually.

Unless we're spelling Definitely. Then it's just chaos.

CHAPTER ONE

*"Odin has many names; Hangi, Grimnir, and Allfather
among them. He created the realms and those that dwell in
them. He has many children, who are each powerful gods in
their own right, and all of them are sons."*

—*Asgard Historical Records, Volume 1*

They say it's courageous to persist in the face of overwhelming odds, but whoever said that obviously wasn't dealing with Odin.

A cloud of dust kicked into the air as I swung down off my horse and landed on the stone with a thud. I straightened my skirts, the gold-embroidered navy blue discoloured with blood and dirt. There was a tear in one of the sleeves, the low collar drooping to one side. Remnants of a mission gone awry.

Odin was off his horse a moment later, stomping towards Valaskjálf. If I let him, he would disappear into the corridors of his great hall, into one of his many rooms, and I'd never find him. It was one of his tactics to avoid my questions, that much I knew by experience.

"Father." I tried to appear calm as I strode beside him, attempting to keep up with his long gait. I knew the answer like I'd known it every other day, but I asked anyways. "So? What do you think?"

Odin huffed, taking the first of several stone steps up into the double doors that opened into Valaskjálf. The hall was decadent, like Odin himself, made of grey and white stone, and trimmed in gold like he would never run out of it.

I cleared my throat. "All things considered, I think it went well."

"If things had gone well, we'd have come home with treaties, not bloody clothes."

I hiked up my skirts to keep from tripping; he was picking up speed. "There was never going to be a treaty, and you knew it the whole time. It was just another grab for power from idiots who think they can defeat gods. Their choices have nothing to do with my competence."

I gave him a moment, and when it was clear he wasn't going to respond, I tried again. "I think I did well. None of your men were killed, I healed every wound before the ride home, and my shields provided more than ample cover—"

"You were sloppy." Odin rounded a corner.

If I weren't accustomed to that kind of insult from him, the words might have stung. "I was not. I did everything right. What more can I do to please you?"

Odin ground to a halt, turning to glare at me with that single piercing eye. His salt-and-pepper beard was wilder than usual. He folded his arms across his broad chest, the armour glinting silver and rust-red where today's blood had dried. A splatter had even made it up to the leather patch that covered his missing eye. "Sigyn, stop interrogating me every time I bring you anywhere. You think you're ready for a title, but you're not."

I flexed the fingers of both my hands, breathing as deeply as I could manage. "And why not? I've worked harder than anyone else had to. All Thor did was break one Jotun skull, and you gave him everything he ever wanted. The Trickster has a title, and he's *exiled*. So please, tell me why I don't deserve one."

"Because you're not ready. Be patient." He started to walk away.

I moved in front of him. "Last week you told me to be more assertive. Last month you wanted more dedication to my studies, and the month before that, you said I was spending too much time in my books. You don't really have a reason, do you?"

Odin stepped toward me. I'd been alive for nearly eighty years, but he was still wagging his finger like he was scolding a child. "You don't have a title because I haven't given it to you, and you won't have one until I see fit. You're impatient, demanding, and too sure of yourself. If I hear another word about this, I swear by the Nornir, I'll have you fed to a troll."

He whipped past me and stormed away.

It was all I could do to keep my feet planted. My whole body itched to run after him, to berate and beat him until he gave me what I wanted. The frustration built under my skin until it burst from me in an exasperated scream. My voice echoed off the cavernous walls, decades of frustration boiling over. But he didn't turn around.

It didn't matter. This wasn't the end of anything.

I turned around and headed back out of Valaskjálf. Odin's halls were the centre of the city of Asgard, and there were so many other places I could be. Anywhere else.

The Goddess of Nothing At All

Looking up, my eyes fell on Yggdrasil, the World Tree. The branches spanned out over most of the stone and wood city, so tall and all-encompassing that the clouds played among the leaves. Every time the breeze caught the tree, it shimmered jewel tones, pinks and purples and blues. And, as usual, that's where I went.

I followed my feet into the busy streets, past horses and carriages, travellers and locals. I pushed my way through the market, where the stalls were selling all manner of wares to Elves and Humans and Jotnar of all shapes and sizes. Each familiar tavern and tannery passed in a blur as I wove through the streets, and by the time I'd reached the outer edge of the city, my rage had started to fade.

The bluster left me the way it always did, and the slow certainty crept back under my skin. The overwhelming knowledge that Odin had all the power. That he was not one to be swayed once he'd made up his mind. And I was at his mercy.

What play could I make if he held all the dice?

As I passed the last homes on the edge of the city, the view ahead became a wall of leafy woods, each of them rustling in the breeze. To the left was a well-worn path that led into the forest, and I stepped onto it, grateful for the familiar scent of soil and greenery, the scurry of critters, and the trill of birds. A balm for my heart.

The path let out into a clearing a few minutes later, and everything was as it should have been. In the middle of the grass sprang an enormous tree trunk, so wide that it took a full minute to walk around it. Yggdrasil rustled above me, tossing in the wind and letting sunshine dance on the grass.

Tucked up against the treeline of the forest was Idunn's tiny wood cabin, nearly obscured by the flowers she'd planted around it. The flourishing garden, full of fruit and vegetables, was larger than the cabin itself.

Laughter rose up from the direction of Yggdrasil. Wooden scaffolding was pressed against the side of the trunk, a series of platforms and ladders all for the purpose of plucking golden apples. The voices were coming from up there.

I trekked across the grass, skirting around the four deer who lived at the base of the tree, each of which refused to budge an inch. The first step I took onto the ladder shook the scaffolding, and the voices quieted. A head peeked over the side, alarmed, but the moment her eyes caught mine, Idunn's face lit up.

"Sigyn! You're home! Come up, and tell us about your trip." Her sky-blue eyes danced with excitement and her single thick, blonde braid dangled in the air, laced with white flowers. She held her hand out to hoist me up.

Idunn settled onto her knees, careful to avoid the blanket laid out with food. The platform was tight with the three bodies and the lavish spread crammed onto it, so I sat with my legs close to me.

3

"I see you two have been keeping busy without me." I scooped up a handful of nuts and berries from their picnic.

Freya was next to me, sitting cross-legged in a casual violet dress. Normally, she was a woman of two sides: extravagant jewelled gowns or shimmering plates of armour. She pushed her flowing auburn hair back behind her ear, and my breath caught. A motion so simple shouldn't be so alluring, but she wasn't called the most beautiful woman in all the realms for nothing.

"The world doesn't stop just because you leave." There was bite in Freya's playful tone, and it reminded me immediately that beauty isn't everything. "Who else was going to eat all this cheese?" She reached out, the broad muscles in her arms flexing and relaxing under the sheer fabric of her sleeve.

Idunn looked me over, taking in the blood and dirt on my dress. "I take it things didn't go well?" Her lips knotted up in a frown, a look that was out of place on a woman who was made of softness.

"Let me guess," said Freya. "It was a trap."

I rolled my eyes. "It's always a trap, isn't it? I don't want to say that all trolls are mindless, but there seems to be a pattern."

"And you missed us so terribly that you couldn't even wash the musk from your body before you visited?" Freya smiled crookedly as she filled her cup with Elven wine and passed it to me.

"Pour a bucket of water over my head if you think it'll help." I took a hearty drink, wondering for the hundredth time what Idunn saw in Freya. But they were both staring, so I answered the silent question. "He turned me down."

Idunn put her hand on my knee. "I'm sorry. I shouldn't have encouraged you to ask again." She sighed. "It's just…I thought with all the training you've done and the end of this newest apprenticeship…" Her gaze fell from mine. The sadness on her face brought tears to my eyes.

I squeezed her hand. "As if any of this could be your fault. If it weren't for you, I'd have given up decades ago."

Freya snorted. "I don't see how he can keep denying you. No one else had this hard of a time."

I made a face, not sure if I should take that as comradery or an insult. "Maybe he's run out of titles and can't admit it. Even if the youngest gets the scraps, you'd think he'd make me Goddess of Sheep Herding or something." I drained the wine from my cup and held it out for a refill, which Freya obliged.

Idunn started to shuffle her bottom toward me, and I held out a hand to stop her. She meant well with her kind words and cuddles, but I couldn't stand the pity. I wanted to go back to my hall, get very drunk, and cry where no one could see me. So, I swung my legs over the edge of the platform, making an attempt to leave. "I'm going home. No sense in ruining your sunny afternoon with all my clouds."

"Nonsense, I love complaining about Odin. It's almost a hobby at this point." Freya took back my cup and gave me a sincere smile. "Things will work out. He's a crotchety old man, but he has to give in sometime, right?"

I nodded, tears blurring my eyes. I blinked them back and fumbled my feet onto the rungs of the ladder. "I'll see you later." I kept my eyes on my descent as they said their farewells.

By the time I was on solid ground, the tears were streaking over my cheeks, and I was trying to hold back that annoying inhale of breath that would give my crying away. I strode across the grass, wiping them away and wishing it wasn't such a long walk back to the centre of the city. It wouldn't help my case if Odin found out his only daughter had been caught weeping in the market.

I was nearly at the path when Idunn called out behind me. Her always-bare feet clapped against the grass as she ran. Damn. I tried to compose myself and turned to face her. Her white dress billowed out behind her, making her look ethereal as she passed through a patch of sunlight. There was a golden apple in her hand.

"You didn't need to bring that." I gestured to the apple, trying to seem happy. "You gave me one last week. I know I look horrible today, but I don't age *that* quickly."

She stopped in front of me and held it out. "It's not for you. I...I have an idea. I've thought about this a lot, but I know there's a price to pay for offering it, so I waited. I thought that Odin would come to his senses a long time ago, but he hasn't. So...I know someone who might be able to help you."

I sighed. "I've tried everyone and everything. You have no idea the lengths I've gone to for this title. Who could possibly be left?"

Idunn's fingers tapped on the apple. She hesitated. "You know how each month I take a walk to the woods on the border of Asgard and Jotunheim?"

My eyes darted open. "You can't be serious!"

Idunn hushed me. "Not so loud. If Freya finds out what I'm telling you, she'll lock you in the dungeons before you have a chance to think it over." She held out the apple and waited for me to take it. When I did, she wrapped her hands around mine. "He is many things, Sigyn, but he's not as bad as they say."

"Then why do they call him Trickster and Silvertongue as if they're afraid to say his name out loud? Half of the city thinks those woods are cursed because of him. He stole, lied, cheated—"

"You weren't here in those days, but I was. If there was something to be afraid

5

of, do you think I'd go out there alone?" She stared into my eyes, all compassion and urgency. "Think of the stories you've been told. Power like that could change things for you. He's complicated, and doing this could land you in trouble, but he knows how to use seidr in ways that most of us never will. It could be just what you need."

I looked away, my eyes searching the clearing as if the answers lay between the blades of grass. The Trickster had been exiled before I'd been born. People said he could walk on air, shapeshift, control the elements. Freya swore up and down that he had once broken into her chamber and stolen the necklace from around her neck while she slept. He'd been gone from the city for nearly a hundred years, and the tales had only grown with time.

Idunn pulled me out of my thoughts. "Give him the apple and tell him I sent you. If you enter the forest near the boulder at its edge, then follow the river, you'll find his cabin. But please, wait until morning. The woods are thick with wolves, and I don't want you getting caught off guard."

I took a deep breath, my mind working over the details. Aligning myself with the Trickster behind Odin's back was a bad idea. But when was the last time anything had sounded this promising? How many more decades could I spend studying botany and war history with no end in sight? I was calculating the distance to the woods when Idunn shuffled her feet and turned to leave.

I grabbed her hand. "Thank you. I have no idea what's going to come of it, but I'll find out tomorrow."

She smiled, a look so warm and contagious that it spread to my lips as well. "Be safe, Sigyn. And say hello for me." She gave my hand a squeeze, then pranced her way back to Yggdrasil.

I turned and walked down the path as fast as I could without breaking into a run. My heart was thumping in my chest, my mind racing in every direction. Another chance. I wasn't proud of the lie, but I'd run out of patience years ago.

A couple of wolves were hardly going to stop me. I was going tonight.

CHAPTER TWO

*"From this day forth, the God of Lies will be exiled from
the city of Asgard. If spotted within these walls, citizens are
expected to report the incident immediately. He may appear
in many guises, so remain vigilant..."*

—City Notice - Historical Archives

The mountains of Jotunheim loomed in the distance, grey and peeked with ice. The sun was disappearing behind them, seeming at first as if it were being swallowed by an enormous wolf, orange and red filling the gaps between its teeth. Below that, the forest stretched out before me, already bathed in shadow.

I dismounted at the tree line and tethered my borrowed horse to a strong branch. I checked everything again—an axe on my belt, rations in my bag, my thudding heart in my chest. Though there wasn't a soul around to see, I put on a brave face and stepped into the underbrush.

There didn't seem to be a path, and no wonder. I'd heard the city folk say the woods were full of beasts and spirits, and the Trickster was the worst of them all. He was the god so full of spite and treachery that Odin had cast him out of the city. The thought brought a lump to my throat. I tried to swallow my nerves down, reminding myself that time makes mountains out of molehills.

It didn't line up. Idunn had told me about her visits before; she always reserved a whole day for her journey, not because of the length of the walk, but because she stayed for supper. If he were so evil, why would he cook for her? How could he be both these things?

The forest underbrush was thick and uncomfortable to navigate. After a while, the last of the sunlight faded until there was only black sky visible through the cracks in the treetops. I hit my toe on a rock, cursing. I couldn't afford to twist my ankle on a root or wander past the cabin in the dark. I'd need a light.

I took a deep breath and cupped my hands in front of my mouth. I pressed myself down, grinding the soles of my feet into the soil. Energy lived in all things, and those who practiced seidr knew how to find and harness it. I called upon it, and it came, sliding up through the soles of my boots, warmth slipping under my skin. Gooseflesh crept across my arms, a long-familiar sensation. I whispered the runes for a lantern, letting them slip over my tongue and across the barrier of my lips without a sound. My breath escaped as wisps of light, flowing slowly into my cupped hands, turning round the shallow space until my palms were full, a ball of light coursing and churning. The lantern remained after my whispers stopped, casting just enough light to see by.

Carving a straight line through the trees was nearly impossible, but I tried, always listening for the rush of water. The woods were black, and the silence was only occasionally pierced by the scurrying of something in the brush. There was so much I couldn't see, and the fear of it settled into my chest. Anything could be out there. A rustle in the trees could be a squirrel *or* a bear.

My mind raced. Idunn had told me not to come so late in the day. Perhaps I was a fool to have come out here at all. I wanted my title more than I wanted the air in my lungs, but maybe this was too far. Maybe there was a reason that—

Crack.

Something was behind me. I whipped around to face the noise. There was nothing but darkness in the distance, my lantern unable to pierce it.

Crack.

This time from the side. Again, there was nothing. Whatever was out there was keeping out of the light. I tossed the lantern into the air above me, where it stayed suspended. I pulled the handaxe from my belt, the weight of it reassuring in my hand.

"Show yourself," I snapped, turning a slow circle, watching the trees for some indication as to who or what had found me. The answer came not as a word but as a low, rumbling growl.

Wolves.

One growl became two, then three, half a dozen, more, until I wasn't sure where one started and the other began, circling around me as I turned. I could fight off a few, but this…this was a problem.

The light caught a pair of bright yellow eyes as they took a step closer. From the corner of my vision came another pair. Another crack behind me. I planted my feet firmly and slowly raised my palm out in front of me, whispering. A glimmer surrounded me, like the glint of sunlight on ice.

The wolf in front of me gnashed its teeth and leapt forward. Its body crashed into the barrier I'd summoned, and it fell to the ground in a stunned heap. Another lashed out, clawing at the invisible wall, tearing gashes in its surface. The barrier had bought me a moment, but nothing more. I let it fall.

I swung hard, bringing my axe down on the head of the confused wolf. The blade lodged in its skull. It crumpled into a heap, and I pushed down on its body for leverage, prying the axe back out. Blood poured from the wound, and bits of gore stuck to the blade. There were at least two more, and I needed to get out of danger.

Pain shot through my calf, and I screamed. One of the wolves had bitten into my leg, its teeth caught in material and flesh. Enraged, I beat the wolf's head with the blunt side of my axe. Bone cracked under the blow, but its jaws only clamped down harder. I screamed again and drove the handle into its eye with all the force I could muster.

The wolf collapsed, releasing me. My knee gave out, and I dropped down beside it, something warm and wet seeping down my leg. I pulled the axe back up, ready to fight, the pain twisting through me. The burning ran up my leg and down to my toes. My vision swam. I blinked and pushed it away. This wasn't my first wound, and it *would not* be what killed me. Not if I could help it.

A new wolf came out of the darkness to take the place of its fallen friend. There were more. How many could there be? What if I bled out alone in these woods? They were coming, they were coming—

Teal flames lit the air within the darkness of the trees, flashing bright and then burning out almost immediately. Only seidr wildfire could have a colour like that. One of the wolves yipped and cried out somewhere in the darkness. Branches snapped as something approached. A growl rose up from behind me. I turned away from the flame to face the next hungry maw, and I stumbled. My head was spinning again.

Focus. Kill the wolf and live.

It stalked closer, and I drew back my axe to strike.

A ball of teal flame hit the wolf, setting its fur ablaze. It yelped and jumped back, falling to its side to try to douse the fire. The sound of boots stopped behind me.

A man, towering over where I knelt, flame-red hair falling over his shoulders in waves, skin as pale as ice. A Jotun. Tall and lean, his open palm full of wildfire. It was *him*. It had to be.

More growls came from the darkness. I crawled to my feet, all my weight on my good leg.

The Trickster's gaze travelled to the bloodstain on my trousers and back to my eyes. "Let's end this, shall we?" His voice was low and coy, a small smirk on his lips.

9

I nodded, gritting my teeth against the pain. The Trickster's lips began to move, no doubt summoning up his own runes. The wildfire in his hand churned, and with one swooping movement, he lobbed the flame at the ground. It hit the dirt and burst upward, illuminating the woods like a lightning flash. I covered my face with my arm, the heat of the fire bursting against my skin. Chaos fell through the ranks of the wolves as they leapt back, whining and screeching. Then they were gone, three more wolves disappearing into the trees.

The Trickster flicked his wrist, tightening his open palm into a fist, and all at once, the enormous flame died out. All that was left was the blackened ground and the soft lantern light that shone down from above us.

Exhaustion swept over me. My leg started to give way again, but an arm caught me as I fell. The Trickster held me up, shifting my body like I was a ragdoll. My face was nearly pressed against his chest. He smelled like honey and cinders. I looked up, hazy. He was at least a head taller than I was. Small for a Jotun, really. And his face…it was sharp. Like a knife.

He settled me back onto the ground, and the pain of it shocked me back to my senses.

"Don't think me too untoward, but I need to see your leg." The Trickster knelt down in front of my feet, hands firmly planted on the ground next to him.

My head felt thick, but I managed a nod. I carefully pulled the leg of my trousers up over my calf. The bite was deep, made of dozens of punctures on either side of my calf, each running with blood. My skin and the leather of my shoes were painted red. My stomach lurched. I preferred my blood on the inside.

The Trickster pulled a knife from his belt and cut a long chunk of fabric from the bottom of my ruined travelling cloak. "We'll need to get you to my cabin. I have supplies there." His fingers brushed the underside of my calf, holding the fabric in place as he wrapped it around. I cried out, the wound burning as he tightened it. "It needs to be done, if I don't—"

"I know. I'm a healer," I hissed through clenched teeth.

He paused for a moment. "Good." His hands deftly wrapped the fabric around and under and over. "I am not. You can get yourself in working order once we've cleaned it out. Don't want to get slavering sickness." A little smirk played on his lips, his emerald eyes on mine. He tucked the last piece of fabric into the binding. It was already soaked, nearly black. "Are you ready?"

I nodded. He stood and took my hand, pulling me to my feet. I readied myself to lean on him and stumble my way to the camp, but he bent down and picked me up before I could so much as protest.

"What are you *doing?*"

"You'd rather walk?"

I wouldn't, no.

He pushed his way through the trees, into the blackness of the forest. He skirted between bush and branch with long strides, careful not to hit my legs on anything. Meanwhile, I was cradled against the chest of a stranger, one who was possibly very dangerous, and bleeding out through my leg. It might've been awkward, if I'd felt well enough to care.

There was a tiny pinprick of light in the distance, glowing teal. "I suppose that's your cabin."

"It is."

"Naturally I'd get attacked two minutes from the place I need to be. Why not?" I hissed as another wave of pain rushed up my leg.

"That tends to happen when you travel in wild places in the middle of the night. Why did you?"

I cleared my throat. This hadn't been how I'd planned to ask him. "I was looking for you."

"For me? Well, isn't that interesting." He laughed, though I wasn't quite sure what was funny. "I wonder if that makes you very brave or very stupid."

I bristled at the comment. "Excuse me?"

"I'm sorry; I assumed you'd heard of me. Loki Laufeyjarson, Trickster, God of Lies, Sky Treader, Silvertongue, disreputable male völva, master to the beasts in the woods and eater of babies. Pleased to meet you."

"Eater of babies?"

"Ah, that one didn't stick? Too gruesome, I suppose. You can only spin so many tales before they become too tall. And for the sake of honesty, I also don't control the *beasts.*"

I tried to make out the features of his face, but I couldn't see anything but the outline of his sharp jaw. "You started those rumours?"

"Of course. It ensures a certain amount of peace and quiet."

Loki stepped out from the brush and into a clearing. The teal campfire roared in the middle, illuminating part of the small clearing. A pair of wooden benches sat at the fire's edge, and the barest outline of a log cabin was tucked into the shadows. He hurried me over to the fire and sat me down on one of the benches.

"Lucky for you, I keep a large stash of alcohol." He left, bounding his way up the stone path to his cabin.

Pain shot through me again as I pulled my leg up onto the bench. There would be no getting around it. I found the end of the fabric and started to unwind it, gritting my teeth to keep from crying out as it peeled away from the wound. The bleeding had slowed, but red was still seeping down my calf. I pulled my bag from my back and rummaged around for my water skin. The water burned the moment it hit the open wound, and I tried not to scream. I breathed deeply, exhaling through my teeth. After I gathered my wits again, I leaned toward it, twisting my leg at odd angles, looking for anything lodged in the flesh that didn't belong.

Loki's boots crunched down the path toward me. He handed me one of the two dusty glass bottles in his arms. It was already open, and as I put it to my lips, I caught the smell of spiced honey mead. I gulped down a few mouthfuls.

Loki sat down next to me. "Let me look." It was hard to see inside the wound, so I was in no position to argue when he lifted up my foot and placed it on his leg, my knee propped up across his lap. My white-knuckled hand gripped the side of the bench as he used the tip of his knife to edge pebbles out of the tooth marks.

I poured more mead down my throat. "Is it clean?"

"I think so," he said, taking another look.

I poured the mead over my leg, soaking both of us. There was no holding back that scream. The alcohol burned into the wound, my vision darkening. Hands clasped my shoulders as I wavered. The bottle dropped from my grip and clunked against a rock. I blinked away the darkness, coming back to myself.

"Breathe." His voice seemed far away, only a low whisper. "Are you able to heal yourself?"

I forced myself to focus. If I couldn't concentrate, there would be no way for me to fix the wound. I took a few deep breaths and held my hands over my calf. The first runes I whispered weren't correct; I knew it as I spoke. Another attempt left me with that familiar warmth under my skin as I drew up energy from the ground. This time was right.

Loki's hands stayed on my shoulders, steadying me as I worked. I kept whispering, using runes to protect against sickness, bind tissue, and grow skin. The pain was lessening, little by little. The holes became shallow, the blood stopped leaking, and eventually, all that was left were faint silver scars in the shape of a wolf maw.

When I was finished, every part of my body was aching for me to lie down. I stretched out my leg, removing it from its awkward placement on Loki's lap. At least I was whole again.

"Impressive," Loki said, turning toward the fire and pulling at his mead-soaked trousers. "It's been a while since I've seen seidr like that."

"I could say the same for you." I pulled my torn, stained trouser leg back over my calf. "That wildfire was extraordinary."

"Just an old trick." Loki picked up a still-corked bottle of mead from beside him and pulled it open. He took a drink. "So, tell me, which goddess are you?"

I froze in the act of examining the damage done to my clothing and looked up at him. "I never said I was."

He started counting on his fingers, holding up another for each point he made. "The common folk don't wear such extravagantly embroidered cloaks, especially out to the woods. Your seidr is far more complicated than what they use for weaving and home-making, and, if my lipreading is still accurate, you used some of the same healing runes they use in Asgard's infirmary. Not to mention, you knew where to find me."

"You're jumping to a lot of conclusions." I crossed my arms and stared at him.

"And how many are true?" When I said nothing, he continued, "Polite society demands a name, goddess, especially since I helped drag you out of the woods."

I sat straighter, as if I could somehow give an impression of grace after everything that had happened. "Sigyn Odindottir."

Loki barked a laugh. "Oh, I should have guessed. You don't look much like him, though. You're a bit more darkly complected. Thicker hair, friendlier. Two eyes."

I bristled, pushing down the comments that came to mind. My features had always stood out in the halls of fair-skinned and smooth-haired gods. I looked more akin to the ebony Elves than the Aesir. My mother had been a human woman from Midgard, someone who had had the bad luck of catching Odin's eye.

"You're very condescending for someone who lives alone in the woods." I glared at him, refusing to break the stare.

Loki just smiled. "Fair enough. Now, what is it you want from me?"

I tried to loosen my tensed body, shifting myself to the far end of the bench. "You asked me which goddess I am, but I'm only a goddess by birth. Odin refuses to give me a title and make it official."

His brow arched, and he leaned forward, elbows on his knees, waiting for me to continue.

"I want to buy a favour. Odin says I'm not ready, even though I've spent decades studying everything I can. I'm a warder, disenchanter, curse breaker, and healer. Hel, I even tried to learn smithing in case *that* was what made the difference, but nothing's worked. I've heard the stories. Maybe you can teach me something that will change his mind." I took another drink, finally feeling the warmth of the alcohol under my skin, softening the edge of the world just slightly.

"You want me to be your teacher? Ymir's breath, if someone had told me when I woke up this morning…" Loki took a long drink of mead. "You understand that whatever Odin says is law, don't you? If you think he's stubborn now, what do you think he'll do when he finds you tangled up with me against his wishes?"

I stood up and walked to the other side of the fire, my tattered trouser leg dragging in the dirt. "What did you do to get yourself banished from Asgard?"

"You see, you should have led with that question. Maybe you'll regret asking the first." He reached down into my travel sack. Before I could protest, he pulled out the cloth bag of rations and laid it out on the bench next to him. "Let's give the highlights, shall we? I lit a few sets of drapes on fire. Some expensive, well-aged mead went missing from the stocks. I took more than a few emissaries to bed with the goal of influencing the outcomes of some trade deals, sometimes at Odin's request and sometimes not. I snuck into Freya's room and stole her precious necklace, also at Odin's insistence. That bridge-troll brother of yours, Heimdall, fought me and took it back, and he's hated me ever since. Oh, and I once let some wild boars inside the halls while everyone was asleep. They didn't find it as funny as I did."

I stared at him, waiting for him to continue. He didn't. "Wait. That's it?"

He shrugged. "That's it."

I threw up my hands. "I was expecting something…heinous! Murder and treason! At your worst, you're a mildly irritating thief. What did he banish you for?"

"He doesn't like disobedience, and I was tired of obeying. Being his Blood-Brother comes with too many caveats." Loki sifted through the rations and plucked out a couple of nuts, popping them into his mouth. "I'm going to be honest with you, Sigyn. In my experience, Odin never gives anything freely and never against his will. If he doesn't want you to have a title, there's nothing you can do about it."

I stared him down. "Maybe you would give up that easily, but I haven't. I've worked too hard. I'm too close."

"I used to say the same thing." A smirk ran across his lips, but something else was underneath. "And after what you know about me, you still want me to teach you?"

It was a fair question. He wasn't a good influence, but if half of what he said was true, it meant accessing locked rooms, the strength to take on other gods, command of elements, a strategic mind. All that and more. It wasn't smart, but I'd been trying smart for decades. Maybe it was time to try sly. Besides, how bad could the price really be?

"Do you really have boots that let you walk on air?"

Loki shook his head. "Stolen by a dwarf. Such a shame; I do like the name Sky Treader."

"How did you earn the title God of Lies?"

"By lying, one assumes."

"Will you lie to me?"

He shrugged, nonchalant. "Not if I can avoid it."

"And if I don't believe that?"

"You'd be the wiser for it."

"What do you want in return?"

Loki leaned back, eyes on the night sky. He thought for a few moments. "Affluence. I want to use the hot spring baths in Valaskjálf again. Sleep in those plush beds, eat those dainty pastries. New clothes, fine Elven wine, newly forged weapons, a hot meal I didn't make myself. All of it. Treat me like a king again."

That complicated things. With all the ways Odin had to spy on the realms, there was a good chance he had already seen me coming to the woods. If I brought Loki back to Asgard to lavish in comfort, Odin would have me strung up in the rafters in Valhalla for the disobedience.

Luckily for Loki, I was feeling reckless.

"And if I arrange this, you'll teach me whatever I want?" I went back to sit on the bench.

Loki looked at me. "Whatever I know."

"Prove it. Teach me wildfire."

"Now?"

I nodded.

"Alright. Turn around." He whipped one leg over the bench, straddling it. I did the same. He shuffled closer until our knees were nearly touching. "Give me your hands."

I stretched them tentatively. It was a candid thing to do, having known him for the entirety of an hour. But he'd also pried dirt from my bare calf, so touching hands was frankly a bit of a step backwards. I held them out.

He cupped his hands underneath mine, holding my palms skyward. They were larger than mine, his pale skin against my bronze. Soft. And warm.

"Do you need a boost? It's been a tough night, and I can lend you some energy if you'd like." His skin was warming, an undercurrent of heat building in his hands where the energy was gathering. The look on his face was deceptively kind, and though I was trying to be on my guard, it felt too easy to just fall into it, to trust him.

I shook my head. "As long as I don't have to close another wound, I'll be fine."

"Suit yourself. You know the runes for wildfire?" he asked.

I shrugged. "I've read them, but it was a long time ago. I never had much skill for offensive seidr."

"Doubtful. Practice makes perfect and all that bearshit." He leaned in, waiting for something. After a moment, he twitched an eyebrow. "Well?"

I leaned in as well. To use a rune, one had to whisper it into existence, a secret on a breath. To say them aloud was to strip them of that power, to expose them to the

15

world. Even written runes only held a small fraction of their power. And so, to teach a rune, one had to learn it through a whisper.

Loki leaned in further. His face was dangerously close to mine, our skin nearly touching. When he whispered the runes into my ear, his breath spilt over my skin. Gooseflesh ran across my body, a small shiver betraying me. When he pulled away, it was clear from his grin that if he hadn't noticed the shiver, he had certainly seen the blush in my cheeks.

Summoning my focus away from the lingering sensation, I stretched my neck and readied myself. Exhaustion was creeping in, but I was able to draw up more than enough energy for the task. He lifted our hands, mine cradled in his, and I let the runes slip off my tongue.

Nothing.

"Try again. Watch your pronunciation." He was watching my lips so intently that it was nearly disarming.

I drew in a deep breath, let it go, and whispered the runes again, changing the inflexion slightly. A spark flashed in my palm and disappeared, like flint striking on stone. "Oh!"

"Good, keep going." He was leaning closer to our hands, the tension of the moment coiling up like a snake in the grass.

Another breath, another rune. And this time, the spark caught, a tiny lavender flame coming to life in the palm of my hand, flickering and dancing.

"Yes!" I leaned in to examine the flame, joy springing up under my skin. "But it's a different colour."

Loki stole back one of his hands and lit a teal spark on his fingertip. "Everyone's is. Yours suits you."

After a moment, the exhilaration of my accomplishment faded, and I realized how closely we were sitting, and how his hand was still on mine. I cleared my throat and moved away, shaking the flame to snuff it out. "I suppose that settles it."

"I suppose it does."

Silence settled in, neither of us quite knowing how to disarm the moment. And then I caught a sliver of gold peeking out from inside my bag. I reached down, plucked out the golden apple, and handed it to him. "Idunn says hello."

A genuine smile lit up his face as he took the apple, brushing it off on the front of his cloak. "We have a friend in common."

He stared into the fire as he cut slice after slice from the golden apple with his knife. I watched, curious to see what type of rejuvenation the apple would bring him. The change didn't take long. The faint smile lines around his lips and across his forehead faded, leaving it as smooth as white ice. He hadn't seemed all that old to begin with, but now he had the youthful look of a man in his prime. Another month on the tally of his life, however long he'd lived.

It was hard to say how much of him was honest, but I didn't need him to be genuine. I just needed him to give me an edge towards the one thing I wanted. There would be a price; even if Odin saw logic, there would be more than one God in Asgard that would be furious with me for bringing him back. But I'd been furious for the last two decades. What did I care if it was someone else's turn?

When he was finished, Loki tossed the ravaged apple core into the fire. It cracked and sizzled, filling the night with the scent of baked apples. He licked the tips of his fingers and turned to me. "Time to rest our heads, I think."

He stood and started up the stone path to the cabin, and I assumed that I should follow him. When we reached the door, he turned back to the fire, and with the whisper of a rune and a clasp of his hand, the teal flame quenched itself, the clearing falling dark.

The cabin was pitch black as well, but in the space of a heartbeat, Loki had a spark of wildfire on his fingertip. He used it to light the hearth, illuminating every inch of the tiny, single-room cabin. There was a small kitchen with shelves, and a water basin not far from the hearth. A quaint bed was pressed up against the opposite wall, space enough for one. Most of the room, however, was taken up with bookcases, each one overladen with books.

I walked to the bookcase without waiting for permission and ran my fingers down the spines. '*Into the Deep: An Elven Perspective on Dwarven Culture.*' '*Cast in Moonlight: Seidr at Night.*' '*Myths of Midgard.*' I picked one up and turned to Loki, staring incredulously.

"What?" he asked, straightening out the unmade furs on his bed.

I slipped the book back in place. "I wouldn't have taken you for the reading type."

"No, I don't imagine you would." He held out a fresh tunic, still folded. I hesitated, and he shrugged. "Unless you want to sleep in your own blood."

I took the tunic.

He gestured to the bed. "I'll take the floor tonight, since there's a feather mattress waiting for me in Asgard." He thought for a moment. "That or a funeral pyre. I suppose we'll see."

He pulled a sleeping roll down from a hook on the ceiling and laid it out in the middle of the floor. He turned his back to me and started to change into drier trousers. I blushed and turned immediately, taking it as an opportunity to get out of my torn clothes. My cloak and trousers were torn, some of it stained a deep red. His tunic was big on me, but it still only came down to my knees. I hurried under the furs of his bed and pulled them up over my chest.

"Why did you agree to come back if you think Odin may kill you for it?"

He turned to me, a grin on his lips. He tossed a pillow toward the head of his sleeping roll. "I've been gone almost a century, darling. I've travelled, and I've behaved—more or less—and I'm bored. It's time to do something new." He sat down on the furs and pulled off his tunic, revealing a lean, muscular chest. A thin scar snaked from his navel to his side and a trio of scars ran over both shoulders. Claw wounds, likely. He looked up and caught my stare. "Besides, I want to see the look on their faces."

I pulled the furs tight against my chest at the same time he crawled into his bed roll and turned toward the fire. "Goodnight."

"Goodnight," I murmured back. I shifted my head, getting comfortable on his pillow. My limbs were heavy, and I felt like I'd melt down into the mattress and never return. The smell of cinder and honey floated at the edge of my senses until, eventually, I fell asleep.

CHAPTER THREE

"The fir-tree that stands in the grove fades;
its bark and needles give no shelter:
so it is for a man whom nobody loves,
how shall he live for long?"

—*Hávamál 50*

The sunrise was still below the branches of Yggdrasil when Loki and I approached Asgard the next morning by horseback. The light danced and glinted on the metal and gold that covered the city. Odin's halls shone from the centre of everything, only challenged in height by Yggdrasil herself. It was built to look extravagant, desirable. To anyone unfamiliar, the city would seem a paradise.

"They know we're coming." It was the first thing Loki had said since we left the woods. He was doing his best to be polite and leave room between us, but that was difficult with two bodies on one horse. Why would he have a horse, he'd said, when he could fly.

I followed his finger skyward. Two ravens circled above, keeping pace with us. Huginn and Muninn, Odin's nosey pets. "Of course they do. Odin wouldn't be Odin if he wasn't two steps ahead of everyone."

"I'm surprised you got as far as you did last night."

I chuckled. "I haven't been worth keeping an eye on for a very long time."

One of the ravens screeched and dove down to land on the shoulder of a rider in the distance. There were five; four dressed in the red and gold of Freya's militia, and in the middle was Freya herself, dressed head to toe in leather and steel armour, her auburn hair tied back in a severe set of twists and braids.

19

I cursed under my breath. Of all the people Odin might have sent.

We approached cautiously, but none of them moved. Freya looked ready for blood, her lips curled back in a snarl. "I should kill you where you sit," she spat as soon as we were in earshot.

Loki leaned over to give a dramatic wave of his hand. "Freya, it's been too long. You can't imagine how good it is to see you!"

"Shut your mouth, snake." Her head turned to me. "And you. I knew you were desperate, but if I'd had any idea how much… This isn't the way to your title. You brought him here without a thought for anyone but yourself."

I took a deep breath. "I don't expect you to understand. How am I supposed to explain this to you? You've always had everything you've ever wanted."

She threw her hand up in exclamation. "I came to Asgard as a hostage—"

"And yet you hold two titles, a stretch of land of your own, half the dead souls of Midgard, and you train Asgard's völur. They call you the most beautiful woman across every realm, and the people of Midgard worship the ground you walk on." I put my fingers on my chest. "I've carved out what little reputation I have line by line, one favour, one conversation, one lesson at a time. I have *bled* dedication. And it still isn't enough for him."

The raven on Freya's shoulder squawked, and she looked up at it, a heavy line set across her lips. He'd hear everything I said, but I didn't care anymore.

She shook her head. "This isn't going to change anything. Odin will have him thrown back into the woods, or worse, if we're lucky. And you'll be fortunate not to spend the rest of your days sweeping pork rinds with the kitchen staff."

Loki snickered, and all eyes turned to him. "If you think Odin is foolish enough to send his daughter to work as a maid, then you're an imbecile. He couldn't have the leaders of the realms thinking he's *lost control* of something, now could he?"

He wasn't wrong.

Freya stared him down as if she hoped he'd spontaneously catch fire.

She waved her hand, and her tiny militia moved forward, two swinging their horses around to our flanks, trapping us between them. "Let's get this over with," she snapped, then turned toward the city. Not having much choice, we followed behind.

Loki leaned in over my shoulder, his voice low. "Are you having regrets yet, goddess?"

"Not one." I tried to keep the tremble from my voice. I wanted to believe my father would see reason, would see how fucking desperate I was, and that he'd let it go. This had to work somehow. I couldn't see any other path forward.

After we passed the farms on the outskirts of the city and the houses became dense, pressing against each other in rows, the people took notice. Asgard was full of gawkers. They whispered and stared openly, but not at me. All eyes were on Loki. Some of their faces changed from confusion to shock as others whispered in their ears, surely revealing the name of this newcomer to those who hadn't been in Asgard long enough to know his face. The tension was closing around us like a fist, but no one dared move against Freya and her militia.

When we arrived, we were forced down from the horse and escorted through the main entrance of Valaskjálf, down its rich corridors like a pair of common criminals. I knew where she was taking us. Father had a flair for the dramatic and nothing was more dramatic than Gladsheim.

We turned the last corner and were met with Gladsheim's doors, so large and intricately inlaid with gold carvings that it had taken a team of dwarves two straight weeks to complete. Through the doors was the great hall itself. If ever something was built to intimidate, it was that room. It was cavernous in depth and height, empty but for the row of golden seats that sat high on a dais overlooking the hall. At the centre was a throne, and on it was Odin himself.

He was leaning forward, his elbows on his knees, staring us down with his one good eye. The raven perched on Freya's shoulder leapt off, flying across the room and landing on Odin's arm. It turned upward, whispering in his ear. Odin nodded, and the bird found a new perch on the back of the throne, right next to its brother.

Every excuse, every wish, every possibility ran through my mind as we approached. The things I could say or do to convince Odin to give me this chance. Because there had to be a way.

"*Grimnir*. It has been an age, hasn't it?"

I looked up, torn from my inner turmoil. No one had called Odin that in a very long time.

Before anyone could stop him, Loki had sprinted towards the stairs, heading straight for Odin.

"You know, I would've stopped by, but there was this small problem with my being exiled." He stopped at the foot of the stairs, the soldiers clambering after him. "I do wish you'd written. I was beside myself, thinking about how you'd survive without me doing all your dirty little deeds for you."

It was all I could do to keep my jaw from hitting the floor. No one spoke to Odin that way and lived to tell the tale.

But to my surprise, a small smile cracked on the corners of the Allfather's lips. "You've never been anything but trouble, Loki Laufeyjarson. What makes today any different?"

"Nothing and everything." Loki took one step up the stairs and then another.

21

Every muscle in my body tensed; my breath caught in my throat. Then he sat down in the chair beside Odin as if it was his gods given right to be there.

Leaning back, Loki draped his legs over the arm of the chair, looking every bit as comfortable and casual as a cat. "I'm sure you already know why I'm back."

Odin sighed, sitting up and turning toward him. "My impatient daughter thinks you'll be the key to her title. She may have brought you here, but you came willingly, so who do you think bears the most blame?"

Loki arched an eyebrow. "Did you really think this little arrangement would last forever, *Hangi*? I've played nice, but you know it hasn't stopped me, don't you? Exile is just a word, after all."

Odin huffed, wagging his finger at him. "Don't think I haven't seen you stumbling your way around the nine. I knew every time you came into Asgard in disguise and every time you made trouble somewhere else. Word always gets back to me, in the end."

Loki leaned his elbow on the arm of his chair, his chin resting in his hand. "As if *you've* spent the last century being innocent. I bet you're still up to the same old things." He turned to stare down at Freya. "Like that time you had me sneak into Freya's chamber and steal that pretty little necklace from around her neck."

Freya's leather-gloved hand went straight for the dripping chains of gold and amber around her neck, but the scowl was pure fury. "You're a liar. This had nothing to do with Odin."

Loki laughed. "Oh, darling. You had your reasons, didn't you, Odin?" Loki turned back to him, waiting for an answer.

Odin neither confirmed nor denied, and the scorn on Freya's face shrivelled into doubt.

Loki swung himself out of his seat. "Now, if we're done getting reacquainted, shall we get to the matter at hand?" He held out a hand in my direction, the movement full of flourish. "Would the lady care to speak for herself?"

The lady would. I cleared my throat and stepped forward. "You've been underestimating what I'm capable of, and I'll claim my title by whatever means necessary. I sought out Loki because by all accounts he is more skilled in seidr than many of the masters I've studied under. He's a wasted resource out in those woods while I'm stuck here begging for opportunities." The words felt bold on my tongue. It felt like someone braver than I was, and I couldn't bear to push them back down. "I want him reinstated in Asgard with rooms in Valaskjálf and access to whatever he needs, and in return, he will provide me with lessons that may *finally* convince you that I've earned my seat up there." I gestured toward the empty chairs. "I understand he's caused issues in the past, but I guarantee that I can keep him under control—"

22

Odin burst into laughter. After a moment, he took a deep breath. "You think you can keep him under control? Then you truly have no idea who he is." Odin stood, his posture growing stiff as the laughter faded. He turned to Loki. "This has gone on long enough. You're here next to me like you still belong here. You don't." Loki didn't wither under Odin's gaze like I would have, but I could feel the chill of his words from where I stood. "I should have *you* killed. And you..." He turned back to me. "I should disown you for going behind my back. He was exiled to protect the realms, and that includes you."

I crossed my arms over my chest. "I don't need your protection, and I don't care about your permission. You think I'm incapable of keeping him under control because you don't know anything about me. He'll be my responsibility, and you will pry this opportunity from my cold, dead fingers." Though I was staring Odin in the eye, I could still see the intrigued smirk on Loki's face.

"I vouch for him as well."

I turned to see where the new voice had come from. Idunn strode toward the dais, the white silks of her dress trailing behind her, her bare feet peeking out from beneath it. Even with such a stoic look on her face, Idunn radiated serenity.

She stopped beside me and took my arm in hers. "I've had more contact with Loki in the last century than the rest of the realm put together. If anyone has the right to judge his character, it's me."

Odin examined her and huffed. "You're overstepping your role. This doesn't involve you."

"I disagree." She left me to ascend the stairs, stopping in front of Odin. "Even with your ravens and your high seat, you don't see everything. Loki has more than served his penance for the crimes committed, and your daughter is drowning while you keep her at arms-length." She took Odin's hand between hers, clasping it gently. "You are wise, Allfather. Do the right thing."

He glared at Loki, and Loki winked in response. Then Odin's gaze landed on me. His lips pursed, the only thing I could read on his face. Finally, he snarled and ripped his hand from Idunn's. "Fine. You have three weeks. Prove to me that he is capable of returning *peacefully* and has taught Sigyn something worthy of a title, and you'll all get your way. If he steps out of line, I'll make good on my threats. Are we clear?"

Freya stormed forward. "You must be joking. You can't invite this fox back into our home. He's going to destroy us from the inside again! I won't allow it!"

Odin whipped around to face her. "Quiet! Three weeks. There will be no more discussion." He stomped past all of us, down onto the stone floor of Gladsheim, past Freya's troops, and straight out the door. Freya was quick to follow, her soldiers right behind her. And then all was silent.

When I turned back to the others, Loki had a bright smile on his face, his arms held wide. Idunn stepped into his embrace, squeezing him tightly.

"Impeccable timing, darling." Loki straightened one of the lilies braided into Idunn's hair.

She stepped back, waving a hand. "I knew where Sigyn was heading, and I kept my ears open. Some of the people in the market were talking about the return of the Silvertongue, and I couldn't stay away."

I stepped up beside her and put my hand on her shoulder. "Thank you. I hope this won't get you in too much trouble."

"I'll tell you a secret." Idunn took my arm and led me down the stairs. "When you're the only one in the nine realms who can pick the apples that keep the gods young, you have a little sway in the house of Odin."

I laughed, letting some of the tension run off my body. At some moments, I may have even forgotten to breathe.

Loki skipped down the stairs, his presence filling the empty space next to me. Nothing about his demeanour suggested that his life had just been in danger. "Call me impatient, but I'm ready to exploit Odin's treasury. Anyone care for a trip to the market?"

Idunn shook her head. "Another time. I've got to get home to Bragi before he sets off on another of his trips around the realms." We stopped outside the doors of Valaskjálf, ready to part ways. Idunn planted a kiss on my cheek and gave Loki another hug. "I'll see you tonight in Valhalla. And Loki, be gentle with her. She doesn't know you like I do." She gave him a wink and turned on her heel, gliding off into the corridor.

Loki shrugged casually. "That leaves you, Siggy."

"Don't call me 'Siggy.' I'm not a pet, and I don't want to go to the market."

"What if I promise you'll learn something?" Loki started walking down the hall backwards, clearly expecting me to follow.

Damn it. Two seconds inside the city lines, and he already knew how to twist my arm.

CHAPTER FOUR

"Of course I'd seen him. Half of the city had probably sold
something to Loki while he was exiled, whether they knew it
or not. I just wasn't stupid enough to look him
in the eye and say no."

—Anonymous Merchant - God of Lies Revealed

It was clear that Loki still knew his way around the city. He led me away from Asgard and toward the market without a single wrong turn, and when we arrived, he shot a straight path for Áshildr's stall, one of the best bakers in Asgard. He ordered two warm apple pastries and had me pay for them. As we left, he passed me one. I took it, still sizing him up.

"You're staring." He bit into the snack and brushed the crumbs from his aged blue tunic.

"I have a lot I need to learn," I said impatiently, barrelling past the niceties. I reached into my cloak with my spare hand and shook a slip of parchment open. "I have a list."

"I see that." Loki took it from me, a crooked grin on the corner of his lips. His eyes scanned the page, and after a moment he folded it up and pressed it back into my palm. "You won't be needing it."

"Excuse me?" I sidestepped in front of him, attempting to cut him off. "What does that mean? I spent a long time on that."

Loki skirted past me, slipping into the open stall of a man selling furs. He ran his hands across the line of soft pelts laid out on the table, sparing a quick glance at me. "I'm going to need you to breathe. Can't have you passing out in distress." He picked

25

up a beautiful silver wolf pelt, examined its edges, then slung it over his shoulder. He made a sweeping gesture with his hand, from me to the shopkeep, and I pried a few coins out of my purse with a sigh. The merchant took the coin, but his terrified eyes were on Loki the entire time.

Loki turned back out to the market with his new prize, and I stayed directly on his heels.

"Please take this seriously. I brought you here to help me, not to take advantage of me."

He gave me a look of mock surprise. "I'm insulted. For someone to assume that I, Loki, would take advantage of someone when they don't know a thing about me…why that's *never* happened to me before."

Guilt curdled in my stomach. Had I been letting the doubts of others affect my opinion of him? None of the beastly stories sounded anything like this oddly charming and vaguely infuriating Jotun in front of me. Then he swivelled into another shop and had me pay for a new belt, a leather travel sack, and a coin purse.

While I was busy thinking, still following Loki around the bustling market, he reached out and plucked a pear from a fruit merchant as we passed. The motion was subtle, meant to go unseen. Hel, I nearly missed it myself, but he simply slipped it into his new bag and kept moving.

My mouth dropped. "Honestly? You can't just steal from people!" I turned back and hastily dropped a bronze coin into the confused merchant's hand, then rushed back to Loki. He'd already moved on without me, and as I caught up, his hand reached out and slipped a bottle of wine from a table and into the bag while the shopkeep was arguing with a customer. My eyes shot wide. How was I supposed to keep him from stealing everything that wasn't tied down?

I rushed to pay the wine seller, then wound my way through the other market-goers. Loki was reaching out for something else. I grabbed his hand, pulling him toward me. "What are you *doing?*"

"Giving you your next lesson." He wiggled his hand from my grasp.

My frustration released as a hiss, tempered down from a scream. "How is your thieving supposed to teach me anything?"

"Because, goddess, you insist on looking at the distraction instead of the main event." His gaze travelled over my head, back in the direction we'd come from. The scent of smoke hit my nose at the same time I saw the teal flame creeping up the side of one of the merchant's stalls.

No one had noticed yet. I summoned up all my focus, drew up the energy for runes, and let a string of them slip from my tongue. The air pushed away from the space around the stall, snuffing out the flame in a blink and leaving the people nearby gasping for breath. A moment later, the air rushed back in, and the crisis was averted.

I whipped around, ready to snarl at the man causing me so much grief, but he wasn't there. I scanned the market, searching for that flaming head of hair until I found him leaning against a wall at the edge of an alley. Blood boiling, I stormed toward him, dodging everything that got in my way. He looked up as I approached, not a care in the world, with that godsforsaken smile across his face.

"Why would you do that? Someone could've been hurt or had their livelihood ruined!" It was all I could do to resist the urge to slap him and cause a scene.

"Nothing was going to happen," he said, pushing himself away from the wall with his foot, nonchalant.

I gaped at him. "You can't know that!"

"Of course I can. You were there." He gave his head a nod to the other end of the alley, walking away from me.

The words tumbled in my head like I'd been shaken. What in the nine realms did that mean? Was it a good thing? Was I dependable, reliable? Or predictable? I didn't have time to decide; he was already far enough away that I had to run to catch up.

Before I knew it, we were at the outskirts of the city, away from the homes and shops built nearly on top of one another. There were fields as far as the eye could see, some with grain and vegetables, others full of cattle and goats. Loki pulled us off the path and into the grass, heading for a lonely tree next to a boulder.

He laid the wolf pelt across the grass and gestured for me to have a seat. I sat. He threw himself down across from me and tipped the bag over, emptying its contents like an avalanche. I'd only seen him steal the pear and the wine, but there were cloth sacks of cheese, a loaf of bread, a gold inlaid knife, a handful of hazelnuts still in their shell, a hand-carved wooden statue of a goat, and half a dozen other oddities.

My face must have been the picture of dismay because Loki started to laugh. Not the cackle of someone evil, but the innocent laughter of a boy who thinks he's told a good joke. When I didn't laugh with him, he wiped a tear from his eye and started making himself something to eat.

"And what *precisely* was I supposed to glean from this?" I fingered through the pilfered goods, guilt festering in my stomach that I'd essentially let him get away with it. I'd never stolen anything in my life, and here I was, accomplice to grand theft picnic.

"Plenty." He settled onto his side, propped up on his elbow, relaxed as could be. "Misdirection is everywhere, especially in Asgard. Never let anyone tell you where to look, because while you're staring off into the distance, they'll be pressing a knife to your back."

I rolled my eyes. "Don't you think that's a little paranoid?"

"Better to be a little paranoid than a lot dead." He winked and popped a piece of cheese in his mouth.

Odin's hanged body. Though I didn't want to admit it, there was a possibility I'd bitten off more than I could chew.

CHAPTER FIVE

*"Odin might have hung himself from Yggdrasil to gain
knowledge of the runes, but I mastered them and gave seidr
to the world. Some things only a woman can do."*

—*Freya - Asgard Historical Record Volume 4*

We spent the better part of the afternoon debating the ethics of thieving and developing a baseline for which of us had what knowledge of seidr. As a whole, seidr was many things: divination, healing, warding, elemental, psychological. My estimation of Loki had been more or less correct; he was very nearly my opposite in abilities. Everything he knew was flashy, impressive, or deadly. He expressed a disinterest in anything medicinal or protective and dismissed my offer to teach him something in return, stating only that he'd already earned his title.

When the pilfered food was gone and our legs were tired of sitting, we rolled up the wolf pelt and returned to the centre of the city. It would be nearly time for supper, and Loki was chomping at the bit to get to Valhalla. He'd been greedily listing everything he planned to eat during the entire walk.

Supper was already well underway when we arrived. The hall stretched out before us, the rafters made of spears, the roof built from shields, and the walls featuring more doors than could be counted. Tables filled the hall as far as the eye could see, packed with rowdy warriors. No matter how many arrived, there would be room for everyone, the hall stretching to accommodate its occupants. The benefits of building a place with seidr.

The einherjar were eating, laughing, and arm wrestling all through the hall, filling the room with a welcoming pandemonium. They were Odin's warriors, the humans of Midgard who had died bravely and been chosen to serve in his army. There were people of all shapes and sizes, young and old, and of all complexions. Anyone who had proven themselves worthy. One day they would fight for their god during Ragnarok, but for now they spent their days training until it was time to drink.

Loki and I headed toward the high table at the end of the room. It stretched across the width of the room with a long row of seats behind it, each one meant for a god. More than half the gods were missing; it was rare for them to be in Valhalla all at once, but their seat was there regardless. Odin sat at the centre, his wife Frigg next to him. The rest sat next to whomever they pleased, and, given my present company, I wondered who would be pleased to sit with me.

Worry gnawed at my stomach as I stepped onto the platform, but Loki was clearly feeling differently. "Hello, old friends! I've come home! Aren't you happy to see me?"

The table grew silent, all eyes moving in our direction. I froze like a spooked deer. Something thumped against the table, and a chair scraped against the floor. Thor stood, his face grim underneath the red-blonde of his beard. Every piece of his body was broad and muscular. He was still covered in dust and scrapes from whatever he'd been fighting that day, his hair tied back in an unkempt tail. When he stepped toward us, I moved out of the way, having no desire to get between anything and Thor's fist.

"Loki, you old dog. How have you been?" Thor pulled the Jotun in for one of his bone-crushing hugs. Loki squeaked in discomfort, and Thor loosened his grip.

I started breathing again.

With a cough and a brush of his shoulder, Loki slung his arm around Thor's neck. "Exiled. Didn't you know? Or are you still suffering from air between your ears?"

Thor howled a laugh. "Oh, I've missed your jokes, you mongrel. Come on, sit next to me, and let me pour you a drink. I want to hear all about your adventures." Thor whisked him off to the other side of the table.

No one else moved to greet him.

I took my normal seat next to Idunn, letting my body sink into the cushions like a sigh. Idunn leaned over and gave me a peck on the cheek. "I hope you aren't tired already," she said, selecting portions of roast boar, baked root vegetables, and seed bread, and setting them on my plate.

I didn't argue, just leaned my face into my palms, exhausted, and told her about the scene Loki had made at the market.

Idunn just smiled. "No one said it would be easy."

"It doesn't need to be easy," I groaned, picking at my supper. "but he's…"

"Chaotic?"

"Exactly."

An arm appeared between us, setting two horns of mead on the table. I smiled up at the woman and thanked her. She nodded in return, the swan wings on her back rustling. She was one of the Valkyrie, another staple of Valhalla. Each woman was stunning in her own way and entirely deadly. They were dressed in white gowns that draped over their battle-hardened bodies, their hard-earned scars peeking from beneath the fabric. Sometimes it was hard not to stare.

"Loki tends to test people's limits," Idunn said, drawing my attention back. "Some people handle that better than others. Did I ever tell you about when I first came to Asgard?"

I looked up. She was still busy with her plate, pulling and cutting things into smaller pieces. She didn't look at me, and I knew she wouldn't; Idunn didn't like talking about sad things.

"A little. You told me that it was hard for you. Fitting in."

"It was." She slipped a piece of roast boar between her lips and took her time chewing it. "I didn't know that Bragi was a son of Odin when I met him. He was kind and beautiful, full of poetry. Not like the rest of your half-brothers. I was in love so quickly that when he did tell me, it was already too late. I would've followed him anywhere."

Her cheeks were pink, a smile on her lips, like every time she talked about her husband. But the smile faded. "I didn't know a single other soul when I arrived. Everything was loud and violent, and I didn't belong here. Nothing was mine, nothing except Bragi. A few days after I arrived, I got upset and ran out of Valhalla crying. And Loki was late coming to supper. I nearly knocked him over. He took me by the shoulders and said, '*What in the nine could be wrong with the woman made of sunshine?*' I'll never forget that.

"Afterward, he made time for me. Talked with me during meals and brought me seeds for my garden when he went travelling. When Bragi was on the road, bringing poetry to the people, Loki would keep me company. He was my first friend in Asgard."

I hesitated to ask. "Were you two... involved?"

"Hmm?" She looked up, puzzled, then less so. "Oh, no, he's just a friend." She paused for a moment. "Loki is a strange creature. He's kind to those who show him kindness, when his spite and pride don't get in the way. Just... give him a chance to show that part of himself."

Well then.

We talked casually for the better part of an hour while the hall slowly emptied out. Every time I looked up, the room seemed to shrink a little more until there were only a few straggling tables of warriors left.

As was tradition, the gods took their drinks down to one of the empty tables so they could talk amongst themselves face to face. Thor and Loki were the first, and a few others trickled down after. Odin and Frigg were quick to leave Valhalla entirely. Idunn and I sat together, and I found myself across from Freya, who looked just as unimpressed with me as she had earlier in the day.

The last to arrive at the table was Hod, another of my many brothers. His walking staff clicked on the floor as he approached, feeling his way towards us. His chestnut hair was cropped short and swept to the side, his skin a pale pink. A blue wool sweater hung loose and open over his tunic, despite the summer weather. Hod was always cold.

Loki jumped up from his seat at the end of the bench. "Hello, you. You're as dapper as ever."

Hod tilted his head, staring in the direction of Loki's voice with cloudy blue eyes. "Loki Laufeyjarson. I knew they couldn't keep you away."

"And you haven't lost your knack for voices. Come and sit." Loki took Hod by the elbow and directed him to the now-empty seat. When Hod was settled, Loki leaned against the tabletop rather than sit somewhere else.

Sif was eyeing him from across the table, discomfort written on her face. Distress bubbled in my stomach as Loki took notice and stared right back. When she said nothing, Loki brushed his hand through the length of his hair. "I know, I'm entranced by these beautiful locks as well. I could give you tips if you like. Yours seems to have lost some of its shine."

Immediately, her cheeks went red and she retreated back into her long, wavy mass of golden-blonde hair—the hair proclaimed as the most beautiful in all the realms—as if they were a set of drapes to hide behind.

Loki grinned and turned his attention back to Hod and Thor, slipping into conversation with the skill of a practised socialite.

Meanwhile, Freya was still glaring at me.

I sighed. "How long will you keep this up?"

"Until you find some way to undo this." Freya pointed at Loki. "No one wants him here."

I leaned toward her. "*You* don't want him here. You've got an awfully big grudge against him for stealing your necklace. But that's not all it's about, is it? You think he's argr."

She sneered, confirming my suspicions. "He is. There's never been any question about that."

"He's a male völva, not a pussing boil." I waved in his direction. "Why should he be forbidden to practice seidr?"

Freya prodded the tabletop with her finger. "Some things aren't up for discussion.

The Goddess of Nothing At All

Seidr is for women. It's built into the history of mothers and daughters and sisters, and I did that on purpose. Men have enough in these realms that's just for them, so we made something extraordinary out of woman's work. Would you give a man a loom and ask him to weave a new fate with seidr? No, of course not. A man doing a woman's work is not a man, he's argr. And what about the parts of divination that aren't just about blood magic? Using sex to reach a higher consciousness and see the future? Those acts would make a woman out of him."

I rolled my eyes. "Have you heard of *The Horn and Stag*, the brothel down near the Smith quarter? It has a *thriving* market of men looking for other men. There are male völur popping up all over the realms. This obsession these realms have with maintaining masculinity is appalling. Things are changing. You can't stop it."

She only stared at me.

Like divine intervention, I heard my name. Loki was staring in my direction, still perched on the edge of the table. "They want to know what I'm teaching you!"

I opened my mouth to answer, but Freya was ahead of me. "How to become a deviant, one assumes."

"Freya," Idunn said her name like a song. "Why don't we go for a walk? Talk about this."

Freya sat up straight, bracing her hands on the table. "No, I don't think so. You're not going to convince me to forgive his ways, no matter how good a peacemaker you are."

Loki pouted. "My ways? Whatever could you mean?" Sauntering around to Freya's side of the table, Loki slid his fingers across the wood like a caress, finding his way up the arm of Thor, who looked thoroughly confused. He ruffled Thor's hair, and as he drew closer to Freya, every muscle in her body grew rigid. He never touched her, just leaned towards her ear and whispered, "I could tell you *such* stories."

Freya leapt out of her seat, fist wound back to strike him, but Loki had already pranced backward, out of reach. His hands were up, palms out, an innocent smile on his face. "Don't be so jumpy! You'll scare someone."

I stood and leaned across the table, eyes on Loki. "Are you finished?"

Freya was breathing as if her head would pop off her shoulders, like she was one wrong move from going for her knife.

Loki just tilted his head and grinned. "Of course, Siggy. That's all I needed." He winked at Freya. "Besides, there are other souls to say hello to." Then he turned and headed towards a group of einherjar a few tables away, taking very confident strides for a dead man.

Sif was pulling at Freya's sleeve. "Sit down. You can't let him bother you like that;

33

it's only going to encourage him."

"I don't know why you ladies despise Loki so much." Thor leaned on his elbows. "I think he's funny."

Sif glared at her husband. "He wasn't so funny when he was taking you off to all sorts of places and getting you into trouble. It's been *calm* since he's been gone."

"I wouldn't say that," Hod piped up. "You've spent plenty of time fighting amongst yourselves since he left. He gave you a common enemy, that's all."

Something in the corner of my vision caught my attention. A brown and white cat was padding towards our table. Its fur was thick around its entire body, white streaking down from its mane and onto its belly.

"Look," I said to Idunn. She followed my gaze and squealed in delight. Holding out her hand, she waited for the cat to sniff her skin and approve of her. It did, of course, pressing its head into her palm. Then it hopped up onto the table.

The others ooed and aahed appropriately, but the cat seemed to have its sights on Idunn and I. Idunn scratched behind its ears for a moment until it wriggled loose and sat down in front of me. Its mewing was so adorable that I cupped its face in my hands and planted kisses all over its head.

On the other side of the table, Freya's foul mood shifted. "Come here darling, let me look at you." She tapped her fingers on the table, trying to lure the cat away.

The cat scooted backwards, out of my reach. It winked with one emerald eye before turning to the noise.

Something itched at the back of my mind. Cats didn't wink, and certainly not on purpose.

"Oh, aren't you glorious?" Freya's hands were deep in its fur, scratching and petting, eliciting deep purrs from the wild cat. "You look just like my Astrid, yes you do." She pulled the cat onto her lap and held it to her chest, sighing like a woman thoroughly pleased. "Why aren't there more cats in Valhalla? This is much better than putting up with that horrible man."

Sif reached over and stole a touch, the cat leaning into her hand. "A head full of lice would be better than Loki." The cat stretched out its front paws onto Sif's lap and kneaded its claws into her dress before Sif shrieked and pushed it away.

I turned to try and catch a glimpse of the table Loki had been heading towards, but he wasn't there. He wasn't anywhere.

I looked back at the cat. Its green eyes said it was very pleased with itself.

Himself.

"You'll need to learn to get along with Loki," Hod said. "Unless Odin changes his mind and throws him out, he's going to be here a very long time."

"Three weeks!" Freya pulled the cat away from Sif's dress. "He has three weeks to prove himself useful, and then I get to toss him out of the realm for the last time. Yggdrasil above, I hope I can."

I'd been keeping my eyes on the cat, but the comment left a bad taste in my mouth. "Ah yes, please sit here and tell me how much you want me to fail."

"That's not what I meant, and you know it." The cat was pawing at her chest, trying to get more of her attention.

"But that's what'll happen. I need his help, and you want to take that from me."

"You do not need him." Freya could barely keep the cat under control. "You would've been fine without him. Odin would've eventually—" She was cut off as the cat turned round and presented its bottom dangerously close to her face.

Freya screeched in frustration and picked up the cat. She plopped it onto its bum on her lap. "What is wrong with you?"

The air around the cat shifted, colour and space changing and distorting until I couldn't stand to look anymore. I blinked, trying to make sense of what I was seeing. The air popped, and Freya screamed. Sitting on her lap was Loki, legs crossed, the biggest grin on his face. Once a shapeshifter...

"What? Don't you want to cuddle?" He threw his head back and howled with laughter.

He wasn't the only one. Thor was laughing from his gut, trying to explain the stunt to Hod between each gasping breath. Idunn was giggling behind her hand while Sif screamed about the mangled state of her dress.

A smile crept onto my lips, pleased at this tiny moment of revenge. Loki caught my eyes and grinned back, and I froze. I'd kissed that cat's head. Oh, gods.

Having no choice but to touch him, Freya pushed Loki backward, knocking him onto the table. He was still laughing uncontrollably as she pulled the knife from her belt and drew it back above her head.

A hand was on her wrist before any of us could react. One of the Valkyrie had come from behind her. Alruna. Her chiselled face was neutral, the picture of cool strength. One braid hung over her shoulder, every hair pulled away from her face, leaving her severe, intimidating. All this wrapped into soft, flowing white fabric. Her vivid blue eyes were locked on Freya, and my breath caught. Alruna didn't play games; it was part of what I had loved about her.

"I expect this from the einherjar, but not from you." Alruna said this mere inches from Freya's face. "If you're going to kill each other, at least have the decency to do it *away* from where we eat. My people have enough work around here."

"Get your hands off me." Freya yanked back her arm and looked towards the table. The embarrassment started to creep onto her face. Her eyes locked on mine, and then back to Alruna. "That makes sense. You two may not be sleeping together anymore, but you'll always be idiots for each other." She rubbed at her wrist for a moment, composed herself, and stormed off toward the door. Sif wasn't long stumbling after her.

I stood and went to Alruna. "Thank you for that. Things got...a little out of hand."

Alruna leaned in, an old familiarity in the way she did it. "Between you and I, it was hilarious. But I don't want to spend tonight wiping Jotnar off the floor." She gave me a smile then left me with the others.

When I turned back, Loki was rolling himself rightside-up on the table. He sat where he was and looked around. "Alright, who wants a drink?"

CHAPTER SIX

*"It was time for him to rejoin us. His exile was never meant
to be permanent, and the gods are eager to welcome him
back. Loki has a lot to offer, and we're
happy to have him home."*

—Odin - *Asgard Historical Records, Volume 13*

I woke to the sun stretching through my window, its light snaking slowly into the room and up the sheets. I stayed where I was, curled up underneath the furs, my head fuzzy and my mood sour. I'd been dreaming that I was lost in the woods and that something was chasing me, but no matter how far I ran, the woods never ended. So many of my dreams were like that now.

I eventually forced myself out of bed and pulled my morning gown over my satin nightdress, shuffling out to the main room. I knelt in front of the hearth and stacked a few pieces of wood around a pile of kindling. I tried to summon up a flicker of wildfire and failed. Too sleepy to bother, I settled for flint and steel instead. It sparked, and the kindling smoked, fire creeping up the twigs. Waiting for the wood to catch, I looked around the quiet, empty house.

When Odin had told me he was commissioning a hall for me as well, he was vastly overselling it. Any hall belonging to any other god was large enough for a dozen families, built on enough land to stretch acres. In contrast, mine was a handful of rooms cramped so close to Valhalla that my father could likely see in my window from his own chambers.

I didn't need more space; it was devastatingly lonely inside as it was. It was the principle of the thing. Sol and Mani had literally been given the sun and moon for free.

37

There was blood under my nails from clawing my way towards everything I'd earned.

What made me so different from everyone else?

I sighed. It took effort not to be ungrateful, especially on melancholy days. I'd seen the drafty, sod-roofed houses in Midgard and the families trying to make a life with a rocky field and a pair of goats. There were worse things than being underappreciated, I knew that. Sometimes.

I got up and poured a cup of water, leaning against the wooden counter, trying to shift my mood. The kitchen felt like home at least, its walls covered in herbs drying on hooks and shelves laden with jars and bottles and mortars. One side of the long dining table was piled high with loose parchment, charcoal, and unfinished books. A corner of the world that was undeniably mine.

When the fire was hot and the food was finally ready, I sat at my place, the chair padded with furs and cushions, and picked up the most recent book Hod had lent me. He was a collector of stories. He'd been born blind but had an uncanny ability to make others feel seen. People came from across the nine realms to gift their stories to him. This one was from Midgard, and I was 15 pages in before the first mention of Thor's heroic, selfless rescue of some poor villager and how the family fell to their knees in gratitude.

I marked the page and put it aside.

I didn't *like* myself this way. I didn't *like* the bitterness. But it had been building up for decades, and I wasn't sure how to keep pressing it down.

I took a deep breath. I would fix it. Loki would teach me everything I needed to know, and I would prove that I was valuable and needed and worthy. The others would respect me, and that would be enough. The past wouldn't matter, because I'd be sitting alongside my family, not in their shadows but in their light.

Looking up at the window, the sun was still in the line of sky between the horizon and the edge of Yggdrasil's branches. I still had a little time before the lesson.

Picking through my wardrobe, I found a rose-coloured dress, something I could still move and breathe in. I sat down to pull a pair of short stockings on and caught sight of the silver scars on my leg. The wolf bite.

I ran my hand along it. Loki had only been back a day, and he'd already ignited old feuds. There would be nothing simple about this. But whatever he was, he had saved me once already from a mediocre death. He might still save me from a mediocre life.

A familiar laugh spilt out from the hallway as I approached the guest quarters of Valaskjálf. I rounded the corner to find Loki with his arm around Frey's shoulders, not a care in the world. Frey, God of Abundance and Fertility, on the other hand, was clearly looking for an escape.

"Good morning, boys," I said, drawing their attention.

Loki looked up, that sly grin still on his face. "Good morning! I was just asking Frey about one of the sects in Midgard that worship him. Every one of them is a man, and every one of them practices seidr. Even the *naughty* stuff. Did you know that, Sig?"

Frey, who was normally the picture of young confidence, started to stammer. He pushed back his short auburn hair, trying to seem more relaxed than he was. His lips were pursed underneath his beard and moustache. Only the silk and gold trim of his luxurious Elven clothes looked composed; the rest of him was quivering. "That's not true. There's no such thing happening in *my* name. In yours maybe, but not mine."

Loki pulled him closer, the two of them nearly cheek to cheek. "Don't lie to me. I've seen it with my own eyes! What do you think Freya would say about that? Surely your sister doesn't *know?*" He tsked, talking to him like one might reproach a toddler.

"Loki, leave him alone." I took a step closer, hands on my hips.

"Oh, you're no fun." Loki sighed dramatically. He pulled Frey in, kissed the top of his head, and let him go. It flustered the poor god, turning his cheeks a brighter red than his hair. He gathered himself and practically ran away, leaving Loki laughing in his wake.

It was my turn to scold. "Do you exist to aggravate others?"

He looked like he was thinking it over. "Perhaps. Though I'm certain I have other skills."

"Like what?"

"None that I can talk about in the presence of a lady." He winked and turned on his heel, walking away.

I rolled my eyes.

As we left Valaskjálf, I pressed him for information. "Do you have something planned for today other than petty theft?"

He chuckled, leading me through the city but skirting the market entirely. "Something tame, I promise. Conventional learning for the sake of your poor heart."

"*My poor heart.*" I scoffed. "Like I'm a delicate flower."

"Fine. If you won't spare yourself, have a thought for me. You may have left Valhalla early last night, but I didn't and keeping up with Thor is a task all its own." He gave me a forced smile, and I caught a glimpse of the weariness beneath the mask.

"Will you at least tell me where we're going?"

"A little bird told me that if I came to Yggdrasil before midday, I'd be given a warm meal and a comfy chair to eat it in."

"That does sound like Idunn."

39

"Hasn't changed a bit."

We fell into silence as we walked through side streets and around bustling city corners. His hair alone made him an easy sight, and more than a few people stopped to stare at The Liesmith.

"Tell me about the Valkyrie," he said abruptly, interrupting my wandering mind.

"Excuse me?" So much for small talk. It occurred to me to ask him '*Which Valkyrie? Whatever do you mean?*' but I had a very distinct feeling that we both knew what he was talking about.

"The Valkyrie," he said, low and conspiratorial like an old woman looking for gossip.

I chewed at the inside of my lip before answering. "Alruna is the commander of her own Wing of Valkyrie, 30 women strong. She's tough and very good at what she does."

He gave me a sidelong glance. "Well, that was rather dry."

"What else do you want to know?"

"Tell me what her lips taste like."

I bristled, mouth dropping open. "How dare you ask something so personal?"

"Ah, you see," he waggled his finger, "the response of plausible deniability is '*how would I know?*' Your answer gives you away. You loved her."

"You can't know that."

"You're not exactly a closed book, and I'm good at what I do."

I paused, letting the length of an entire street pass before I spoke again. "It was a long time ago. I'd have married her if things had gone that way. But they didn't."

"Why not?"

If I didn't tell him, someone else would. I'd heard what other people said about us, and it wasn't true. "When Alruna first went to compete for her spot as commander, she failed. In one of her tests, they convinced her I was in danger and made her choose between my life and the realm's safety. She chose me."

Loki let out a long, empathetic sigh. "I bet Odin loved that."

"He was furious. He'd chosen her for the promotion himself. He gave us an ultimatum; if we remained together, I would never get my title, and she would never get her position as commander of a Wing."

"How long ago was this?"

"60 years, give or take."

"And you still don't have your title." Loki kicked a rock down the path. "*Hangi's* always been a bit of a bastard."

"More than a bit." It slipped out before I could stop it. I looked up at him, afraid that I may have betrayed myself.

He only laughed. "Don't worry, I won't tell. I've got better things to do than get on his good side."

I cracked a smile. "Does he have one?"

Loki snickered and threw his arm around my shoulder, jostling me. "Have you ever made faces at him from his blind side?"

Yes, I absolutely had.

Idunn was in her garden when we arrived, clothed in one of her plain linen dresses and a layer of dirt. By the look of things, she'd been tearing up a new patch of grass and tilling the soil underneath. She looked up as we approached, wiping her cheek with the back of her hand and leaving a new streak of dirt among the others.

"Good morning!" She hopped up from her knees and brushed her hands on her apron. "You're a bit earlier than I expected. I need to get this soil turned before the rain comes tonight."

"We could help." I reached over to pull the shovel out of the ground, but the moment my hand touched it, Idunn slapped it away.

"No. I can handle this on my own. The two of you should make the best of your time together." She stared at me, very directly, as if she knew something I didn't.

Loki just shrugged. "As long as someone feeds me today, I don't care what else happens." Loki ruffled Idunn's hair, eliciting a delighted squeak from her, then trotted off toward Yggdrasil. "Come on, Siggy. Let's get to work before I decide to get drunk again."

I pushed down the urge to complain about the name and hurried to catch up.

He started talking the second I got close enough. "How do you draw your power?"

"From the ground, of course. What other way is there?"

Loki stopped in a patch of sunlight, halfway between Idunn's cabin and Yggdrasil's trunk. He swung himself down and sat cross-legged in the grass. I sat across from him, tucking my dress under my calves.

"Have you ever used seidr in Jotunheim?" He picked out a section of his hair and nimbly twisted the strands into a thin braid before starting on the next.

"Not often, but when I did, it was…challenging."

"The connection to the ground is weaker in the mountains. Too much stone, too much ice and snow. But you knew that already."

I nodded. "Your people also use seidr, but no one seems to be able to tell me how they can sustain it."

"It's a well-kept secret. Gives an edge over the Aesir any time Asgard decides to ride into Jotunheim. Now, I'm in a precarious spot, my mother being Aesir and my father being Jotun; I have mixed allegiances. But I'm assuming this is a secret you can keep?"

I looked him in the eyes. "With all the talk about tricks and betrayal, I never took you for a *keeper* of secrets."

The emerald in his eyes seemed to light up for a moment, full of life. "You'd be surprised what kinds of things I know. So, will you play along, or should we sunbathe instead?"

Damn that incorrigible smile. "I won't tell a soul."

Loki stretched his shoulders and shook the tension from his body, letting his hands rest on his knees. He closed his eyes. A focus exercise then. I followed suit, relaxing my muscles and coaxing myself into long, deep breaths.

"Ignore the instinct to do as you were taught. Don't feel for the ground beneath you or the roots or whatever nonsense your mentors told you. Wait for the breeze."

The breeze. That made perfect sense. What's more universal and accessible than the air?

He didn't say anything else. We sat in silence as I put myself to work on the new task. It felt odd to reach skyward rather than down, but I trusted him—enough.

A slight breeze brushed against my skin. I gave it all my attention, focusing on the cool flutter of it, the way it slid across my cheek like a lover's caress. It moved through my hair and left gooseflesh on my neck. I drew it in, filling my lungs and exhaling, focusing on the push and pull of each breath, the way it filled me up and left me empty.

I had lots of practice with focus, and it was easy to let my thoughts flow over me, in one ear and out the other. I lost track of time, hearing but not listening to the sound of ground being churned and the leaves rustling and the birds chirping. We stayed that way for a long time. It was hard to feel for something that didn't always have mass or force, but I felt a spark of something every time a breeze flitted across my skin. I was getting there.

Then a burst of concentrated wind spread across my face, breath that smelled like breakfast, sparking heat into every pore. I jumped, rubbing my hands across my face to get rid of the tingling sensation, then broke into sneezes.

Loki fell on his side in the grass, laughing hard enough to pull a muscle. "I'm sorry," though he was clearly not, "I couldn't help myself."

I frowned, trying not to laugh. I wanted to take it seriously. But it was also a little funny.

He stayed where he was, head propped up on his hand. "Your skin was glowing when the breeze hit. It's going well, I take it?"

"I just need a little practice."

"And the wildfire?"

"I can't do it anymore."

"Show me."

So I did. I failed the first few times, and even when I managed to summon up a spark, it was a small, fragile thing. He told me to do it again, leaning in close to listen. I repeated it until my tongue was tripping over the runes. By the end, I was summoning it seamlessly, snuffing it out and igniting it once more.

"Well done. Time to throw some oil on the fire then." He leaned in and whispered another set of runes, similar to the original but full of catalysts. Runes meant for a larger flame.

I rolled my shoulders, focusing on the runes and the space between my hands. I whispered them, and flame burst out of my palms, igniting the air in all directions and knocking us both onto our backs. The shock to my focus snuffed the flame out immediately, but the scent of scorched hair lingered.

"Are you alright?" Idunn called from the distance, hands on her hips.

"We're fine," Loki called back, gaping at me. The fire had charred off the bottoms of his new braids. His gaze travelled up to Yggdrasil, then back to me.

I threw my hands over my face and cried out in frustration. "I'm going to end up burning down all nine realms, starting with that tree!"

He moved to kneel in front of me, smelling more like cinders than ever. With a gentle insistence, he pried one of my hands off my face and gave me an empathetic smile. "I blew a hole in the roof of a barn my first time."

I sniffed, tears of frustration welling in my eyes. "No, you didn't."

He bobbed his head and made a face, caught in a lie. "No, I didn't. I burnt my mother so badly, she had to go to the infirmary. The point is, you're doing fine." Loki looked over his shoulder. Idunn had pulled over her apron and was heading for the cabin. "Now's as good a time to stop as any. There'll be plenty of time to burn down Asgard later."

CHAPTER SEVEN

"Flowers blossom most thoroughly when given time, affection, and kindness. This is, I suspect, true for most things in life."

—Runes for Botanical Remedies

Three Weeks Later

Loki was already leaning against the outer door of Valaskjálf when I arrived, looking far too excited for the matter at hand. In contrast, I looked exactly the way I felt: sleep deprived and harried. Day 21 had arrived. It was time to prove myself worthy to Odin, sink or swim.

"I told you not to come." I barely looked at Loki as I passed through the doorway. My stomach was already doing flips, and I didn't need him making it any worse.

Loki slipped up behind me, matching my pace. "I know, but that would be rude. I couldn't just let you walk in there alone, could I?"

"You really could have." I rounded a corner, heading for Gladsheim, my heart beating out of my chest. The doors were right there. I was ready.

Wasn't I?

A hand wrapped around my wrist and Loki pulled me to a stop. "Are you alright?"

I shook my head, blinking back the tears welling in my eyes. The panic was setting in. I couldn't slow my breathing. "We've done nothing but practise for three weeks, and it's not going to be enough. It's just like every other time, and then what? What else can I possibly do to change his mind? I've tried everything."

And it really felt like I had. Loki and I had spent nearly every waking hour together, pouring over books in my study, practicing rune sequences, making failed attempts at shapeshifting. 21 days wasn't enough to learn everything he could offer, let alone master it, and it didn't matter that we'd sat shoulder to shoulder day after day, night after night. It wasn't going to be enough.

"Don't think like that." The mirth dropped from Loki's face. "You deserve this."

"Does that matter?" A tear threatened to spill over, and I wiped it away with a finger before he could see. "It never has."

"Sigyn." Loki put his hands on either side of my face, pushing some of the stray hairs away from my eyes. I drew in a breath. I'd gotten used to the way he could touch people so casually, like touching people meant nothing, but this was so much more personal. "Look at me. Pay attention. I know what I said about Odin never bending to anyone, but I was wrong. You're going to prove me wrong. You are better than him, and me, and everyone else in this city. You're going to take all those smarts and that stubborn spirit and you're going to make your father give you that title. Do you understand me?"

I swallowed hard and took a deep, centring breath. Then another. Pushed the fear down. "Yes. That's what I'll do. Because you're all wrong."

A slight grin slid back onto his lips as I slipped out of his grip and turned towards the doors of Gladsheim. As I reached for the handle to push the door open, I looked back. Loki had propped himself up against the wall and pulled a book from somewhere. He looked up.

I cleared my throat. "Thanks."

He didn't say anything, just nodded towards the doors, then went back to his book.

I pushed open the heavy door and slid inside. Odin was already in his chair, thumbing through a stack of papers. Frigg sat at his side, staring into the distance. The rest of the chairs were empty. A handful of guards stood around the room, their eyes on me. My body started to hum with worry again.

No.

Loki was wrong. Odin was wrong. This was mine to take.

I strode forward, telling myself that I was more confident than I really was, and stopped in front of the dais.

"Good morning, Father."

Odin looked down at me, and after a long moment, he set the pile of papers on the floor next to his chair. "You're ready to show us all your marvellous new tricks?"

"I've learned a lot. I think you'll be surprised." A voice in the back of my head begged me to walk away, but I drowned it out. "I've done good work."

"Right." He slumped down into the seat and propped his head in his hand. All the finery of his furs and embroidered clothes did nothing to hide the fact that he already seemed bored.

I looked to Frigg, hoping for a warmer reception, but that was a lost cause. She had yet to register that I was even in the room. Aside from being Odin's true wife, the Goddess of Marriage, and the mother of Hod and Baldur, she could also see the future. Her mind was somewhere else, watching another time and place. All that was left was a frigid, blonde shell in an icy blue gown, a cold attempt at a stepmother.

When no one said anything, I looked back at Odin. "I'm ready to start."

"Well, go ahead."

I pursed my lips and looked around, then back at him. "Will someone be attacking me, or do you have some other test in mind?"

Odin shifted in his seat, one ankle coming to rest on his other knee. "It won't be necessary. Just demonstrate what you've learned."

"Won't that be…anticlimactic?" Some of the things I'd learned from Loki weren't all that obvious to the naked eye. Better reflexes, the ability to read people's actions rather than their words, using a second energy source. These things needed to be proven.

"If you're not ready—"

I didn't let him finish the sentence. I'd been storing energy since the moment I walked in the room. With a single string of runes, I called up a burst of lavender flame on the stairs in front of him. Its heat sprang out in all directions, its tips reaching skyward. I let it sit for a moment, crackling and dangerous, then reached out, pushing my hands together in the empty air. The fire shrunk until it sparked out completely, leaving a wisp of smoke in its wake. Summoning up another burst of flame in my palm, I tossed it from hand to hand. I lobbed it into the air and snuffed it out again.

I took a deep breath and let a long string of runes slip from my tongue. The air crackled as static raced down my outstretched arm, pooling in my hand. The bouncing, living light writhed in my cupped hands, and I stretched it into a spear. I pulled back my arm to launch it across the hall—

"Is that all you've learned? Some flashy tricks to keep the crowds entertained?"

My heart dropped from my chest so quickly that the lightning snapped and died in my palms. I stood there, slack jawed, unable to form a word. I'd barely gotten started, and it was already over.

"This is the trouble with learning from Loki; he's all show and no substance." Odin yawned. "How will this help you when you're at the negotiation table with emissaries, vying for a piece of land? What good will it do when you're working to broker peace between two cities?"

I attempted to brush the shock from my face. "I spent five years studying under Forseti for that, learning the laws and rites of each realm. I spent months with historians to learn Elven etiquette and tradition. When I told you about that, you told me I needed to learn to defend myself." I pressed my face into my hands, holding back a scream. "I've forgotten more things than most of the other gods have ever known. When will you make up your mind?"

Odin leaned forward in the chair, glaring down with that one eye, a scowl under his grey-streaked beard. His pet ravens rustled and squawked from the back of the throne. "I'm waiting for you to show me something worth rewarding, and I haven't seen it yet, not in the least. Give up on this maddening chase; I'll tell you when you're ready."

"I worked for this! I can't just give up!" I pressed my hand into my chest, emotion boiling over. "You expect me to settle for scraps like a dog while the rest are handed everything they'll ever need! I want their respect! I want a place, a meaning. Why are you keeping me from it?"

He took a deep breath, his hands gripping the arms of his chair. "You. Aren't. Ready."

I threw my hands up in exasperation. The tears were welling in my eyes, and if I cried it would only make me look weak. "Fine. What now? You'll exile Loki back to the woods, and I'll get to go back to begging others to teach me things? Because this was all for nothing?"

Odin was about to speak, but Frigg reached out, setting her hand on her husband's knee. He stopped and looked at her. She nodded, cool and collected, then looked down at me. "No." Even her voice was like ice. "You've learned something from Loki, as the arrangement stipulated. He's caused no real trouble since his return, and there are still things Asgard will gain from him. Things we need. He stays."

I squinted at her, confused. Frigg didn't often overrule Odin, but we'd all seen it before. She knew things the rest of us didn't, and though Odin wasn't accustomed to bowing to the will of anyone else, he always listened to his wife.

"Is nothing ever straightforward with either of you?" I snapped. "Am I supposed to keep working with him, or should I go back to learning Dwarven table manners?"

"The direction of your life depends solely on you, Sigyn," Frigg said, her voice as smooth as glass. "Each choice you make weaves a stitch into your fate, and the Nornir watch you, as they watch us all. Choose wisely."

I stared at her, wondering if her cryptic bullshit only made sense to her, or if I was the one left out of the joke.

Odin slapped his hand on the chair and stood. "There are other things I need to attend to. Collect yourself before you leave." Frigg rose as well, though with more grace, and the two of them started down the stairs and out the doors, leaving me standing in the empty hall.

I reached up to touch my face. The tears had spilled over. Ymir's breath. I was so furious I hadn't even noticed.

Everything grew so quiet that I could hear my own breath, feel the race of my heart under my skin. I made my way up the dais, one step at a time, approaching the closest chair. The metal was cool under my fingertips. I slid them along its arm, feeling the imperfect gold plating, each groove and knot and scratch from some part of Asgard's history.

It was suddenly very clear to me that I would never be that god. They had been right. Odin had already decided who I was, and I had spent decades beating my head against a wall. For nothing. It would never be me sitting there, helping to shape the realms and fight back the tides of Ragnarok.

I was doomed to stand at the bottom of the stairs and look up at my betters.

A sob took my breath away. I bent my face into my hands and cried. Every useless night spent studying, every sacrifice, every wasted effort. I couldn't remember ever really losing hope before, because I had always felt like it was coming. Someday.

This felt like never.

The echo of boots on stone pulled me back to the world. I turned away from the door, wiping my face in my sleeve. The last thing I needed was to be seen snivelling in the shadows.

"Well? How did it go?" Loki came bounding up the stairs, a lilt in his voice. I didn't answer, didn't turn toward him. I felt him approach, stepping in front of me. "Did he—oh. I guess not."

He put his hand on my shoulder, and I finally looked up at him. There was concern etched all over his face. My lip started to quiver. He let out a long sigh and pulled me against his chest.

Perhaps it was just the kindness of the gesture, or perhaps it was because it came from him, someone who had no reason to care what happened to me. Whatever it was, I cried the bitterest, loudest tears I'd ever cried. I pressed my face into his chest, soaking his tunic, a floodgate of misery and self-pity. He held me, one hand lost in my hair, the other around my back, as if he might shield me from the world. It had been so long since I'd taken comfort in someone else like that, I thought I might melt into him and never come back.

When I could breathe again, he looked down at me with the softest smile. "I want to show you something."

I wiped my eyes with the back of my hand, no doubt smearing black kohl and tears across the entirety of my face. His tunic was a mess. "What is it?"

"Something your father doesn't want you to see. Will you come with me?"

I sniffed and nodded. It could hardly be worse than this.

He released me from his grip and led me down the stairs, out of Gladsheim. The moment we were outside the doors, he stopped and looked around. There was no one in sight. "Alright now, as quick as you can, but keep quiet." He took off running, light footed and sure, and I had to hold up my skirts to keep up with him.

He wound us through corridors and around corners. We were getting dangerously close to Odin's chambers. He couldn't possibly be planning to break into them, could he? But then he took the wrong turn. He took the corridor to Hlidskjalf.

I fell in beside him. "You can't be serious. No one's ever broken into Odin's tower."

"You only think that because no one's ever caught me." He stopped in front of Hlidskjalf's door. It was barely an impression in the wall, its edges flush with the stone. There was no handle, no lock to pick.

His lips started moving in long strings of runes that I couldn't catch. The air stopped making sense in front of my eyes, and I was forced to look away, blinking the blur from my vision.

When I looked up again, I startled backward, nearly hitting the wall behind me. Odin stood there, as large and overbearing as always. But the grin under his beard was out of place, too sly and playful to be his.

"What has one eye and no sense of humour?" His voice was a growl, the same as Odin's, but the light, carefree movements belonged to Loki. "Your father." He laughed at his own joke and pressed his hand flat against the door. Something behind it hissed and groaned, and the door moved, sliding back and away, letting me peek inside for the very first time.

It was a plain grey room, a cylinder big enough for three to stand comfortably and not an inch more. No window, no stairs, nothing.

"Honestly, I'd expected more from a secret tower." I stepped in and turned around, trying to see if I'd missed anything. I hadn't. When I turned back to the door, the shape of Odin had sloughed off, and Loki was himself once again.

He stepped in behind me and pointed upward. "Look."

The tower stretched up further than I could see. There was no visible way to get there, though there was clearly a platform overhead.

"Last time I used my flying boots, but with them so tragically lost, perhaps you could use the air to push us upward..."

Right. That would work. It could get me in a lot of trouble, but what did that matter now? I was never getting a title, and here was Loki, acting like I was capable of floating us into the sky. And all I wanted was for once, one single time, for someone to believe in me.

I strung runes together, choosing them carefully, repeating them over and over. After a moment, the air around us began to swirl, batting our clothes and hair. I pushed down with my hands, and the movement concentrated the force toward our feet. Gradually, we rose from the ground.

It was a slow process, getting all the way up there. Loki didn't say a word, quietly watching the ground move further away, knowing that any break in my concentration would mean a deadly fall for us both. My mouth was parched and my tongue tied by the time we reached the top. But the view was more than worth the effort.

The room at the top was small, plated in silver and gold. There were no walls, only curling iron bars to hold visitors inside. The bars held up a tiny roof, protecting two ornate, plush seats. Everything else was open air.

Hlidskjalf was Odin's private tower, one of the ways he kept his eye on the realms. His wife could see the future, and his son Heimdall could see leagues into the distance, and his ravens brought him news from everywhere. It was an obsession of his, knowing everything. Like he was worried that one day he would miss something and that it would be the last straw that hurdled us towards Ragnarok.

But the view.

The realms stretched out around us for miles. Far in the distance was the white walled city of Vanaheim, built into the side of a cliff and bordered by waterfalls. In the other direction were the icy mountains at the far edge of Jotunheim, and behind us was the magnificent blue of the sea. We were so high that even Yggdrasil's branches seemed to be within reach.

"I've never seen anything like this." I walked to the edge of the room and placed my hands on the swirling steel bars, staring over the edge toward Jotunheim. As I watched, the top of one of the far-off mountain peaks crumbled, raining snow down the steep slope.

Loki came to stand beside me. "It's not a title, but it's what I can give you."

"It's amazing. Thank you." I took a deep breath, watching him from the corner of my eye. "Frigg said you could stay in Asgard. What will you do?"

Loki gave the most exasperated, exaggerated sigh I'd ever heard, then tossed himself down onto one of the two seats, a place only the Allfather and his wife would have ever sat. Legs slung over one arm, slouching into the cushions, it felt vaguely disrespectful. "I've got all these *things* now. The books and the bags and all that. It would be a terrible inconvenience to bring them back to my shack in the woods. The gold wouldn't even match the rot."

"You poor thing. We can't have that." I pushed down the doubt and sat down in the other chair. It took effort to appear as nonchalant as he was. I wiggled, trying not to feel stiff and disobedient, and laid back with my legs strung out next to his.

"Sigyn, you look like you're going to die of stress. Relax." He kicked my boot playfully, then shifted one leg on top of mine, tangling us up.

I sighed and demanded the tension leave my body. Easier said than done, but his company helped. "So, you'll stay then?"

Loki smirked. "You've clearly got more to learn. What choice do I have?"

CHAPTER EIGHT

*"The staff have been questioned and punishments doled out,
but the bottle of 140-year-old Elven Sapphire is still missing.
Odin's going to have my fucking head."*

—*Valhalla Record of Inventory*

Loki and I met the next morning, as usual. But this time we didn't set out to teach or be taught. Instead, we sat under the shade of Yggdrasil, drinking Elven strawberry wine and telling scathing jokes about the state of Odin's beard. It was strange at first, to just sit and be with each other, but the wine helped.

I'd barely slept. I'd spent the night alone, sitting against the headboard and clawing the depths of my mind for some kind of purpose. It felt useless to read or study, but I didn't know how to do anything else. I tried to imagine myself as a traveller, an emissary, a thief. None of the things came close to the future I'd wanted. None of the possibilities kept me from crying myself to sleep.

So this was good. The sun was shining, the wine made me feel light, and there was company for my misery. Whatever Loki was, good or bad—or something else entirely—he knew his way around a good story and a drink.

But by noon the wine was empty. Loki stood up and reached out a hand to help me. "Come on. I'm not ready to sober up."

I slumped back into the grass, holding myself up by my elbows. "I don't want to go anywhere. I'm sure Idunn has something to drink in her cabin."

"Ah, but what she won't have is the 140-year-old bottle of Elven Sapphire that Odin keeps in the cellar of Valhalla."

I sprang to attention. "Oh no. I'm not going to Valhalla. I can't see my family.

Everyone will know by now and I just...I can't."

He crouched down in front of me. "No one says you have to. I'll steal the bottle, and you get something to eat from the hall, and we'll disappear into the gardens like a pair of crafty rats. Come on, you deserve a little fun."

I *did*, didn't I? I'd clearly spent too much time focused on one thing. As heartbroken as I was, there was a small part of me that revelled in the idea of giving up, the freedom of it. So what if it was spiteful to raid the cellar and drink Odin's wine? I *felt* spiteful.

I pulled myself off the grass, brushed off my skirt, and let him lead the way to my father's wine. As promised, Loki disappeared down one of the corridors leading off of Valhalla, and by the time, I'd gathered a tray full of appetizing morsels from the empty kitchens, he was back. There was a suspicious bulge under his shirt, but he was carrying on as casually as if it were a normal extension of his body.

We left through the opposite side of Valhalla, a door which led out into the garden. A wall of sprawling green bushes and trees divided it from the rest of the city. Flowers bloomed among the greenery, brought in from all corners of the nine realms. Fiery red vilanis from Vanaheim, crawling crimson farenum vines from deep in Svartalfheim, sunset plumeria blossoms from Midgard. A sandy path ran from Valhalla down to the stone fountain at the furthest point and back again.

We settled ourselves in front of the fountain, spreading out our stolen loot. Above us, a looming gold statue of a Valkyrie rose from the water, her wings outstretched as she pulled a fallen warrior from the depths.

Loki pulled the wax seal from the bottle of wine and sniffed at the opening. His eyes lit up. He passed it to me. It smelled pure, light, like if sunlight glimmering on the blue of a lake had a smell. I tipped the bottle to my lips. The taste was impossible to place, airy and fresh. Something only Elves could make and only the lucky could afford.

We passed the bottle back and forth, chatting over our patchwork lunch, lying conspiratorially in the grass, telling stories as easily as if we had been doing it for years. It wasn't until we heard a lilting song at the other end of the garden that we came back to the world.

I sat up, peeking over the bushes that lay between us and whoever had arrived. It was Sif. She had a basket slung over one arm, a pair of shears in the other hand. She sang as she combed through the flowers, holding one out, snipping the stem, and placing it in the basket with the rest. Her hair, that precious waterfall of blonde locks that she valued more than anything in the world, flowed along with her every movement, and I felt compelled to run my fingers through it. It probably felt like silk.

Loki cracked his knuckles.

"No. Please, don't cause any trouble." I put my hand on his arm, trying to push him back onto the grass.

"But she's *such* an easy mark." He pouted.

I started to argue with him, but the wine had already gone to my head, and I was suddenly very sure that I didn't give a fuck. What was the point of staying out of trouble anyways? I flopped back into the grass and waved a hand noncommittally. He flashed one of those grins and leapt up, sneaking past the brush toward Sif.

I could see everything from my vantage point behind the bush, my body hidden away. As he snuck up behind her, I languished in the grass, not quite feeling like I was inside my own skin. It was some *damn good wine*. The grass was cool, and the sun was warm, and Yggdrasil Above, my heart hurt so badly when no one was around to distract me. The silence felt like an eternity. I didn't want to think about what I'd lost. I wanted Loki to make me laugh until I forgot again.

Sif didn't notice Loki, not even when he was practically breathing down her neck. He leaned in next to her ear and bleated like a sheep. She screamed, nearly jumped out of her skin, and dropped all her carefully cut flowers into the grass. I smiled a little despite myself.

Then she slapped him.

I scraped myself off the ground and shuffled over, a sinking feeling brewing in my gut. This would not end well.

"That was a dirty trick, and you're a complete imbecile." There were tears in her eyes; she really had gotten a scare.

"So you're afraid of sheep now, are you? Life must be so difficult for you with Thor's pet goats around." Loki shoved his thumbs into the loop of his belt, a smug look on his face.

"I am not afraid of sheep! I'm afraid of wild Jotnar half-breeds sneaking up on me in the garden!"

I stepped between them. "Please don't. It's a beautiful day, and it was all just a joke. Can we make peace and move along?"

She turned her steely eyes on me. "If you hadn't brought him back, none of us would have to worry about him at all."

I sighed, the largest part of me wanting to find a quiet place to lie down while they finished their spat. "Frigg was the one who decided he should stay, not me. If you're so opposed, you should take it up with her."

Sif picked up her basket and held it against her chest like a shield. "You know he used to get Thor into all sorts of trouble, don't you? Taking him on these long journeys around the realms. I was never sure if he'd come back in one piece or if he'd come home at all. Things have been quiet, but now that he's back—"

I held up my hand, confused. "So you were only worried about Thor when Loki was around? How many times has Thor gone off alone to fight something three times his size?"

"Sigyn." She said my name the way a parent might patiently talk to a disruptive child. "You weren't here. You can't understand. Trouble is part of his blood."

"Is it?" Something in Loki changed then. He straightened out, tense and ready for something. "Do tell."

"It is." She wiped a stray tear from her cheek and squared her shoulders like it might lend her some credence, her eyes locked on Loki's. "Your people have never been our friends. Everyone knows the Jotnar will come for us at Ragnarok. It's part of the prophecy. When Laufey ran off to Jotunheim and brought back a half-breed baby and your ice-blooded father, we gave her the benefit of the doubt. But we shouldn't have. You've caused nothing but trouble since. Your mother was naive and dim-witted, and it was her own fault she died!"

Loki's lips moved, a split-second reaction. A rune, a breath. And then Sif crumpled to the ground before my eyes. Her legs had given out beneath her. She was sprawled out on her chest among her flowers, her impossibly long hair fanning out like a sunlight blanket.

I stood there uselessly, too addled by the drink. I waited for something to happen that would tell me what kinds of runes he'd used.

She began to snore.

Loki stared down at her sleeping body, his chest heaving with each breath, his teeth ground together in a snarl. It was a patient anger, one forced down and tempered from practice. After a dozen deep breaths, he crouched down, gathered all of Sif's hair into one hand, pulled the knife from his belt, and sheared the whole bundle off.

The moment that followed was one of the longest in my life. Loki opened his hand and let the wind take the mass of hair from his palm. Strands untangled and tumbled in every direction. They caught on every bush and branch. Gold scattered across the grass like straw after the harvest. It blew into the fountain, hooking itself on the corners of the bronze Valkyrie. It was everywhere.

He stood, brushing his hands together to get rid of the last strands. And Sif slept on, her hair cropped and jagged like wheat stalks.

All at once, the panic set in. My heart racing, my breaths coming short and quick. The wine was losing its hold on me, everything suddenly too real. And Loki was just standing there, staring at Sif.

I pushed him. He startled out of his quiet and snapped at me. "What?"

"What have you done? Thor's going to hunt you down and kill you!"

"Let him try." He brushed off the front of his tunic, where some of Sif's hair had gotten caught.

I grabbed him by the chin, forcing him to look at me. "He will beat you to death with his bare hands."

He pried my hand away. "I was his friend longer than you've been his sister. I know he will."

"Yggdrasil shade us," I mumbled, both a curse and a prayer. I looked around. No one in sight. I grabbed him by the arm, trying to pull him along. "Come on."

"Why?"

I stopped and faced him, jabbing my finger against his chest. "Because she was right; it's my fault you're here, and I'm not going to let you get us *both* killed."

He pursed his lips, thinking about it for a moment, then begrudgingly shrugged.

I pulled off my cloak and slung it over his shoulders. It was too short, but it would cover the evidence long enough to get him back to his room.

As we rounded the corner into the hall, I looked back. If it weren't for the angle of her body, it might almost look like Sif was taking a nap.

CHAPTER NINE

"Guilt is like a weed. Plant a little in the soul, and it will consume the whole garden."

—*Elven Proverb*

Every sound and footfall startled me as we walked through Valaskjálf. I thought for certain that everyone who passed would know what had happened. By the time we were at Loki's chamber, my hands were shaking. He unlocked the door, and I pushed my way in, desperate to be out of sight.

His room was like any of the other guest quarters, aside from a spattering of his own belongings. A set of drawers stood against one wall, a lush bed covered in furs and pillows across from it. A full-length polished metal mirror stood next to the fireplace. A small pile of his books were on the night table, and lying on the floor was a pair of sleeping trousers.

My heart was thudding against my chest as I willed myself to think past the haze of danger. Loki, on the other hand, seemed just fine. He pulled my cloak off his shoulders and slung it over the end of the bed, as casual as could be. I looked down. Long wisps of blonde hair were scattered on the floor.

I waved a hand at him. "Take off your tunic."

He didn't move, so I took hold of the bottom of his tunic and yanked it up. It got stuck around his shoulders, and he stumbled as I pulled, bending and wriggling.

"What the hel are you doing?" He tried to resist, but I slapped his arm and pulled the tunic all the way off.

I turned it right-side out. It was covered in Sif's hair. "Make a fire."

"Sigyn, calm down. You—"

57

"Make a fire! Now!"

He stared at me for a moment, eyes wide. Then he turned to the hearth and did as he was told.

I cracked the shirt like a whip, trying to shake the stray hair from it. Strands fluttered to the stone. There was still more. I picked off every strand caught on it, tears running down my cheeks, my breaths short and panicked. I wiped them away and went back to picking the tunic clean. The floor. My shoes. It was everywhere. I dropped to my knees, raking my fingers along the stone, trying to find an end to all this evidence.

"Sigyn." Loki crouched next to me. "Hey. Sit down. Everything is fine."

I threw the hair into the fire. It sizzled and curled in the flame, the acrid smell filling the room. It stuck to my hand, tangling and clinging to my skin like guilt made solid. I glanced at my dress. They were there too, spread over everything like a pox. No matter how much I picked off, there seemed to be another one to take its place.

Loki put his hand on my shoulder, and I whipped around to face him, seething. "Why? Why did you do it?"

He settled onto the stone, legs crossed underneath him. "Because she deserves it."

"She was mean to you. How does that even compare to this?"

"It's just hair."

"It's *assault*, Loki. Her hair has always been her pride and you *know* that, we all do. And depending who you ask, this is just enough of an insult to warrant killing you for it. So what makes it worth your life, hmm?"

He looked down at his trousers, plucked a hair from his knee, and tossed it in the fire. "You don't know about my mother, do you? The real truth. If you did, you wouldn't ask me that." He shook his head. "Or maybe you would, I don't know."

I leaned forward on my palms. "Just tell me. Please. I need to understand this, or I can't...I can't be around someone who would just *do* things like this, Loki."

There was a silence after. A long, heavy moment of weighing options. Of deciding what to say. Loki stared at the stone in the hearth, his eyes far away.

When he spoke, his voice was quiet. "My mother's name was Laufey. She was there from the beginning, when Valhalla was built. She helped breathe life into this city along with the other gods. But she did something unforgivable. She married a Jotun."

"Your father?"

Loki nodded. "Mother had gone out into the realms to make her own way for a while, and she came back with a family. I was just a baby at the time. The gods lost their minds. The Jotnar are enemies, and it's all good fun to *fuck* one—Thor's mother is Jotun, for godsake—but no one had married one before. But my parents loved each other, and the gods all but cast her out for it. The way people looked at us, the sneers, the things they said…it made everything hard. Impossible. My parents fought all the time, and it made them bitter towards each other. My mother didn't care what the gods thought, but my father was always trying to follow the rules, so no one had an excuse to hate him. After a while, it didn't matter what we did, and when my mother had two more sons—"

"You have brothers?" No one had ever mentioned them, not once.

"Somewhere. I don't know where. But my mother wanted to pass on her gifts to someone, and I suppose I was the closest thing she had to a daughter. She taught me seidr when no one else was looking. And I was good at it. Like I'd always been meant to use it. It took years for my father to find out what we were doing. And he killed her for it."

I sat back, the tenderness of his story taking the bluster out of my anger. Loki was so good at laughing, at being carefree; how could he have so much tragedy under his skin? "How did he do it?"

"Poison." He still hadn't looked up. There were no hairs left to remove from his trousers, so he started to scratch away the skin around his fingernails. "The night he caught us practising, he hit her so hard, it split her cheek open. I hid under the table, knowing he'd do worse to me; he couldn't stand to have an *argr* son, a coward. But she peeled herself off the floor and burned the shape of her hand into his chest. The smell of burned flesh…it's what I remember most. Farbauti never touched her again. He didn't have the guts."

He stared into the fire, his body seeming to curl in on itself, his elbows against his knees, face hidden behind a curtain of hair. "It was only a week later that she started to get weaker. Sicker. Even though gods rarely get sick. No one could figure out what was wrong with her. Or maybe they didn't care." He drew in a long breath. "I didn't find the vial until after she was gone. She'd been dying for months, and he'd been slipping poison into her food every day."

"Loki…" I reached out for him but withdrew my fingers. "I'm so sorry. What happened to you? Where did you go?"

"I told the gods, and my father ran. Heard later that he was killed for information about Asgard by his own people. Odin took me in. Raised me here, started calling me Blood-Brother, made sure I was taught the things he'd need from me. He took more from me than it was worth." He rustled, wiping at his face with his hands, then sat straight again. There was the slightest hint of red around his eyes. "So now you know. Does Sif deserve it?"

I turned my gaze away from him. What should the cost of insulting someone's murdered mother be? Is the price a head of hair? Is it more or less than that? "What you did was wrong, Loki. There's no getting around that. And I can't defend that action. But I might have done the same, I think, if I'd had a mother I loved like that. Lost like that." I tucked my hair behind my ear, unsure of what else to say. "I'm sorry. You must miss her."

He nodded slowly, and then the room grew quiet. I wanted him to speak, to say something, anything. To see him quiet, somber, was like watching a shell of him. Someone hollowed out. There was something so desperately unsettling about knowing what was underneath all the quips and sly grins. That he carried the weight of bodies on his shoulders.

The wood in the hearth crackled, spreading a new wave of warmth across my front. The smell of burnt hair was weaker, returning to the smokey comfort of burning wood. The adrenaline in my body was fading, and all I felt was tired, right to my core.

Someone was going to find Sif. After I'd failed to get my title, I'd been sure that I had no future. Now it might really be true.

I leaned my head against Loki's shoulder and closed my eyes. If it was all going to end, at least I wanted a little peace before it did.

CHAPTER TEN

*"Loki's always had a taste for pranks, but this one went too
far. To cut off Sif's hair just for fun—what kind of monster
does something like that?"*

—*Frey - Godly Endeavours*

My bones rattled, waking me from a dead sleep. The long, droning blow of the Gjallarhorn was loud enough to seep through the walls, but it didn't need to. Every god could feel it, no matter how far away. A summons. Someday, it would blow and signal the end of everything, but not today.

My stomach curdled like old goat's milk. I already knew what it meant.

Loki had put on a fresh tunic and was leaning against the mantle, eyes on me. I stared at him, catching my breath, the vibration still under my skin. He must have felt it too, but he looked so composed. After a century in exile, he'd probably gotten used to ignoring it.

I wasn't sure how long I'd slept or how I'd ended up in Loki's bed. The fire was dead in the hearth, only embers and ash remaining. My mouth tasted like smoke, and I was parched, my head wringing with sobriety.

"I'm sorry I got you involved in this," he said at last.

I hesitated. I believed that he meant it, just the same as I believed he would do it again in a heartbeat. So I gave him a nod. There was nothing to say.

I crawled out from under the furs and went to the mirror. I brushed back the bed-mussed tangle of curls in my hair and tried to wipe away the smudges of kohl around my eyes. In the reflection, Loki was staring across the room at nothing, his thoughts a thousand miles away.

61

There were only a handful of gods present when we arrived in Gladsheim. Odin was in his high seat. The twelve council seats were empty, and the few gods that had shown up stood at the bottom of the dais, chattering to each other. Freya and Frey were whispering back and forth, thick as thieves. Idunn was with Bragi—he must have just come home from Midgard—and they were smiling too broadly.

They didn't know yet.

I walked over, my hands clasped together so they wouldn't shake, willing myself to act normal. Everything I did felt fake, like my smile was enough to give us away. And Loki, he just…was. How could he be so *calm*?

Bragi reached out and shook Loki's hand, confident and pleasant as always. "Idunn told me, but I didn't believe her. Welcome home, old friend."

Bragi always looked a little tired around the edges when he came home, but he cleaned up nicely. His coarse black hair was kept in thick locks which he'd tied back, and his beard was immaculately brushed, silver bobbles woven through it. His mother was Elven, and he had their umber skin and their penchant for poetry. The only thing Odin passed on to him was his sharp blue eyes. Lucky him.

Loki gave him a pat on the shoulder. "Where were you this time? Get lost in a troll cave?"

"*Erual*," Bragi cursed in Elven, laughing. "That was once, and I'll never hear the end of it. I was in Midgard, but it was time to come home. I had somewhere more important to be." He put his arm around Idunn's waist, and her smile was bright enough to light the room.

"What's the matter with him?" Idunn whispered, pointing to the far corner of the dais. Thor was sitting with his head in his hands, every muscle coiled like he could barely contain his rage.

"Who knows?" Loki waved it off. "Probably lost a fight or something. Your brother never has been a good loser, has he?"

He was looking at me, nudging me for a sign of life.

"No. He hasn't."

Odin slammed his fist down on the arm of his throne, and I nearly jumped out of my own skin. All eyes went to him.

"There's been a crime," Odin bellowed, his anger echoing from the walls of the chamber. "And someone will pay dearly for it. Sif, step forward. Let them see."

The Allfather waved a hand, and Sif stepped from the shadows behind his throne. Her head was bound with a shawl. She was trying to remain composed, but her grief was thinly veiled as she removed the shawl and exposed her mangled scalp. Shock spread on the voices in the room, and it was enough for Sif's resolve to crumble. She broke down into tears, her shoulders shaking with each sob.

Satisfied with the display, Odin spoke again. "Sif has already told me who it was. Are you going to come forward, or are you determined to be a coward about this?"

"Yes," Thor growled, standing up. "Admit that you attacked my wife so I can give you what you deserve. No one, *no one* insults us like this and gets away with it." Both of his fists were clenched, skin white around his knuckles.

No one spoke, no one moved. Of course they didn't. Because it was us.

Loki took a sweeping bow, staring up at him. "You could've just come to my room and beat me to death in private, but you've always got to go for the dramatic, don't you *Hangi?*"

There was a scoff. Freya. "As if it could be anyone but you. At least you'll prove me right."

"So you admit it?" Odin leaned forward in his seat.

Loki shrugged, looking up at Sif. "She knows who she insulted, don't you, sweetheart? Maybe in the future, you'll mind your manners."

Thor screamed, moving towards Loki with his fist wound back to strike.

My reaction was instant; I'd seen this play out a thousand times before with a thousand other targets. I let a rune slip from my tongue, and a barrier shimmered into being just as Thor struck. His hand collided with it, and he recoiled, teeth gritted against the pain.

"Sigyn, don't get in my way."

The venom in his voice... Thor had been angry a lot over the years, but never at me.

Loki hadn't flinched. He just snickered, tilting his head a little. "Why? Are you afraid you won't be a match for her?"

"A man doesn't need a woman to fight for him," Thor snapped. "Frey. Get her out of my way."

Frey knew enough to clasp his hand over my mouth when he grabbed me. Without the ability to whisper, my seidr was useless. The barrier fell. He pulled me back, away from Loki and Thor. I struggled against him, my scream muffled by his skin, but he refused to let me go.

"Don't make this worse than it already is," he said. "Please."

Thor's eyes stayed on me. "How could you help him do something like this? You, of all people."

I wanted to defend myself, but I had no voice. *I* hadn't done anything. And why was no one interested in what *Sif* had done?

Thor turned on Loki, who was mid-whisper, but he wasn't fast enough. Thor hit him, and the strength of the blow sent Loki flying backwards. He collided into the floor and slid back until he came to a crashing halt against the wall. There was already blood. Then Thor was on top of him, striking him again and again.

Thor would kill him.

I bit down on Frey's hand. He hissed and pulled it away, and I elbowed him in the gut. As he hit the ground, I bolted forward, runes on my lips. The air stirred around me, and I swept my hand sideways, the air whipping up to toss Thor across the room like a ragdoll. He struck the dais, and something cracked.

The hall was in an uproar. Someone was crying; Bragi, Odin, and Freya were screaming at each other. But none of that mattered. I knelt next to Loki and pushed back the bile in my throat. His skin was purple and swollen, his hair painted with the blood from his face.

"Hello, darling." He coughed, wincing from the pain. "Come here often?" Too self-assured, as usual.

I heard Thor before I saw him, running toward us, hel-bent on finishing what he started.

"Thor, enough!"

The command halted my brother in his tracks. His chest was heaving, his clothing spattered with Loki's blood. His whole body twitched, wanting to move, but Odin's word was law.

Odin stood and made his way down the steps, heading toward us as leisurely as he could. I put myself between them, trying to shield Loki from whatever was coming next. My hands were raised, ready to fight.

But Odin stopped at my feet. "You've insulted Sif and, by extension, her husband. If you want to live to see another day, you'll fix what you've done."

Loki spat, blood splattering onto the floor. He laughed. "And here I thought we were friends."

"How dare you!" Thor moved towards us, his feet slamming into the stone with each step.

"Don't come any closer!" I summoned a burst of wildfire in front of him, and he reeled back, checking his face for his eyebrows.

"Enough!" Odin waved a hand at Thor, but he came anyway, straight for me. As quick as a breath, Thor lifted me from the ground by the collar of my dress and held me up for the room to see. Some of them yelled for him to stop, but it was Loki who was most desperate.

"Alright! She didn't *do* anything, you giant oaf!" He struggled to get up and failed, blood seeping out over his lips and dripping to the floor. "Get your hands off her, and

The Goddess of Nothing At All

I'll fix it. Just put her down."

My brother stared at me, teeth grinding together. There was nothing there but rage. All those years of violence he'd laid out across the realms, and he'd never laid a hand on me. My collar was biting into my neck, and my head felt like it would pop clean off, but I wasn't going to beg.

And then he put me down.

I fell to my knees, fear making my legs weak. Loki slid himself closer, nursing his side. His hand landed on mine, staining my skin with blood.

Odin turned to the others. "If Loki can't find a way to restore Sif's hair by the new moon, then it's within Thor's rights to take his life." He looked at me. "And you, daughter of mine…you'll go with him, since you've so aptly promised to keep him 'under control.' Consider yourselves lucky you're not already dead."

Odin turned, the others parting to let him through. He ascended the stairs again and sat back in his throne. Freya was the first to follow him, and then Frey.

Thor didn't look at anyone, just gathered up Sif and left.

With the danger subsided, Bragi let go of Idunn's arm, and she ran to us. She was crying, wiping tears away and choking out words with her sobs.

"Oh, Loki." She took his free hand.

"What?" He wheezed as he caught his breath. "Aren't I handsome?"

But I saw the look on Bragi's face. The friendly demeanour that had been there before was gone. Because he knew what I knew; Idunn would forgive anything, but Loki had proven he was capable of more than just a trick.

"Help me get him up." I stumbled to my feet. Idunn and I took Loki underneath his arms and pulled. He cried out but managed to stand. His eyes were swelling into bulging purple bulbs, and his nose sat crooked on his face, dripping blood down his lips. When I pushed him to walk, he leaned on me, nursing his left leg. He moved slowly, gritting his teeth against the pain. But the strained sound of my name on his breath was what drove the knife into my chest.

"Let's get him to the infirmary." Idunn shifted under his weight.

"No. Stay here; I've got him." She gave me a sharp, hurt look, but she backed away. She meant well, but the truth was, wherever she followed, Bragi would come too. And I couldn't bear the judgement in his eyes.

It took forever to get Loki to his chambers. We shambled down the corridors, past startled visitors and staff, shock on their faces and scandal in their whispers. Maybe I could've fixed him in Gladsheim, but there were too many people gawking, too much worry about turning my back to them. I needed to concentrate.

I fished the keys out of the pouch on his belt, struggling to hold his weight and unlock the door at the same time. I kicked the door open and pushed us through. Loki collapsed onto the bed with a pained hiss, and I slammed the door shut.

"I don't suppose you have anything for healing?" I asked, knowing he absolutely wouldn't. His answer came as a stilted chuckle. "Alright then. The bare minimum it is."

I went to the bed and used a knife to cut his tunic off. I found exactly what I thought I would: a dark patchwork of bruises pooled across his lean chest. Likely a broken bone or two, and something was bleeding.

"Sigyn—" He coughed, cutting the words from his mouth.

I hushed him. "Shut up. I'll mend what I can, but first I need to set your nose." He nodded and gripped the bedsheets as I bent over him. I jammed the corner of one of his pillows into his mouth, and he bit down. Without the tools I'd normally use, I'd have to rely on my fingers and seidr to put everything right. The bridge of his nose was off centre, and when I applied a bit of pressure, it realigned. Loki clenched his teeth into the pillow. He was crying.

It was a horrible sight, watching him like that. Guilt bubbled in my stomach; I had to hurt him to heal him, but it didn't make it any easier. I put my hand on his, and he grabbed hold, squeezing so hard I had to bite back the urge to pull free.

I gathered my focus. The longer I waited, the more pain he would be in. If my time in the infirmary had taught me anything, it was that these injuries were going to take more energy to heal than I had in me. But I would do it anyways.

As the pain of his nose subsided, I stole my hand back. Holding both of them over his chest, I started to whisper a complicated string of runes. In a perfect world, I'd have poultice and rune ink and more strength, but I didn't. I set my mind on the repetition of the runes, willing them to stop the bleeding, to put everything back where it belonged. I persisted, whispering long after my mouth had dried out and my legs started to shake from exhaustion. Then finally, something shifted under his skin, and he screamed so loud I thought my ears might bleed. More of the bruises disappeared with each passing moment, the crack in his lip and the bulge of his eyes mending and softening.

He wasn't healed, not yet. But it was all I could give. He'd stopped crying, and he was out of trouble, but there were still patterns under his skin and swelling in his face. It would have to wait. Any further and I'd end up with rune fatigue.

I pulled my hands away from his skin, now nearly snow-white again, and finally stopped whispering. "That's all I can do for now."

"Well. I guess it'll have to be enough." A smirk settled onto his lips, but it was gone quickly. He was blinking to stay awake.

I forced myself to keep moving and went to the bedside table, where a fresh bowl of water and a washcloth lay, one of the many perks of living in a hall full of dutiful staff. I brought them to the bed and sat at Loki's side. I wrung out the cloth and gently ran it across his forehead. His eyes were closed, something peaceful falling over him as I washed away the leftover blood.

As I cleaned his neck and his chest, the bowl turned a deeper and deeper pink. I fought back the urge to lecture him. I could remind him how stupid he'd been and how close he'd come to his own death, but his breathing was settling into the deep, drawn-out rhythm of sleep. So instead, I finished my work, pulled the furs up over him, stole his keys, and slipped out.

I locked the door behind me. For his safety and everyone else's.

CHAPTER ELEVEN

*"Witnesses said he begged for mercy as Thor pummeled
him, beating him within an inch of his life.
Mercy was more than he deserved."*

—*God of Lies Revealed*

When I returned in the morning, I found Loki still asleep. He had his pillow in a loose embrace, his head on its upper half. His breathing was shallow, and a book lay cover-up on the bed next to him, the open pages pressed against the furs. *Asgard: A History.*

I closed the door gently. He didn't stir. I tiptoed to the bed and carefully picked up the book. The cover was worn, its edges frayed. It was open to a page that had seen more use than the rest, the glue of the binding breaking. On one side was a drawing of a woman, each line of her face sketched with black ink and a thin point. She had long hair, a finely angled face, and kind, piercing eyes. The runes beneath read *Laufey*. After a quick inspection, the inside of the cover also said *Property of the Archives of Asgard.*

Feeling intrusive, I set the book down on the side table, open to the picture of his mother, and set a hand on his shoulder. He inhaled sharply, his eyes fluttering open.

"Good morning." I leaned over him. "I need to check your wounds."

Loki yawned and uncurled himself from his pillow. He moved to stretch but stopped short, hissing through gritted teeth.

"Well…" He cleared his throat. "I've felt better."

"Lie on your back."

There were still faint bruises on his face and a slight tear in his lip, the same as the night before. I ran a gentle hand over his chest where the bones had broken, and he flinched, crying out. I muttered an apology, trying to remain clinical and ignore how tight my chest was as I moved my fingers along his skin. That, and the intensity on his face as he watched me.

"Your neck—"

"Is fine," I interrupted. I'd already seen it, the yellow and green bruises that the collar of my dress had left under my jaw. It was tender, but Thor was capable of much more. I was lucky.

Loki pursed his lips and let the topic slide. "You look tired."

"I'm fine." The truth was, I'd barely slept. I was exhausted from head to toe, but my mind had run circles all night. Ethics, morality, duty, pride. I'd spent my life walking the razor's edge of Odin's approval, trying to keep my every action in line with his expectations, and in a single day, I'd thrown it all out the window. So much of what had just happened pressed against the boundaries of what I knew was right and wrong. Too many contradictions fighting for attention and not enough answers.

But it barely mattered. We had a handful of days before the new moon. If we didn't do something quickly, we'd both be dead soon.

So I'd heal him, and we'd go off and save our own lives. We didn't have time for being tired. I pulled a brush and inkwell out of my bag and set it on the side table.

"You brought a catalyst?" Loki asked.

"I did." I uncorked the inkwell and glanced back at him. His face was set with concern.

There were several kinds of catalysts, ink being the most common. Most catalysts were used preemptively, to keep a völva from expending too much energy at once. Ink was one of the staples of infirmary work, letting one practitioner help twice as many patients as they could without it. Loki was smart. He would know that using it after the fact meant I was trying to conserve what little energy I had left.

He watched as I dipped my brush in the ink and scraped the excess on the side of the jar. I carefully drew runes along his ribcage, each one a small piece of a long string. The black was a stark contrast against his skin.

"Where did you get these scars?" I asked, the silence too uncomfortable.

He looked down curiously, almost as if he had forgotten he had them. "Ah. That one" —he pointed to the long scar that snaked across his stomach— "was a close call with a knife and an Elf. The claw marks are a gift from your brother."

I stopped writing and looked up at him. The scars were vicious, three jagged lines running over both shoulders like pauldrons. "Which brother?"

"Heimdall, when I took Freya's necklace. The man is obsessed with morality. He didn't think it was 'right' or 'honest,' so we had a scuffle. Did you know he can shapeshift into a bear?"

"I think I know that story."

He winked. "I'm a thing of legend."

I sighed, refusing to reward him with a laugh. "You know that he hates you, right?"

"I know. Maybe that's because I won."

A smile snuck onto my lips. "That's not the way I've heard it."

"*Skít,*" he cursed in Jotun. "Can't blame me for trying."

With the last rune finished, I held my hands over his chest. The runes were the same ones I'd used yesterday, but the ink made the weight of it different, easier to bear. The longer I whispered, the fainter the ink became, sinking down into his skin, disappearing a little more with each repetition. Then slowly, the lines and cracks in his face mended. The last of his bruises faded, and hopefully, the pain would go with them.

The exhaustion had been building as I worked, weighing on me like a rock around my neck. My legs were weak, threatening to give out under me. I slumped down onto the mattress. Loki moved quickly, making room for me on the bed, and I let myself collapse onto the welcoming softness of the furs, my head at his feet. My body was so very heavy.

"And what will we do now?" I mumbled.

"Go to Svartalfheim."

I squinted, trying to make sense of it. "You're running away?"

Loki ran his fingers through his hair and found it tangled. He reached for the comb on the bedside table and started working out the knots. "Never. The Dwarves can make anything. A new head of hair isn't even a challenge for them."

I did the math in my head. "That's three days ride from here, and the new moon is in 10 days. If you want to get back in time, we'll have to leave—"

"Today." He'd finished brushing his hair and was working a thick braid into the side of his head, just above his ear. "I hope you don't have anything pressing to do, since your father decided I need a chaperone."

"You *do* need a chaperone." I yawned, covering my mouth with my palm.

"Maybe." He caught my yawn and looked out the window. "Odin's hanged body, Sigyn, it's barely even daylight."

I murmured a response, something I was vaguely sure hadn't made sense.

Loki leaned forward, pulled a spare fur from the bottom of the bed, and threw it over me. "You can't ride all day with rune fatigue. Go to sleep, and don't wake me until it's well past noon."

I wanted to argue, but I was already slipping under. I took the pillow I was offered, and the last thing I felt was the shake of the bed as Loki rolled over, back to the comfort of sleep.

CHAPTER TWELVE

"Dwarves are famous for making something out of nothing.
Give them a hammer, a forge, and enough time, and they
could rebuild the realms themselves."

—*Forging the Belows*

To travel to Svartalfheim, Loki and I had to cross into Midgard. The easiest way was the Bifrost. So we took a pair of horses from Odin's stables and led them down the shimmering rainbow bridge that sloped down from Asgard into the human realm. It took three days of riding, camping, and rationing to make it to the entrance of the Dwarven realm. We travelled by main roads, but never stopped in human towns; too many unfortunate things happened when gods involved themselves with humans. That's how legends—and gods like me—were born, and we didn't have that kind of time.

The entrance to the realm was a cave, a secret kept only from the humans. In order to keep them out, the cave was dressed up like a dragon den, sun-bleached bones littering the path outside. Only a fool would approach it.

Loki hopped down from his horse and walked closer, and the moment his foot neared the edge of the cave, a pair of short, fully armoured soldiers stepped out into the light. White smoke spilled out of the nooks and crannies of the metal suits where the sun hit them. Dwarves.

"Halt." One of them jabbed his spear toward Loki. "Why are you here?" The second Dwarf took a few steps towards me, armour creaking and squeaking as they shambled forward.

Loki cleared his throat. "The Goddess Sigyn Odindottir and I are here to

71

commission the Sons of Ivaldi. We come in the name of Asgard and—"

The Dwarf slammed the butt of his spear into the dirt, cutting him off. "Alright, alright, shut your trap and get inside before the sun boils us alive." He turned and stomped back into the cave, muttering something about long-winded Jotnar. The other followed.

Loki turned to me, a triumphant smile on his face. "After you, my lady."

I stepped down from my horse and went inside. The space was larger than I'd guessed from outside. It was a fully functioning stable, packed to the brim with all manner of animals, load bearing and otherwise. Stable hands rushed to and fro with buckets of feed and bales of fresh straw. There were people from all realms headed in and out of the entrance to a stairway marked *Svartalfheim*.

Loki guided his horse toward the stable, looking around. His eyes fell on a tiny Dwarven girl, so young that her beard hadn't started to grow in yet. She was sitting alone on an overturned bucket, as sullen as could be. He headed straight for her.

"I've got these two horses." He crouched down. "And they need exceptional care. Someone kind and gentle. Is that you?"

She nodded. "I can take your horses. But not for free, if that's what you're getting at."

Loki chuckled. "Nothing in the realms is for free. There's a handful of silver in it for you if you take care of them overnight. Half now and half in the morning."

"Deal." She held out her hand. Loki shook it, and she held fast, examining the detail on his embroidered Aesir leather riding gloves.

He eyed her closely, a smirk on his lips. "I like you. Fine, the gloves as well." He slipped them off and handed them to her. "Not a scratch on those horses, right?"

"Not a scratch, sir."

When the horses were in her care, Loki ambled toward me. I peered at him suspiciously. "I didn't think you'd be fond of children."

He strode past me, turning on his heel to walk backward. "When are you going to learn that you don't know anything about me?" He gave me a wink and headed for the stairs.

When indeed.

The way down to Svartalfheim was wide enough to accommodate the constant foot traffic in both directions. As we descended, others were returning to the surface with the treasures they'd hoarded from below. Intricate sword hilts protruded from ornate scabbards, saddle bags stuffed to the brim with chalices and jewellery and axes. The staircase wound down in wide circles, the descent long enough to make me dizzy. It was easier to focus on the murals along the walls that told the history of Svartalfheim and its treasures.

The Goddess of Nothing At All

By the time we hit the last step, I had lost all sense of time. The stairs emptied out into an enormous cavern. The roof was so high that it looked like a starless midnight sky. Enormous pillars had been carved out of the rock to support Midgard above.

Loki stepped in front of me, interrupting my admiration. "What? Don't tell me that with all your studying, you've never come to visit?"

"It didn't seem important," I said, trying not to look embarrassed. "I've never had a life that didn't revolve around Odin."

Loki's face tightened for a moment, then he swept a hand out, dramatically gesturing to the bustling realms in front of us. "No time like the present. Once we book a room at the inn, you'll have plenty of time to explore."

"Right." I turned to look through the people that moved around us. A signpost towered above us, pointing out the direction toward the market, the business district, and The Belows. "What are the Belows?"

Loki led the way through the crowd, presumably toward lodging. He pointed to a dank looking cavern entrance, clearly marked. "The forges are deep underground, and every forge has a bellows, so they call it The Belows. That's where I'll be while you're taking in the sights."

I dodged a Jotun loaded to the brim with iron shields. "*You* will? And why not me?"

"You can join me if you like, but the Sons of Ivaldi are temperamental." Loki swerved out of the stream of bodies and up to a charming building nearly six stories tall, carved entirely out of the side of the cavern wall. "It could take a while to convince them to do the work, and it would be a shame for you to see nothing but sweaty, sooty Dwarves on your visit. You know, in case your brother kills us both."

Loki opened the door of the inn, and I followed him inside. The front room was a tavern, and a long bar stretched out in front of us. The walls were lined with drinking horns and bottles of wine, mead, and ale. Behind the bar was a Dwarf. Her eyes were lined with kohl that ran down both sides of the bridge of her nose. Her deep brown hair was pulled back, and her beard was plaited with round golden beads, each inscribed with a rune. She looked up from the cup she was washing and came to a dead stop.

"No. No, no, I won't have you here, not again." She put down the cup and cloth, palms pressed into the bar. "Not after last time."

I turned to Loki, arms crossed. "What did you do last time?"

The Dwarf poured two fingers of dark rum and drank it like it was water. "He stole two sacks of gold chalices from one of the smiths *after* taking the virtue of my niece."

I turned on him. "Loki!"

"What?" He shrugged his shoulders, disbelief on his face. "Those chalices were just lying there, and I can tell you definitively that your niece not only knew her way around a man's bedchambers already but was very happy for the company."

The Dwarf slammed her cup on the bar. "You have the biggest, brassest balls to come into my bar and talk about my kin like that. I swear by Rathsvith and all the lineage of my house that I—"

"Wait!" I'd studied enough about Dwarven customs to know that if I let her go any further, we'd end up consigned to a duel and dead by morning. I stepped up to the bar and placed my hands on the wood. "I'm Sigyn Odindottir. Loki and I are here on an errand for Asgard. We need room and board, and if you grant it to us, I will personally see to it that Loki keeps his mouth shut and his hands to himself."

She leaned toward me. "How am I supposed to believe that? You could be just as big a snake as he is."

I unhooked the coin purse from my belt. It had nearly half of what I'd brought with us. I dumped the coins onto the counter, a small deluge of chinking gold. Each was stamped with the rough mark of the raven, one of Odin's symbols. "If the markings prove nothing, then perhaps the coin will speak for itself. Put us up for one night, and this is all yours."

She brushed her hand over the pile, spreading the coin so she could see it properly. I could practically see her tallying it in her head, imagining what she could buy for such an exorbitant amount of gold. Her face twitched, nose wrinkling until— "Fine. One night. And if I hear one peep, *one complaint* out of my other guests, I'll take him down to the furnace and press that pretty face of his into the coals. Are we clear?"

"Perfectly." I turned to look at Loki.

He was as nonchalant as ever. "I think you're both overreacting." He turned to look at the Dwarf. "Besides, I know what else you sell here."

The Dwarf narrowed her eyes at him, then scooped up the gold and pocketed it before turning around to fiddle with something under the cabinet. She emerged with a key and stepped out from behind the bar. The bar must have had a raised floor, because when she came around to us, the tip of her head only came up to the middle of my torso. She walked right past us, skirting by the mostly empty tables, calling instructions as she went.

"Dinner runs until nine bells. You want something after that, it's cold scraps and warm ale. The staff stay on until ten bells, then it's just the night watch until first bell. Breakfast is first bell to third, and I'll be selling your room at fourth." She started up a set of oaken stairs, and we followed.

She led us down a hall and stopped at a door with a rune etched into the wood that matched the tag on the key. She held the key out to me. "Any damage caused in the duration of your stay is *additional* to what you gave me."

The Goddess of Nothing At All

I took the key. "There won't be any damage, I assure you."

"Right." She pushed her way past Loki and headed back downstairs.

The room was cosy. It had a hearth against one wall and two small beds. An oversized broadsword hung over the hearth, inlaid with more gems than would be practical. It was doubtful the blade was even sharp.

Loki didn't come in, just stood in the doorway.

I turned to look at him, hands on my hips. "Do you have enemies everywhere?"

"You don't live an eternity without ruffling a few feathers." He leaned against the frame, his hair sweeping down from his face in a way that made me avert my gaze.

"Stealing isn't just ruffling feathers, Loki. If you don't stay out of trouble, I swear on the roots of Yggdrasil—"

"I will, I swear it!" He backed out of the doorway, hands in the air. I followed him. Somewhere outside the building, a loud bell clanged five times. Loki stopped at the top of the stairs and turned to me. "Fifth bell. I'll be back before seven bells. Go have fun." And then he bounded down the stairs, past the bar, and out the door.

I found myself wandering the streets of Svartalfheim, trying to get my bearings. There was an incredible amount of people, and the closer I got to the market, the busier things seemed to get.

I'd expected to see Dwarves smithing metals right before my eyes, but it seemed that was kept exclusively to The Belows. Instead, I got to glimpse some of the most beautiful craftsmanship I'd ever seen. Merchant stands lined both sides of the wide street, their tables so full of shining metals and glistening gems that I thought I might go blind.

The stall in front of me was covered head to toe with weapons. Pikes stood on display next to a heavily laden table of axes, daggers, and bows. A collection of short swords was strapped to a tall metal rack against the stall walls. I stopped to look more closely.

The shopkeep was busy with another customer, haggling over a price. As he talked, the back of his stall opened up. Two children ran out, one after the other. They each had wooden swords and shields, charging off to battle.

I couldn't help but smile. What a wonderful thing to be full of joy, not a care in the realms.

As the first one ran out into the street, his foot caught the bottom of the rack of swords. He hit the ground hard, and the rack shook, tilting forward, into the path of his little sister.

My hands were up and the runes on my tongue before I had a moment to think.

75

Wind summoned from nowhere held the rack and all the loose swords at an impossible angle, hovering above the little girl, who was crouched beneath, hands over her head and screaming.

The shopkeep came running and pulled his daughter out from beneath the rack. When they were safe, huddled on the ground in each other's arms, I tipped my palms forward, pushing the rack back into place. I let the runes die on my breath, and three swords hit the ground with a clatter.

A whistle sounded behind me, followed by some clapping, and a few scattered cheers. I turned, startled. A hand clapped me on the back, a towering, beautiful lady Elf. "Well done," she said, and moved on, disappearing into the crowd.

Something in my chest untied itself, and relief flooded through me. I was smiling, though I didn't mean to. It was just...I had done good, and someone had noticed.

The shopkeep got up, holding his little girl against his chest. His cheeks were slick with tears. Pushing down my own self-centred thoughts, I approached him. "Is she alright?"

The girl turned to look at me, still sobbing. It didn't seem there was a mark on her.

"She's alright, thanks to you." He looked around, eyes flitting between the onlookers and me. "If you weren't here, she'd be—" His voice caught. "Who are you?"

"Sigyn Odindottir, sir."

His eyes lit up. "The daughter of the Allfather himself! Look Lif, you were saved by a goddess! How blessed we are!" He dragged his hand across his face to clear the tears. "You can't know what you've done for us. You must take something as a gift. It's a small thing to pay back such a big debt, but please, choose something."

I started to protest but made myself stop. Dwarven culture was built around honour. To refuse a gift offered by a Dwarf was one of the greatest insults you could pay, right before insulting his mother's beard.

"Thank you for your generosity." A sniffle came from behind me. and I moved aside to let the young boy past. He latched himself to his father. As they spoke to each other in hushed voices, I let my eyes run over the weapons around me. I'd never been much for hand-to-hand combat, but some of the daggers were carved with runes, seidr worked into the metal. Catalysts, and every one of them beautiful. I knew just what I'd take.

When the door of our room opened, two bells later than promised, I was sitting on the end of my bed, examining the dagger I'd chosen. Loki looked like he'd seen better days. His skin had a sheen of sweat to it. His hair was matted, there was coal dust on his arms, and all in all, he needed a bath.

"What happened to you?"

He fell onto his bed with a sigh. "I ran into some delays."

I put the dagger down and shifted to face him. "I told you not to get into trouble."

He wiped his hand across his forehead, and a line of soot came with it. "I wasn't in trouble. I was in a hot, dank cave next to a forge with a bunch of surly Dwarves. It's dirty work."

"Did you get the hair?"

He coughed like he'd been inhaling smoke all day and put on a tired grin. "I did better than that. The Sons of Ivaldi *and* the brothers Brok and Sindri will come back with us to Asgard to compete for any future patronage from the gods."

My mouth dropped. "This isn't what we agreed on."

"No, it's better. Both sets of Dwarves make three gifts tonight, and your family will be in such awe of their new possessions that they'll practically be in my debt. We'll leave tomorrow at six bells and ride by moonlight, so the Dwarves don't melt in the sun. Back in Asgard just in time."

I didn't know whether to be impressed or angry. "And there's no catch?"

"None whatsoever." He nodded toward the dagger next to me. "What's that?"

I passed him the blade and told him the story of the girl in the market as he inspected it. The hilt was gold, its design split in two along its length. The bottom side was inlaid with sapphires, while the top was etched with runes. The blade itself shone like a mirror, flat and deadly.

He stood up and flipped it from one hand to the next, stabbing at empty air. "It's light. I like it."

"I have no idea how to use it, but it was too beautiful to leave behind."

Loki summoned me with his hand. "Get up. I'll show you."

There was a very large part of me that didn't want to. I was tired and a little embarrassed that I didn't already know how, but he'd turned so enthusiastic at the idea that I felt compelled to play along. So I took the dagger from him and stood at the end of the bed.

"Daggers are about stabbing, not about slashing. I assume you know that?"

I nodded. "I grew up in Valhalla; I've seen a few einherjar stab each other in the neck."

"Those are the good nights." Loki smirked. "If you're attacking someone in plainclothes, you'll have more opportunities to break skin, but if you're fighting someone with armour, you're looking for openings." He pointed to different places on my body as he spoke. "In the neck, where the shirt stops. Under the arm if there's no plating. Under the chest piece if there's place. It's about precision, not brute force."

"Ah, that explains why Thor doesn't have one."

That earned a laugh. "Why be precise when you can crush someone with your fist?" Loki moved behind me and pushed my foot into position with his. "Keeping your feet together is asking to be knocked over. Stand with them apart so you can brace yourself against attack."

He put his hands over mine, and I was keenly aware of his chest pressed against my back. I blinked, trying to push down the rising butterflies in my stomach, but his breath swept across my neck, and it sent a shiver down my spine.

"If you're aiming for the neck, you want a motion like this." He guided my hand up above my head, then back down. I repeated the motion. "Good. Keep your empty hand ready so you can defend yourself."

I huffed, feeling foolish in so many ways. I raised both hands dramatically. "I feel like a bear. Rawr."

He chuckled, his chest moving against me. "You're better company than a bear. Try it again but with some speed."

I stabbed at the air, leaning out of his grasp and then back. "Good." His voice was soft, his head close to my ear. "Again."

My heart was thrumming. Having Loki this close was distracting. I couldn't focus on anything except the heat of his hands and the smell of him, and when I tried to strike again, I stumbled. I fell back against him, and he caught me. My body was suspended in mid-air, his arms wrapped firmly around my waist, one hand settled on my hip.

I swallowed and looked up, embarrassed and overwhelmed and foolish, and he was so close. There was a grin on his face, like he was pleasantly startled. Even covered in soot, with his hair mussed and the scent of smoke heavier on him than ever, he was handsome.

Handsome? Where in hel had that come from?

I bolted out of his arms, smoothing out my skirts and pushing back my hair. Subtly, I'm sure. "Thank you. I'll keep practising."

There was something in his expression that felt...content. "Don't go picking any fights just yet. There's more to it than standing and stabbing. For another time, maybe." He rolled his shoulders and stretched out his neck. "Now, what do you say we get something to drink? It's been a long day, and I've got this horrible taste in my mouth that I just can't shake."

I followed him to the door. "From all that bad air in The Belows, I suppose."

"Yeah." He nodded. "Something like that."

CHAPTER THIRTEEN

*"I knew what he was doing. Loki's too cocky for his own
good, so I made him an offer he couldn't refuse..."*

—*Brok - God of Lies Revealed*

We arrived back in Asgard in the dead of night, one day before the new moon. Loki and I rode in the front, with seven ponies trailing behind us; five for the Dwarven smiths and two hauling the carriages of treasures they'd crafted. They hadn't let us see inside, but something was rustling around in one of them. The hatch was cracked open several times a day so an armful of food could be shoved inside, followed by yet more rustling and snorting. I didn't dare ask.

As expected, when we hit the border of the city, the Gjallarhorn blew. The sound of it penetrated my bones. The gods would be on their way soon, despite the hour.

We guided the riding party through the city, up the main road, and straight to the doors of Valaskjálf. The stable hands came quickly, helping our guests with their horses. Some were instructed to take the carriages inside, into Gladsheim. Loki and I followed behind.

"It's almost over," I sighed, allowing a small bit of relief to wash over me. I was ready for my life to go back to being calm and peaceful.

Loki stopped so abruptly that it took me a moment to realize it. I turned back to him. His eyes were on the floor, and the knuckles of his fists were white.

"Are you alright?"

He shook his head and came over to me, standing too close. "Sigyn, if things go badly, promise me you'll run."

"What?" I stepped back. "A moment ago, you were telling me that everything

79

would be fine."

Loki closed the distance between us again, his voice a whisper. "Maybe it will be. Maybe everything goes to plan, but maybe it doesn't."

I stared him in the eyes, searching for the truth. "What did you *do*?"

There was something in his face, like he was fighting himself. And then he gave in and sighed. "If the brothers Brok and Sindri win, they get to cut off my head."

"*Loki*," I hissed, hands flying into the air like a question. "Are you stupid?"

"It won't happen, Sig." He looked down the hall. Everyone else had already disappeared. "I sabotaged the gifts. No one is going to pick theirs."

I pressed my hands over my face, exasperated. "Why would you do something so stupid?"

He looked around again, searching for anyone who might be close enough to hear. "I was trying to earn some leverage with Odin. Bring him some shiny baubles in exchange for my being allowed to *live*. It got… a little out of hand. I'm apparently not popular with either of them."

"I can't believe you—"

"Come on you two!" Frey's voice rang out from down the hall. He was leaning out the door of Gladsheim. "Everyone is waiting!"

Loki walked away immediately, likely happy to have an exit from the conversation. It took everything in me to make my feet move. How could he be so callous? Careless? What about his life? What about me?

A few of the gods were already in Gladsheim when we rounded the corner. Odin was on his throne, with Frigg at his side. Thor and Sif were next to each other, hands clasped, the scarf still tightly wrapped around her head. Frey, Idunn, Baldur, and Hod were all there, along with a handful of others. The carriages were parked close to the dais, one on each side. Both families of Dwarves were whispering among themselves, casting the occasional menacing glance at the other.

I turned my head to the door at the sound of clicking boots. Freya was dressed as if she were ready for a grand celebration in a flowing red and yellow Vanir silk gown that moved against her like living flame. She gave Loki a snide smile as she passed. "Today is a good day to die, isn't it?"

For once, he said nothing.

When Freya was seated, Odin called for order. The room grew silent. "Loki. Explain this. You were told to fix the crime you committed, and instead, you've come back with a retinue of Dwarves."

Loki cleared his throat. "The Sons of Ivaldi as well as the brothers Brok and Sindri are here to compete for the patronage of Asgard. I've commissioned a new head of hair for Sif, as promised, but also a great deal more. Three gifts from each Dwarven family, for Odin, Thor, and Frey, which you will judge the quality of. The most impressive will continue to work with Asgard on future necessities."

Odin huffed. "Well now. I don't like to make a habit of praising you, Loki, but it seems you've done a good job. We'll soon find out."

Brok stepped forward. "Loki's left out the last piece of our agreement."

Odin turned toward him. "And that is?"

"If my brother and I win this contest, we get Loki's head."

Whispers darted around the room, the shock of the news setting in. Only Freya was grinning from ear to ear. The rest were dismayed, and Idunn had her hands over her mouth.

Perhaps they would veto this. He'd fulfilled his part of the bargain, surely someone—

Odin started laughing, rubbing his hands together. "I expected this would be eventful, but you've outdone yourself!"

"Father, please." I looked up at him, trying to get his undivided attention. "This is ridiculous. The debt has been paid—"

"He made an oath, goddess." Brok was picking at the forge dirt under his nails, unconcerned. "He's bound by his word."

I looked back at Loki, and he nodded, unable to meet my eyes.

There really was no way around it then. We would just have to wait and pray.

"Let's begin." Odin stood and descended the stairs to be on even footing with his guests. Frey and Thor went to stand with him.

The Sons of Ivaldi stepped forward. One of them approached Thor and gave him an ornate wooden chest. "As requested," said the dwarf, opening it. Inside was a gleaming wig of golden hair. "This hair is finer and more beautiful than any in the realms. It's crafted from the thinnest, purest strands of gold and will bind to the head of whoever wears it."

Thor motioned for Sif to join him. She stepped forward. Blushing, she removed the scarf from her head. With all the affection of a gentle lover, Thor placed the golden hair on her bare scalp. She winced, but the look of discomfort quickly passed. The hair fell into place, it's golden tresses sweeping over her shoulders and her back, brushing against the stone floor. She bundled the hair up against her face and began to weep with joy.

Thor ran his hands through her hair. "You've brought back my wife's smile. That's worth more than any amount of gold."

That had to be a point in our favour. It had to be.

The middle brother approached Frey, pulling something from the pocket of his travelling cloak. He held out his hand and placed a tiny ship into Frey's palm. "This is Skidbladnir. She's small now, but cast 'er into the sea, and she'll grow larger than any ship in the nine realms. The breeze always blows in your favour, and when you're done with 'er, you fold 'er back up and put 'er in your pocket."

Frey examined the tiny ship and laughed. "What a fantastic idea! And I can already see all the details in the bow. This is fine work."

"And what do you have for me?" Odin asked.

The last of the three Sons of Ivaldi approached Odin with a long, intricate spear. It was a thing of beauty. Gems had been inlaid in the metal between knotted patterns that ran all the way up to its hilt. The blade looked sharp enough to part a man from his head just by staring at it too hard. "This is the spear Gungnir. It'll find its target no matter how poorly it's aimed. It never misses."

Odin held the spear in his hands, feeling the heft and smoothness of it. "I've never seen a spear like this one. I can feel the power in it. This is good craftsmanship." He looked at the other two gifts, then back to the Sons of Ivaldi. "These are wonderful gifts. Thank you."

The dwarves bowed and stood back, letting Brok and Sindri step forward.

"Mighty Allfather, we've brought you something to please the eye and fill your coffers." Sindri presented Odin with a golden ring, shimmering and simple. "This is Draupnir. Every nine nights, it will drop eight new rings, identical to the first, to use as you please. Give them as gifts or keep them for yourself. Your wealth will continue to grow so long as you have it."

Odin inspected the ring and slipped it on his finger. "Now this…this is impressive. A man could buy the realms themselves if he were patient enough." He stared at it, lost in thought, and I knew immediately that no spear would ever stand up to endless wealth.

My eyes moved to Loki. He was scratching at the skin around his thumbnail. I tried to slip my hand into his, to offer some kind of comfort, but he pulled away immediately, crossing his arms over his chest. I flinched at the sharpness of it, withdrawing my hand. His expression was…nothing. A mask.

Sindri opened the door of the carriage and reached inside. His hand came back with a leash and attached to it was a half-grown boar. Its hide was pure gold. It jumped down and shook itself, the light from the torches glinting off him like sunlight.

Brok stepped forward. "For the god Frey. This beast is named Gullinbursti. It runs faster than any other across air, land, and water. You can travel through any darkness, with its golden fur to light your way."

Frey knelt down and held out his arms. The boar sniffed at his hand. It hesitated, then nuzzled its way into Frey's embrace. He hoisted it up—not without a little effort—and the boar nestled against Frey's chest as if they were long-lost friends. "He's stunning!" Frey kissed its head, and the boar snorted, drawing laughter from the room. He scratched behind its ears. "And so friendly! Aren't you? Yes, yes you are!"

I moved closer to Loki and reached for him again, leaning in. "I thought you sabotaged them?" I whispered, panic setting in under my skin.

"*I tried,*" he hissed. "This shouldn't be happening."

The air in the room felt thick. If his plan didn't work, all of this would be for nothing. Loki would die, and I would watch, and even if they let me live, I'd have to go back to existing without him. And he had done harm, yes, but every single one of my days had been better with him in it, with the exception of this latest catastrophe. I'd gotten used to warmth and laughter every single day, and they were going to take it from me over my dead body.

Brok pulled the last gift from the back of the carriage. It was a war hammer. Both ends were blunt, the whole thing made of cold iron. There were knots etched into the edges, and the surface had been blessed with runes until the entirety of it was covered in them. He presented it to Thor. "This is Mjolnir, a hammer fit for the strength of the God of Thunder."

The moment Thor hefted it into the air, the flaw was obvious. The handle was half as long as it should have been. There was only enough space for a single hand. Finally, I could take a breath. The hammer was faulty.

"You see," Loki whispered, leaning toward me. "I took care of it." But he was sweating, and every bit of that slick confidence was long gone.

Thor took the hammer and held it up, scrutinizing the details of it. "But the handle..."

"Aye, it's true that it has a shorter handle than most. There was a...complication in the smithing process." Brok's eyes darted to Loki. "But it's a small price for a weapon like this. Mjolnir won't shatter, no matter how hard you swing it or what you hit with it. If you throw it, it always strikes its target and always returns to your hand."

Thor's eyes widened as the dwarf spoke, his enthusiasm growing with each word. When Brok was finished, Thor tossed the hammer. It flew across the hall, above the heads of the gods, each of us scrambling to avoid decapitation. The hammer stopped at the end of the hall, changed direction, and flew directly back into Thor's hand.

"This is the best gift I've ever been given. Absolutely the best." He sniffed a little as if forcing back a tear, then held the hammer over his head like a trophy. Some of the gods gave an enthusiastic roar.

Fuck. Fuck, fuck, fuck.

Odin motioned for the crowd to be silent. "These are all fine gifts. They'll be put to good use, and for that, we thank you. Your work truly is among the best in the nine realms, but there can only be one winner." He looked to Frey, who was doting on his new companion, and then to Thor, who had taken to tossing the hammer in the air to test its reliability. "I believe the winner is clear. Brok and Sindri, you've earned the patronage of Asgard."

The crowd clapped politely, but my eyes were on Loki. My heart was racing, trying to escape the confines of my chest. What could I do? There had to be something. I could almost see the calculations happening under the surface, Loki's alert eyes scanning the room in some false semblance of calm. Then he took a slow step backwards. He was going to run.

I wasn't the only one to notice.

Brok pointed in our direction. "Don't let him leave!"

A few of Odin's guards stepped forward. With a string of runes and a flick of the wrist, I sent them flying back against the wall, trying to buy Loki time.

He made it halfway to the doors of Gladsheim, but Thor was quicker. He grabbed Loki by the tunic and dragged him back to the feet of Brok. Loki thrashed, cursing Thor as he did, but it was no use. Thor was stronger than all of us.

There were a thousand things I could do to Thor—electrocute him, set his hair on fire—but he was still my brother. I wouldn't risk one death to prevent another.

"Father!" I strode up to Odin, who was simply watching. "Hasn't this gone far enough? Loki's done exactly what you asked. You can't let this happen!"

He stared down at me with his one cold eye. "I thought you had him under control, Sigyn? Shouldn't you have prevented this from happening in the first place?" He chuckled, as if anything about this was funny. "Loki swore an oath. Asgard is not a city of oathbreakers. It may have been idiotic, but he's bound to his word. No god will intervene."

"This is cruel. Look at how you've benefited from what he's done, and you'll still let him die?" But my words fell on deaf ears. He was already watching the horror that was about to play out in the centre of the room.

"Hold him steady." Brok pulled a blade out from the sheath on his belt. Sindri had pulled Loki's arms behind his back, wrenching them so he had no choice but to stay on his knees.

"Don't you think this is a bit hasty?" Loki's question was answered by a twist of his arm, and he hissed in pain.

I started toward them, runes on my tongue, but before I could summon the wildfire, Thor's beastly arms wrapped around me, crushing me to his chest. He hauled me off my feet, destroying my concentration. I kicked, screaming for him to let me go, and when he didn't, I bit down on his forearm.

Thor wailed and threw me. My head cracked against the floor, and my vision blurred, the world spinning. Everything was muffled, turning, writhing. I tried to push myself up, whichever way that was, and my hand slipped. The only thing I was sure of was the cold radiating from the stone.

"Sigyn!" The foggy shape of Loki had risen to his feet, but someone bigger pushed him to his knees again.

Someone touched me, gentle hands lifted me up, cradling me against a soft chest. Straw coloured hair and kind blue eyes. I blinked, trying to bring the world into focus. Idunn's fingers ran across my scalp, and I heard her voice through the fog. "She's bleeding!"

More hands were on me. I fought them off, swinging my arms in all directions, clawing at anything that came too close. My elbow connected hard with something, though I couldn't see what, and the hands retreated. I rose to my feet, the world still turning, and whispered the runes for wildfire. But the flame wouldn't come. Everything was too dull, too unfocused. I managed to stumble a few steps forward before crumbling to my knees.

I stared until the world calmed around me, watching the shapes of Loki and Brok and Sindri, willing myself to move but unable to do it.

Then, Loki laughed. The laugh grew into a cackle, his voice full of condescension. "As you wish. If you want my head, take it, but I haven't wagered my neck. If you touch my neck at all, you'll have broken the terms of the oath. You want my face for your mantle? You'll need to think hard."

A murmur rose around me. Odin stomped his foot on the floor, and there was silence once again. He let out a long sigh, annoyed. "Fine. You may only harm his head."

Brok was furious. "How do I take his head without damaging his neck? I want the *whole* head. What good is half a head for mounting above my forge?"

Odin shrugged his shoulders and just watched. As if he should have expected it to go this way.

The Dwarf threw his blade across the hall, livid. "This is treachery. You foul fucking Jotun, there's nothing in the nine realms I hate as much as you, and someday, mark my words, I'll have that head of yours." He turned to his brother. "Get me leather and an awl. I'm going to sew his lying, scheming mouth shut."

No.

They were going to take his laugh, his smile, his runes, the sound of his voice. They couldn't.

I tried to protest, to move, but Idunn's hands were on me again, holding me fast. I screamed, unable to help. The tears mixed with the slow trickle of warm blood that ran from my hair, staining everything red. The price was too steep for what he had done.

Loki thrashed, futile protests. Brok approached him with the awl and a thin strap of leather. Sindri tilted Loki's head toward the ceiling, holding his jaw closed. I couldn't see past their bodies, but I didn't need to. Loki's blood-curdling cries were enough.

Idunn held me tightly, whispering things to me that I couldn't hear, things that were no comfort as his pain spilt through the room. Each stitch changed the sound of his screams as they bound his lips shut. The work couldn't have taken that long, but it felt like an eternity. And when it was done, the brothers stood triumphantly over Loki as he sobbed, his chest heaving in agony.

"It's not a head, but it'll do for now. Perhaps you'll all get a break from his bullshit." Sindri laughed. Others laughed as well, some nervous, some triumphant.

Thor knelt down next to Loki and balled the front of Loki's tunic in his fist, forcing him to meet his eyes. "Remember this the next time you think to disrespect my family." He growled and dropped him, kicking him in the chest. The single blow was enough; there was no satisfaction to beat out of Loki anymore. Instead, Thor returned to the dais and took Sif's hand. They left together, her new hair cascading behind them as they walked. The other gods trickled out behind them, gossiping and laughing as they went. Even the Dwarves were busy packing up their carriages.

Just as I looked away, I caught sight of the hem of Freya's dress passing by, and a glob of spit landed on the stone next to Loki. She didn't say a word, only grinned like a cruel child who'd just gotten away with murder.

Each of them passed Loki, paying no mind to the broken god bleeding onto the stone.

Idunn released me, and we went to his side. He was struggling to lift himself from the floor, and I caught him just as he tumbled down. Even with what was left of the blur in my vision, I nearly retched. His face...

The leather was soaked red, stitched messily into the skin just on the border of his lips. Not all the stitches had been clean-cut; some stretched thin lines away from his lip, a rip in the canvas of his face. Blood seeped from the corners of his mouth, trickling down his neck and staining his tunic. There was madness in his eyes.

I held him to my chest and cried with him while Idunn sat helpless next to us. Her dress was stained red where she had cradled me.

"We're going to fix this," I said softly, stroking his hair. Loki nodded and pressed his forehead into my shoulder. The three of us stood, Idunn and I helping to lift him from the ground.

"He needs to go to the infirmary." Idunn shifted until his arm was around her neck. "I'll come with you, and we'll find someone to take care of your head."

I shook my head. "No, I'm taking him to my hall. I have everything I need there."

Idunn scowled. "Sigyn, please. You don't need to take care of everything alone."

"I have it under control."

The worry was etched on her face. "And who will take care of you? At least let me help you get there."

Loki's head was bobbing down. If he fell unconscious, I knew I'd never get him home. "Fine. We need to hurry."

We dragged him through the corridors of Valaskjálf as gently and quickly as we were able, his feet barely underneath him. We got him outside and down the path to my hall. As I struggled to pull my keys from my chain, I realized I was having an odd sense of deja vu.

How many of his wounds would I need to heal?

Idunn and I got him inside and set him in one of the chairs at the table. "How can I help?"

"Go home," I said. "I have this."

"But—"

"I mean it. Come back tomorrow. He'll be fine."

Idunn gave me a wary look, but she also knew from experience that I wasn't going to back down. So she left me with Loki, who had slung himself over the tabletop, his face staining the wood red.

CHAPTER FOURTEEN

*"And the Dwarf bound his lips, promising the gods he
wouldn't be able to waggle that silver tongue
for a very long while."*

—*Asgard Historical Record, Volume 14*

L oki stared into the hearth fire, the light casting dancing shadows on his face. A
blood-soaked wraith in leather-bound lips, strands of his flaming hair stuck in
the blood crusting along his neck.

Without a word, I took his chin in my fingers and turned his face to mine. His
eyes caught mine for just a moment, then fell away to stare at the furs beneath our
legs. The ends of the leather hung loosely on either side of his mouth, trailing over his
bottom lip like a broken seam. I reached out to touch it. He recoiled.

"Oh, Loki…" I hushed him, blinking my tears away. I cupped the curve of his jaw,
wishing I knew how else to comfort him. He was cool and sticky to the touch.

I concentrated on the skin under my fingers, speaking in whispers. After a
moment, the creases in his face softened, the pain fading under the effect of the runes.

"It won't last. I can't concentrate on the runes and take out these stitches at the
same time. I'm sorry."

He nodded.

As carefully as I was able, I severed each of the seams, one by one. It was simple
enough to cut the outside with a pair of sewing shears. Working on the inside would
stretch the leather and rip at his skin, though. Pulling out the stitches would be agony.
Snip after tiny snip released the front of his lips. I wiped my hands on my lap, smearing
red across my dress. Deliberately, gently, precisely, I opened his mouth to sneak the shears

inside. He flinched. Without maintaining the spell, the runes were already fading.

Each piece of leather inside his mouth soaked the blade in blood. His teeth and lips were stained with it. I drew closer to his face, trying to keep my aim steady. His breath was rancid, metallic. Loki wanted to fight me off, push me away; I saw it in the tightness of his closed fist, in the furrow of his eyebrows. He wanted to stop the pain. And then at long last, the final piece was cut, and his lips were free. He stretched his jaw, wincing with each movement. Then he started sinking down, too tired to keep going.

I urged him back up. "It's not done. Not remotely." He said nothing, just braced himself against the floor. I held his chin steady and pulled the first piece of leather through. Even having cut the strap short, it was slow work to bring it through the skin. Loki fought against a scream, his teeth ground together in agony. When it came clear of the wound, the strap left a vicious hole. It oozed blood, dripping over the curve of his lip and onto the furs below.

I fished around for the supplies beside me—clean water and cloth to wash the wound, poultice to sterilize it. All the while, he cried. Just waited and cried.

I worked slowly, and as I worked, I sang to him. I sang the melodies the wet nurses used to sing to me when I was a child about treetops and mountain ranges, open seas and creeping forest. When those ran out, I sang any silly tavern song I could think of. In the end, I made up songs of my own. And one by one, the leather straps came out.

Each one seemed more painful than the last. He dug his fingers into the rugs, holding onto them as if they were the only thing keeping him from falling off the edge of the world. Halfway through, he retched into the bowl of water. I cleaned him up, his eyes full of shame and regret. I began again. When the pain was more than he could bear, he put his hands on mine and squeezed, and I simply held him, singing to him until he was ready to go on.

"Last one." I held his face in my palm for a moment, then pried the stitch from his lip. Loki fell forward onto his hands, chest heaving, blood and spittle dripping to the ground. He collapsed under his own weight, his head in my lap. I washed and treated the last wound while he lay there. His eyes were closed, his face twisted with pain.

I whispered the runes for sleep. The ones he had used in the garden, the ones that had gotten us here in the first place. As I whispered, I ran my fingers delicately over his scalp. Gradually, his body relaxed, his breathing weighted and steady. I stayed with him at the fireside, not daring to wake him. I washed the blood from his hair and wound it into thin braids, and all the while, his blood and tears seeped through the folds of my dress, onto my skin.

CHAPTER FIFTEEN

"There are things that we do to each other that no man deserves. Oh, to live among the gods, where surely they are beyond such things."

—*Stories from Midgard, Volume 13*

I woke in my bed with no memory of how I got there, a sharp sound piercing my sleep. There was a kink in my neck, and my head throbbed where I'd hit it. Hadn't I fallen asleep in the kitchen? Next to the fire and—

I looked at my hands. There was still blood under my fingernails. But where was Loki?

There was the sound again. The throat-catching squeak of someone repressing pain. I wiped the sleep from my eyes. Loki was sitting in the chair across the room, bare-chested, still in yesterday's bloodstained trousers. There was a pillow behind him and a blanket at his feet, but he was awake, his hands clasped over his mouth.

I pulled myself out of bed, trying to shake the weariness away. His eyes followed mine across the room, full of panic. A tendril of red was oozing through the cracks of his fingers, snaking around his wrist.

"Let me see." I knelt down in front of him, trying gently to pry his hands from his mouth. When they came away, both palms were coated in blood. The poultice had come free, and the wounds were dripping. "This should've healed, at least a little. They shouldn't be wide open..."

He'd thrown last night's tunic onto the ground next to him. I scooped it up and pressed it to his lips. "Hold this tightly, to help with the bleeding. We need to go to my study."

Loki followed behind me, the tunic pressed to his lips. I took him across the kitchen and through another door. My study was lined with bookcases, hundreds of books spanning across them with room for hundreds more. In the centre were a set of luxurious chairs, covered in linen and stuffed with down. The windows let in enough light during the day, and there were candles all around the room after nightfall.

"Sit down. I'm going to try something." He sat, and I bent over him, pulling the tunic from his hands. There was still so much blood.

I drew up energy, more than enough for a wound like this. I touched the tips of my fingers to the skin around his mouth, whispering runes that were more powerful than needed. And nothing changed. I gave the tunic back. He took it from me and put it back in place, worry in his eyes.

I went to the bookshelves, letting my fingers slide against the covers until they found the right one. *Hexes, Curses, and Other Maladies.*

I brought it back, sitting across from him as I hurried through the pages. The descriptions inside were as horrifying as the sketches, each one describing the curse and how one might reverse it but never how to cast it. The others were so mortifying that I nearly missed the one I'd been searching for; it was almost innocuous in comparison. *Ever-bleeding Wound.*

"Damned Dwarves. I think they cursed the awl. If I don't remove the curse, you'll bleed until you're dead." His eyes widened, his back straightening in the chair. "Don't worry, I can help you. Besides, you're too pretty to die."

The comment had meant to elicit a smile but only earned me an arched eyebrow.

The runes were costly ones. If it were easy to undo a curse, they wouldn't be half as fearful as they were. "When I've removed the curse, there won't be enough energy left to heal your wounds. You'll need to do that yourself."

He shook his head. Yggdrasil above, he'd never learned.

I was puzzling over my options when he leaned forward and placed his hand on my wrist. His skin was abnormally warm, the heat of rune energy spreading through my skin. I pulled my chair closer to his. "That would work. It's going to be one hel of a case of rune fatigue, but we don't have much choice."

Loki nodded, though there was doubt in his eyes.

I took his face in my hands. The tunic was wet, and he looked paler than usual, if such a thing were possible. I placed my thumbs close to his bleeding lips.

The runes that I needed were long and winding. Some were familiar, a common set used for disenchanting, but I kept needing to refer to the book in my lap for the others. After a dozen choruses of the same chant, I stopped looking down and simply moved my lips in silence to the flow of the runes.

Loki's hands covered mine, pushing his own energy into my skin. The rush consumed me, pushing its way to my core. My heart was racing, my body alert to the overwhelming power under my fingertips. It felt like there was nothing I couldn't do.

I kept working, the runes running faster on my tongue until I thought I might lose track of them. Repetition after repetition, until at last, black pus began to trickle out from the holes in Loki's lips. The curse had broken.

I pulled one hand away long enough to wipe the blackness from his skin, then cast a series of runes to heal the wounds. The only thing keeping me moving was the energy that he was pouring into me, and even that was fading.

The bleeding stopped gradually, most of the wounds becoming thin silver scars that cracked the surface of his lips. Some were simple. Others were jagged creases in the meat of his lips. The worst of them were still an open, angry pink, but it would have to be enough. "There," I said, dropping the runes. "As beautiful as ever." And it was true. Mostly.

He didn't move his hand away, but he was closing off the flow of energy. The warmth slowly faded, and my eyelids fluttered. The room went dark for a moment, and when I opened my eyes, I was in his arms. He'd caught me.

Loki picked me up and cradled me against him. I fell in and out of consciousness, my cheek pressed into his bare chest, jostling as he walked. He laid me out in my bed and pulled the furs over me. Just as I was fading back into the blackness of sleep, he leaned over and whispered in my ear.

"Thank you."

CHAPTER SIXTEEN

"Loki was too cruel to have the company of anyone for very long. Prone to acts of bitterness and contempt, he was only ever concerned for himself."

—*God of Lies Revealed*

I slept like the dead. The sun was already low in the sky when I woke. My pulse beat inside my skull, thump thump thumping. There was nothing I wanted more than to sink back into the sweet oblivion of sleep, but my stomach clawed at itself. I forced myself to sit up. It had been a very long time since I'd felt like this, and I hadn't missed it.

When I opened the door to my bedroom, I was immediately graced with the savoury scent of broth and smoke. The boiling pot was hanging over a small fire in the hearth, the water inside slowly simmering. I shuffled over, my body protesting every step, and pulled the ladle out. Venison, potatoes, a mix of root vegetables. It seemed nearly done.

I went to the counter and put a cup underneath the pipe that ran to the basin. I whispered a rune and tapped twice on the metal. Water rushed into my cup until I tapped it again to stem the flow. I gulped it down and went back for more, then turned to take in the room. The floor in front of the hearth was clean, the bloody furs gone. My eyes went to the table. There was a permanent stain where Loki had lain over the surface, but it was clean. Papers were scattered nearby, all in Loki's sharp scrawl, and next to them was a quill pen. A bowl with fresh golden apples sat next to a platter of pastries.

Fingers straying to the papers, I shifted one after the other off the pile. A one-sided conversation, paper by paper.

Speaking proves a bit difficult yes

It comes and goes. It's worse when I try to sleep

Please don't. You have nothing to apologize for.

I mean it Idunn, <u>stop</u>

She's alright. I think. She's been sleeping since sunrise yesterday.

Yes, she's breathing.

Because I checked!

It's only rune fatigue. I've done it to myself before, ignoring my limits.

I will. I owe her that much.

The front door opened. Loki startled when he saw me, his arms full of quartered firewood. He gave me a glare and nodded his head forcefully down. When I didn't properly interpret his meaning, he pulled out a chair one-handed and nudged me until I sat.

He settled a piece of wood onto the coals, stacking the rest neatly against the side of the hearth.

I pointed to the papers. "So you're not speaking?" He shook his head. "Can I help with—" A throb burst in my head so suddenly and violently that it took my breath away. I leaned against the table.

Loki knelt down next to me, trying to catch my eye. He cocked an eyebrow.

"I don't know what you want," I groaned, pushing my forehead against the tabletop. He reached over me. There was the ruffle of paper and the scratch of a quill. I looked up to see him holding a paper.

Are you alright?

"No," I whined. "I'm sore and hungry, and my head is pounding." I kept my head pressed against the table, the pressure serving as a kind of relief. His boots shuffled across the floorboards. The ladle scraped against the iron pot. Then the subtle splash of water and the tapping of boots coming nearer. Something clunked down next to my head. I peeked up. A bowl of stew.

I wanted to cry. No one had served me dinner in my own home for a very long time. "Thank you. You didn't need to do this."

He tapped his finger twice on one of the notes.

I will. I owe her that much.

A blush ran to my cheeks, and I deigned to eat instead of speak. The stew was delicious. There was a rich, thick flavour to it, something that I hadn't tasted in Asgard before. Certainly, nothing the cooks in Valhalla would know how to do. I ate it as quickly as I could manage. Loki came back to the table and set a steaming mug of something next to me. I pointed at the empty bowl. "That was fantastic. And what's this?"

Loki faked a wince and held his forehead, like a man suffering from a headache.

Whatever it was, it smelled like something from the infirmary, bitter and piney. I blew on it, hoping to cool it enough to drink. It was still hot, but I was in too much pain to wait. It tasted exactly like a tree. I gulped it down and slammed the mug on the table, making a face. "Horrific."

Loki huffed, a laugh on the corner of his scarred lips.

I pushed back my chair, trying to ignore the wobble in my legs. I reached up and took Loki by the chin, pulling his face closer so I could see the damage. The wounds that had still been open yesterday were redder than I'd hoped.

His eyes were impatient as I twisted his chin back and forth. I touched one of the wounds as gently as I could, and he hissed. "This needs more healing. You'll get an infection if you're not careful."

He rolled his eyes.

"I mean it. Sit down so I can help you—" And then the room started to spin.

Loki held me steady, his fingers digging into my shoulders to keep me from tumbling over. He shook his head and gestured impatiently back to the seat. I ignored it, holding onto his arm for balance, just aware enough to blush. "Fine. Go to the infirmary then."

He shook his head, brows narrowed.

I sighed, not feeling well enough to fight him. "Alright. There's poultice mixture above the water basin. Moisten it and use it on the wounds."

His head lulled to the side a little, rolling his eyes as if I were talking to him like a child. He started to pull me back toward the room, but I stopped him.

"You should stay here for now, until you're better. I can keep an eye on the wounds. Make yourself a bed in one of the guest rooms instead of sleeping in that chair."

A thin smile spread across Loki's wounded lips. It was broken immediately by a wince. He sighed, nodded, and walked me towards my bedroom. It was taking real effort to stave off sleep, and I knew there was no sense in fighting it.

He brought me to the bed and lowered me down, his arm the only thing keeping me from collapsing entirely. I'd barely hit the mattress before I lost myself to dreams once again.

CHAPTER SEVENTEEN

*"What Ulla wanted more than anything was something she
could never have: a home. It burned in her, that desire. And
the touch of his hand felt more like home than
anything she'd ever known."*

—*Back Towards Daybreak*

Rune fatigue was no joke. I slept until the next morning, ate, and then went back to sleep for another half a day. When I *was* conscious, I felt positively useless.

Loki and I settled into an odd routine. He slept in the bedroom across the kitchen from mine. He woke me for meals, all of which he cooked, though he ate next to nothing himself. Then I would check his wounds and attempt to stay awake for a while longer, if for no other reason than to give him a little company.

It hurt to see Loki so dejected. He had been silenced, just as Brok had planned, and even when his eyes lit up, ready with a joke, he'd open his mouth, and the pain would stop him. He reopened the wounds twice that way. I was still too weak to heal him, and he was too proud to go to anyone else. He learned not to smile at all.

The two of us made for a lazy, forlorn pair. We spent our days playing dice games at the table or curled up in opposite chairs in the study with a book. I spoke more than my fair share, telling stories about godly dramatics that he had missed while he was gone or things that had happened to me over the years. I did it to fill the silence, but somehow, I knew that he would have listened even if he'd had his voice.

I knocked on the door to Loki's room. It was already open, and he was sitting on his bed reading a book, the deep blue cover reading *Back Towards Daybreak*.

His room. His bed. How quickly things had changed.

He looked up and a slight smile slid onto his features. "Well, hello."

It had occurred to me many times that the realms would be a duller place if he never smiled or laughed again, and to see him trying it on, no matter how subtly, gave me hope.

There was nothing on his feet and a pair of soft tan trousers were the only stitch on his body. He was clearly ready for bed, but he knew I'd be coming, like I did every night. I went to the side of the bed and sat down at his side, spreading out the supplies I'd brought with me: poultice, a damp cloth, a jar of salve.

Loki marked the page and sat up, legs crossed beneath him. All routine now.

"Let's see what the damage is."

"Damage? That's my face you're talking about."

"Oh, how I have missed your biting wit," I teased, leaning forward to take hold of his chin. I tilted his face so I could see his lips in the firelight.

Their condition had improved immensely. They'd stayed closed for days, even if he smiled, and it seemed like it would stay that way. I squinted, focusing on one of the thin scars that ran into the meat of his lip, one that had been especially fussy. The silver started above the bow in his upper lip and tore a deep line into the curve of the flesh. I touched it gently with the pad of my finger, but he didn't flinch.

I looked up, realizing that I'd drawn my face so close that there was barely space for a breath between us. I blushed. While I'd been inspecting, those curious emerald eyes had been watching me. That look was so soft, so utterly at peace. And in that long, drawn-out moment, my heart hammering in my chest, his hand rose up. His fingers delicately tucked a lock of hair behind my ear, lingering to slide along my jawline.

His lips pursed and loosened again. My breath hitched, so focused on the imperfect curve of his mouth, that look in his eyes like he was waiting for something. For me to make a move. The longing coiled inside of me until I couldn't resist the one thing on my mind. I leaned forward and kissed him.

It was such a nervous, impulsive, desperate kiss that I immediately felt ashamed and pulled away. It was sloppy, I was sure of it. And who was I to assume he'd wanted to be kissed? Friends touched each other's hair all the time, didn't they?

But then his hand cupped the back of my neck, keeping me from retreating. He drew me in again. His lips were soft, even with the imperfections, each brush against mine sparking like flint until I was certain that the warmth would melt me. He pulled me closer, leaning back against the headboard, making me chase his kisses. Gods did I want them. My hands found his shoulders, trailing my fingertips over the lean muscle of his chest. The feather-light touch coaxed a deep breath from him, his lips resting against mine for just a moment, and his grip tightened on me, like he was holding back. I wondered if I had ever truly wanted anything in my life the way I wanted to see where that kiss could lead.

I drew away. It would lead nowhere.

This longing was so familiar. Wanting something so badly, being so close to having it. But what future was there in a kiss from Loki? I could already hear the scorn from the others in Valhalla. Thor, Sif, Freya.

Odin.

He would never approve. He never did.

It would be just like before, and I couldn't break like that again.

Loki's brow furrowed as I pried his hand from its root in my hair. He'd felt my eagerness, I knew that. It would have been impossible not to. Underneath the doubt, I felt it too.

"Did I do something wrong?" he asked, still close enough to whisper. The smokey silk of his voice was so foreign now, so rare and precious. There were so many sounds I wanted to hear him make, the sigh of my name among them, but—

I disentangled myself from his hands and got off the bed. "No. Yes. I don't...I just can't."

I gathered my things, a small part of me hoping that he'd say something, that he'd reach out and pull me back into his arms. But he just sat there and watched as I left, shutting the door behind me.

CHAPTER EIGHTEEN

"The mind alone knows what lives near the heart;
alone it sees into the soul.
Worse for the wise than any disease,
finding nothing that makes one content."

—*Hávamál 95*

The night faded under my watchful eyes, the sun coming up on the horizon. I'd like to lie and say I slept. I wanted the pride of having gone back to my room without any weight on my shoulders, without the taste of his lips lingering in my memory, the feel of him under my hands, but that's not how it went. The tension under my skin wouldn't let me lie down, let alone rest. I went to the door a dozen times, ready to race back to him, but I didn't. He had woken my body with his stupid hands, and it wasn't until I used my own to quiet it that I had any peace.

Finished with pacing the floor, aching for him, I laid in bed dreading the consequences of that kiss. It was hard to say which felt worse. They were both tiring, and neither let me sleep.

For the first time since Loki had been staying with me, I was the first to the kitchen. I gathered meat and bread and cheese from the cellar and set to work cutting, slicing, cooking. When the door opened, I didn't turn to look. "Good morning."

"Good morning." His steps made no sound, but he soon appeared in my vision, kneeling next to the hearth to take the skillet from the fire. As I wrapped the rest of the bread back in its cloth bag and set it aside, Loki set the skillet on the potholder.

Plate the bread.

Set the table.

Put the cheese away.

Fill the pitcher with water.

Bring the cups.

Silence.

It had been quiet since his lips were sewn shut, but this was worse than any of the silences we'd had before. The other kind had been punctuated with turning pages and casual touches and gentle company. This had a weight to it, heavy with all the things I didn't know how to say.

When I ran out of reasons to stay standing, I slid into my chair, keenly aware of how much closer I was to having to confront things. Loki gestured to the food, and I took my share, scraping things onto my plate with slow, deliberate actions. He waited for me to take mine, then helped himself.

He slid a knife through the middle of his bread and began to lather it in salted butter, not looking up. "Did you sleep?"

The question stopped me. "I…no."

"That makes two."

I skewered a piece of bacon and brought it to my lips, trying to buy time. Chewing slowly, I kept my head down just far enough to see the movement of his hands around his plate.

"Thank you for cooking." He still hadn't taken a bite of anything. He was delaying too.

And how long could we keep up a dance like this?

There was still a flask of mead between my stacks of books. I snatched it, drank straight out of the flask, then set it down in the middle of the table. Loki ignored it. I tapped my fingers on the table, drumming up the courage. "Alright. Neither of us is going to pretend it didn't happen, so I guess we're talking about it."

Loki put the second half of the bread on what was now the top of a very strange, anxious-looking sandwich, butter on every layer, bacon and cheese covered in salt and jam. Inedible. "I'd prefer that."

My guts were twisted. The things I wanted were clashing with the things that were trying to protect me. I wanted to accept whatever it was he was offering last night, but love left so many scars. I was already covered in them.

"I'm sorry, Loki. What I did wasn't right. I shouldn't have."

He stopped toying with his ungodly creation and finally looked up with disbelief. "Yes, you should have."

I couldn't meet his eyes.

"You really don't see it, do you?" Loki pushed his plate aside. He hesitated for a

100

moment, his finger sliding across the scars on his lips. "Every single time you get near me, my heart stops. And when you do touch me, it's more than I can stand. I've been waiting for that kiss since...gods, I don't know."

That made me look up. "Since when, Loki?"

He hesitated, picking the skin around his nails. Nervous. "Two nights before your trial with Odin."

"Why then?"

He looked up at the ceiling, clearly uncomfortable. "We'd all had a few drinks, and you just...laughed. You were so happy." The corner of his lip twisted up as he paused. "You snorted. Your guard was down, and I could see you without all the weight on your shoulders, just yourself, and I knew I...That was it."

It was too simple, wasn't it? It sounded so pure.

I leaned my face into my palms, struggling for the words. "This wasn't supposed to happen. You were supposed to help me earn my title, and I would help you get your place back in Asgard. We would respect each other, and it would be a mutually beneficial deal and... My father is going to feed us to his wolves."

Loki leaned forward. "Is that what this is about? *Grimnir?*"

"It's about everything." I couldn't look at him. "You know what happened with Alruna. Every time I reach for something for my own, someone takes it from me. Usually him. I can't do that again, Loki. I'm tired of getting hurt."

He got up and came to sit in the chair next to mine. Leaning in, he forced himself into my line of sight, his hair sweeping down over his shoulder. "He doesn't *have* to have that power over you, Sigyn. He thinks he controls everything, but he doesn't. When I stopped letting him manipulate me, he had me exiled, but that didn't change anything. I was still me. What happens between us isn't about him. It's about us."

I didn't speak. I couldn't. If I opened my mouth, I'd fall apart. It never mattered what I wanted. Never.

Loki reached out, his fingers finding my chin, directing my gaze at him. The kindness on his face was more than I could bear. "Sigyn, you belong to yourself."

In almost a century, had anyone ever said that to me?

The tears started with a desperate hitch of breath. I fell into his arms, face pressed against his chest as the fear bled out of me in sobs. I wanted so badly to belong to myself, to be worth something that no one could take.

He held me tightly, whispering affirmations in my ear. I was tucked so deeply against his chest that I was barely on my own seat, and he slid an arm under my legs to hoist me onto his lap. It startled me but pressed up against him so tightly...I felt safe. This man who had come out of nowhere and believed that I was capable and powerful and valuable. He planted hurried kisses on the top of my head, trying to soothe me. I arched my neck, and the kisses slowed, moving to my temple and down to my cheek as I turned my head to receive them. Before I had time to tell myself no, I was kissing him, my fingers lost in his hair, his thumbs brushing the tears from my cheeks.

If I'd had no need to breathe, I think I might've kept kissing him forever. Our lips parted, and I rested my forehead against his. His eyes were so full of life. I needed that spark to keep my own fire burning.

And he was watching me, still so unsure. Like he was waiting for me to change my mind. Part of me wanted to, but...

"I want this," I whispered against his skin. Making a choice.

He placed a kiss on my lips. "So do I."

CHAPTER NINETEEN

"It was too hard without him. She needed him there, in the
little moments, to remind her that she
was still alive and well."

—*The Too Long War, Levaine Theavin*

The days after were unlike any that had come before. The Loki that revealed himself to me in soft-hearted confessions and gentle kisses was different than the one who boasted and cajoled in Valhalla. With the walls pulled down, he was generous with his affection, wanting to be close, to help, to be part of everything. I'd seen glimpses of it already, but this was a Loki very few people saw.

On the fifth day, I woke to the sun creeping up the length of the sheets through the window. There were birds chirping outside. I was snug and warm, and beside me was the gentle rise and fall of Loki's steady breath as he slept.

I took in every detail of him: the way his flame-coloured hair fanned out over the pillow; the tidy perfection of the newly twisted braids that ran over his scalp above his ear; the kohl around his eyes that he'd forgotten to wash off, which had smudged over the bridge of his nose; the occasional long breath as he dreamed.

We'd been reading together last night in my bed, the hearth fire warming our entangled feet. He'd fallen asleep with his head on his arm, his book still open on the sheets. I hadn't had the heart to wake him, so I'd marked his page and gone to sleep. We'd been wrapped up in each other for hours, but he hadn't pushed for more than I was willing to give. Maybe he knew what I did. That if he pushed too hard, too fast, I'd spook.

But now I knew something else. I wanted so many more mornings waking up next to him.

As gently as I could, I moved closer and ran my fingers along his cheek. A smile drew across his lips, and his eyes fluttered open. Then his arm found my waist and pulled me closer.

"How did I get here?" His sleepy voice was low and seductive, coaxing a shiver from me.

"You never left."

"Mmm, I made a good choice." He pulled me against him, his hand pushing against the small of my back, his lips finding the crook of my neck. I could feel his excitement—in more ways than one—but I had something else in mind.

"Loki." It came out as an unintended sigh. I cleared my throat. "Don't you think it's time you left the house?"

He hesitated for a moment. "Why leave when I have you all to myself?"

I gently pushed him back. He resisted being torn away from me, playfully biting at the air like a wolf trying to reach its prey. "Because you've been here two weeks and never once gone out that door. Even Idunn is worried about you."

"There's nothing to worry about." He cupped my cheek, smiling in a way that almost made me believe it.

"I'm withholding my kisses until you go outside."

He blinked. "You're what?"

"You heard me. We've been in this house attached to each other like a pair of youngsters in heat. And if you want to keep kissing me, you're going to need to leave this house."

"This is utterly unfair."

I untangled myself from his arms and swung my feet over the side of the bed. "Isn't it though?"

Loki followed me out to the kitchen, dragging himself the whole way. "Does it have to be today?"

I set about making breakfast. "Why not today?"

He came around to the table, where I was cutting thick slices from a loaf of seed bread. He put his arms around my waist, tucking his chin into the curve of my neck. "Because I want to spend it with you."

"You've done nothing but spend the day with me since you got here."

"And I love that."

I put the knife down and turned around, still locked in his embrace. "I'm not blind, Loki. You're afraid."

His lips pursed, jaw clenched. "Hardly."

"You know there's no one out there waiting to hurt you, right?"

"Would that really be so ridiculous to think? It hasn't gone well for me, historically."

Craning my head up, I kissed him, a kindness. But the way he kissed me back was too longing, too desperate, and I remembered why I'd been denying him.

"You of all people know that nothing lasts forever in Asgard. Nothing would ever get done around here if all we did was bicker and hold grudges."

Loki nuzzled his nose into my cheek. "But this is good, Sigyn. We could just be happy here and never go back."

"The Loki I know would never let anyone else win." I ran my fingertips along the scars on his lips. "And he certainly wouldn't let anyone keep him from Áshildr's apple pastries."

Clasping my hand in his to keep it against his cheek, he sighed. "I suppose."

"And afterward, we can go see Hod."

"Must we?" He pulled my chin up with his finger, pouting.

I covered my mouth with my hand, and he finally started to smile.

We arrived on the steps of the archives with four warm apple pastries wrapped in cloth. The building itself was tall and made entirely of stone. Its peaks stretched upward, a smooth warm grey against the blue sky, the front doors intricately carved with winding pictures telling the creation story of the realms.

Loki held the door open for me as I cradled the pastries in my arms. Inside, the smell of old parchment, ink, and leather lingered on the air. The cavernous room was lit only by floating seidr lanterns, like walking through a field of bright fireflies. Specks of dust floated along, finding their home upon the rows of shelves. A few apprentices wandered through the stacks, taking notes, refreshing lanterns, and shelving books.

If there were a more complete collection in the nine realms, I would've liked to see it.

Hod was standing at the edge of an expansive table with his scribe, Eyvindr. The scribe was taller than Hod, his straight black hair tied in a tail that hung over his shoulder, loose strands framing his face. His skin was desert gold, and he was wearing a finely embroidered grey tunic, every bit of him well put together—all except the ink stains that were always on his fingers.

They were speaking low enough that we couldn't hear as we approached. Hod's fingers danced across a loose page. He shook his head, and the scribe slid another paper on top of the first.

Eyvindr looked up. He caught my eye and whispered something to Hod.

"I hear we have visitors." Hod straightened out, running his hand along the edge of the chairs, making his way around the table.

"You do indeed." I met him halfway, pulling him in for a hug. "I've brought you something."

"Áshildr's pastries?"

Loki chuckled. "Can you really know that by smell alone?"

"No." Hod gestured to take a seat. "It's the only thing she ever brings."

Loki pulled out a chair for Hod, and the four of us sat down, trying not to interrupt the piles of stories strewn across the table. Each paper was covered in special runes, etched into thick pages in order to leave a mark that could be felt underneath Hod's fingers.

"I hear you have quite an interesting new tale to tell, Loki."

"Oh?" Loki's eyes dropped to what was left of his pastry. "And what are they saying?"

Eyvindr, who always remembered everything, spoke up. "Thor said you're 'an idiot with stupid hair.' Freya was elated to 'watch you get what was coming to you.' Idunn cried for ten minutes when I asked her about it."

Loki shrugged. "Nothing unexpected."

Hod felt along the neck of his tunic, wiping away pastry crumbs where he found them. "I went to your chambers, but you didn't answer the door. I assumed you didn't much want to see any of us after what happened, but Idunn told me you were with Sigyn."

"His wounds needed tending, and he refused to go to the infirmary," I said. And it was true. It just wasn't the whole truth.

"That I can understand. The infirmary might be my least favourite place in the nine." Hod tilted his head a moment, thinking. "Maybe you should know something else. There's been a certain amount of suspicion about the relationship between the two of you. Once it got out that you were in Sigyn's hall and hadn't come out in two weeks…well, you know how tongues wag."

My chest tightened. Maybe Loki was right. We should've stayed home, where things were easy, and no one knew. Where there weren't any consequences to our choices.

"You don't have to say." Eyvindr had put on a polite smile. He knew as well as any of us that a hesitation like the one in the air might as well be a yes.

Loki's eyes were on me, and it made me want to hide. Saying anything else would be an insult to everything he'd given me, but it took more effort than I wanted to admit just to say, "We're together."

A smile spread across Hod's face. "I'm glad to hear it. I try to stay neutral when it comes to most things, but I have to say, I was hoping so."

Loki leaned over and kissed my temple, and I laughed in relief. All the fear, for nothing. "And why is that?"

"Because everyone needs someone." Hod got up, taking his walking staff from the place he always propped it against the wall. "I've got a new book, something I think you'll both be interested in. Care to join me?"

That was enough to get Loki out of his seat. "What kind of book?"

"The daring, adventurous kind. Eyvindr, finish up with those last pages, and I'll be back soon."

Hod led the way through the chamber, counting the rows by tapping them with his walking stick. Loki and I followed behind, giving him more than enough room to navigate. He walked us alongside stack after stack, past the iron-barred cage of the rare texts, and towards the far end of the archives.

Loki's hand slipped into mine. I startled and nearly pushed it away, but I reminded myself that there was no reason to. We were safe here, with our old allies.

Stopping at the next bookcase, Hod turned a corner, and we followed. Each shelf was lined with etched runes. History, linguistics, culture, fiction. He slid his fingers along them until he'd narrowed it down to the correct shelf. "I've taken you this far; you can find the book yourselves. You're looking for the newest work of one Levaine Theavin."

I squealed and scanned the shelf, but Loki had already dropped into a crouch, fingers hurriedly running across the spines. He stopped when he realized I was staring at him.

"The both of you have always been smitten by her work," Hod said. "Now you'll just need to fight over it. I've got another for you, if I can find it..." He started trailing off toward the end of the stack, fingers searching the shelves.

I narrowed my gaze, suspicious. "You read her books?"

Loki held up a finger. "Don't say it. She's one of the best Elven storytellers, and you *should* have expected it."

"She writes love stories!" I teased.

He scoffed. "And why should I not want to be wooed?"

I laughed, the happiness bubbling over every inch of me. It was such a small, innocent coincidence, but it buoyed something in me, a lightness I hadn't felt in years.

He must have felt it too, because his hand found my waist, and he leaned in expectantly.

I lurched away. "What are you doing?"

"I've left the house. By your rules, I can have a kiss."

"Hod is here."

He nodded toward the now empty corridor. "Around a corner somewhere. It's just a little kiss, Sig."

I drew a breath, trying to calm myself. It was just a kiss. A kiss I wanted, and no one would see. I licked my lips, and that was enough permission for Loki to pull me close and claim them.

A little kiss. God of Lies indeed. I got lost in it. His hands were on me, backing me up against the bookcase. My focus was torn between the trail of his fingers and my wavering will to keep quiet. My mind was so set on keeping the moan off my breath that I didn't hear the boots.

"What in the *nine?*"

Fuck.

Freya stood at the end of the stacks, only a stride away from us. Her cheeks had gone scarlet, rage seeping to the surface. "You can't be serious!"

I pulled myself out of Loki's grip, pushing past him. "Freya, you need to listen—"

"Fuck you!" She was pointing at me, finger nearly jammed into my collarbone. "I'd heard the rumour, but I thought *surely* you weren't that dumb. I warned you about him. Do you think you're the first person he's wormed his way into bed with?"

Loki shifted his weight to one leg, arms crossed over his chest. "If I knew you were jealous, I'd have invited you to join us."

"Loki!" I reached out a hand to Freya, but she batted it away. "Please, Freya. You don't understand. He's...he's good to me."

"Of course he's good to you!" Her voice was echoing through the archives. "Why would you let someone cruel share your bed? He's a parasite. He needs someone to protect him, keep him fed and dry. It's a self-serving lie, just like all the rest!"

The click of wood on stone came from the other end of the stacks. Hod. "Someone had better be dead, because you're disturbing everyone in this building."

"Did you know about this?" Freya asked. "That Sigyn and Loki have been running around together?"

Hod sighed, his head tilting back in annoyance. "Does it matter if I did? It has nothing to do with you or I."

Freya's face bunched up in frustration. "You could've done something!"

"What, Freya? What should I have done?" Hod drew closer, holding his walking stick like a weapon. "Should I have forbidden them to see each other, as if it would have stopped them? And precisely why would I want to see my own sister alone and miserable instead of with a good man?"

Freya's venomous laugh rippled through the room. "Good man? Ymir's breath, you're supposed to be smarter than the rest of us put together. Nevermind. I'm taking this to Odin."

I grabbed her by the arm. "Don't. Please. I can't do this again."

She shook her hand from my grip, her stare boring into me. "Then you should've made better choices." She stormed off toward the archive doors.

Something inside me collapsed. We'd had a few minutes of serenity, and it had all come crashing down, just when I'd allowed myself to hope.

Loki put his arms around me, his face pressed into the top of my head. "It's alright. They have no power over you."

I sniffed, blinking back tears. "You were right. We shouldn't have left the house today."

"You and I, we don't run, hmm?" He gave me a squeeze. "They can't touch us."

Hod stepped tentatively forward. "I think it's best you follow her and face this head on. She'll throw you both under the wagon if you let her."

Loki looked up at him, a hint of himself back in his voice. "Let her try."

Though we'd lost Freya between the archives and Odin's halls, it wasn't hard to find her once we arrived. We only had to follow the yelling.

She was with a few of the other gods in a small council chamber off the side of Gladsheim. Odin, Thor, Idunn, Sif, Frey, and Tyr were standing around an enormous table with the map of the nine realms on it, collections of wooden clan markers sitting in strategic places across it. But when we entered the room, all eyes were on us.

"You see?" Freya hissed at Odin. "Everyone was talking about it, and you wouldn't listen. And now it's too late."

Thor was the first to make a move. He rounded the table toward us, looking straight at me. "How can you touch him after what he did to Sif?"

I stared at him, open-mouthed. The nerve. "How can *she* touch *you* with all the blood on your hands?" I took a step forward, closing the distance, tiny in his shadow but trying to seem large. "Don't pretend that all your deeds were justified, brother. We both know better."

Thor scoffed. "You don't even deny it. You should at least have the decency to be *embarrassed*."

"*You* want to talk about embarrassed—"

"Stop this nonsense. You're being unreasonable." Idunn came to our side, pushing us away from each other. She couldn't budge Thor but managed to force me away. She looked straight at me, her back to the rest of the room. "Is it true? You're together?"

I nodded. Idunn's face lit up. She mouthed a silent, overly enthusiastic exclamation that only Loki and I could see, then turned soberly back to the others.

Loki was forcing back a grin. It was good to have an ally in the room.

Odin had his arms crossed over his chest. He was distinctly quiet, which never amounted to anything good. "This ends at once."

Loki strode across the room and hung his elbow off Odin's shoulder, leaning against him. "Oh, *Grimnir*. What makes you think you have any say in the matter?"

"Because she's my daughter, and I'm telling you it's done."

"Ha! Do you really think you get to tell me what to do anymore?" He walked away from Odin, taking slow strides around the table. "You haven't had that privilege for a very long time. Besides, aren't I just finally putting all your lessons to good use?" The grin he flashed him was like knives.

"What I choose to do and who I choose to see is no one else's business," I said.

"The destiny of Asgard is always my business." Odin's one eye was on Loki, predatory.

"My destiny has never been important to you. I'm not in any of your prophecies, and you won't give me a title. The least you can do is leave me alone and let me love someone."

"Do you love him?" Frey tilted his head like an inquisitive child.

My cheeks turned red. "It's been a week, Frey. At least give me time to decide."

"There's so much that you don't know, Sigyn," Odin started. "You don't understand—"

"I understand enough." I was finished listening to it. "I know that Sif said things to Loki that we'd have strung *anyone else* from the rafters for saying. If it weren't for him, you wouldn't have your hammer, or your spear, or your godsforsaken shiny boar. You talk about his morality, but the only person in this room with a clean conscience is Idunn. I know the lies of more than half of you, and each of you either smells like your secret lover or has blood under your nails."

I came round to Odin and jabbed my finger into his chest. "And you're worst of all. Sticking your prick in things until you have a host of motherless children, giving your favour to leagues of battle-hungry humans only to take it away when you're ready to claim the bodies for your own collection. The single greatest murderer that's ever walked the Nine. And you want to pass judgement on us."

The room was silent. Even Loki had stopped breathing. I couldn't quite believe what I'd said, but there was no taking it back. Odin's face was as red as a sunset, teeth ground into a snarl. He was about to open his mouth, presumably to order my execution, when Frigg walked in.

"Leave them be." She stood in the doorway, regal and ethereal, her eyes unfocused on the scene in front of her.

Odin didn't look away from me. "This mutiny can't stand." His knuckles were white, and I could vividly imagine them around my neck.

Loki stepped in beside me, his shoulder between my father and I, as if he could ever be enough to keep Odin from getting something he wanted.

Frigg drifted into the room, her long, wispy skirts trailing along behind her. "If the Nornir have bound their fate together, then who are we to keep them apart?" Her eyes had yet to focus on anything, as if she were barely there at all.

110

The Goddess of Nothing At All

"To hel with the Nornir." Odin reached out for Loki, and in the blink of an eye, Frigg was between them.

She stared her husband down. Her full presence in the room was like a thundercloud, changing the atmosphere. When she was quiet, it was easy to forget her strength, but it only took a moment to be reminded. When she spoke, her voice seemed thick with other voices, travelling through her all at once, cold and unwavering.

"There are still things that must come to pass."

A shiver ran down my spine.

Odin lowered his hand, taking one deep breath after the other. The pressure in the room seemed to fade as he calmed, and Frigg led him by the hand to the distant corner of the room. She smoothed out his clothes, whispering to him.

The room was still. No one dared make a move, as if anything could stir up Odin's violence again. That is, until Idunn tiptoed to my side and touched my shoulder.

"We should go." Idunn took my hand and one of Loki's, pulling us gently away from the others, who all seemed to be fixated on Odin. Thor glared at us as we left the room, but didn't dare approach, not against Frigg's will.

When we were safely out of the room and out of earshot, I looked to Idunn and then Loki. "*Things must come to pass.* What the hel does that mean?"

"I don't know," Loki replied with an uncharacteristic stillness that worried me.

"I'm sure it's nothing." Idunn hooked her arms in ours so that she was tucked between us as we walked.

"It didn't sound like nothing."

Idunn tightened her grip on my arm. "Even dessert is still something that must come to pass. It's an eerie comment, but it's hardly a prophecy. It's not important." She gave a tug on our arms, an enthusiastic squeal on her voice. "But this! This is incredible! Two of my favourite people in the nine, together? I'm going to make you something to eat, and you're going to tell me absolutely everything."

CHAPTER TWENTY

*"Loki was beautiful. It's indisputable, all the stories say so.
Beautiful and so very good with words. I think, perhaps, that
it's cruel for us to blame her for that. Would any
of us have been able to resist?"*

—*God of Lies Revealed*

"No, just leave the bottle on the table, please."

Idunn laughed and passed the berry wine directly to me. "You be careful! I haven't seen you drink this quickly since that time you ended up in bed with the Elven Princess."

Loki gasped. "Which one?"

"Miranel." I took a drink. "She was a bad influence."

"So is her oldest sister." Loki shot me a conspiratorial grin. "Or was I a bad influence on her? We'll never know."

"Listen," I interrupted before he could ask more questions. "I will get precisely as drunk as I want. What happened today was truly the most reckless, stupid thing I've ever done."

"Clearly, you need a more exciting life." Loki held his cup out to be filled.

I obliged, stopping only when the wine was threatening to slosh over the top. "I would argue that that's exactly the opposite of the truth."

"Then darling—" he planted a kiss on my cheek "—you're barking up the wrong tree."

Idunn squeaked her delight and set down a platter of sizzling pork, plated in the middle of a medley of freshly grown vegetables. She was skirting around the kitchen of their cabin, adjusting and fetching and plating. The room was large, but so much of it was already home to other things. Bronze cooking pans decorated the wall behind the hearth, and there was a corner to sit in that clearly belonged to Bragi, notebooks towering on a corner table next to a lute. Plants hung in pots from the ceiling and every windowsill was home to some flower or another. In one corner, vines crept up the wall and trailed across the ceiling, a lush paradise for two.

When Idunn finally slid into the chair across from us, she sighed, resting her chin on her hands and gazing dreamily at us. "This is everything I've ever dreamed of."

Loki reached across the table to take his helping of supper. "You dreamed that an irresistible bronze-skinned beauty would come and sweep me off my feet?"

"Well not so specifically, but yes." Her eyes were shimmering, like she was about to cry. "I always thought you needed someone to love."

There was that word again. "Well, it's good *you're* enthusiastic. Other than Hod, I don't think we have another soul on our side."

She waved a hand. "They'll come around."

"I really don't think they will. Odin might have skinned us both if Frigg hadn't stepped in with her '*things must come to pass*' speech." I took a long drink, eager to get the image out of my head.

"He can skin me when he can catch me." Loki pried the bone from his cut of meat, ripping off a bite-sized piece. "Frankly, I think I'd make a fetching rug."

I shuddered, that image far too vivid in my mind after all that had happened. "How can you be so casual about this? Every time one of them gets their hands on you, I have to put you back together again."

He kept his eyes on his plate. "This is only new to you, Sig. It's an old dance for the rest of us."

Idunn waved her hands, her face scrunched in discomfort. "No more of this depressing conversation, please. I want to celebrate the good things instead." She scooted her chair closer to the table, honing in on us with her dreamy smile. "Tell me how this happened with the two of you. And no lying; I know it must have been full of sparks."

Loki's fingers were clasped in mine as we waved goodbye to Idunn and stepped onto the path back to the city. We'd stayed late, and the night was quiet; leaves rustled in the trees and small animals skittered unseen in the bushes. The sky had clouded over since we'd arrived, and it smelled like rain was coming.

"What are you thinking?" Loki lifted our joined hands and kissed my knuckles.

"I'm thinking that this was the perfect way to make up for everything else."

"That woman's gotten me through a lot over the decades," he said, something wistful in his voice.

I knew exactly what he meant.

A few tiny droplets had started to fall by the time we stepped out from under the trees. We strolled easily through the streets, still hand in hand. Light poured out the windows of tiny houses, raucous shouting from the open doors of full taverns. We passed very few people in the streets, but either I was getting used to the stares or they had grown more accustomed to having Loki back.

We were halfway to my hall when an overwhelming crack of thunder roared across the sky. All at once, a great deluge poured down onto the city. I shrieked, holding my hands over my head, cursing myself for leaving my cloak at home.

Loki was laughing, arms held out and face up to the sky as the rain streaked down his cheeks and into his clothes. "Thor must be livid about something." He wiped the water from around his eyes. "Do you think it might be us?"

"Does it matter? This could last hours! Come on!" I started running, pulling my skirts up in my hands so I could move freely. The road was already slick with mud.

Loki was on my heels in a moment, the two of us racing past packed up merchant carts and drowned out torches. The thunder rolled again, far too close, lightning illuminating the sky a moment later. We careened through the streets of Asgard as fast as our boots would take us.

As we ran towards the exit of a tight alley, a bolt of lightning snapped down into the street ahead, lighting up everything around it. We startled back and waited, my heart hammering in my chest. Loki was laughing again, but I could barely catch my breath.

"Maybe we should wait a minute, stay under cover." Loki guided us under the overhang of a roof, a small piece of reprieve from the torrent of rain. But it also meant pressing ourselves into the small space, my back pressed against the wall, Loki's body tight against mine.

The alley was dark, but a sliver of light poured out of a window not far away, and I could see the shadows and angles of his face, the droplets of water running over the lines of him. The kohl around his eyes had run down his cheeks, and it only amplified the hunger on his face. The wanting.

And gods did I want. I ran my hands up his chest, his wet tunic sticking to every line of him, carving him out like stone. Solid under my hands. He drew a trembling breath and brought his hand up to my face, cupping my cheek, gently arching my head as his lips lowered to my exposed shoulder and kissed up to my neck. I melted against the wall, a moan spilling from my lips. He pressed against me, warm against my cold clothes, his breathing shallow as he nipped my ear and the corner of my jaw with his teeth. The fingers of one hand entwined with mine, and he held it above our heads, against the wall, looking at me with an urgency I could feel through my whole body.

I pulled him down by the back of his neck, kissing him desperately. His response was immediate, his hands pressing up my side, sliding against my breast, stealing my breath. His tongue slid against my lip, and I met it, and he felt so fucking good under my hands, so burning with need.

Then a shiver racked its way through my body so violently that Loki pulled away from the kiss and looked me over, concerned.

"Sorry," I bit my lip, wanting to ignore the cold in my bones and go back to the warmth curling in my belly.

He pressed his forehead against mine. "You're freezing. We're going home."

"Loki…"

That grin of his slipped back onto his face, and he leaned into my ear to whisper, "There'll be more chances to fuck in an alley, darling." A thrill ran up my body, and I gaped at him, which only earned a chuckle. He took my hand and pulled me towards the next street. "Come on."

The rain had barely let up; Thor was clearly having a bad night. But we were close to my hall, and a few minutes later, we were barrelling through the front door, dripping water and shivering from head to toe. Loki slammed the door shut and leaned against it, panting for breath, laughing. And then we were both laughing, sopping wet in the dark, the silliest, most carefree thing I'd done in a long time.

"Alright," Loki said, pushing himself off the door and coming towards me. "How do you feel about getting out of those clothes?" I stammered, both from chill and nerves, and then he was pressing me against the hearth, his lips on my cheek. "Shall I?"

I drew a sharp breath, my body arching against his, betraying my wants. His mouth was open just a bit, and I ran a finger across his lip. "Please."

He hoisted me up, startling me, and pushed my back against the stone. I wrapped my legs around his waist to keep from falling, his hands already forcing my dress up to my hips. The way he kissed me, needy and deep, sent a wave of heat through my body. Then his mouth was on my collarbone, trailing lower, and I drew in a breath, tangling my fingers in his hair and curling into him as he explored everything above the line of my clothes.

"Loki…"

His lips found mine again, and he whispered, "Yes?"

"Warm me up."

The grip of his hands tightened and growled against my skin. "*Fuck*." And he bit gently on the ridge of my shoulder, like an animal holding back.

He let me drop to my feet, his hands lingering on my hips for a moment. Then turned me around, one hand on my ribs while the other unhooked the clasps on the

115

back of my dress. I closed my eyes, savouring his fingers running across the bare skin on my back, leaning against him as he pushed my hair from my neck and ran his tongue along my skin. My body thrilled against him, and his hand followed the arc, palming my breast.

"I've waited so long to hear you breathe like this."

Pursing my lips, I swallowed hard. "I have no idea what you mean."

Loki hummed a disapproving note against my jaw. "That won't do." The length of my dress moved, Loki hiking it up to bare my thigh, and he traced the line of my hip with his fingers. The gasp of an *oh* escaped me, and he chuckled. "Like that, beauty."

I turned in his grasp and wrapped my hands in his collar, pulling his head down to kiss him. Slipping my hands under the edge of his shirt, I peeled it off his body and tossed it toward the water basin. He dipped down to kiss me again, one hand on the hearth, keeping me between them, and I stopped him. "I want to see you," I spoke against his lips.

His fingers snapped and a flicker of wildfire lit in his hand. Trails of water ran down from his hair, over his skin, dipping and curving around muscle, glistening in the light. His shoulders moved with shallow, lusting breaths.

I ran my thumbs under his eyes, removing the worst of the kohl. "You are, without a doubt, the most beautiful man I've ever seen."

Something softened in him then. The way he stood, the set of his face. He closed his eyes for just a moment. "You flatter me, Sigyn."

I toyed with the ties on his trousers, never breaking eye contact, then tucked my fingers under the line of the cloth and pulled, walking backward. Forcing him to follow.

"Where are you taking me?" He laughed, snuffing out the wildfire.

I bobbed my head. "Wherever I please."

But he didn't let me. A moment later, he'd scooped me into his arms and was carrying me into the bedroom. "You have to understand," he said, putting me down next to the bed. "I'm feeling very inclined to get you out of this dress, and you are *still* in it."

I pushed down the sleeves of my dress one after the other, and then his hands were there, his fingers slowly pulling it away from my skin, revealing me by degrees. The cloth slid over the tips of my breasts and down to my hips, and the sight stole Loki's breath. He peeled the last clinging pieces away from my body, underthings and all, and it fell to the floor, leaving me bare in front of him.

Pressing kisses on my lips, his hands on my skin, he urged me to the bed. I backed myself onto the mattress, but he didn't follow. Another snap of fingers, and he was lighting candles on the bedside table. I rested my head on my arm, watching him, waiting. Then he started to untie his trousers *achingly slowly*, eyes locked on mine, mischief in his smile.

"Don't want to get the bed wet." He let them drop and stepped out of them, crawling towards me. Stopping to run his tongue along my skin, he worked his way up to my ear, on all fours above me. "Just you."

I ran my fingers over the claw scars on his shoulders, wanting to feel his skin on mine, but then he was moving away, trailing his lips down my chest, over my stomach, until he was kissing the inside of my thighs.

Oh. So that was what we would do.

The first touch sent such a spark through me that I had to dig my fingers into the mattress just to bear. Then it was a soft, building ache, a patient progression as he discovered what made my hands curl in his hair. I languished in it, this captivating Jotun on his knees for me. The heat swirling in me. And oh, he was good. I wrapped my legs around him and whimpered as he brought me closer to the brink. Then his fingers were there as well, and I held him in place, begging him to keep going. And then it was done, my hips bucking against his mouth, Loki's hand dug into my thigh as I cried out, gripping the furs on the bed.

I tried to catch my breath, running a hand across the sheen of sweat that had started on my belly. Loki was looking up at me, a satisfied grin on his face. He kissed my thigh and came up to lie against me, face tucked against my shoulder as my heart kept racing.

His fingers trailed down my chest and ran over the curve of my breast. "You are *so fucking beautiful.*"

I turned towards him, pressing his warm skin against mine. "And that was divine."

"I'm only getting started with you." He pulled me flush against him.

Kissing him, I reached down and ran my fingers along the length of him, waiting for the hitch in his breath. It was quick and impatient, and he gripped my face with both hands, snaking his tongue against mine.

"I want you," I breathed.

"You have me." He sat up, pulling me onto his lap, sliding carefully inside me. My head lolled back, pleasure rushing through me as he drew me close, his face nestled into my neck. His lips were everywhere. I held him against me as I moved my hips on top of him, growing bolder with each noise I earned. When he eventually pulled back from my skin, his face was awash with a bliss I'd never seen on him before. His eyes were closed, fingers digging into my hips, lips parted.

But my legs were begging me to slow, and as I did, Loki's eyes fluttered open. I bit my lip in apology, and he planted a kiss on my jaw. With one hand on my back, he lowered me to the bed and stayed on his knees. I bit back a moan as he hoisted my hips up to meet his and slipped back in.

I wrapped my legs around his back, my fingers entangled in the furs above my head, trying to hold on as Loki gave in to what he craved. He was moving faster, each thrust pouring static through my body until I was crying out. His fingers dug deeper into my thighs, and I felt how close he was, knew that if I just squeezed a little— My name spilled like a prayer from his lips. He kept going, and I lost myself to the feeling as he cried out one last time, head tipped back, the pleasure coursing through him.

It was fucking beautiful to watch.

Then he cursed. "Oh, Sigyn, I wasn't thinking, fuck. It just—"

I hushed him and tugged his arm until he collapsed down next to me. "I have something. It's fine. Gods…more than fine." There were herbs in the cupboards for a tea, and I wasn't going to let it bother me yet. We'd get up in a moment, have something to drink, languish near the fire. For now, it felt too good to get up. Every muscle was relaxed. Blissful. I wanted to melt into the bed and never come back.

"The perfect end to a perfect evening." Loki laid his arm over my waist. "Are you happy?"

I pressed my hand to his chest, feeling the race of his heart. "Of course. I have you."

He looked at me, his eyes sleepy and content, and he smiled. "You'll always have me, goddess."

CHAPTER TWENTY-ONE

*"I hesitate to think about how horrible it must have
been inside those walls. To be at his mercy.
Sigyn must have had nerves of steel."*

—*God of Lies Revealed*

The sun was up by the time I woke, curled up in bed. Loki's whole body was tucked so tightly against mine that I didn't dare move. My hair tickled the back of my neck as his breath grazed my skin, his chin snuggled into my shoulder.

"Good morning," he whispered against my skin, his arm tightening around my waist.

"I thought you were asleep." I turned to face him, resting my hand on the sharp angle of his bare hip.

"I didn't want to wake you. You snore."

I covered my face with my hand, blushing. "I do not."

"You do, just a little. It's adorable." He reached up and pushed a stray lock of hair back from my face. "I like waking up next to you."

A thought was bubbling up in me, one I'd had again and again. And it was so hasty, but it was overwhelming. So I just said it. "Then don't go back to Valaskjálf."

He eyed me suspiciously. "Do you mean that?"

"I want to keep doing this." I ran my palm across his chest. "Waking up together, cooking together, coming home to you. I don't want to go back to living here alone, only seeing you sometimes. I don't think I could stand it."

A thin, cautious smile found its way to his lips. His fingers traced the curve of my shoulder. "If you're sure."

I took his face in my hands, pulling him down for a long, reassuring kiss.

When we parted, he pressed his forehead against mine. "Well, what can I do but say yes?"

I walked my fingers down his bare chest, biting my bottom lip. He drew in a breath as my hand reached his stomach, his mind clearly already lost on delicious pursuits. "You can say you'll help me."

He grabbed me and flipped me onto my back, kneeling over me. His sleep-tangled hair fell around our faces, his lips hovering just above mine. "Oh, I can help you," he growled.

"I need to break into the archives."

The confusion on his face was priceless. "I'm sorry, come again?"

"Later." I wiggled out from under him. "First, there's something I need."

Loki fell onto his side, still bewildered—and clearly disappointed—at the change of pace. "Well, it's not as if they charge admission."

The pitiful look on his face coaxed a hint of guilt from me. I took a section of his hair and began to work at the tangles with my fingers. "I want access to the rare texts, and they still keep them under lock and key."

"Wouldn't Hod just let you in? He trusts you."

"Odin only gives permission to a small list of people, and you'll be absolutely shocked to know I'm not one of them."

He peered at me. "Sigyn Odindottir wants to do something against the rules. If you're not careful, you're going to make it into a habit."

"I want another chance at my title." My fingers nimbly braided a section of his combed hair and moved on to the next. "I don't want to give up on it, and maybe something in that room can give me the edge I need."

"Aren't I the edge you needed?" He chuckled and pulled me against him, prying the half-finished braid from my hands. "You don't need a title to be worth something."

The words bruised me. I turned away. "I don't know what I am without all this. It's the only thing I've ever really wanted, and if I spent all those decades working toward it for *nothing*...How do I just give up on it?"

His palm found my cheek and gave me no choice but to look at him. "It's not for nothing. No one can take that experience from you. All the things you learned, the power you have. That's yours."

The familiar bitterness rose in my chest, willing itself to the surface. I stared him in the eyes as it poured off my tongue like poison. "That's easy for you to say. You have yours."

He withdrew his hand, like I'd burned him. "Are you jealous of my title? God of Lies? Because that would be a very stupid thing to be jealous of. You don't know what it took to get it, and you don't want to."

I sat back, unable to look him in the eyes. "Could it really be any worse than what I've done?"

"Sigyn. There's always worse. Always."

When I dared to look up, his eyes were glistening. A knot twisted in my stomach, and I pushed back the bitterness, reaching a hand out to him. "I'm sorry. You can tell me."

He sat up, elbows on his knees, picking the skin from around his nails. "Everything comes at a price with Odin. He took me in, made me feel like I owed him for it. Taught me how to spy for him, bring back the information he wanted. Before I knew it, I was sneaking into rooms, stealing things, flirting with important people, killing. Sometimes he needed someone to change their mind, so he sent me. I could change shape, become whatever would appeal to them. Get the job done. Whatever it took."

I knew what he was alluding to and I wished I didn't. "Loki, that can't be true."

"It is. I've taken emissaries and councillors and princesses to bed and changed their minds with the flick of a tongue or at the point of a knife. Whatever Odin needed."

"He sold your body for favours?"

He reached out and took my hand. "Odin will never stop taking. Do you think you're the only person he's used at the price of a title? Do you think I am? What price do you think the rest of the gods paid?"

I hardly knew what to say. How long had I been blind to it? How many things had I done for him in the last half a century, hoping it would be enough? "But you got your title. How?"

He laughed, bitter. "He exiled me and gave it to me as he pushed me out the door. It didn't come with a council seat or any of the perks. Just a dagger in my back that I can't dig out."

I sighed, deflated. "I'm sorry."

He pulled my hand, bringing us both back down to the mattress. I tucked myself against his side, my palms on his chest, and he buried his face in my hair. "You have nothing to be sorry for."

We laid in silence for a long while, my head pressed against his skin, his heartbeat in my ear.

"I'll help you." He tucked his finger beneath my chin and tilted my head, planting a soft kiss on my lips. "You deserve a title, and if this is the thing that gets you there, who am I to say no? But Sig…he can burn your life to cinders."

"Let him try. I won't let him ruin this. One last try, and then it's finished."

Half a smirk appeared on his lips. "You never give up. I love that about you." He rolled over suddenly, playfully pinning me beneath him. I squeaked, laughing at his change of mood. He dipped his head for a longer kiss, and I melted under his touch. He spoke against my lips. "But we have a whole day before sundown. How will we *ever* keep busy?"

Most of Asgard was asleep by the time we arrived at the doors of the archives. This was by design, naturally. Hod and Eyvindr would need to be fast asleep. Both of their living quarters were in the archives themselves, and we needed to get in and out without being seen.

It wasn't as if the building was locked up tightly; we were probably the only ones in the nine realms eager to break into a place where they kept books. All it had taken was a small boost through an open window leading to a storage room, and we were inside.

Excitement mingled with fear inside my chest, both fighting for dominance. I'd never broken into anything before, and despite recent events, I still wasn't used to breaking the rules. Not that Odin had explicitly forbidden me to go in there. He just hadn't given me permission.

The main hall of the archives was low-lit, most of the seidr lanterns having faded over the course of the day. We padded down the room, weaving our way between the stacks until we came to the back of the building, where the private quarters were located. It was an effort to make no noise at all; my mouth was dry, and my heart skipped every time my shoes made the slightest scuff.

We stopped outside Hod's door. Loki slowly turned the handle, but nothing happened. He'd promised me that he could get the key but hadn't explained how. Now that we were here, he put a finger to his lips and motioned for me to stay put. In the dim light, I couldn't make out the runes he whispered. Eventually, the air around him shifted, blurring before my eyes until I was forced to shield them. When I turned back, he was gone.

I looked over my shoulder. He wasn't behind me either. He had shapeshifted of course, but into what? Something buzzed next to my ear, and I nearly raised my hand to swat at it.

Oh.

I squinted until I could follow the path of the fly in the dim light. It swooped down and landed on the handle of the door, then skittered down around the knob and into the keyhole. Curious, I knelt down and peered inside. There was nothing blocking the way, and other than a beam of moonlight, the room was black. Then the shape of a man stepped into view, skirting around the room.

That sneaky fox. It had always driven Freya mad, not knowing how he'd gotten into her room in the first place. What a handy, devious trick.

122

The Goddess of Nothing At All

I backed away from the door, keeping watch around the corner. The archives were always quiet, but now, every second of silence was full of that guilty anticipation of being caught. Of having to explain myself and watch the disappointed look in everyone's eyes. The moments crawled by, every second timed with a dozen thumps of my heart. How long could it take him to find a key?

The smallest click came from behind me. The door slid open. Loki crept out and closed it gently behind him. Clasped tightly in his other hand was a ring of keys. He came to me and showed them off, but the panic under my skin was too loud for me to be impressed. He cocked his head at my lack of enthusiasm, so I pressed his empty hand against my chest, so he could feel the drumming.

He leaned in to whisper. "You are brave and bold and beautiful." He nipped at my ear, distracting me, and for just a moment, the thrill drowned out my fear.

He took my hand, and we tiptoed to the gated section of books. Loki examined the lock and chose a key that seemed to match. After the third attempt, the lock clicked. The gate creaked open, setting me on edge again. They would've heard that. I stood still, eyes darting in all directions, trying desperately to see our inevitable captors.

"Sig, hey." Loki grabbed my shoulders, staring me down. "If you don't calm down, you're going to knock into something and *really* get us caught."

I drew a breath. I could do this. I could be a petty thief.

We left the gate ajar and stepped into the tiny room. Loki took one side, and I took the other, skimming the spines of the books with my fingers. The ones closest to the front were dull, most of them private journals of important figures from around the realms. There wouldn't be anything tempting where the common eye could see it. The real goodies would be in the back.

The process was a long one. Over and over, I picked up a book based on its title and skimmed its contents only to decide it wasn't anything special. Lists of poisons and curses, risky imbalances of nature like raising the bodies of the dead. Nothing I needed or wanted. Loki passed me books he thought were worth considering, but none of them felt right.

I stopped to stretch and yawn, wondering how long we'd been inside. When I turned to him, Loki was skimming through a ratty old book, eyes wide. There was the slightest tremble in his hands.

He noticed me looking and cool composure slid over him.

"What's that?" I whispered.

"Some old stories about the realms. Nothing special." He cleared his throat.

"You said you wouldn't lie to me." I crossed my arms over my chest.

"I'm not lying."

"Loki."

"Fine," he hissed. He took a deep breath, pushing down whatever anger I'd stirred up. "It...there's something about my mother."

"Oh." I don't know what I'd been expecting, but it hadn't been that. "What does it say?"

He closed the book and ran his hand over the cover. "I'm not sure. I didn't read much, but there was a picture."

"Oh, Loki." I took his hand. "Can I see it?"

"I—" His grip tightened on the book. There were tears in his eyes. "I'd rather not. It's just... I just found it. I'd like to keep it to myself for a little while."

"Of course." I took the book from his white-knuckled grip and slid it into the bag over his shoulder. "Take all the time you need."

He gave me a weak smile and straightened his shoulders. "Have you found something?"

I shook my head. "Not yet. Let's keep looking." I knelt down next to him, looking over the shelf near his feet.

He was quiet for a moment. "What do you know about Ragnarok?"

"The same as everyone else. Why?"

Loki bent to look at the shelf above my head. "Let's call it a distraction."

I sighed and gave in, careful to keep my voice low. "I know what everyone knows. First comes the Fimbulwinter, three endless winters that will have the people of Midgard killing each other to survive. The enemies of Asgard will march on us, and Heimdall will blow the horn that calls the gods to battle. And we'll die. Every single one of us."

Loki huffed. "You take all the joy out of storytelling."

"Fine." I stood to get a better look at the top row, reciting the prophecy the way it had been told to me. "Thor will fight an enormous serpent, bigger than anything the realms have ever seen. He'll slay it but die from its poison. Odin will fight a wolf so large it makes the realms tremble with its step. The wolf will eat him alive. Frey will be killed by the fire giant Surtr. Everyone else goes unnamed in the prophecy. Is that detailed enough for you?"

"Seems odd they haven't learned anything new since I was away, that's all." Loki passed me a book about increasing the growing speed of plants, and I quickly dismissed it.

I made a face at him. "I don't think that's how prophecies work. They don't evolve over time."

"Maybe, maybe not. What about that?" He pointed over my shoulder.

124

The Goddess of Nothing At All

The book was bound in red leather and detailed with inlaid gold. The spine read *Intention*.

It was incredibly heavy for its size. I flipped it open and whispered the introduction. "The contents of this book are delicate. If you're reading this, then you are one of few, as this volume will be locked away upon its completion. Intention is a subtle art, and one that has only existed in small doses before now. Many call it a sixth sense and have only a dash of it in their blood, but I have gone too far and learned too much. Choose carefully what you learn from this book. You may wish you'd never found it at all."

"Well, that's ominous." Loki rested his chin on my shoulder, his hands clasped around my waist.

"*The Source of Intuition. Body Language. Avoiding Poisoned Food.* Whoever wrote this was truly paranoid. But look, runes for sensing intention. If I could understand what exactly is going on in Odin's mind, maybe I could turn things in my favour."

"Are you sure this is the right book? It's not all that impressive on its own."

I kept shuffling through the pages. "It doesn't need to be. Think how useful it would be to know if someone was lying, if you were about to be taken advantage of." I snapped the book shut and turned to tuck it into Loki's bag. "This is the one."

"If you insist." The words trailed into a yawn. "Does that mean we can go to bed?"

We locked up the gate and reversed our steps, putting the keys back where Loki had found them and leaving back through the window. There wasn't a single soul still awake as we made the short trek back to my hall. We went straight to bed, where I curled up in Loki's arms, his hand stroking the top of my hair until I fell asleep and dreamed of the future.

CHAPTER TWENTY-TWO

"3 cloudberries
2 raspberries
3 cherries
Small spoon Venerium*
Dash of powdered Elderroot
Pinch of Sugar

*Adjust dosage depending on desired effects."

—*Recipe for tea*

Sliding out of bed unnoticed was difficult, but I managed it. I tiptoed from the room, leaving Loki deeply asleep, and closed the door behind me. The pilfered book was lying there on the kitchen table, begging to be read. I sat right down, not bothering with anything as trivial as breakfast.

I'd already picked it up and opened the cover when I noticed that Loki's book was missing.

I shrugged and wrapped the furs from the back of my chair around me, settling in, legs curled to my chest. A few pages turned into a few chapters as I read through dry, increasingly paranoid primers that hinted at incredible possibilities. My stomach growled, but I ignored it, willfully ignorant about the time of day. The next chapter detailed the theory behind instinct, and it was not as if I was going to stop *there*.

The door to the bedroom opened, and Loki shuffled out. There were shadows under his eyes, and his hair was more of a mess than usual. He circled around to the far side of the table and gave me a peck on the cheek before he slumped into the chair beside me.

126

"You look awful." I marked my page and set the book down with only a little regret.

He gave me a sarcastic smile. "Thank you."

"I didn't mean it like that, and you know it. Did you sleep at all?"

He rubbed his hands across his face. "Eventually."

Sometimes, Loki had nightmares. He'd startle me awake in the middle of the night in a cold sweat, gasping like something was chasing him. Whenever I asked what he had dreamed about, he just said '*Monsters.*' I suspected he meant the human kind.

"More bad dreams? Surely not about last night. Robbing a library must have been child's play for you. Was it the book?"

Loki shook his head and tried to brush out the tangles in his hair with his fingers. "I'm fine, Sig, just tired and hungry."

My stomach roared in agreement.

He leaned in and cupped my cheek in his hand. "How about I summon my strength and go to the market to find us something special for breakfast? Whatever you'd like."

I stole a kiss. "Surprise me."

And so, Loki dressed and left me to my reading. Not long after he was gone, my legs started to complain about having sat all morning, urging me out of my chair. I flitted from chore to chore, casting runes to make the broom sweep the floor, tidying my workspace, and starting a fire to cook with.

I went into the bedroom and pulled all the crumpled sheets and furs from the floor. A corner of the bedding had come loose on Loki's side, so I yanked it tight and pushed it back between the two mattresses. My hand struck something hard, and I shimmied it out. It was the book that Loki had taken.

He had asked me not to look. But I was curious, and it was only a drawing. Everyone else had seen so much of his life, and I'd seen so little. I just wanted a glimpse of it. I sat down on the bed and opened the cover.

> *The contents of this book are not for the eyes of anyone else. It contains*
> *the prophecy of the seer, transcribed as accurately as I could manage. No*
> *one is to read the contents of this book, not even you.*
> *I'll return for it when it's time.*
>
> *—Odin*

Alarmed, I opened the book to the middle. Loki had said the book was—but it wasn't. The lines were skaldic poetry, some that I'd been familiar with since I was a child. Odin had gone to the seer long before I'd been born and had come back with a prophecy foretelling Ragnarok, the exact story I'd told Loki when—

The front door opened. "Sig?"

That snake.

I said nothing, too stunned to even move. I only looked up when he appeared in the doorway, a full satchel on his hip. His mouth opened, but his eyes caught the book in my hands. "*Skit.*"

"What is this?"

"It's nothing."

I stood, shaking the book. "If it was nothing, why would you lie?"

Loki paused before answering. "How much did you read?"

"Does it matter? It's the lie that—" There was a page earmarked. I flipped it open.

"Sig, no, please." He reached out to take the book, and I twisted away from him. I only caught the runes for both our names on the page before he pressed the book shut, refusing to release it. "Please let me explain."

"Why are our names in the prophecy of Ragnarok? They were never there before!" The panic was rising in my chest. It was impossible. I was no one, so why was my name there?

Loki pried the book from me, holding my hand so tightly, it nearly hurt. "Come sit down. I'll tell you what I know. Please."

I tried to get my breathing under control. His arm went around my shoulder, guiding me to the kitchen where he pressed me into a chair. I stared at him as he moved from water basin to hearth to shelves, emptying his bag and putting water over the fire to boil.

"Well?" I snapped. "Are you going to tell me or not?"

He stopped, pressing his palms into the tabletop. "I didn't know before last night. I wish I didn't know at all."

"Know what, Loki?"

"When Odin told the realms the prophecy of Ragnarok, he left out some things."

I shifted in my seat. "How much?"

"Only a little, but..." He took a long breath. "Sig, he left *us* out."

The water over the fire bubbled, interrupting him. He went to take it away from the hearth and over to the counter. He filled two cups and put the boiling pot back. He reached into my own jars and then into pouches he'd brought home moments ago, taking pinches of this and that, his back turned to me. A wooden spoon scraped on metal, stirring. At last, he turned toward me, placing the cups on the table.

I took a deep breath. "Just tell me. You're making me nervous."

Loki sat down next to me. "I'm sorry. I want to say it the right way. It's more than just what the book says. What it means, what they must have known all this time...I don't want to hurt you."

"Tell me Loki, or I swear on the roots of Yggdrasil Herself—"

"Okay, alright." He pushed one of the cups toward me. "Breathe."

I took the cup and lifted it to my lips. Pieces of dried raspberry, cloudberry, and cherry floated at the top, giving off the faintest scent. It was too hot by far and deceptively tart.

"Your father has been hiding this from you, from both of us. This prophecy was new when my mother was young, and if what it says is true...they've known about this, between us, for a very long time."

I stopped drinking, the cup already half empty. "But that's impossible."

He shook his head. "Divination is imprecise but it's never exactly wrong. Are you sure you want to know this?"

I wasn't. My head had started to spin. I took another drink, cursing the sudden headache. "If he knew, why would Odin keep it a secret? Why...why would he...Loki, nothing in that prophecy is good."

"I know. And I'm sorry. I can't lose you, you're the..." He was still speaking, but his words danced in my mind, just out of reach. I tried to grasp at them, but I couldn't.

I leaned against the table, tea splashing over the side of my cup. "I...I don't feel well."

He took the cup from my hand and set it aside. "Are you alright?"

The light from the window was too bright. My temples ached, my mind shrivelling up like fruit in the sun. What had we just been talking about? I grasped at fleeting thoughts, trying to pull them back to me, but they refused to stay. "I had something to say, but I can't think of what it was now..."

He smiled, taking an unfamiliar red and gold book from the table and holding it up. "You were just complaining about the book I found for you, remember?"

Had I? "*Influence*. I've never heard of it."

He kissed me on the cheek and set it in front of me. "I found it at the market, but you told me it's a lot of nonsense. All folklore and no real seidr. I guess I'll sell it back."

"What a waste..." I grimaced, my mind swimming in all directions. "The whole room is turning."

"Come on. You should sleep it off." He took my arm and led me back to the bed, where the furs were lying haphazard on the floor. Who had left them there?

I laid down, burying my head in the pillow to ease the ache, and everything went black.

CHAPTER TWENTY-THREE

"Trust is the foundation that all good love is built on.
Remove it, and the rest crumbles."

—*Winter Wilds, Levaine Theavin*

L oki had taken the useless book and come back from the market with a new one, a book about manipulating water. On his insistence, we were sitting in the sun outside my hall, me with my new book and him napping with his head in my lap. I'd just finished a chapter about controlling the tide when the sky clouded over, and a clap of thunder rolled above our heads.

Loki peeked an eye open. "Well, that's not good."

"What do you think he's mad about now?" I stroked a hand across Loki's temple and down his cheek, drawing out an easy smile.

"Maybe he's just jealous that he doesn't get to lie in your arms." His face shifted, disgusted with his own comment. "No, pretend I didn't say that. Pretend I said something better."

I laughed. It was horrendous, but it was nice to see that he couldn't smooth-talk his way through every moment.

Another roll of thunder crashed overhead, and Loki sat up, brushing himself off. I marked my page, not wanting to ruin my book when the sky broke open. We were almost through the door when the sound of scraping gravel drew our attention. Thor was stomping towards us, his face set in a snarl, his fists balled up at his sides.

"Oh, that is *really* not good." Loki rolled his shoulders and stretched his neck before taking a step towards my brother. "You know, if you're going to visit, you could at least bring a little sun with you."

"Mjolnir is gone," Thor snapped, stopping just out of arm's reach of Loki. And a good thing too, since he looked eager to break something.

I stepped in beside Loki, freeing up my dominant casting hand, just in case. "Your hammer has nothing to do with us."

"Doesn't it? There's half a chance he's got it in your cellar."

Loki shrugged. "I don't have it."

"You really don't?" Thor turned, looking around like he was lost. The clouds above softened, and the rumble grew more distant. He kicked a rock and sent it soaring into the city. "Hel take me, if you haven't got it, then where is it? You have to be lying."

Loki stared him in the eyes, unflinching. "If I wanted to hurt you, I could think of better ways."

Thor's shoulders fell with a great heaving sigh, the tension between them fading as quickly as it had come. He slumped against the side of my hall, head in hands. "What am I going to do?"

"It's just a hammer," I said, still bristling from the accusation.

"It's not *just* a hammer. It's *my* hammer, and I've been telling everyone about it and killing everyone with it, and if the realms find out it's gone, then not only will *everyone* want to pick a fight with me, I'll look like an idiot."

Loki cackled. "Don't you always?"

Thor looked up at him, practically pleading. "You have to help me." I couldn't recall ever seeing tears in my brother's eyes before.

"Why me?" Loki shifted his weight to one foot. "Last I checked, you loathe me."

"It has to be you. You're crafty and devious and smarter than I am, and—"

Loki waved a hand, smirking. "No, that's all I needed to hear. Come inside. Let's see what can be done."

Thor was away from the wall and past me before I could think to move. Yggdrasil shade me, had they always been like that? Neither friend nor foe?

The men were already at the table, Thor having tracked dirt in behind him. I sat down next to Loki. "Where did you see it last?"

"I put it down at supper, and I thought I brought it to my room, but I'd had a lot to drink and…well, you know. Maybe I didn't?"

Loki extended his arm across the table to Thor, palm down, like he was talking to a child. "Tell me you looked in Valhalla."

"Of course I did. The Valkyries haven't seen it. Couldn't you do that thing you do? Where you turn into a bird and go scouting?"

I turned to Loki. "Scouting?"

He put his arm around my shoulder. "Once or twice, I may have shifted into a hawk to find things worth finding. Usually an enemy, occasionally a lost keg of ale."

"That was good ale." Thor sighed wistfully.

"Alright." Loki smacked the table with his palm and stood up. "How far could it have gone anyway?" Without another word, he went outside and closed the door behind him, leaving Thor and me alone.

It was so silent that I may as well have been alone. Thor was staring off to the far end of the room, tapping his fingers on his own bicep. When it was clear he wasn't going to say anything, I stood up. "Mead?"

"Yes, please."

When I brought back two tall, flat bottom horns, he was at least looking at me again. He drank down half of his at once.

I sighed. "Say what you want to say and be done with it."

Thor wiped the mead from his red-gold moustache with the back of his hand. We stared at each other for a long moment before he finally spoke. "I don't like it."

"Don't like what?"

The horn clicked against the table as he put it down. "You shouldn't be with him. You're better than that."

"But it's okay for you to be his friend? Or whatever you want to call this strange relationship?" I took my own drink, realizing just how badly I was going to need it.

He huffed. "I don't have to trust him to be his friend. Letting him live with you and sleep next to you, that's something else."

"Let me ask you this." I leaned across the table. "Have you ever thought I was dumb?" He shook his head. "Irresponsible?" Another shake. "Easy to manipulate?"

"Sigyn, you just don't understand—"

"People just keep saying that. I do understand. I understand that there is no absolute truth, and that everyone is guilty of something, especially in Asgard. And if you knew how unwaveringly good Loki is to me, how fantastic it is to have someone who believes in my skills—in *me*—then you wouldn't be sitting here telling me not to be with him. You'd be happy for me."

Thor sat back, his tree-trunk arms crossed over his chest. "And what about what he did to Sif?"

"You weren't there. She said horrible things about his mother. He shouldn't have done it, but you'd have torn the head off anyone who talked about your mother that way. Yggdrasil shade me, that kind of insult is a crime punishable by death in more than half the realms."

His lips protruded from his face as he turned it over in his mind. "I knew Sif said something, but she won't say what. But that would be just like Loki. I've seen him break bones defending his mother's name."

"So, can we just let this go? He's out there being helpful, and I don't want us to be enemies because you don't like who I'm with."

Thor nodded absentmindedly, then met my eyes, a playful smile on his face. "He's that good in bed then?"

I gasped and threw my empty horn at him. He bellowed a laugh as it bounced off his chest.

Things were better by the time Loki returned. Not perfect, but good. Even Loki seemed surprised to find us both alive and well. But he was also empty-handed.

"I couldn't find it. I checked everywhere worth checking, but I don't think it's in Asgard anymore."

Thor threw his chair back. "Not in Asgard? How?"

"You gave them plenty of time to ride off with it. It could be anywhere by now."

"You have to keep looking, you have to." Thor put his meaty hand on Loki's shoulder and shook him in desperation until Loki's face started to turn green.

"Just let go—" He swallowed hard and pushed Thor's hand from his shoulder. After a moment of composing his stomach, he sighed. "I'm tired, Thor. You want me to search half the realms on a whim. I can't keep the form of a hawk all day and do all the work of flying on top of it. It's too much."

"There's got to be another way."

"The falcon cloak." Their eyes turned to me, both seeming to have drawn a blank. "Freya's seidr cloak. Though she's not going to be happy to give it to you."

"She'll give it to me." Thor pushed Loki out of the way and opened the door. "I'll get the horses." And he was gone.

"Well." Loki smacked his lips. "Just like old times."

CHAPTER TWENTY-FOUR

*"With the most likely candidate eliminated, Thor forced Loki
to help him in his search for Mjolnir."*

—*Asgard Historical Record, Volume 15*

Racing across the realms on the back of a horse had always been one of the small joys in life. Wind whipped through my hair, the drum beat of hooves sounding in my ears as our horses bolted toward the horizon. My heart thudded in my chest, only the restraint of common sense keeping me from letting go of the reins, leaning back, and pretending I could fly.

Thor was far enough ahead of us that our horses struggled to keep up. His mount was a Jotun breed, bigger and stronger, built to hold heavier bodies. The perfect thing for a god built like a stone house. As he rode, the sky clouded over, giving me a distinct impression of his mood.

Loki was grinning from ear to ear, bent over the neck of his horse as if that were enough to will it to run faster. His hair whipped behind him, snapping like flame, his travelling cloak billowing out over the animal's flank. In that moment, I was very aware of just how handsome he was.

He turned his head to me, catching my stare. The eager rush of excitement on his face shifted into something coy, his eyes smouldering. He bit his bottom lip. A shudder ran through me, and I turned my eyes back to the path ahead, willing my body to quiet itself.

The moment we crossed the shallow stream into the fields of Fólkvangr, the enormous stone fortress Sessrúmnir came into view over the far ridge. It had none of the glittering gold of Asgard, and its stone ramparts were dotted with soldiers. Where

Odin had built himself a paradise, Freya had made a stronghold.

A horn blew, announcing our approach.

We slowed the horses just before the doors and hopped down. A pair of red-and-gold armoured guards stepped forward as if to ask us what business we had but took a step back when they caught sight of Thor. One could call it cowardice, sure, but it was more likely a healthy respect for the god who could snap your neck with his little finger.

Instead, the guards pushed open the looming iron doors and let us into the main hall. Freya was already waiting inside the doors, hands on her hips, dressed head to toe in leather and chainmail. Even with all that, she still wore Brísingamen, the necklace dripping amber down her throat. "What are you doing here?"

Loki pouted. "Aren't you happy to see us?"

"I'd rather have my monthly bleeding than let you in."

"Oh, I understand," Loki said, hand on his chest with exaggerated empathy. "My monthly bleeding usually comes as a beating from Thor, but it's never well-timed or comfortable."

Freya's teeth ground together, her hands clenched into fists. "What. Do you want?"

"We need your falcon cloak," Thor said.

That drew a dry laugh from her. "As if I would give something so precious to you. You don't have the seidr to use it, and I'm hardly going to hand it over to this Silvertongue."

I crossed my arms over my chest. "I could do it."

"No, you couldn't. I let you try it *once*, and you couldn't get off the ground."

"That was decades ago. I must be better at it now."

"I very much doubt that."

"Freya." Thor stepped forward, palms out, a desperate look on his face. "Please. Give Loki the cloak. Mjolnir is gone."

She groaned. "You lost it already?"

"I didn't lose it!" Thor scratched his head. "I just can't find it."

Freya dragged her hand down her face, exasperated. "You have rocks between your ears, I swear it. The Dwarves make you an unstoppable weapon, and you just *let* someone walk away with it." She turned around and strode down the hall. "Well, come on!"

We hurried into step behind her, past the red and gold banners that lined the stone walls. As we neared the end of the hallway, the ringing of steel and the clamour of soldiers filled the air. The doorway opened up into an expansive courtyard where more than two hundred soldiers were sparring against each other. As they fought, their weapons glanced off bodies without so much as a scratch, not a drop of blood to be seen. An effect of Freya's seidr, no doubt.

Freya took us to her fur-covered, sun-bleached wooden throne. She sat down, crossed her legs, and looked at us. There was nowhere to sit, so we stood.

Loki glanced around. "Are you going to give us the cloak, or should we dance for you instead?"

Freya beckoned the help with a crooked finger. A young woman approached the throne. "Bring the falcon cloak."

The woman nodded and left, staying close to the walls of the courtyard and disappearing into the fortress.

Freya leaned forward. "You'll return it to me in the same condition. If there's a single feather missing, if it's dirty, if it's disenchanted, if it so much as *smells* like you, I will have you killed. I won't even bother to soil my own hands doing it. You'll just be dead."

Loki laughed. "Well, I hadn't thought to do anything to it, but now that you bring it up…" He shrugged.

The woman appeared again, a heavy brown feather cloak draped across her arms. She stopped next to Freya and waited for a command. Freya waved a hand toward Loki, who graciously took the cloak from the woman. He ran his hand along the outside, then pressed it to his face, staring Freya in the eyes. "So soft."

Freya stood, her face red and her teeth bared. I stepped between them, hands up. "Just tell him how to use it."

She glared past me. "Put it around your shoulders, summon energy, and get the fuck out of my keep."

I turned and pushed Loki back a few paces. The conniving look on his face normally meant trouble, and that was the last thing any of us needed. I took the cloak from him and stood on my toes to wrap it around his neck. It came down to his ankles, concealing almost his entire body. "You're going to get us in trouble, Loki."

He brought his gaze back to me, a warm smile on his scarred lips. "It's fine. Don't miss me too much."

I tightened the collar around his neck and tilted my head to kiss him. "I won't."

His fingers found the back of my neck, holding me there for another kiss, then he touched his nose to mine. "Always."

I backed away, giving him room to shift. The change was no different than normal, a ripple in the air so bright it hurt to look, then a pop. A large falcon stood on the stone. It hopped a couple of times, and then flew off, a single feather floating down from the sky. I held my palm out to catch it and looked up to see Freya's exasperated groan.

Knowing that there was no shortcut to scouring the realms for a hammer, Freya had the kitchen bring out food. A small table was set out for us to eat at. Thor barely touched a thing, but I was famished. Freya ignored us for a while, handing out orders to captains and staff or reading through a stack of letters, but eventually she came and sat across from me.

"Thor." She looked up at him. He'd been pacing across the hall for a while now, chin down and staring at the ground. "You're going to stomp a trench in my floor. Sit down and eat."

Thor mumbled something under his breath and came to the table. "How long is he going to be?"

"As long as it takes. This is what you get for being so careless." Freya unhooked the chainmail over her chest and pulled it off, revealing the muscled curves of her arms. "As much as it pains me to say it, you may as well get comfortable."

I pulled a piece of bread off and handed it to Thor. "Please eat."

He took it and stared at it for a moment, then put it down. "I can't eat. My stomach is bubbling, and I can't stand it."

I looked at Freya. "He's nervous. I think this is a first."

Thor huffed. "I'm not nervous. I just don't like this." His face screwed up, and a vein in his forehead bulged out. He stood up suddenly. "No. I can't. I'm going outside to wait." And he did.

"He really didn't get any portion of the brains in your family." Freya took a long drink, then set her horn down. "Though neither did you, it seems."

My eyes rolled involuntarily. "How long were you holding that in for?"

"A while." She cut a large piece of smoked boar in half and took her share, pushing the platter toward me. "You know exactly how I feel about Loki. You've always known."

"Yes, and I've always known you're a woman of extremes. Extremely beautiful, extremely bloodthirsty, extremely hateful, whenever it suits you. Blessed are those on your good side and Yggdrasil shade the rest of us. Too judgemental to understand anything."

"At least I know my convictions. I know who my enemies are, I know what I want, and I know what's best for seidr. Do you have any idea what you want, other than a title? Which apparently you'll go to any lengths to get."

"When did you get so bitter?" I snatched up another wedge of cheese. "Were you always like this, or was it only the last 50 years?"

A crease formed in Freya's forehead. "I've fought for everything I have. Don't tell me what I am."

I gestured in confusion. "You'd think that would make us allies, wouldn't you? That we both feel like we fought tooth and nail. So why doesn't it?"

"You made your choice."

"You had years to help me before Loki came around, and you didn't. We're not friends, we've never been friends. You're too rigid for that."

Freya chewed slowly. "I know you don't believe me, but you need to end this thing with Loki before you figure out just how bad he is."

"Listen, if we don't change the subject, I'm going to shove that attitude down your throat so far even your little army won't be able to find it."

Thankfully, the doors burst open before I had any need to prove myself capable of such a thing. Thor came running in just as a falcon swooped down into the courtyard. The air shimmered as it descended, and Loki landed in a crouch, the cloak billowing out around him. He stood, a grin plastered across his face.

He waited a moment, brushing down the feathers. "No? No one's going to comment on the entrance? Alright, your loss."

Thor was on him in an instant. "Did you find it? You must have found it."

"I'm not going to tell you anything if you keep shaking me. Stop."

Thor backed away, hands up. "You don't have it."

"No." Loki went to the table and picked at the scraps of lunch. "It's in Jotunheim."

"Jotunheim." Freya covered her face with her palms. "You let that hammer fall into the hands of the exact people you were going to use it against. I can't believe you've survived this long with that little in your head."

I went to Loki and helped him take the cloak off. "How did it get there?"

Loki planted a kiss on my forehead. "That's still a bit of a mystery, but Thrym— the Jotun who took it—knew exactly who I was, even as a falcon. He called me down, we talked, and he admitted to hiding it."

"Where?"

"He wouldn't say. He wants to make a trade. We get the hammer, and he takes Freya as his wife." Loki sat down on the end of the table, looking right at her. "Really, I don't understand everyone's obsession with you. You're on the top of everyone's list, but clearly no one has *met* you."

Freya's face turned scarlet. She jumped up from the table and got as close to him as she dared, snarling up at him. "Insult me again."

The sneer on Loki's face was malevolent. "How many nights in Dwarven beds did that necklace cost you?" He reached out and flicked one of the amber jewels. "Four, wasn't it? That's a high price for something so tacky; I'd have haggled."

She cried out, enraged, and shoved Loki. He stumbled back, laughing, and that only fuelled her anger.

I moved to get between them, but Thor grabbed my arm. I shot him a look.

Thor shook his head. "Let them work it out."

Freya's hand went to the necklace. "You think I care what you think of me? That the beds I've been in amount to anything tallied next to yours?" She tore on the chain, and Brísingamen came free from her neck, the steel links snapping like glass. "If I'm a whore, what are you?" She swung at him.

Loki jumped out of the way just in time. "Darling, you're awfully riled up for someone who doesn't care!"

She backed him up into the table and slammed her open palm into Loki's face, the amber and metal cutting his skin. A line of red appeared on his cheek, and he grinned as the pain bit into him.

"That's enough." Thor stepped towards Freya. He grabbed the back of her armour and a chorus of metal rang out around us. The training had stopped, and her army had turned their blades on us.

"It's only enough when he's dead." Freya's free hand went to the knife on her belt.

Without a second thought, I swung at her.

Freya turned her head to me, more annoyed than hurt. "Are you serious? Where did you learn to punch? Your—"

Then Loki disappeared from under her. She fell onto the table, barely saving herself from smashing her face into the wood.

Something leapt from the surface, scurried across the stone, and clambered up the outside of my cloak. A mouse. I picked it up, caught a glimpse of its emerald eyes, and sat it on my shoulder.

"Where is he?" Freya whipped around, blade out. "Come out, you filthy fucking rat."

"Close," I said, pointing to my tiny companion. "Not quite."

She made a move, but Thor stepped in front of her, grabbing her arm. She screamed in frustration, but there was no fighting it. Thor was Thor. He held her in place. "This isn't the time."

Several of her army had gotten close enough to strike Thor, but none had tried. He looked at them. "Is this a fight you really want to pick?"

They looked at each other, considering their options, then backed away.

The mouse nudged my face with its nose and ran to the edge of my shoulder, squeaking. I carefully set it down on the ground and gave it space. A moment later, Loki was back, sitting cross-legged on the ground, wiping the blood from his face.

"If you're done failing to kill me, I think we have more pressing matters at hand." Loki winced as his finger caught on an open gash.

"I won't be sold to a filthy Jotun for a hammer! Traded like a fucking horse every time some god owes something!" Freya screamed, throwing her knife wildly toward Loki and missing by a wide margin. "Asgard can burn for all I care!"

139

Thor pushed Freya back, holding her shoulders as if her stillness would translate into calm. "I'm getting Mjolnir back, whether you help me or not. And if you don't, then I don't much care where you end up." He let her go and walked away, towards the entrance to the hall.

Loki gave Freya one last sneer, got up, and followed Thor out.

Freya's eyes met mine, and there was something desperate there. "I won't do it. Sigyn, they can't just sell me off."

"They won't. I'm not going to let that happen." I didn't do anything as foolish as reach out. I just…stroked her ego. "*You're* not going to let it happen. You're the Goddess of War. No one tells you what to do."

She huffed and squared her shoulders, drawing a long breath. She pulled the chainmail from the back of her chair, fastened it back over her chest, and walked past me. "No. They do not. Now someone get me my horse. I've got places to be."

CHAPTER TWENTY-FIVE

*"And Freya, benevolent and understanding, gave Loki the
falcon cloak without hesitation. 'I would give it to you even if
it were made of solid gold.'"*

—*Asgard Historical Record, Volume 15*

"So what are we going to do?"

Loki had just finished telling the room of assembled gods what he had seen,
though he'd left out some of the more obscene things that had occurred between
him and Freya. Or perhaps they were still coming.

Odin had his head in his hands, elbows leaning on his knees. It reminded me of
the times I'd gotten in trouble when I was young; he just didn't have the patience for
such childish endeavours.

"Asgard hasn't always been my home, but I've helped build this place as much as
any of you." Freya's arms were crossed over her chest, defiance written on her face. "I
won't be married off like some shepherd's daughter to settle a debt. And even though it
doesn't much matter to you, I already *have* a husband."

Necks craned to look around the room. Baldur said what everyone else was
thinking. "Has anyone *seen* Od?" The question was met with silence. "I guess not."

"I'm not doing it." Freya sat back in her chair, balancing one ankle on the other
knee, and watched us.

"Then the question is what we *can* do about this." Odin scratched at his beard.
"You're a room full of gods; one of you has to have an idea."

Baldur spoke first. "We could propose a different trade."

Loki shook his head. "I don't think he's the type to barter. They somehow got inside Valhalla without anyone noticing, waited until Thor let down his guard, and walked right out of Asgard with the damned thing. He knows how valuable it is. If we give him a counteroffer, he might escalate the problem."

"Can't we find the hammer ourselves?" Thor asked.

"If the Jotun is telling the truth, we can't. He says it's buried deep underground. If we assume it's in Jotunheim, which it most certainly is, it could be anywhere. The border is thawed, but after that, you're talking about an endless stretch of ice and mountains. We'd never find it." Loki's brow was furrowed, and he was restless, something I rarely saw in him. This puzzle was bothering him.

"I might have a solution."

Heimdall. He rarely came down from his home next to the rainbow bridge, and when he did, it was usually to assist with something dire. My brother had changed very little since I'd seen him last, his long hair braided with gold beads and tied back behind his head, his beard trimmed into a tidy patch on his chin. A massive sword was strapped to one side of his hip, and the Gjallarhorn, engraved with runes, hung from the other.

"Thor, once the hammer was back in your hands, you could kill Thrym, correct?"

"Of course!" Thor puffed up, a picture of ego.

"Then you'll need to go to Jotunheim and get it back." Heimdall gestured with his hands as he spoke. "Go in place of Freya. Convince Thrym to give Mjolnir to you, then strike him dead."

Thor dismissed the idea with a wave of his hand. "If he's smart enough to steal the hammer, he'll never put it near me. How could I convince him to do something that stupid?"

A smile cracked the lips of the ever-serious Heimdall. "He'll have no idea that you're there, because you'll be disguised as the bride."

"What? No." Thor's eyes widened, and he took a step back. "Disguise me as Freya? No. I won't go riding about the nine realms dressed like a woman. You're insane! I'd never hear the end of it!"

Loki clapped his hand on Thor's shoulder. "You know, I make it a point not to agree with Heimdall. Part of my moral code, really. But it's a good plan. I mean, it's just a dress."

"No! It's not just a dress! It's the things people will say! You know how stories travel. I'm a warrior, not some *argr* völva like you! I'll have no respect after this."

Loki's eyes narrowed, clearly bristling at the word *argr*, but he tried to reassure Thor anyway. "You're protector of Midgard, the people will *hardly*—"

"They will." Thor glared at him. "They will, and you know it. You of all people."

"You have *seen* Thor, right?" I gestured at him. "He looks like a bear. It's never going to work."

"You'll make it work." Odin walked down the steps. "We need Mjolnir back, and trying to storm an ice keep in the middle of the mountains isn't going to accomplish that. Loki, I assume you'll be accompanying him, since you're somewhat of an expert."

The silence was horrifying. Loki didn't laugh, didn't say anything snide in return. He just painted on a smile, his teeth like knives. "Of course. The expert. I'd love that."

"It's settled then. The two of you—"

"I'm going too," I cut in.

Odin's single eye landed on me with enough scorn that you'd think I'd pulled the wings off one of his ravens. "And why would you need to go along?"

"If you want Thor to pass for a woman, don't you think it would help to have a woman along for the journey? Surely with Loki and I there, Thor stands a better chance than he does alone."

Loki's smile softened, his shoulders relaxing. "It would be strange for a goddess of *such renown* to be married off with only one handmaid to help her." He shrugged. "Realistically, you can give Sigyn permission to come, or I can let Thor go alone. Dealer's choice."

Odin's eye narrowed. That threat wasn't going to earn us any favours in the future. "*Fine.* Have word sent to Thrym and see that the provisions are prepared. You'll leave in the morning." He gave Thor a firm pat on the shoulder and whispered something in his ear before leaving the hall.

"By the Nornir," Thor groaned. "I can't believe it's come to this. Can't you do something? Use your seidr to change my face, so no one will know it's me?"

Loki slid his arm into mine and led us past Thor. "No, I'm afraid not. I have my own shape to change; I can't be responsible for yours as well. Besides, why would I do that when I could watch them call *you argr* for once?" Loki laughed and left Thor to wallow in self-pity.

The fire in the kitchen hearth crackled to life, lavender flame snapping at the air. I looked over my shoulder as Loki kicked his boots off. He'd barely spoken on the way home, and something sour had settled into his features.

"Are you alright?"

Loki let out a breath. "Nothing new, Sig."

"That's not what I asked." I took his face in my hand and checked the cuts Freya had carved into his cheek. They were minor, and they'd stopped bleeding a while ago. I put my fingers near the wounds and started whispering.

He held still to let me work. "I'm fine. Just…tired. Flying across the nine will do that."

With the small cuts closed, I licked my thumb and wiped away the last of the crusted blood. "You know you can talk to me, don't you?"

He leaned his head against my palm. "Of course I do. Just…not right now, please."

The urge to fix his problems was eating at me, but I wasn't going to push. "Do you think the disguise will be enough to fool Thrym?"

"It's possible, but Thor will still be a boar in a dress, no matter how much makeup we put on him." He kissed my cheek and walked away.

I went to the table and leaned on it, watching as he stretched his muscles. "And you? You said you're going to shapeshift. You've hinted at changing your looks before, but will it be difficult? Is it only a glamour?"

He looked up, something curious in his eyes. "I could show you."

"If you're tired—"

"I'm sure I'll manage." He smirked, then made a series of flashy movements with his hands, unnecessary showmanship to add dramatic flair to the moment. His lips moved in complicated runes that I quickly lost track of. My vision crackled and distorted. A moment later it cleared and standing in his place was a woman.

She wore his tunic and his trousers, but underneath the fabric were new curves. Her hair hung around her in the same waterfall of flame over her chest, but her eyes were lined in fresh, thick charcoal, alight with familiar mischief. Her lips were fuller but still marred with thin silver scars. Her cheeks and jawline were softer. She reached out a hand to touch me, her long, slender fingers grazing the skin of my cheek.

"Amazing," I breathed. But that wasn't even the beginning of it. She was stunning, and I was dumbstruck.

"Am I convincing?" Her voice was distinctly more feminine but still as smokey and entrancing as Loki's. She struck a pose.

"You look real." I reached out to touch her. She was solid under my fingers. She tilted my head up with a single finger, drawing closer, pressing her body against mine. My heart raced. Every movement she made belonged to Loki, beautiful and dangerous.

"Because I am. It's not a glamour; I'm a woman, inside and out." Her lips brushed the words against mine.

I nodded. I clasped the back of her head in my hand and held her in place for a long kiss. Her tongue flitted against my lip, and my breath hitched.

Her lips stretched into a grin, pleased. "Do you want to try?"

I slid my hand up her neck to pull her in for more. Satisfied with my approval, she grasped my thighs and hoisted me up. I hooked my legs around her hips as she sat me on the table, bending me, running her tongue up the length of my neck, heat rising in me. My hands ran over her new shape, up under her tunic, exploring, drawing a long breath from her. Our hands kept working, knots loosening, fabric falling away.

Piece by intimate piece.

CHAPTER TWENTY-SIX

*"I went there once. In that house. It was darkness in its purest
form. It felt sick, like those walls had seen all manner of chaos
and perversions."*

—*God of Lies Revealed*

We collapsed on the furs around the hearth, spent. The perspiration on our skin glistened in the firelight, night having fallen around us. Loki laid on her stomach next to me, her head propped up on her arms. She watched as I caught my breath, a delighted grin on her lips.

"Did you enjoy yourself?" She tucked her hair behind her ear.

I covered my face with my hands, blushing and smiling all at once. "Your imagination puts me to shame."

"Me?" She held a hand to her lips, mocking offence. "That thing you did with your tongue! What *were* you getting up to with that Valkyrie of yours?"

I rolled my eyes, pushing down a grin. "You've spent time in other bodies. Learned things. You must know something I don't."

She looked into my eyes, pressing the tips of two fingers into my chest. "You make your home here. I'm just passing through."

"But you must have done this a thousand times before." I reached out to run my fingers over her skin; her body was softer, rounder, with fewer sharp angles than his. "Were there really so many people who wanted you to be something else?"

Her smile wasn't a true one. "I took whatever shape I needed to. Some of the emissaries wanted someone of the opposite sex, and others wanted something closer to home. But you know Asgard; stick two women together, and it's a fantasy. If you're

146

a man and you let another man 'make a woman out of you,' no one will speak to you again." She scoffed. "All this talk about my 'expert' *argr* behaviour, but it was Odin who encouraged it first."

I pursed my lips. "I wish you could've told me earlier."

Loki looked away, staring into the distance. "It's Asgard's worst kept secret, Sig. No one wants to confirm it, but the gods know enough to speculate. I play the game with them, antagonize them, but no one wants to catch me in the act. It's far too uncomfortable for them to look at."

I made an effort not to look away. "Does it bother you? Changing again?"

She reached out and curled my hair around her fingers. "No, darling. It doesn't. It wasn't my choice, not at the start. Some encounters were good. Mutual. You make the best of it. Other times, it wasn't. But when I was free to choose for myself, I knew from experience that I wasn't just attracted to women and that I wasn't just a man. I can't imagine a life confined to one thing or the other. It was easy outside of Asgard to be whoever I wanted every day. Here, it's…less so. I have to be a man or a woman they won't recognize. I can't be this." She gestured at herself, and her voice quieted. "Just me. A womanly man is a joke here. It's like living in a prison."

There was the slightest hint of a tear forming in her eye. I reached out and wiped it away with my thumb. "I'll stand by you no matter what shape you take. And this is your home. You're safe here. I can't change outside for you, but I want you to feel comfortable in these walls."

Loki nuzzled her face into my skin and drew a breath. Her body relaxed against mine. "Thank you."

She was still, her breath brushing slowly over my neck. I ran my hand over her hair, letting her hide away. And after a bit, she came back, settling with her nose close to mine. There was a blush to her cheeks and a tear had trailed down her skin. She was looking so intently at me, lips pursed. Scared.

She started to speak.

Stopped.

Took a breath.

"Sigyn, I love you."

And there it was. The words that I had been feeling for weeks in her actions, in her touch. Every day. I flushed, thinking of all the tiny moments where I had thought it and refused to say it. Protected myself. And here she was, heart in hand.

"Oh, Loki. I love you too." I took her face in my palms and pulled her in, trying to show her in each desperate kiss that I felt it too. That I was with her. Relief bubbled in her, tiny laughs rising between the brush of our lips. Her fingers wrapped around my wrist, holding me in place even after my breath was gone.

And we just laid there for a while, wrapped up in each other.

"You know," I said eventually, "I used to think there was something wrong with me. There were so few women around who outwardly preferred women. I'd find someone here or there, and some who were interested back. But I spent years wishing for more. More people who would understand and accept it without me having to contextualize my desire into a neat little box that 'made sense' to other people."

"I hope you've already figured out that there's nothing wrong with you." She let her hand trace to my middle. "If my past taught me anything, it's just how many people who are out there wishing they were free to be themselves or to love who they wanted to. It takes courage to be authentic in a place like this."

I placed a kiss on the tip of her nose. "Then that makes you very courageous."

She blushed, giving me a rare glimpse of a bashful Loki.

"I wish I had known this about you. I'm glad to know now."

She smiled languidly, relaxed in my arms. "It's good to be known."

I leaned over to kiss the bear claw scars that ran across her shoulder. "I've been calling you 'she' in my head. Can I do that in public? Should I call you another name?"

"'She' is fine," Loki chuckled. She rolled onto her back and pulled me down with her. I curled into her, and she kissed the top of my head. "Would you name me something else?"

I thought about it. "No. You're Loki, no matter which form you take. No other name would suit you." She smiled and snuggled closer, her eyes fluttering as she prepared to doze off. "How long will this shape hold? How long do I get to keep you?"

"It's simpler than most changes. I need to refresh the runes twice a day. And you get to keep me forever, you fool." She yawned and closed her eyes, entwining her fingers with mine, my arm draped across her belly.

She fell asleep gradually, her breath slowing, her chest softly rising and falling. Her skin flickered orange and gold in the firelight, as if she were made of flame. The dance of it lulled me until I fell asleep in her arms.

I woke to the sun rising through the windows. Loki had rolled away from me during the night and had pulled one of the furs lazily over her body. She was still sleeping, her back and bottom uncovered. A long scar snaked over her side, from the middle of her back and over her hip.

What a curious night.

I leaned over and swept her hair away from her face with gentle fingers. "Time to rise, my beautiful goddess," I whispered in her ear. She stirred, rolling over. Without even opening her eyes, she nuzzled her head into my chest, readying herself to go back to sleep.

"Come now, we have somewhere to be," I ran my fingers along her arm. She moaned in protest and rolled away as if that would be enough for me to leave her alone.

I ran kisses over the back of her neck until her skin prickled with gooseflesh, and she was forced to admit defeat. She gazed up at me with sleepy eyes. "Sig, we've made a fatal mistake. I don't have anything to wear."

"Of course you do. You can wear something of mine."

I brought Loki to my wardrobe, and though she was still wiping the sleep from her eyes, there was a slight grin on her face. Just when I was about to offer suggestions, she dove right in, pulling out dress after dress. She hung the rejected offerings back up with a dismissive *No* and slung the lucky prospects over one arm until she was wearing a dozen layers over her elbow but not a stitch on the rest of her body.

There were dresses of all makes and colours that I'd collected over the years, many of them too extravagant to belong to a handmaid, but who was I to ruin her fun? She giggled as she slid one over her head, its sky-blue satin draping down to the floor, thin plates of steel sewn over the shoulders like armour.

She spun around, the bottom of the dress whirling out around her. "What do you think?" She grinned and struck a pose.

I cupped her face in my hands and gave her a kiss. "It's beautiful."

Loki actually blushed. "Hmm. I can't travel in satin, though." She pulled the dress off, threw it onto the bed and went for the next.

And so it went, one dress after the other until she'd nearly tried on the whole wardrobe. I followed behind her, giving praise and hanging up the ones that didn't pass her criteria. She twirled and laughed and sighed, running her hands down especially soft fabrics and savouring the feel on her skin. She wrapped fur scarves and delicate cloaks around her, pairing the most expensive, outrageous things she could find.

Eventually, we settled on a pair of dresses more suited to riding, with stockings for the frigid weather in Jotunheim. They were simple pieces, without embellishment or embroidery, things that wouldn't give away our plan. Loki was practical enough to choose them but not generous enough to love them.

As she stared at herself in the mirror, pouting just a little, I wrapped my arms around her waist. "You can wear the beautiful ones whenever you like."

She froze in my arms and something in her face changed. Her eyes were glistening. She turned to me, pulled me close, and kissed me. Then she ran her thumb down the curve of my cheek. "Thank you, Sig."

"Of course." I gave her a gentle kiss, afraid that any more than the tenderest affection might shatter the moment.

And it did. Her lips pursed in a fragile smile, and she blinked rapidly, moving on as if she hadn't just made a dramatic confession. "They'll be here any minute, and we've got more to do. We'll need road rations and bed rolls, for a start."

I watched her, the spring in her step as she folded up the other dress, piling things together. The lilt in her voice as she named all the things we would need, and the cascade of happy tears she wiped away when she thought I wasn't looking.

When the riding party arrived, Loki was made up with fresh, smokey kohl around her eyes and faded red on her lips. She stepped out the door with a flourish. "Good morning! I—Ymir have mercy."

Thor sat on his horse, front and centre, barely contained in a long red gown and hooded brown cloak. His thick arms were masked by flowing sleeves, and Brísingamen had been repaired and hung around his neck. Someone had done his makeup, but it had hardly helped matters. They'd even shaved his beard clean off.

I walked up to him. "Hello, Thor."

His sad eyes caught mine. "I don't like this."

"Won't it be worth it to get your hammer back?"

"Yes…"

Loki strode over and gave him a slap on the leg. "Aren't you excited? Soon you'll get to meet your new husband."

"Shut up, Loki." Thor's teeth ground together, and the grey clouds that had been hanging around all morning began to churn.

Loki held her hands up in defence, grinning from ear to ear. "Suit yourself." She turned to the riding party. "Now which of you strong men brought me a horse?"

CHAPTER TWENTY-SEVEN

"Then bound they on Thor | the bridal veil,
And next the mighty | Brisings' necklace.
Keys around him | let they rattle,
And down to his knees | hung woman's dress;
With gems full broad | upon his breast,
And a pretty cap | to crown his head."

—*The Lay of Thrym*

Thor's mood didn't improve much over the next six days. The clouds followed us through the fields as the eight of us rode to the border of Jotunheim, into the woods and out again, and up the rock path that led into the endless snowy mountains. While Loki was enjoying herself to the fullest, I couldn't help but feel a little bad for my brother. He was just so…miserable.

We made camp under an outcropping of stone on the sixth night, expecting to reach Thrym's keep the next day. We built a sizable fire, leashed the horses to a hook Thor had ground into the mountainside, and settled in for the night.

When I woke the next morning, Loki was curled around me. We weren't the only ones sharing a bedroll for warmth, but likely the only ones enjoying it.

"Good morning," she whispered, blessing me with soft, slow kisses. Her hands roamed under the furs, tracing my curves.

I shivered under her touch. "Loki! Not with everyone else here."

"No one will know." She nipped at my bottom lip.

I looked up. Thor was sitting next to the fire, his eyes downcast, but definitely looking in our direction.

151

Loki followed my stare and laughed. And, presumably just for Thor's benefit, she gave me another long, passionate kiss before crawling out of the bedroll.

The camp woke up slowly, dragging themselves from the warmth of their beds to the fireside. Hard seed bread was broken and passed around, and salted meats were warmed on the stones close to the flame. There was an undercurrent of excitement in the riding party, but Thor was gloomier than before.

"Thor, you need to eat something." I was busy rummaging through my pack for a few modest accessories, like one of the headscarves some of the city folk wore. I wrapped it around my head, but my hair refused to be contained.

Loki helped twist it into a more manageable shape as I secured the entire thing. Thor still hadn't said anything.

"You're going to make a very sad bride if you don't learn to smile a little," Loki teased. The frown sunk deeper.

With a sigh, Loki dug into my travel pack and brought out a tiny container of kohl, lip paint, and a shining metal mirror. "This is the problem with the men in Asgard," she whispered to me. "Brave enough to fight dragons but take away their raging masculinity, and it scares them to their core."

She rounded the fire and sat next to Thor, taking his face in her hand and yanking it to the side. "You listen to me. If you want Mjolnir back, you're going to need to play the part. We're going to make you beautiful, you're going to dazzle Thrym, and then you're going to kill him. Doesn't that sound like fun? It's all just one big game."

"I really want to kill him," Thor mumbled just loud enough to be heard.

"And you will. It will be brutal and violent and bloody. The manliest thing you've ever done. Now, eyes shut."

"If you draw a nutsack on my face, I'll throw you down the mountain."

Loki gave him a pat on the cheek. "No funny business, I promise. But only this once."

She used a steady hand to apply the kohl, tracing the applicator along the curve of Thor's eyelids. She smudged it in the right places, creating a look fierce enough for Freya herself. Then she used her finger to apply the red paint to Thor's thin lips. She even shaved the stubble from his face with the edge of a blade, talking all the while about the burly things Thor could do when he got his hammer back.

Decapitating Jotnar, for a start.

It wasn't long before Thrym's keep appeared on the horizon. We were still out of earshot of the walls when Loki called for the riding party to halt. "I know everyone's been having a great time these last few nights, snickering about *argr* men while you thought we weren't listening, but this is where it ends. As far as you're concerned, the woman before you is the goddess Freya, and we are her handmaids." She gestured to the two of us. "If you make the mistake of addressing any of us by our true names, your death will be my deepest pleasure. Understood?"

The soldiers nodded in agreement, their faces solemn. Loki turned to Thor. "You understand your part, yes?"

Thor groaned, exasperated. They'd stuffed him into a regal sky-blue gown, something worthy of a goddess' wedding. He spoke through the thick lace veil over his face. "I'm aware. No speaking or touching or doing anything that draws attention to me."

"Exactly." Loki turned her horse around and started up to the icy gates of Thrym's keep.

I fell in beside her. "Here goes nothing."

"This may just be the greatest day of my life." She grinned and reached out to squeeze my hand. "Very validating."

The keep loomed over us, sheets of ice coating the high stone walls. It looked like a proper place to freeze to death. On either side of the gates stood a lookout, where the guards were yelling down into the keep. As we approached, the gate swung open. Behind it stood Thrym, arms open and a broad smile on his face. He was nearly two heads taller than Loki, with skin just as pale wrapped around an enormous broad frame. An icy blue sheen ran just under the surface of his skin. He was dressed for a banquet, his royal blue tunic embroidered with gold. A scar ran across his cheek, but underneath, he looked like someone had just made all his dreams come true.

The captain of the riding party stepped down from his horse and addressed the keep's master. "It's our honour to present Freya, Goddess of War and Love, blessed ally of the Aesir, descendant of the Vanir, rightful overseer of half of Midgard's worthy dead, most beautiful woman in all the realms. Your bride." The captain gestured towards Thor, who sat sulking on his horse, the thick veil obscuring his face.

Thrym scratched his beard. "This is Freya? Everyone talks about how strong and beautiful she is, but no one has ever mentioned how...large she is."

My breath caught in my throat. Everything in me itched to take control of the situation, but I fought it back. One wrong move might reveal the entire plan.

Loki pulled her horse up beside the captain, interrupting before he could continue. "Mighty Thrym," she spoke coyly, surely stroking his ego. "The tales of Freya could never encompass her true beauty. We've kept it a bit of a secret, but there may be a tiny touch of Jotun blood in her veins. I trust that won't be a problem for someone as esteemed as yourself."

Thrym straightened his back, standing proudly. "Of course not! I had no idea. She's practically family already!" He waved us in, stepping out of the way. "Come in!

You're going to love it here! We've prepared a feast bigger than anything you've ever seen. Join us inside when you're ready!" Thrym stomped off, a swagger in his step.

Astonishing. It baffled me how someone could believe what Loki was saying, despite the evidence to the contrary sitting right in front of their nose.

The stable boys came forward and helped the riding party with their horses. Loki accepted the hand of a lanky young man who helped her step down from her horse. She blushed and dropped to the ground, as demure as could be.

I slid down of my own accord, jealousy brewing in my stomach. Loki caught my eye and skipped to my side.

"You're playing the part awfully well, aren't you?" I pouted.

She took my hand and kissed my knuckles. "What is life but a series of parts to play? My love for the stable boy pales in comparison to my love for you, darling. But yes—"

Thor leapt off the back of his horse and landed with a ground-shaking thud. For just a moment, his wedding gown flew up, exposing his thick, manly legs.

Loki whipped around and marched toward him. She jabbed him in the chest with her finger, her snarling face an inch from his. "Behave yourself!" She drove her fingernail deeper into him. "Or do you want us all to be ripped to shreds by Thrym's guards? Act like a lady for once in your life!"

Loki turned on her heel and marched off, taking me by the arm as she passed and dragging me toward the keep.

Before long, we were all seated in Thrym's stone dining hall. The Jotnar had done their best to make it seem cozy, setting large fires in the hearths and hanging excessive decoration along the walls. Shining gold platters and polished drinking horns, everything glimmering. The room was warmer than outside, but the cold still found its way in. Icicles hung from the cracks in the stone, dripping from the ceiling.

Thrym sat at the head of the table. He'd insisted that his bride sit next to him. Loki sat between Thor and me. The rest of the riding party followed down the length of the table. Across from them were a line of Jotnar that Thrym had named and I hadn't bothered to remember. His sister was next to him, overdressed and sour looking. With the exception of one, every one of them was larger than us, and each had an outfit that was accented with a weapon on their hips.

The woman directly across the table was smiling at me, her black hair wound in a thick braid over her shoulder. But the smile wasn't warm, and neither was the axe hooked to her hip.

"Honoured guests, I hope you'll make yourselves at home here. We have everything you could possibly need, so just ask." Thrym clapped his hands, and several of the staff came into the hall carrying platters of food. They laid out roast duck, pig, and salmon. A heaping platter was set at the head of the table, heaped with roasted cuts of an entire ox. Casks of mead were placed along the table, and each of their cups were filled to the brim.

Thrym was staring at Thor, waiting for his bride to speak. I cleared my throat. "I'm afraid Freya's barely said a word for days. She's been so eager to finally meet you that she could hardly bear it. But her voice should return in no time." I held up my drinking horn. "To you, Thrym, and your generosity. This meal is—"

My words were drowned out by the deafening screech of Thor dragging the platter of ox meat across the bronze table, stopping only when it was safely in front of him. It took all my willpower not to cover my ears with my hands. He ate from it voraciously, handfuls of greasy flesh disappearing under his veil.

Loki set her hand on my thigh and gave a frustrated squeeze.

To say that Thrym seemed put off was an understatement. I half expected him to recoil right out of his chair. "Freya...what an appetite! I've never seen a lady eat with such enthusiasm..."

Thor reached across the table with his grease-slick hands and snatched up three salmon, which he tossed on top of the rest of his food. They slapped onto the platter, sliding against the pile of meat. He reached for another platter, but Loki moved it away from him. I couldn't be sure, but I was certain Thor growled at her.

Loki turned to Thrym. "Freya was so excited to hear the news of your proposal that she hasn't eaten a single bite for eight days and eight nights. I can't say what a *relief* it is that her appetite has returned. It must be because she's finally in your company."

Thrym nodded, his gaze softening as he looked on his bride. "I know the feeling too well. I've spent my whole life waiting for you. Eat as much as you like, my beautiful goddess. Anything you need is yours."

Thor grunted and reached for another platter. He dumped it onto his own, stealing an entire platter of pastries. Good thing I'd lost my appetite since he'd already taken a bite out of everything in reach.

Thrym's sister rolled her eyes.

The group ate quietly, everyone watching Thor from the corner of their eyes as he demolished plate after plate. It was up to Loki and me to keep up conversation with Thrym, chatting about the weather and the state of life in Asgard. By the time the table had been cleared, Thor had inhaled eight salmon, the entire ox, all the pastries, and three casks of mead.

I pulled a handkerchief from inside my dress and passed it under the table to Loki, who slid it to Thor. He grunted again and the fabric disappeared under the veil. He wiped the residue from his mouth and tossed the dirty fabric onto the table unceremoniously.

Yggdrasil shade us. The only thing working in our favour was the fact that every Jotnar at the table was too uncomfortable to look at 'Freya' too closely.

"Mighty Thrym," Loki leaned forward, as charming as she could be, "when can we count on the return of Mjolnir to the people of Asgard?"

Thrym chuckled. "Soon. First, I want to claim a kiss from my beautiful bride!" He reached out to pull the veil aside, but quickly jumped back. "Freya! You have eyes like a wild beast!"

Loki's hand was on Thor's bicep, trying to keep him from leaping out of his seat.

"You'll have to excuse Freya," I said quickly. "She's been so excited to be married that she hasn't slept since she found out. She swore she wouldn't go to any bed until she could go to bed with you. Isn't that right?"

At the other end of the table, one of the riding party choked on their drink.

Loki nodded. "She's been exhausted. Probably why she caught a chill so easily. Stubborn thing, but *surely* you appreciate her commitment."

Thrym relaxed into his chair. "I've never met a woman so eager to be bedded before. I'll be sure not to disappoint." He winked at his bride, and what little I'd eaten curdled in my stomach.

"This is all well and good," Thrym's sister—Inara? Ira? We were going to kill them, it didn't matter—said. "But no one's said anything about the bride gift. You've asked for your hammer, and now I want to know what you're going to give us for housing Thrym's voracious new wife."

"Sister, we can figure these things out later." Thrym put his hand on her shoulder. "Why don't you fetch the hammer so Freya and I can finally be married?"

She crossed her arms. "I don't think so. The Aesir have enough wealth that they can spare some for us. Freya's going to cost us her weight in gold just to keep her fed, not to mention *two* handmaids...as if anyone could need that much help getting into a dress."

Loki eyed the sister over the rim of her drinking horn. "We've been instructed to pay a sizable amount for Freya's care. You'll have it once Mjolnir is returned to the captain."

"You see?" Thrym waved a hand in Loki's direction. "All things in time. Fetch the hammer, sister."

She rose from the table in a huff and stormed out of the room.

Loki leaned into me, her lips beside my ear. "Be ready. This is where things get *fun*."

I counted the Jotnar along the table. Thrym and his sister and seven others. Plus the rest of the keep, if they decided to intervene, though we could never be sure. I put my mind to gathering energy.

The Goddess of Nothing At All

The sister returned in short order and set Mjolnir down at the head of the table with a thud.

"If that settles it, we can begin with the ceremony." Thrym rose from the table, rubbing his hands together in anticipation.

A deep chuckle rose from the veiled bride. It sent a shiver down my spine as it built to a cackle. Thor stood and reached out for Mjolnir. With the hammer in hand, he ripped the veil from his head and turned on Thrym.

"What's this?" Thrym cried out. "You aren't Freya!"

Loki rolled her eyes. "Well obviously not." She pulled the curved dagger from her belt and vaulted over the table, kicking Thrym's sister to the ground.

I spat a string of runes under my breath, summoning a burst of wildfire and tossing it into the face of the woman across from me. She screamed and batted at her hair as I scrambled over the table. I snatched up a platter and smashed it into her face for good measure.

The room shook. Thor had thrown Mjolnir into Thrym, driving him across the room and into the wall. Thor caught the hammer as it rushed back to him, his scream of rage rising above all the clamour. He hurled himself at Thrym, hammer raised above his head—

Don't get distracted.

My mark had fallen to the floor, using her own shirt to put out the wildfire. I leapt down from the table and kicked her in the jaw with all my strength. She stopped moving.

Loki climbed to her feet next to me. The sister's body was a mess, gruesome bone and muscle peeking out from the slash across her throat. Red was splattered across Loki's cheek and down her lips, blood dripping from the dagger in her grip. "Next."

A pair of Thrym's soldiers had cornered one of ours. Loki snared one from behind and twisted him around. With a nod, she tossed him at me, and the Jotun fell into my grip just as the current of electricity shot from my hands. He seized, the smell of charred flesh filling the air. His eyes rolled back into his head, and I let him go. He continued to writhe on the floor as I turned my attention to the next Jotun in line.

"Sig!"

I whipped around. A woman in a flour-covered apron was brandishing an iron pan and about to knock me out cold. I ducked as she swung and backed away from her, arms out. "You don't need to do this. Stay out of the way, and everything will be fine."

She screamed, shaking the pan but making no move towards me.

"Would you like to be the master of this keep?"

She blinked.

"Round up the rest of your people and keep them safe, and I'll give it to you."

157

"Liar!" She swung the pan in my direction, missing by miles.

Loki slid up behind her and set the edge of her blade against the woman's throat. "That girl is my world, so test me, darling. Please do."

She dropped the pan. Its clatter was loud enough to rise over the screaming and the metallic ring of weaponry. "I'll go," she said, her hands raised in the air.

Loki ruffled her hair and pushed her off. "That's a good woman." We didn't bother to watch her leave.

Our soldiers seemed to have things under control. There was only one Jotun left standing. Thor was still in the corner, toying with Thrym. He had the poor man pressed up against the wall by his throat and was breaking his fingers one by one.

"Did you just give this place to a scullery maid?" Loki asked, slipping an arm around my waist.

"I might have." A childish grin slipped out. "Father will be thrilled."

The doors burst open, a rush of cold air pouring in from outside, along with another dozen of Thrym's people.

"Back to work, I suppose." Loki shrugged.

"Wait. I want to try something." I pulled up my skirts and slid the dagger out from the sheath strapped around my thigh.

Loki threw me a smile and bounded back into the action. I followed behind and was quickly knocked on my back by a fist to the face.

"Ymir's asshole!" Pain shot through my skull, and my teeth jarred. The Jotun stood just above me, so I whipped up a leg and kicked him between the thighs. He squealed and dropped like a stone, and I stabbed the dagger into his throat. The blood sprayed hot across my face. He choked, the sound wet and bubbling, then collapsed into the growing puddle of red.

A hand reached down to take mine, and the captain of the riding party hoisted me up. He turned his back to me at once and elbowed a Jotun in the face.

One after the other, the Jotun fell. As we stood there, trying to catch our breath, I realized that some of the noise of battle was still ringing. Specifically, a hammer on stone. Thor was still in the corner with what used to be Thrym.

"Do. Not. Touch. Me." He repeated it over and over, bringing the hammer down again after each word, coating the walls and floor with blood and shattered bone.

The whole riding party, even those who had been wounded, watched Thor's descent into madness. There was nothing left to the body, and yet Thor kept hitting. Blood was soaked through his wedding gown and ran down his face in streaks.

Loki wrenched her blade from the fresh corpse of a young man and wiped a hand across her face, smearing more red across her cheek. "Yggdrasil above, what is he doing? Thor!"

When he didn't respond, she picked up a thick femur from the dining table and tossed it. It struck Thor in the back of the head. He whipped around, his eyes as crazed as any berserker, looking for the enemy.

"Brother! Come back to us. It's all over." I held my hands out, ready to summon a shield if he ran at us. A berserker could kill 20 men in a rage without blinking an eye, and that wasn't accounting for the fact that this was Thor.

His whole body shook with each breath. He threw his hammer down one last time, spraying the room with entrails and cracking the stone. "None of you say a word about this to *anyone*. Do you understand me?" he roared.

Loki tossed her hair back and grinned. "Well, that's unlikely."

CHAPTER TWENTY-EIGHT

*"Thor and Loki returned with the hammer, having killed
Thrym and everyone in his keep. The two gods were welcomed
back to Asgard with a feast, and Thor has since learned to
take better care of his things."*

—*Asgard Historical Record, Volume 15*

A nd that's how a Jotun keep came to be ruled by the servants, and how Thor
got his hammer back. They housed us for a few days, long enough to burn the
dead and rest our bodies, and then sent us home with deliciously fresh rations.
And, as I'd suspected, Odin was not pleased with what I'd done.

After a pointless lecture and a good long bath, life went on. Loki returned to his
masculine form, Thor came around to visit more often, and I kept studying. Before we
knew it, the days were getting shorter, and the air was growing chill.

Thor shook his cup, his hand over the top to keep the dice in. He loosed them onto the
table, and they rolled to a grand total of five.

"Balls." He scooped them up, put them back in, and passed it to Loki. Behind
him, the rest of Valhalla was carrying on much the same, including an arm-wrestling
contest between a Valkyrie and an einherji.

Loki tossed the dice, coming out with 17. He flashed Thor a grin. "That's four in a
row, friend. One more, and you owe me a bottle from your old man's stash."

Thor pointed a finger at him, eyes narrowed. "I swear you're either the luckiest
man alive, or you're cheating."

Loki's arm went around my neck and pulled me closer. His cheeks were already red with drink. "Luckiest man alive, I think."

I rolled my eyes, forcing back a smile. "That's not even cute. It's as feeble as a lame horse, and you should be ashamed."

He nuzzled into my neck and nipped at my earlobe. "But I have the stamina of a stallion, darling."

I pressed my palm into his face, pushing him back. "None of that, you dog." He smirked, and before I could move, dragged his tongue across my palm in a manner that was decidedly unattractive. "Ugh! No more mead for you!" I wiped my wet hand on his tunic.

Thor tossed the dice again. 23. "Finally!" He slammed his fist onto the table, and the dice scattered.

Loki craned his neck. "I only see 14."

Thor was reaching across the table when something else caught his eyes. A pair of armed einherjar were escorting a gruff, burly man into Valhalla. He was road-weary, his beard long and unkempt, his travelling cloak sitting on top of layers of thick clothing. He even carried a staff to walk with, which clopped against the ground with every step.

The three of us watched silently as the einherjar escorted him to the head table, where Odin was eyeing the scene from afar. One of the men came around the table and whispered in his ear for a good long while.

Odin nodded and stood up. "Hod. Freya. Thor. With me."

Thor stood up, grinning at Loki.

"Hey! You owe me Elven wine!" Loki slapped his hand on the table.

"I don't think so. That round didn't count." He shrugged and backed away from the table, not looking the least bit apologetic. "Can't help it. Father calls."

Loki turned to me, lips curled in an exaggerated pout. "So close. Now I'll just have to steal it."

"What do you think that was about?" I took his cup of mead and drank the rest before he could.

Idunn slid into the spot Thor had just vacated. "What was that about?" she asked conspiratorially.

"That's *just* what *I* was asking!" Loki reached out and set his hand on Idunn's. "You're just like sunshine, always reading minds."

Idunn blinked at me, and all I could do was roll my eyes.

"Yes, this is what I'm dealing with tonight. He even licked me." I waved down one of the Valkyrie and begged her for some water.

"I'm an adorable drunk." Loki stretched himself out over the table, his head in the crook of his arm. "Aren't I, Idunn?"

She ruffled his hair, eliciting a purr from him. "You're always adorable." She scrunched up her face at me, pushing down a laugh.

One of the Valkyrie handed me a horn of water. "Loki, I bet you can't drink all this at once."

He popped up from the table. "The hel I can't." He snatched the horn from my hand and tipped it up, gulping the whole thing down. Then he scowled at me. "Water. Dirty trick."

I just winked. "I learn from the best."

Idunn and I continued to fill Loki with water, the three of us gossiping about whatever was happening behind closed doors, until Thor sidled back up to the table nearly an hour later, clapping his hand onto Loki's shoulder.

"Odin wants to see you."

Loki shot me a look, then turned to Thor. "Why?"

"There's a complication that needs fixing."

"Well of course there is. *Grimnir* wouldn't ask me for anything else." He pried the horn of mead from my hands, despite the scowl I gave him. "No. I'm going to need this more than you."

Loki stood and so did I. Thor tilted his head, staring at me.

I raised an eyebrow. "You do understand that there's a tradition where Loki enters a room with Odin, and I have to sew him back up after, don't you? I'm not stupid enough to wait here."

Thor had the decency to look a little ashamed. "Fair enough."

Idunn gave my hand a squeeze but stayed seated. "I'm here if you need me."

Loki and I followed Thor through the crowd of enthusiastic einherjar, weaving our way around puddles of spilt drink and around some sort of jumping competition. He led us out of Valhalla through one of the many doors and into a seldom-used corridor. The man who had marched through Valhalla was seated at the end, outside a pair of iron double doors. His eyes followed us until we entered the room and shut him out.

It was a small council chamber, one I hadn't seen very often. In the centre was a massive table with an intricately carved map of the realms, tiny carved soldiers planted all across it in different colours and cuts. Painted banners hung around the rooms, each depicting a moment in Asgard's history, including the births of each Odinson, from which I'd always been conspicuously missing.

Odin was leaning over the table, his hands gripping the wood edge. He was lost in thought and barely noticed us arriving.

"It's not ethical." Hod was standing across the table from Odin. "I don't think you can agree to this."

"I should say not! You already know my answer." Freya crossed her arms over her chest, teeth bared.

"Perhaps you should catch us up." I walked up to the table and picked up one of the pieces. It was a tiny ebony carving of an elf. "It seems we've missed a lot."

Odin glanced up at me with contempt and sighed. "The man you just passed has offered to build a wall around Asgard. He says he can do it in a year and a half."

"We've been talking about building a wall since I was a kid." Thor leaned against the far wall. "It could do a lot of good for keeping the Jotnar out of Asgard when Ragnarok comes."

Loki scoffed. "*If* Ragnarok happens, no wall is going to save Asgard from fire and floods."

"If it saved a dozen of our people, it would be worth it," Thor challenged.

"It would be up to us to keep it from getting that far." Odin stood straight, cracking his back.

"You're acting like the wall is free. It's not." Freya tapped her fingers on her leather gauntlet. "He wants me in return."

"Didn't we just do that? How is this the theme we keep coming back to?" Loki rolled his eyes and took a long drink.

"Even if Freya was willing to make that sacrifice, it's not the only thing he wants. He's also asking for the sun and the moon." Hod's voice had an edge to it, like the very idea was an insult. "The consequences would be unfathomable. We'd be stripping the titles and duties from Sol and Mani, who have been pulling the sun and moon around the sky since before Asgard was a thought in Odin's mind. If you give that kind of power to a single man, he could withhold sunlight, which would kill off everything in the realms. He could change the moon cycles to pull water out of rivers and flood cities. He'd be more than a god."

Odin straightened out. "Which is why we need to find a way to get the wall without losing anything. We'll save years and men and gold. We won't get another opportunity like this."

Freya shook her head. "Is that really the type of message you want to send the realms?"

"You're talking about oath-breaking," I added.

Odin gestured to where Asgard sat on the map. "Jotunheim sits on the border of our realm. If they assembled their forces, they could march into the city whenever they please."

"Except that's not their style." Loki leaned against the edge of the table, eyeing Odin. "Nearly every encounter we've had with them has been small. Traps on the road, overly ambitious families who want to prove their mettle by killing a god, that sort of thing. Manageable things. The Jotnar are spread over the realm, living in small villages, some of them tucked into mountain ranges like hermits. Assembling the families into a single working unit would be the greatest feat in history."

"And yet that's exactly what the prophecy says will happen at Ragnarok. Or are you feeling biased towards your kin?" Odin glared at Loki, who only flipped him an obscene gesture in return.

I sighed. "What's your solution then?"

"I don't have one. That's why I summoned your irritating shadow." He flicked a hand toward Loki, as dismissive as could be.

"Right." Loki drank back the rest of the horn and pointed to his scarred lips. "Because I can't break an oath to save my own hide but *Hangi* can do it to get himself a new toy. And who better to break oaths with than the God of Lies. Still love that by the way, thank you."

No one said a word. Part of me wanted to step forward and offer comfort, and another wanted to drag him off before he could get himself into any trouble. But you couldn't just say *no* to Odin.

Loki stared at the table for a moment, dragging his fingertips across the wood as the others looked on.

"Make the job impossible," he said at last. "If he can finish the wall in six months, he gets what he wants. Make sure he builds it high. No one can build something like that around a city like this in that short a time. We walk away with whatever he does finish, and he leaves empty-handed. Odin here can empty his coffers to hire someone to build the rest."

The room pondered it. It wasn't a bad plan. But Hod gave voice to what some of us were thinking. "It's still oath-breaking. An oath is sacred."

"No one would be breaking any oaths, technically speaking. It's just an unfair wager." Freya looked around the room, gauging the reactions of everyone else.

"It's too much of a risk." Hod shook his head, worry painted on his face. "You're playing games with everyone's lives, not just ours."

"I don't like it," I agreed. "We don't need the wall. We can find another way without compromising the spirit of the city. Midgard and Asgard are built on a foundation of trust, that when a man swears an oath, he'll come through. This would make you, again, a hypocrite. Father."

Loki shushed me, but too late. The words were out.

Odin's gaze was murderous. "I don't remember wanting your opinion. Save it for someone foolish enough to listen."

I narrowed my eyes at him, trying to find the words to encompass how badly I wanted to beat the shit out of him.

"Excuse me?" Loki took a step toward Odin. "What the fuck did you say, you—"

Odin waved a dismissive hand and gestured towards the door. "Thor. Get the man."

Thor went out into the hall.

I took Loki by the arm and pulled him back. As furious as I was, escalating this would only land someone in the infirmary.

A moment later, Thor was back with the bedraggled traveller at his side. He listened patiently as Odin explained the new deal to him.

The man huffed. "That's a very hard bargain, but I can do it. I'm going to need my horse, though. Dragging stone takes a hel of a long time."

Odin looked to Loki, who nodded. "A horse is only fair. If you're not done by the first day of summer, you get nothing."

"Agreed." Asgard's new wall builder strode around the table and shook Odin's hand. "I'll start first thing in the morning. I imagine you have specifications?"

Odin swept the wooden pieces from the map around Asgard, starting to point out borders. A few moments later, he realized we were still there and dismissed the room with a wave of a hand. Before Loki and I could get through the doors, Thor had his arm around Loki's shoulders.

"That was good work. Very impressive. Sometimes I remember why we're friends." Thor pulled him along, back toward Valhalla.

"Because I was blessed with all the brains?"

"They go well with my brawn." Thor flexed the arm around Loki's neck and squeezed a cry from him. "Come on, let's have a drink."

Loki waved him off. "I've had enough for one night."

"Alright, suit yourself. I'll drink enough for the both of us then." And with that, he strode off into the crowd of einherjar, demanding food and mead.

Loki deflated next to me.

I reached up and cupped his cheek. "What's wrong, my love? Is it what he said to me?"

He nuzzled into my hand with a sigh. "Yes, but not just that." After a moment of withstanding my glare, he gave in. "I don't want to be the one they call when they need things fixed. It usually ends up being my fault when it all goes south."

I pulled him into my arms, resting my head against his chest. "Do you want to go home?"

"Please."

Taking his hand, I led him towards the doors using the path least occupied by half-drunk warriors. It was too difficult to hear through all the clamour, so I waited until we were in the halls to Valaskjálf before I spoke. "How about we light a fire, sit down on the furs with something warm to drink, and see where our hands end up, hmm?"

He gave me an empathetic pout. "Sig, you always know just what to say."

CHAPTER TWENTY-NINE

"When asked, the gods seemed to have come to a consensus
about his demeanour; Loki couldn't be relied on. At the
faintest sign of commitment, he'd run as
far and as fast as he could."

—*God of Lies Revealed*

I spat the lingering bile into the bowl, bent over the counter like a drunk. My stomach had stopped turning, but my mouth tasted like a troll's backside. I got myself a cup of water, wiping the tears from my cheeks. Slow sips. Staring out the frost-edged window, I could already see Asgard's new wall taking shape at the edge of the city in the early morning light. It had only been two weeks.

"Sig?" Loki stumbled out of the bedroom, still half asleep and wrapped in a thick fur. He was rubbing his eyes and blinking. "Again?"

I nodded, moaning like a child. "It's been three days. Why?"

He pulled me into his arms and held me against his chest. "I think you're sick."

"No. I can't be sick. Gods don't get sick."

"That's not true. Every once in a decade, someone comes down with something."

He was right, of course. It did happen. But there was something gnawing at me that I kept pushing down. A possibility that I couldn't look at, let alone give voice to.

I groaned. "I hate this. I feel useless."

He turned me around and nudged me towards the bedroom. "Let's get you back to sleep. You'll feel better when you wake up."

I grumbled in protest but didn't fight him. He pulled back the mussed furs and tucked me into bed. For good measure, he felt my forehead with his hand and planted a kiss on my temple. "Sleep tight, darling."

There were voices when I woke up. Loki's and another. I peeked open my eyes as a familiar face entered the bedroom.

"Eir? What are you doing here?"

I had studied under Eir for years in order to have enough medicinal seidr to practice properly. She had the same severe smile and salt-and-pepper hair as ever, pulled back into a bun at the back of her head. She was still wearing her grey infirmary uniform, though she'd taken off the ever-stained apron. She'd even brought her bag of tools.

Loki came in behind her and was quick to answer. "You're sick, Sig. I got you a healer."

"He's quite concerned about you, you know." Eir gave me a comforting smile and approached the bedside. "I told him there likely wasn't anything to worry about, but that hasn't stopped him."

"There's nothing wrong," I protested, struggling to sit up against the headboard.

"Nausea, vomiting, and lethargy, yes?" She sat down on the bed and put a hand to my clammy forehead. "Warm but nothing drastic." She pulled her bag onto her lap. "There's a test I'd like to run. Will you pull up your nightdress and lay down for me?"

I squinted at her. The request narrowed the possibilities down significantly and was doing nothing to help the creeping suspicion at the back of my consciousness.

I did as I was told.

She laid a cold hand on my stomach, feeling around with her fingertips. "Any tenderness anywhere?"

"I don't think so."

Loki was hovering at the end of the bed, chewing at the pads around his nails.

Eir reached into her bag and pulled out a jar of rune ink and a brush. That narrowed it down even further.

"What are you testing for?" I asked. "Eir? A parasite? Ink can be used for locating parasites."

"I'm not testing for parasites. You're too smart for your own good sometimes. You'll give yourself a heart attack one day." She unscrewed the top of the rune ink and dipped the brush in, scraping it against the side of the jar. "When was the last time you had your bleeding?"

I started to answer, then found I wasn't sure. Recently, wasn't it? But between the trip to Jotunheim and everything with the wall, I'd lost track. I'd been using the birth control I'd learned with Eir to keep myself from being in this exact situation, but... I wracked my brain, trying to remember where I might have slipped up.

Loki's face changed as the realisation dawned on him. "Oh. *Oh.* You mean...Well,

168

how will you know?"

"It's easy. A little ink and some seidr, that's all."

"Like divination?"

"No. This test is as accurate as they come. It either finds a child or it doesn't."

Loki's long inhale was audible even from the end of the bed.

My mouth was suddenly very, very dry. This wasn't a possibility we'd entertained. We'd been together for such a short time, especially in the grand scheme of eternity. Loki was good with children, but did he *want* them? His face betrayed nothing except deep thought and discomfort. But that could mean anything, couldn't it?

The cold ink touched my skin, breaking me away from my thoughts. The brush tickled, but I did my best to stay still. Eir drew hard-angled runes, her lips barely moving as she whispered. As she drew, the ink sunk into my skin, disappearing by slow degrees. I'd seen the procedure a thousand times; hel, I'd performed it often enough on my own. But Loki hadn't.

"What now?" He normally knew better than to speak while someone was casting runes, but I could hardly blame him; the worry was churning knots in my insides too. Besides, Eir had performed through worse.

"The ink will either rise to the surface as a rune or it will come back like a spill." I kept my voice low, trying to be a good patient.

"Which is the good one?"

"That depends." His eyes met mine, and he stared until I felt so uncomfortable that I had to speak. "The rune means a baby."

He nodded and went back to chewing the skin on his fingers.

Eir put the brush back in the jar and placed her hands above my belly. She was still whispering, her palms hovering over my skin. I couldn't breathe.

And then it happened.

I drew a breath, unsure what else to do. I was too shocked to cry and too confused to do much else.

"Congratulations. You're having a baby." Eir squeezed my hand, then took in the utter silence in the room. She wiped the rune brush on an ink-stained cloth, closed the bottle and put everything back into her bag. Before she got up, she leaned over me. "If you need anything, I'm always available. You have options, should you wish to take them. Think hard, and when you decide which path you'd like to take, I'll be there to help you." She closed up her bag and let herself out without another word.

Loki hadn't moved. His knuckles were white, wrapped tightly around the end of the bed. And then, as if snapping out of some thought, his head came up, and he came to sit next to me.

"Well."

I sat up, trying to find something to wipe the ink from my stomach. Loki jumped up and brought back a rag from the kitchen. I scrubbed my skin until it was clean. Neither of us said a word.

For a long moment, we just sat and looked at one another. I couldn't read anything on his face. It was as masked a thing as I'd ever seen. I couldn't stand it. "I'm tired. I'm going to take a nap."

"Alright." Loki's voice was low, barely more than a whisper. I rolled away from him, pulling the blankets up to my neck. He hesitated a moment, then got up and left the room.

Only then did I cry.

The house was quiet when I woke up. I rubbed my eyes. Dried tears flaked away. It took a while to wake my limbs, having been curled into such a tight ball for so long. I looked out the window. The sun was already fading into the early evening of the winter months. I'd slept at least a couple of hours.

I didn't want to leave my bed. Leaving the room meant seeing Loki and discovering whichever truth he'd decided on, and I was terrified of both. But I was thirsty, and I hadn't heard a peep since I woke up. Besides, there was no fighting the inevitable.

I went out.

No one was there.

He's gone. I scrambled around the table. His shoes weren't by the door, and his cloak was missing. But it was winter, and he wouldn't leave the house for *any reason* without them. I went back to the bedroom. His newest book was still on the night table along with a cluttered assortment of the baubles he sometimes wove into his hair. His clothing was in the wardrobe, his favourite soap still in the bathing room. Everything was still there. Except him.

He wouldn't run. Not without his things.

Right?

I was being stupid. Nothing helpful would come from worrying, so I got myself some water and sat down to worry anyway. I flipped through the pages of a dozen books before setting them down again. I tried to scribble a list of things I needed, but that list quickly became a series of pros and cons about babies. All this thought of Loki, but did *I* want a baby? I trailed runes over the page, spelling out everything from soiled diapers to restless nights to long cuddles. A baby had never been part of my plan to achieve glory, but it sounded…good. Mostly. It would change everything. Including the single-minded pursuit of my title.

The clunk of boots stirred me. They knocked on the porch several times, the sound of trying not to drag snow inside. The door handle twisted, and Loki stepped inside, shaking the white from his cloak, his hood still up around his face, royal blue against the flame of his hair and the emerald in his eyes.

He had a basket in his hands, its top sealed shut to keep out the snow. He kicked off his shoes and came to the table. As he approached to set the basket down in front of me, I scrambled to move my lists, flipping them upside down.

Loki sat down next to me, pushing his hood back. His eyes met mine, and he sighed, his shoulders dropping. "Are you feeling better?"

I licked my lips. I couldn't manage more than a whisper. "Still nauseous, though I think for different reasons now."

"I'm sorry."

My voice caught in my throat. "For what?" There were so many things he could be sorry for.

"For putting you in this position. For not knowing what to say. For letting you wake up with no one here." He reached out and pulled the lid off the basket. "But I needed to get a few things."

Inside were piles of mint and ginger tucked around a vial of something that looked like it came from an apothecary in the market. There was warm bread and soft cheese and a tiny cloth bag labelled *cocoa*.

"They recommended these against stomach sickness. The rest was just…"

"Thoughtful," I finished, pursing my lips in pleasant surprise. "What's this?" I reached in and picked up a small oak box from beneath the mint leaves. It was polished and plain, on golden hinges. Simple, but expensive. I started to open it, but Loki laid a hand on mine, holding it shut.

"Sigyn. This isn't what either of us was expecting. I don't know what you want to do, if you want a baby or not. Ymir's breath, we haven't even… There are reasons not to, and maybe I'm one of those reasons. But I would do this with you if you want to."

His hand moved, still cupped over mine, and opened the box. Inside were two gold rings, one thin and one thick. They were plain, the kind that goldsmiths showed to prospective buyers before having patterns etched in. Unfinished stories.

He squeezed my hands. "Will you be my family?"

My eyes travelled from the box to his face and back. Words escaped me. I thought that this wild chariot ride of a day had peaked at the announcement of a baby. And here was Loki, proposing to me. Part of me screamed to say yes, and another...

"You barely know me." I shuffled in my seat. "You're being impulsive, like always."

The look he gave me was akin to one he might give an imbecile. "There is nothing impulsive about this. I love you, Sigyn. It's not the first time I've thought about it. I would've asked anyway. Someday."

"Someday?" I sniffed, tears pooling in my eyes. Anyone could say that after the fact.

"Yes. I'd have asked you someday, in the same way that summer will come someday. You're inevitable."

I chewed at the inside of my lip, blinking back the tears. "This is a lot, Loki. All of these things at once, and what if we fuck it up?" The questions poured out of my mouth as fast as I could think them. "What if I say yes and we get married and we have this child, and you change your mind? What if you don't love me anymore or if you get yourself in so much trouble that you can't talk yourself out of it? What if you die or we both do? What if we're bad parents? What if we ruin their life? And—Yggdrasil shade us, what is my father going to say?" I buried my face in my palms, sobbing.

Loki fell to his knees in front of me, gathering me into his arms. He hushed me. "That's not going to happen, Sig. I'm never going to just *fall out of love with you*. How could I? How am I supposed to find someone else like you? Someone who cares for me the way you do? No one else has, maybe ever. You're my home. I love you, and the rest will come together; it has to. We could take on all of Asgard, you and I."

I tightened my hands around the collar of his cloak. The crying became long, uneven breaths, steady enough to speak. "If we do this, you have to be better."

He pressed his forehead against mine. "I am better, because of you."

"No. You have to mean it. You have to swear to me that you'll be the kind of father this child deserves. Not one who lies and gets beaten by his brother-in-law every second month." I looked him in the eyes. "Not one who doesn't care, like mine. Not a father who doesn't love his child."

His face hardened, brow furrowed. Each breath he took was sharp and deep, his eyes uncertain as if he were waiting on the judgement of his own execution. A lonely tear ran down his cheek.

"I would love that child until my last day."

"Promise me," I whispered.

He took my face in his hands, his fingers gripping me like I was a bird, about to fly off. "I promise. I'll love you both. I *do* love you both."

There was a sincerity in his eyes that I couldn't deny. Whatever trouble he got himself into, whatever bad relationships he'd fostered with other gods, he loved me. It was easy to imagine him putting himself in harm's way for me, sacrificing for me. For a child. And I wanted that. I wanted someone to love me so much that they'd burn the realms for me.

"Alright. Yes." A nervous laugh escaped my throat. "Oh gods. Oh Loki, what are we doing?"

"Something amazing." He kissed me in short, desperate bursts, then reached for the box on the table. "I don't even know if it fits. I just got the same size as my little finger. We can get a new one." He took my hand and slid the smaller of the two onto my ring finger. It slid on, only slightly too big.

I stared at it, my hand sitting so delicately in his. We would have a child. We would be married. Our friends would come, and we'd stand in the gardens at Valhalla in the company of my family, my father—My father.

"Odin is never going to allow it."

"No. He won't." He moved to lay his head in my lap, his palm against my stomach. His breath was hot on my leg, even through the fabric of my dress. There was a glaze over his eyes, a peace. "It doesn't matter. He doesn't have to."

CHAPTER THIRTY

"The only thing more beautiful than two people in love is three people in love. Maybe four."

—Lofn - *The Shape of Love*

I'd never stepped foot inside Lofn's hall. I knew *of* her. I'd seen her a few times a year in Valhalla or in the streets, but she was a solitary goddess. She was rarely home in the warm months and was so far removed from the games and politics of Asgard that no one really bothered with her. Now it felt odd to ask a favour of someone who had never crossed my mind.

Loki and I were bundled up to our necks, hoods drawn around our faces as the crisp wind whipped at our clothes, tossing snow around our feet. It had come down in droves overnight, white drifts leaning against houses, paths dug out through the streets by plough horses pushing steel plates. As we approached Lofn's humble home, there were boot prints in the snow, heading toward the door. Perhaps we were in luck.

Loki knocked. Something rustled inside, and a voice called, "Just a moment!"

The door flew open, stirring up a wisp of snow. On the other side was a tall, bright-eyed woman with an enthusiastic smile on her face. Her skin was still sun-kissed, despite the cold. Her brown hair was parted into locks that wound into a bun at the back of her head. Ribbons, beads, and other oddities were woven in, some of them distinctly not from Asgard.

Lofn threw her arms around Loki, squealing. "I heard you were back! Why didn't you come to see me?"

"I did!" Loki returned the hug, lifting her from the ground. "You're never here!"

Lofn let him go and brushed some snow off the shoulder of his cloak. "I suppose.

The Goddess of Nothing At All

I only got back this month, and I've been up to my ears in bureaucracy from the Allfather. '*Where have you been? What did you find? How can it benefit Asgard?*' He never stops. And did you know we're going to have a wall now? What's that about?"

Loki laughed. "Let us in, and I'll tell you."

Lofn turned to me for the first time. "Sigyn, welcome. I'm sorry, I didn't mean to be rude. I get a bit overzealous with old friends." She took my gloved hand and kissed the knuckles, a flirtatious look in her eyes. I blushed, and she smiled. "Come in, and I'll make us something hot to drink."

The front room was a cosy study. In the centre was a small table with four chairs around it. At the back was an enormous oak desk, cluttered with maps and books, some with writing that vastly differed from our runes. There was a crackling fire in the hearth, and the wood walls were lined with shelves full of statues, clay vases, metal works, and dozens of things I had no name for. A good many of them were of round, ample women, or phallic depictions of men.

I waited until Loki had finished telling her about the wall. As Lofn put water over the fire to boil, I pointed up at the odd collection. "What are all these things?"

"Oh, those are from my travels." She picked one up and handed it to me. It was a foreign, translucent green stone of two people contorted in a *very* intimate position. She laughed at my surprise. "Sorry, I love to see the shock on people's faces. You know what I do, yes?"

"You're the Goddess of Forbidden Love?"

"Correct. But forbidden love takes a lot of shapes. Perhaps someone's father doesn't care for their betrothed, or there's bad blood between families. These things are precarious but straight forward. Other loves are forbidden because of the things we believe. Every society in the nine realms seems to believe something else, so how do I begin to know anything about who should really marry?"

Lofn took the contorted couple out of my hands and pointed at a round stone statue of a man with a protruding belly and no trousers on. "This comes from Jotunheim. It's a carving of a man carrying his first child, placed at the head of the child's bed for protection."

She moved to a carving that looked to be bone. "This is from a tribe of people who believe that your spirit can be both male and female, and that those people have special connections to their gods. Others believe that they transcend their physical form, or they slip between male and female at will. Not unlike our Loki, hmm?" She winked.

Loki sat down on Lofn's desk, grinning from ear to ear. "It's not my fault if everyone wants to be more like me."

Lofn laughed and tossed a wooden statue at me. I scrambled to catch it.

"Recognize this?"

It was a statue of Frey commonly found in the homes of people from Midgard, his engorged manhood front and centre. I cringed and tossed it back. "I wish I didn't."

"All these things, all these people I speak with or traditions I witness, they help me learn the boundaries and limits of love. Where one place forbids two men to marry, another welcomes it. Where one land celebrates the feminine, another destroys it. There are such heights and depths to love."

The water had boiled, so Lofn fixed some tea and brought it to the little table in the centre of the room. Loki and I followed, the scent of mint already filling the room.

She spoke as she cleared a few stray books from the table. "In the interest of full disclosure, Loki has told you, I assume?"

If I'd ever thought myself straight forward, Lofn was doubly so. "Yes, last night."

"It's nothing to worry about, I assure you. Our time was…an experiment. I'm not the type to settle down with anyone, and he's been more valuable as a friend than a lover."

Loki scoffed. "I think I should take offense to that."

"It was hardly forgettable, Silvertongue, don't worry." Lofn passed us each a cup. "I was a bit surprised to hear the rumours, though. The most notoriously by-the-book goddess in Asgard not only bringing the Trickster back from exile against Odin's will but falling in love with him as well? They'll be writing tales about it for centuries."

The blush rose to my cheeks instantly. "I don't know about that."

"Please, I've heard this story a thousand times. A caged bird can't help but fall in love with freedom. And little wonder you did, with Odin so hel-bent on keeping you under his thumb."

"I didn't think anyone had noticed." I blew on the warm drink, trying not to look her in the eyes.

"Lots of people noticed. Most of them kept their mouths shut." Lofn opened a little cabinet and brought out a jar of sun-dried fruit before she finally sat down. "But I get the impression that this isn't just a social call." She turned to Loki, a playful frown on her face. "Shame on you."

Loki hesitated, his grin both guilty and full of mirth. "I swear I'll visit."

"All this time in exile. You *must* have stories for me."

He bit his lip and stared at the ceiling as if pushing down the need to dive right into whatever debauchery he had to tell. "Mmm, yes. Yes, I do. Now focus."

Both their eyes were on me. It was clear they were going to let me tell this tale. I took a deep breath. "Odin is decidedly not supportive of Loki and I being together. I could live with that, but there's been an unexpected turn of events. We're expecting a child."

Lofn's eyes lit up. "This is wonderful news!" She reached across the table and took both of our hands. "Congratulations, truly. You'll make such good parents. One to balance out the other."

The comment drew a smile from me. Though I wasn't quite sure how to take her, I could see why Loki liked her. "We'd like to be married."

"Well, of course you would! You're both stunning to look at, truly. Your child will be so beautiful, people will drop dead in the streets just for looking at them." She gave Loki a wink and slapped a hand on the table before standing up. She went to her desk and rustled through the papers.

"Can you do it?" I asked.

"Of course I can. Has he ever *expressly* forbidden you to marry?"

"He hasn't said 'No, Loki, you may not marry my daughter.' But I do hope he lies awake at night thinking about it." Loki kicked his feet up onto Lofn's empty chair. I gave him a shove, and he just grinned.

"We're walking a bit of a fine line in this case. Normally, I deal with two or more people who wish to be married but a person or circumstance has come between them, not because of something as foreboding as the Allfather. He'll be absolutely outraged when he finds out, but because he technically never forbade it, it will legally be just another marriage ceremony."

She came back to the table with some parchment, ink, and an oddly feathered quill. She jotted down a few lines and passed the paper and quill to me. "Sign the bottom. It's a statement for my records that you're here of your own free will and that you wish to be married to the intended party. In my less experienced days, I had a problem with a marriage that turned out to be a kidnapping. Now I'm more careful."

I quickly read the runes and signed below. Loki followed suit.

"When would you want the ceremony?"

Loki and I looked at each other. "Soon," I said. "With Frigg's clairvoyance, Odin's tower, the ravens…it's a wonder they're not breaking down your door already to stop us."

Lofn took the paper, blew on the ink, and set it aside. "We could do it today, but with this weather, I'd recommend tomorrow morning. You'll need a witness."

Tomorrow. Married tomorrow. My stomach was churning with butterflies.

Loki scratched the back of his head. "Idunn. She's going to be livid that we didn't tell her sooner."

"Hod as well. He'd want to be there."

"Thor?" Loki's eyebrow raised as we both contemplated it.

"He can't keep a secret."

"No, he can't. That's it then. Hod and Idunn."

"And Bragi." Lofn looked up from the paper as she made a few more notations.

"He came home last week."

"*Well*, that explains why we haven't seen her." Loki nudged me with his elbow. "They've probably forgotten how to put their clothes on."

I made a face, trying to force that mental image from my mind. "You can ask her, and I'll go to Hod. I don't need to see anything I can't unsee."

Loki reached for my hand, the look on his face as content as I'd ever seen him. "I'm glad we're doing this."

I gave his hand a squeeze. "Me too."

CHAPTER THIRTY-ONE

*"It's all well and good to make vows, but it's never the
wedding day that counts. It's in the small moments for the rest
of your lives, when you choose love again and again."*

—*Lofn - The Shape of Love*

The mist of my breath rose up every time I exhaled. The weather had calmed, but the clearing under Yggdrasil was white with fresh snow, covered in hoofprints from the deer. Winter birds flitted through the forest, most of the animals tucked away from the cold. Yggdrasil's branches were bare, revealing the grey sky above, threatening to send more snow at any moment. Standing in front of the tree, a nervous warmth running through my body, I had never been so thankful for the chill winter breeze.

Loki was a sight to see. His hair had been tied into a series of intricate braids, bound at the back of his head, and left to drape across his shoulders. He wore a new cloak, midnight blue with white fox trim around the hood. Underneath were the finest trousers and tunic he could find that were still clean.

The details, the cloak, the hair; it had been all Idunn's doing. Apparently, she'd run straight out of her cabin after he'd told her, towing him along with her. They'd bought me a wine-red cloak that had matching fox trim, and she'd picked out a thin gold circlet for my hair. And for the dress, I'd chosen a white satin gown embellished with gold lace and stitching.

Hod and Eyvindr were off to one side, Eyvindr's arm in Hod's. For balance, Hod always claimed, but with the way they were speaking under their breath and smiling, we all had to wonder.

Idunn and Bragi stood on the other side. Idunn was already wiping tears from her eyes with gloved hands, even though nothing had happened yet. She leaned on Bragi, her head resting on his shoulder. He held her, his knowing smile pressed into her hair; Idunn never had dry eyes at a happy occasion.

"If you're ready." Lofn rubbed gloved hands together, shivering. "You'd think I'd learn not to spend time in warmer climates before coming back to a winter in Asgard." She chuckled.

"We're ready," I said.

Reaching into her cloak, Lofn pulled out the ring box. She handed us each a ring, the one that belonged to the other. "Friends, you've been asked here today to bear witness to the union of Loki Laufeyjarson and Sigyn Odindottir. Welcome. Though you are small in number, your love is immeasurable."

Idunn began to cry again, fanning her face with her hand. Eyvindr whispered into Hod's ear, and their fingers intertwined in such a casually secretive way that I almost didn't notice.

Lofn gestured up to Yggdrasil. "Here, under the protection of the World Tree, we ask Her to shade these two as they join hands and journey into the realms together. Provide them shelter from whatever storms may arise and a bountiful life to enjoy for the rest of their days." She took a long breath. "Is there anything either of you would like to say?"

Loki actually blushed. He glanced to the friends watching us, then the ground, then his eyes finally settled on me. "None of this was supposed to happen. When you landed on my doorstep, bleeding and alone, I had no idea how you were going to change my life. You took hold of me so quickly. All the nights I couldn't sleep because I didn't think you would want anything to do with me. And you did, and I—" His breath hitched in his throat. He blinked back tears and started again. "Everything is better with you here. *I'm* better. I love you. Both of you. No matter what."

I choked back a sob. My heart was so full, tears running down my cheeks. How was I supposed to say something if I couldn't breathe? He took my hand, squeezing as if it would give me my voice.

"I'd given up before I met you," I finally said. "Love was for the lucky. But you heard me when no one else did. And I'm scared. I don't know what I'm doing. None of this was part of the plan. I've always had everything under control, but I'm standing in the snow with a baby in my belly, getting married because you asked me yesterday. This is the most outrageous thing I've ever done, and I am *so* happy. You've brought so much light into my life. You're the fire in my veins. I can't live without you anymore."

Lofn reached under her cloak again and pulled out a dagger. At that cue, Idunn brought forth a golden apple. Lofn cut the apple down the centre, splitting it in two. She passed each of us a half. "This apple, which Yggdrasil gives us to bless us with longevity, symbolizes the sharing of a life. Please."

We both took a bite. Lofn took back what remained. "And the rings."

Loki took my hand gently in his. He slipped the ring onto my finger. My heart was thudding out of my chest, my body trembling like a leaf.

I took his hand, the one that had spent so much time on my skin, in my hair, clutching, caressing, loving, and I slid the ring onto his finger. And it was done.

Loki didn't let go of me. Instead, he pulled me to his chest, my feet stumbling with the sudden movement. He held me against him and kissed me, slow and tempered, and I melted under his lips, sure that my legs would give out from under me.

When the kiss was finished, he pressed his forehead to mine. "How do you feel, wife?"

I stole another kiss. "In love, husband."

His thumb wiped a tear from my cheek. "Good." And then he loosened his grip so I could stand on my own feet again, though I wasn't sure I was able.

Lofn had her hands clasped over her heart, her eyes misty. "This is what I live for. May the Nornir weave the tapestries of your lives in stunning colour. I think it's time we go inside and pour a drink for the happy couple, hmm?"

Idunn dried the tears from her face, nodding.

I waved her over. "Come on, come here."

She rushed into my arms, pressing her face into my shoulder. "It's just so beautiful! I love you both so much!"

Loki wrapped his arms around both of us, pressing his cheek into Idunn's head. "If you keep on like this, I'm going to cry and mess up all my kohl. I'll hold you to blame."

Idunn laughed. "I promise I'll stop, I just—"

A drumming rose up in the distance, the thudding of hooves. Loki sighed and stepped away, straightening out the creases in his cloak. "Naturally."

"Too late, Allfather," Lofn laughed, pulling her hood back from her face. We watched the entrance to the clearing together, waiting for the horses to round the corner.

Odin appeared first, followed by Thor and several of the einherjar. Their horses kicked up snow as they approached, slowing from a thunder to a murmur.

The Allfather leapt down from his horse, his face red under his beard. A loud squawk came from the trees, and one of his ravens swooped down to land on his shoulder. How long had it been watching? "What is the meaning of this?"

Lofn stepped forward. "Loki and Sigyn wished to be married, and I married them."

He wagged a finger at her. "I should have you thrown out of Asgard!"

"My *job*, which you gave me, is to facilitate forbidden love. They knew you would never consent, and so it falls under my rights to do so."

"You went against my will—"

Lofn put her hands on her hips. "You never commanded me not to intervene. I've done nothing against your will, because you didn't make your will clear. Their suspicions are not fact, and there is nothing you can do. Go to Forseti. Ask him about the laws. I wrote them with him."

Odin's teeth ground together, his hands looking for something to break.

And Loki, not one to stay out of trouble, moved into his reach. "We wanted to invite you; we really did. We just didn't want it to turn into anything too dramatic."

"You miserable Trickster. Why I let you back in this city, I'll never know."

Loki started to count on his fingers. "Mjolnir. Draupnir. Gullinbursti. All the other Dwarven gifts. The giant wall being built around you. Someone to keep your daughter warm at night."

Odin let out a fit of rage, winding back his fist, and the first thing I could think to do was—

"I'm pregnant!"

Odin stopped in his tracks, eyes wide. But it wasn't anger or shock. It was fear. "No. You can't be."

I drew closer to him, wary, one hand on my stomach and the other held out to him. "I am. And it's alright. We're married, and we're going to look after each other. We're going to do this together. You don't need to worry."

He started to speak, then stopped. While he said nothing, Thor was off his horse and rushing toward me, a grin plastered on his face. He scooped me up in a hug. "This is wonderful news, sister!"

"Gentle!" I cried. "Be gentle!" His grip loosened, and he put me down, arms still around me. "You're going to be an uncle. Again."

"I can't wait! But why didn't you invite me to the wedding?" He started to pout.

"Because you can't keep a secret."

He shook his head. "No, I can't."

Idunn stepped in. "I have soup and warm cider inside. Maybe we should go in." Her eyes darted to Odin, who still hadn't moved. He was slumped over, defeated, and frankly, no one knew what to do about it.

Loki gave Thor a pat on the back. "Join us. Maybe you can help pick a name for the baby."

He started to lead Thor towards the cabin when Odin grabbed Loki by the wrist and pulled him back.

"You know what you've done," Odin hissed. "You have it; I know you took it. You know where this leads!"

"Father! Let him go!" I took Loki's other arm, as if I could pull him away by sheer force.

But Loki just stared at him, blankly at first, then with a sly grin. "Do I?"

"You'll seal their fates."

Loki shook his head. "Don't you think you've done that yourself?"

Odin released his arm, his hand quivering. Not missing a beat, I stole my husband away, back toward the cabin before anyone could change their minds.

I slapped him on the arm. "What was that?"

"Ow. It was nothing. Your Father is losing his mind in his old age."

"That wasn't nothing, Loki."

He huffed, leading me up the steps to the cabin. "Your father is a tyrant. I'm tired of the way he treats you. There isn't a thing he's ever done that has your best interest in mind. He'll never lay a hand on you or make you feel small again, not if I can help it."

"Right." I frowned, certain that something had happened that I couldn't understand. But the cabin was already full of laughter, our friends around the small table, huddled together against the chill. Idunn was serving out thick soup, and Thor was trying to squeeze in an extra chair for himself. And after a moment, I decided to let this evening be a good one. The consequences, whatever they might be, could wait.

CHAPTER THIRTY-TWO

*"The official registration for the marriage of Loki
Laufeyjarson and Sigyn—redacted—dottir has been
received. I recommend leaving it with the divorce
records to save time in the future."*

—Note to Archivists

"Is that the last of it?" I passed the crate out the door, laden with books and clothing.

Loki took it from my hands and put it onto the back of the sled, where he strapped it onto the others. "The last of what's worth taking."

I looked around Loki's little home. The walls were bare, each book, ornament, and cup piled into the back of the sled. A century of his life in a few crates, though I had a feeling it was just a sliver of what he'd seen.

I couldn't help but remember that one odd night. Me, sleeping on what was now the bare mattress in the corner, him on the bedroll on the floor. It seemed so long ago. So much had happened since then. My hand went to my stomach. It still felt no different than it ever had, but our child was in there, and everything had changed.

When I went back outside, Thor was sitting on the snowy ground, scratching behind the ears of his pet goats, Tanngrisnir and Tanngnjóstr. They were enormous as far as goats were concerned. One had thick, curling horns, while the other had one straight horn and one jagged stub. "You can't have much in there. This cabin is as large as my latrine."

Loki raised an eyebrow. "Exiles usually don't get given a hall, do they?"

"I don't know. I never got myself exiled." Thor stood and brushed the snow off his cloak. "Tell me it's finished. If someone doesn't feed me soon, I'll have to kill one of the goats to eat, and then we'll be here all night waiting for it to come back to life."

Loki rolled his eyes and went to lock up the cabin.

It was a slow walk out of the woods as we found the path of least resistance for the goats to pull the tiny sled along. But Loki knew how to get around, and eventually, we made it out to where the horses were waiting.

As I climbed on my horse, Loki dashed over to offer unneeded assistance. "Don't ride any faster than a walk, remember?"

I looked down at him. There was an air of urgency in his eyes, more begging than asking. "I know, the shaking isn't good for the baby. It's just so... slow."

"When the baby arrives, you can race from here to Hel and back, I don't care. For now, you have to be gentle with yourself."

"When exactly did we change roles in this relationship?"

"When Eir gave me the extended list of what could happen to you and that child."

"Loki." I glared at him, impatience bubbling to the surface at being treated like a flower. "Get on your fucking horse."

For a moment, it looked like he might get angry with me, but he just grinned, shook his head, and did as he was told.

Loki and I rode while Thor steered his goats toward Asgard. We laughed most of the way back, arguing all the reasons why we weren't going to name the baby Thor, and no, not Thora either. When we drew closer to the wall and its builder, the discussion stopped short.

"*Skit*," Loki cursed. "That's going to be a problem."

The builder had just finished placing a stone onto the wall, wiping his gloved hands on his trousers. And right behind him was his enormous black horse, balancing on his hind legs, carrying a stone between his front hooves. He put it on the wall next to the other and trotted away like any other horse.

"This is seidr. It has to be." Thor pulled the sled up closer to our horses. "How can that be possible?"

"I don't know." Loki was still staring, nearly lost for words.

"What if he does it?" The tone in Thor's voice was quickly turning to panic. "What if he finishes the wall? You're the one who said, '*let him use his horse, it's just a horse*.'"

Loki turned on Thor like a whip. "How was I supposed to know it was a *magic* horse?"

"We have to tell Odin," I said, trying to remain calm.

"Even if it *is* enchanted somehow, it's a horse," Loki said. "How could it possibly build an entire wall around Asgard before the first day of summer? It's only six months. It can't. It won't."

But if there was anything I'd learned about Loki, it was that his anger and impatience rose to the surface when he was afraid. When he didn't have some careful plan or crafted lie in place.

I looked away from Loki. "Thor, go ahead to Gladsheim. Make sure Father knows. He can decide for himself what to do."

Thor gave me a nod and cracked the reins. The goats sped up on their way to the centre of the city, all of Loki's possessions in tow.

"It's going to be fine," Loki said. And I could almost believe it, if it weren't for the clench of his jaw and the white-knuckled grip he had on the reins.

What Odin decided to do was… nothing. He already knew, and like Loki, he assumed it would be fine. Just a horse, just a man. And so, it was discussed in whispers at dinner and in corridors and away from the ears of the Allfather. How the wall kept creeping higher and higher, how it barely seemed like a challenge at all. Mostly, we did our best to forget about it.

Loki and I had work to do. We moved his last possessions into my—our hall. Books were crammed into shelves in the library, old clothing washed and hung with the rest. All his little treasures found a place next to mine.

We spent time in the market, commissioning new pieces for the spare room we dusted off and put to use. As we shopped, women often stopped to ask questions. When was the baby due? Was the sickness gone yet? Had the other gods blessed its birth? And inevitably the stories turned to the children they'd born in Midgard during their living days. The ones who had survived and grown, and the ones that hadn't. Babies stolen by forest spirits or born broken and left to the elements. I knew that Asgard wasn't Midgard, and that my baby was safe from so many of their hardships, but I held my belly and cried with the women anyway.

Slowly, the new things arrived. First came a bearskin rug. Then a chair. Then a tiny bed. A bassinette was made for our bedroom, carved in pale wood and lined in green linen. We bought diapers and clothing and tiny boots and toys too old for a baby that Loki couldn't live without. Months passed and my stomach grew, and our home began to look like a place for a child.

Storms raged and left again, snow dropping and whisking around Asgard and the realms. It kept us inside, near the fire. Near each other. Then the snow became less frequent, and the realms began to warm again. The full dark of winter gave way to the sun's return.

And despite the sleet and ice and snow, the wall was nearly complete.

"I think you should leave Asgard. Go somewhere safe." I ran my hand over the large swell of my belly, unable to look him in the eye.

Loki kept eating his breakfast. "I'm not going anywhere. It's his bargain, not mine. It's going to be fine."

I brought my food to the table, one hand on my aching hip. I sat down across from him. "You've been saying that for months. Do you really believe it?"

He bristled, the same irritation that came over him every time we talked about the wall. "I said it was fine. And I—"

A rapping came from the front door. Not a knocking, not exactly. Scraping. An unnatural sound. I started to get up, but Loki signalled me to sit back down. And well enough, since this baby was weighing on me like a boulder.

He opened the door and on the other side was...no one.

Something screeched, and a pair of shadows bolted inside, swooping down onto the table. The ravens hopped and skipped across the wood, kicking up egg and meat and parchment with every step.

"Stop!" I swung my arms at them, trying to shoo them away, but they landed out of reach and stared at me. "What do you want?"

Loki left the door open and came back to the table, arms crossed over his chest. "Let me guess. Odin wants to see us."

One of the ravens squawked, though whether it was Huginn or Muninn, I didn't know. It hopped towards me and shook its leg. A note was bound to it with string.

I sighed and fumbled to untie it. "Stop moving. We're not friends, you and I. You're lucky I don't snap your leg clean off."

"Ymir's breath, Sig." Loki was looking at me as if he didn't know who I was.

"These two used to follow me around Asgard, peeping in my windows with their beady little eyes. Didn't you? Telling Odin everything I did, everywhere I went. If Frigg hadn't told Odin to stop, they'd still be spying on me."

I managed to get the string untied and uncurled the note: *Gladsheim. NOW.*

"I'm shocked." Loki trudged over to grab our cloaks from their hooks.

I sighed and wagged a finger at the raven. "Tell that one-eyed old man we're on our way. Now get out of my house. Everything about you bothers me."

The bird screeched and clawed at the table, leaving furrows in its surface. The other left a foul, wet mess on the wood before taking off and flying out the door.

Loki turned up his nose at the raven shit. "I think I'm done eating."

"Do you realize what day it is?" Odin was pacing the floor in front of the dais, his face red and sweaty. "The wall's nearly finished! You swore it was impossible!" He stopped in front of Loki. "How are you going to fix it?"

"How am *I* going to fix it?" Loki snapped. "You knew for months that something was wrong and ordered us to do nothing. It's not as if you didn't notice him out there all winter, stone after fucking stone."

"And did you know what he might be?" Odin sneered.

"After you put him to work?" Loki shifted his weight to his other foot. "Yeah, I had a feeling. He doesn't *look* much like a Jotun but not all of us look alike, do we? He's clearly used to the cold, but he didn't exactly put that in his job references, did he?"

Odin took a step forward, nearly nose to nose with Loki. "You did this, didn't you? Making pacts with your people. You plan to destroy us from the inside."

My eyes darted from between them, cautiously drawing up energy for what seemed to be an inevitable explosion.

But Loki looked almost bored. "Ah yes, my people. I grew up here and Laufey was Aesir, but what does that matter? The Jotnar *must* be *my* people. Loki, destroying everything that Odin built! It's a great story, isn't it? Believe it if it helps you sleep at night."

Odin huffed, like a bull getting ready to charge. He wasn't watching the details. A teal flame cupped in Loki's hand, ready for a fight. Loki wouldn't win, though. Not in Odin's own home.

"Please." I put on my deepest pout, let the sadness seep into my eyes. My hand went to my stomach, drawing my father's attention to the baby, my other hand reaching out for him. A play for compassion. "Don't hurt him."

Odin looked down at me. The rage in his eyes dwindled like a candle snuffed out. I couldn't be sure what he saw or what he was thinking, but there was pity there. More pity than the situation deserved. He took a step back. "Fix it," he mumbled and turned to saunter up the stairs to his seat.

Loki snuffed out the wildfire and smoothed the fabric of his tunic before turning to leave. He looked forward, head up, striding like a proud elk toward the doors. I couldn't help myself. When I turned to look back, Odin was slumped forward on his throne, his head in his hands.

It was my turn to be angry. "You can't meet this Jotun alone. You have no idea what he's capable of!"

Loki plucked a golden apple from the table and threw a thin brown cloak over his shoulders. He pulled his hair out from beneath, and it cascaded over the cloak's fur collar. He ate, as calm as could be, smiling as I berated him at length.

"Say something!" I slammed my fists onto the table, and the baby shifted, kicking me in the side. I winced and slid down into the closest chair.

"There's nothing to worry over, darling. I'll return by nightfall." He tossed the core of the apple out the kitchen window and wiped his hands on his cloak before coming to kneel next to me. He ran his hand across my stomach and pulled my head down for a long, slow kiss.

I pushed him away, wagging a finger at him. "You won't distract me so easily with that silver tongue of yours."

He laughed. "Oh, but I love the way you say it. Be patient, and later I'll remind you what this silver tongue can do."

I blushed and crossed my arms, not wanting to show cracks in my resolve. "Go then. If you're not here by dark, don't bother coming back!"

Loki snickered and kissed my cheek. "I'll see you soon. Keep the bed warm for me."

He opened the door and walked out into the crisp air. I watched his long, confident strides until he was out of sight.

CHAPTER THIRTY-THREE

*"And Loki, who so often gave the gods bad council,
trembled under their wrath. He swore to fix the
matter, whatever it cost him."*

—*Asgard Historical Record, Volume 16*

My neck ached when I woke up. I blinked the sleep from my eyes, trying
to stretch the discomfort from my joints. My book was open to the page
I'd fallen asleep on, and Loki's side of the bed was still made, more or less.
The sun was peeking in through the window. He must have decided not to wake me. I
pulled myself out of bed and went to look for him.

But he wasn't there. Not in the study, or the kitchen, or curled up in his old bed.

It was still early. Things didn't always go to plan. I reminded myself of that over
and over as I stomped around the house, waiting and sweeping the floor, waiting and
slamming cups onto shelves, waiting and resting my poor legs. Every sound had me
checking the door, watching the windows. But Loki never appeared.

Enough was enough. I'd lived with the anxious thrum under my skin as long as I
was able. I pulled on my shoes and cloak and made my way to the entrance of the city's
new wall. My legs wouldn't carry me as fast as I wanted them to, and it added a layer
of annoyance to my already overwhelming rage and worry. Forget that everyone nearby
was watching me waddle bowlegged across the city as if I had a sign strung around my
neck that read '*Sigyn: Victim of Pregnancy.*'

As I approached the edge of the city, the wall loomed over me, taller than three
men and entirely complete except for a handful of stones that lay next to the archway.
Odin, Frey, and Thor were there, talking to the builder. By the look on his face, the

discussion wasn't going well for him.

"The wall's been built!" he cried, pointing to the stones. "Those are all that's left! You have everything you wanted, and you'll still go back on our deal?"

"It's not finished." Odin shrugged. "Leave. Your plan to take advantage of Asgard has failed, and you'll get nothing from us."

"Take advantage of you? My horse ran off all of a sudden, just as we were about to put in the last stones! It reeks of dishonesty, *Hangi*. What did you do to him?"

"The discipline of your horse has nothing to do with us." Thor stepped forward, Mjolnir grasped tightly in his hands. "One less Jotun in the realms is no skin off my back."

"To Hel with you all!" The builder sprung at Odin, but before he could reach him, Thor brought Mjolnir down onto his head. His head cracked like an egg, the sound of collapsing bone enough to make my stomach lurch. Blood and brain sprayed in all directions, covering grass and god alike. The builder's body slumped over, the remnants of his head sunken into the space between his shoulders.

"Well." Odin nodded, wiping the mess from his sleeve. "I suppose that puts an end to our problem."

"Yours perhaps, but not mine." I strode towards them, one hand on my stomach, careful not to slip in the puddles of brain matter. "Loki left yesterday to deal with this and hasn't come back. Where is he?"

Odin stared at me. "How would I know?"

"When I was 15 and snuck out to meet a boy, you knew. When I was 20 and got too drunk in Vanaheim, *an entire realm away*, you knew. You mean to tell me you haven't been keeping your eye on Loki over something as crucial as this? Forgive me, but I smell bullshit." I crossed my arms over my chest. "If he doesn't turn up soon, I'm going to mount both your heads on pikes right next to this stupid wall."

Frey and Thor began to snicker behind their hands. Even Odin smiled, despite the fact that it would probably crack his stupid stone face.

Condescending shits.

Frey put a hand on my shoulder. "No one's seen Loki. Maybe it's best you go back home. We wouldn't want you to strain yourself, for the baby's sake."

I pushed his hand away. "I'm fine, and if you won't help me, I'll find someone who will." I turned and started toward the city.

"I wouldn't want to be him when he gets back!" Thor cackled. I gritted my teeth and pressed on, their laughter boiling my blood.

Two days I waited for Loki to come home. Two days of asking every soul in the city if they'd seen him, but no one had. Two days during which I tossed and turned, unable to sleep, guilt and worry gnawing at my insides.

Where was he?

What had happened to him?

Was he dead?

I fought with myself, springing back and forth between my anger at him and the dread that somehow it had been something *I'd* done. Hoping that he would just come home. But in the end, I was forced to swallow my pride and turn to the one person I wanted least to bend my knees to.

"I didn't think you'd have the balls to set foot here again."

Freya was seated on the floor with a dozen other völur, everyone in the room as naked as the day they were born. Their bodies were painted in sharp patterns, red cutting across their cheeks and chests and along the length of their arms. I'd burst in on divination practice.

I cleared my throat. "Neither did I. But I need to speak to you."

She stayed put a moment, her legs crossed under her, reluctant to get up. But at last, she did. She motioned for the others to stay put and slipped a dressing gown over herself. I stepped back out into the hallway and let her sweep past me.

Freya closed the door and looked me over. I knew what she saw. The circles under my eyes from staying awake for days, waiting for the sound of his boots on my front step. The weathered clothing I'd worn for days and nights as I paced the floor, watching out the windows. A soon-to-be mother who was falling apart at the seams.

"I've seen corpses that look better than you."

I pursed my lips and nodded, pushing back the urge to snap at her. "Neither of us wants to be here, so let me cut to the chase. I know you've heard Loki is missing. I need to find him."

Freya laughed. "You expect me to help you find that snake? Why would I do that? If he's run off back to the mountains, we should all count ourselves lucky."

I put my hands to my chest, gripping at my heart. "Please, Freya. What am I supposed to do? I can't have this child not knowing if he's alive or dead."

"Maybe that child would be better off." She stared me down.

"I don't care that you don't understand. I am begging you. Help me find him. Help my child have a father." The words broke the dam of tears I'd been holding back. I threw my hands over my face and sobbed, too exhausted to do anything but grieve.

The hatred slipped from her face, and she started to reach out, then stopped, her fingers curling back into her palm. She watched me for a moment as I tried to push back my tears, regain some of my dignity. At last, she spoke. "And what do you expect me to do?"

I wiped my face in my sleeve. "Divine a location. Find him. Tell me he's alive, at the very least."

Freya huffed, arms crossed over her chest. She made me wait, but at last she pushed the door open. She swept back into the room, commanding the attention of her students. "You're all dismissed. Take your robes and go. Work on what you learned today and be ready to try again tomorrow."

The women scrambled to gather their things and left one by one. When the room was clear, Freya let her robe fall and sat down. She picked up the blade from the ground next to her and held it out to me. "You know how this works."

I did. Divination required sacrifice. It was blood seidr, life in return for knowledge. I sat down across from her. "How much?"

She shrugged, dipping a cloth into a bowl of clean water. She set about clearing the last session's blood from her skin. "A proper cut. Or are you too cowardly?"

I did it quickly, if only to spite her. The blade bit into my finger, and the blood seeped up onto my skin, trailing down into my palm and pooling there. I hated divination, I really, truly did.

Freya set a small brass bowl at my feet, and I let the blood drip into it. My body hadn't appreciated being opened up and my head was light, but I was hardly going to show it.

"Good." She handed me a cloth to stem the bleeding. Without a moment's hesitation, she took the bowl and dipped her fingers in. She closed her eyes and traced over the perfectly symmetrical patterns on her body, patterns she would have practised time and time again over the decades. The lines stretched across her collar bones, down the lengths of her arms and the curves of her face. As she drew, she chanted runes under her breath.

I could only watch and try to be patient. The waiting was excruciating. I tried not to be too hopeful. Loki could've been anywhere. Something could have killed him. His body might have been half-rotten in a pit somewhere, for all I knew. As I pressed the cloth to my palm, I whispered my own runes to heal the wound, if only to distract myself for a moment. And then, almost abruptly, she was finished.

Freya's eyes blinked open, her pupils shrinking back to normal. Wherever she had been, it took her a moment to come back. I knew better than to press her for answers, no matter how badly I wanted them.

She moaned and leaned forward, massaging her temples. "Sadly," she said, stretching out, "he's not dead."

I inhaled sharply, a hysterical laugh escaping me. "Oh, thank the Nornir! I—I thought he—" I choked, sobbing into my hands out of sheer relief. "Where is he?"

"The Nornir were, in fact, the ones that answered. They spoke in riddles, as always." She sat back up and pulled her dressing gown over her shoulders. "He's close, somewhere within the bounds of the realm of Asgard, but not within the city walls. They told me that no matter how hard you look for him, he won't be found. Not until he wishes to be. *'Your eyes may fall upon him, but you won't see him.'*"

I stared at her in disbelief. "That's what they said? That's everything?"

Freya stood, trying the ribbon around her waist to secure the dressing gown. "That's everything. Now kindly get out so I can mourn Loki's continued existence by getting very drunk."

She hustled me toward the door, eager to have me out of her sight. When I was in the hall, she started to close the door but stopped short. "Oh, right," she said, catching my eye. "They said it's a boy." And she slammed the door in my face.

Idunn stroked my hair as I cried into her lap. She was propped up against the head of the bed, on the side where Loki normally slept. My chest heaved, each desperate breath a sharp hiss. It was too much. He wasn't here. Wouldn't be here. I was alone with this baby. He had promised me so much, and now none of it was true. I wanted to kill him, but I also wanted him next to me.

I wanted so many things at once.

"You're going to be alright." Idunn's voice was little more than a whisper. "Do you know how I know that?"

I wiped the slime of tears and mucus from my face, covering the back of my hand in it. "How?"

"Because you're Sigyn Odindottir. You put up with your father, and with Thor, and with all your brothers all these years. Anyone else would've packed up their bags and left Asgard. You never stopped trying, even when the odds were against you." She passed me a handkerchief. "And because we're going to help you."

I shook my head, trying to pull myself together. "I can't ask for that."

"You're not. Bragi and I will help you with the house and the chores, and tomorrow, I'll speak with the others."

"No Idunn, you can't. You have your own life, and I—"

Her voice grew stern, and her eyebrows furrowed in a way that looked foreign on her. "There's nothing you can do about it. You'll let me in, or I'll have Thor take the door off its hinges."

I choked out a watery laugh. "You would, wouldn't you?"

"I would. We all know you're too stubborn to take help, so this is the compromise I'm giving you. I love you, and I'm going to take care of you." She ran her hand down the side of my face again, the stern demeanour falling away. "Sigyn, he's coming back, and you're going to be okay. I'll make sure of it."

CHAPTER THIRTY-FOUR

*"One strong cat can pull the cart alone, but it will always be
outpaced by a team."*

—*Vanir Proverb*

The baby was restless, kicking every organ within reach. It hurt to sit *and* to lie down, so I opted for something more active. I grabbed the broom and swept the floor in slow, rhythmic motions, hoping to somehow rock him to sleep with the sway of my hips. I could hardly blame him though; my mind was churning with thoughts so loud and upsetting that it kept me awake as well.

I was in the middle of singing him a lullaby when a ruckus came from the other side of the front door, followed by shushing, quiet, and then a knock. Broom in hand, I tottered over to the door; some days it was the only speed I had, and that was as frustrating as anything else about being pregnant. When I opened it, I found a host of gods on the other side.

Idunn was at the front with Bragi. "Good evening!"

"Umm, hello?" I moved aside, not sure I had any other option. They filed in, first Thor, then Hod, Eyvindr, Frey, and even Lofn, each one passing with a greeting. They gathered around the table and sat down as Bragi began to pull food and drink from an enormous bag. Thor set a full-sized keg of mead on the floor.

Idunn took the broom from my hand and nudged me toward the table. "You refuse to come to supper, so we brought supper to you."

Eyvindr was pulling platters and cups from my cupboards while Lofn put water over the fire to boil. Frey was passing food down the length of the table until Bragi had emptied the bag. It was enough to feed a small army, clearly smuggled straight from

196

Valhalla's kitchens.

"This is too kind." I was suddenly very aware that I was in an old nightdress and hadn't bothered to do anything with my hair.

"Everyone needs a little company." Lofn set a cup down in front of me with a wink.

I stared at Frey. "You're...out of place, aren't you?"

"Admittedly, yes. Your husband scares the hel out of me, and my sister would have my head on a pike if she knew, but I'm not one to say no to an invitation."

I couldn't help but laugh. "I appreciate the honesty."

After everyone had settled in and taken their share, the stories began. Lofn told us about her most recent trip to Svartalfheim where she officiated over a secret wedding between three Dwarves. Thor spun a tale about an enormous Jotun he'd killed, which was what most of his stories were always about. Hod gave us a story that had been told to him by a young boy from Midgard, whose father had been an inventor of sorts. Each story was a distraction, something to take up space in my mind so that my own wasn't front and centre.

I winced as the baby kicked and sent pain spider-webbing through my side.

"Are you alright?" Lofn leaned over the table.

"Just a kick. He's a strong one." I tapped my fingers on the table until the pain subsided.

"I bet he'll be wily and sarcastic, just like his father." Thor was grinning from ear to ear.

Everyone grew quiet for a moment, the unbearable silence that comes when someone finally brings up the one thing they were trying to avoid.

"More than likely." I smiled and gave my stomach a rub. "He's just as strong-willed, I can tell you that much, and when Loki gets back, he's going to be so proud."

Frey looked at me with such pity that I could hardly stand it. "How can you be so sure that he's coming back at all?"

"Because I know him." But it was clear that wasn't enough for him. "I hear the whispers. Everyone says he doesn't want to be a father, but they haven't seen him, the way it's changed him. He put a ring on my finger and made me a promise. If something is keeping him away, it's got nothing to do with us."

"It's brave," Bragi said. "Keeping such high spirits."

"No, it's not." I stretched my fingers, resisting the urge to slam my fist on the table instead. "Just because people keep saying he's run off doesn't make it true. Loki is coming home. I just need to be patient."

But I could hear my own desperation even as I said it.

"You're right." Hod nodded, a pained but compassionate look on his face. "Patience is difficult when it comes to the heart, but it'll be worth the wait."

A slow trickle of affirmations turned into stories about Loki. Things he'd done, trouble he'd caused, kindnesses he'd given. It was nice. Beautiful, even. But there was something about it that bothered me. I listened and listened, and the realization crept over me like a cold chill.

These stories...it felt like a wake. The reminiscing about something that was over and would never be again. Like the funeral pyre was burning outside and no one was ready to admit that he was already dead.

CHAPTER THIRTY-FIVE

*"There are many great costs associated with the birth of a god.
The meat and mead alone will cost us a small fortune!"*

—Valhalla's kitchen records

I stared out over the high table in Valhalla, the noise overwhelming. The raucous laughter, the din of metal hitting wood, the occasional fist hitting flesh as the einherjar feasted and fought amongst themselves. The other gods were nearly all present, seated up the length of the table, paying me no mind. It had taken some poking and prodding, but they'd finally convinced me to come back. That the stares of others didn't matter, that people loved me, and that more people missed me than I thought. And maybe they were right.

But now everything felt so surreal. It had all changed in an instant. Like it was split in two. Everything before this moment and everything to come. And no one else had noticed a thing. They were still eating and laughing as the wetness pooled around my thighs and soaked into my dress.

I reached out, still staring wide-eyed out over the room, pawing at the air until I hit Idunn's arm.

She took my hand without looking, still talking to Bragi.

"Idunn."

Her name came out as a whisper. I struggled to say it again. "Idunn. Idunn."

She turned to me, a soft, curious look on her face. "What is it?"

"The baby." I stared down at my lap. "I was so uncomfortable all morning, but *everything* is uncomfortable. I didn't think—"

Confusion fell over Idunn's face. "Sigyn, tell me what's wrong."

199

The words felt like they came from someone else, like I was far away. "My water broke."

"Oh!" She jumped up, nearly knocking her chair over. "Yggdrasil shade us, it's time!" She bolted out of her chair. "The baby is coming!"

Bragi didn't move, just stared at Idunn, locked in place.

"I said, *the baby is coming!*" Idunn screamed it loud enough to silence the whole table of gods, each of them focused on her. No one said a word. "Are you serious? MOVE."

Thor was the first one to his feet. He barrelled past everyone else and knelt down next to my chair. "Are you alright?"

I still wasn't sure I was breathing. I nodded. "I thought I had another two weeks."

Thor pulled the leg of my chair, turning it so I looked at him. "You're going to be a mother."

I blinked. "I'm going to be a mother."

Thor stood back up, grabbed Idunn's cup, poured the rest of her drink down his throat, and screamed out, "The baby is coming!"

The room broke into cacophonous roar, fists and drinks flying into the air.

I couldn't catch my breath. Why was I only full of panic?

"Idunn, I'm not ready. Gods, what have I done?"

Idunn hushed me. "None of that. Everything is fine, and we are going to get you packed up and back home. Yes? Yes. Thor, pick her up and take her home. Bragi, go to the infirmary and tell Eir it's time."

I pressed a hand onto the table to help me get up. My dress stuck to my legs. Before I could take a step on my own, Thor had swept me into his massive arms, carrying me like some inflated maiden. "Nothing to worry about, hmm? I've got you."

Once he reached the end of the platform, he stopped and looked back at the other gods, who were stuffing last bits of food and drink into them as they pulled their cloaks around their shoulders. "Bring enough food and drink to last the night! We have vigil to hold!"

I'd had enough training to know that labour could take hours, sometimes days, but I hadn't been prepared. You think you know a thing, and then the reality of it slaps you in the face.

Things had started so slowly and taken so long. I'd spent hours pacing the kitchen as the gods moved barrels of mead and crates of food, filling every nook and cranny with something for the festivities. Walking was good for the baby, they said. Deep breaths, they said.

The Goddess of Nothing At All

The party was already underway when Eir and her apprentice came. So were the heavier contractions. The first one nearly buckled my knees mid-stride, and Idunn decided it was time to move me away from the drinking brutes. We settled into my bedroom as Eir and her apprentice, Fulla, gathered the things they'd need for the long night ahead.

They'd made the floor as comfortable as they could, with old cushions and blankets to rest on, the four of us sitting together as we waited. They told me stories as the contractions wracked through my body, using laughter to distract me from the pain.

From the absence.

As they kept time, checking my nethers and keeping me focused, the party was in full swing in my kitchen. The familiar voices of Thor, Odin, Hod, and even Freya came through the walls. We'd kept the door closed, but I'd been to a party or two like this before; they'd drink and sing and laugh until the baby arrived, no matter how many hours or days it took.

I reached for the water, and Fulla handed it to me. Sweat was dripping down my face and back, my body protesting what I'd done to it. The contractions were much closer than they'd been. I was so fucking ready for it to be over.

Eir ducked her head under my skirts again. "It's nearly time. Are you ready?"

"No. Not at all. It hurts—" I broke off into a shallow scream. A chorus of cheers came from the other room. Now they knew as well.

Eir tipped her head at Fulla, who riffled through her bag and brought out a bottle of rune ink and a brush. She uncapped the bottle. The brush was barely a tickle as she drew runes across the back of both hands.

"You know what this is?" Eir asked.

"Pain relief," I managed through gritted teeth.

"That's right. Tell me how it works."

I growled at her. "I know how it works; this is hardly the time—"

"Tell me. How it works." The stern look on Eir's face reminded me why I'd never argued with her during my own apprenticeship.

I spelled out the process for her between deep, sharp breaths and pained moans. The reason for each rune, what runes to choose for what types of pain, what alteration could be made. And by the time I was finished, the ink had disappeared under my skin, and the pain was a faint pulse.

I shook my head, sweet relief pouring over me. "Well done, teacher."

Eir just smiled and dipped her head beneath my skirts again. "Alright Sigyn, up on your feet."

It really was time.

Idunn and Fulla offered me their arms, sitting on either side of me as I squatted over the cushions. I strung myself from them, hanging from each of their necks, legs already weak.

"Remember your breathing. As soon as you feel a contraction, push. Are you ready?"

I'd seen this before; I knew what to do. But I wasn't prepared for the way it would feel. I pushed, gritting my teeth and squeezing the hands of the women holding me up. Even with the runes, the pain ripped through me. I screamed, and the kitchen exploded with noise.

"Stop. No screaming, just breathing and pushing. In and out. Again. Push when you feel it."

And so it went. Breathing, bearing down, growling, pushing. Each grunt loud enough to be heard by the others was responded to by the chorus of my friends and family outside the door cheering me on. As I tried to bring this life into the world, they sang bawdy songs, full of tits and slits and fucking. And then I heard nothing, felt nothing, beyond what was happening in my own skin.

Eir's head sunk low to the floor, her hands outstretched beneath me. "I see him. We're almost there. Give me a big push, Sigyn."

I didn't know if I could, I really didn't. But I had to. It felt so impossible, but I pushed, willing my body to work with me, to be stronger than I thought it was. I pushed and felt something move and change, and when I was out of breath, I let the women hold me up, trusting them to keep me from collapsing. Every muscle in my body was shaking with exhaustion.

Eir's head disappeared beneath me. "Breathe deep, love. He's almost here. We're going to breathe in and out and then push one very last time. Can you do that?"

I shook my head, tears rolling down my cheeks.

"Yes, you can." Idunn pressed her forehead against mine. "He's so close. You want to meet him, don't you?"

I nodded, taking another deep, ragged breath.

"Alright. Now, Sigyn."

I gathered up everything I had left and pushed, screaming long and loud, nearly drowned out by the unified uproar in the other room. Something gave, a pressure released.

Eir moved quickly, and I couldn't see over the remaining swell of my belly. She sat up, a wet, pink bundle in her arms. Fulla helped sit me down and went to Eir's side with a new blanket, water, and cloth.

I couldn't believe how tiny he was. Only large enough to nestle in the crook of your arms. He was wet and red and purple, still connected to me until Fulla cut the cord. Eir wiped the slime from his face, and he howled.

The Goddess of Nothing At All

The kitchen broke out into cheers, dancing feet thumping on the floorboards. Someone had found a drum, and the singing began again. A welcoming song.

Eir cleaned the baby while Idunn and Fulla ran warm, damp cloths over my body. I was too tired, too disoriented to care that I was slumped over naked, being washed head to toe. Whatever part of me might want to fight for dignity was lost in the sweet surrender of it being over. And slowly, the dawning of the thought that steps away was the child I had brought into the world. Waiting for me.

They pulled a fresh nightgown over my head and helped me up. My legs were barely mine, and they almost had to drag me to the bed. But once I was in it…gods, had anything ever been so soft?

"You've had a good birth," Fulla said as she propped up pillows for me to lie against. "Very little tearing, and you're both in good health. I need you to stay still, though. I'm going to use some healing runes, just as a precaution."

I nodded. I knew all the rules. As she worked, I turned to Idunn who had settled in beside me, her legs curled under her. My eyes were fluttering, and I needed her to help keep me awake. "Thank you for being here."

She grabbed my hand and squeezed. "Of course I'm here. Where else would I be?"

"You'll be having nightmares about my nethers for the rest of your life." I did my best to crack a tired smile.

But she didn't bite. She just kissed my cheek and squeezed my hand again. "You did so well."

Eir approached the bed, the baby still crying, though softer than before. "He's ready for you."

I reached out, my tired limbs aching to hold my little boy. She passed him over carefully, cradling his delicate head. And there he was.

His eyes were shut tight, his face as wrinkly as an old man. A slick of flame-red hair sat on the crown of his head, and his skin was no longer the red-purple it had been when he'd come into the world. He was something between my bronze and Loki's snow. All ten toes, all ten fingers.

He was perfect.

Eir helped me to feed him. It took forever to figure the damn thing out, but it was just one of the troubles of motherhood, she said. Once he was fed and had dozed off to sleep, it was time for the others to come in.

Idunn went out and closed the door behind her. She was greeted with a cheer, which she quickly hushed. Her muffled voice barely made it through the door, and when she opened it again, the entirety of the party filed in, as well behaved as could be.

They gathered at the end of the bed, all eyes on the baby and me.

Frigg bowed her head. "He's beautiful."

"A little wrinkly, don't you think?" Thor laughed.

"And you're well?" Hod looked tired but seemed to have more wits about him than some of the others.

I nodded. "I'm alright. Very, very tired, but good. Thank you for being here."

Lofn came to my side and pushed my hair back from my face, tucking it behind my ear. "Loki will be so proud of you."

I blinked back tears as the crowd murmured their agreement, then fell into silence, not knowing what to say.

"Does he have a name?" Frey asked.

"He does." I looked down at him, his fists curled up next to my skin, mouth wide open as he dreamt. "His name is Váli Lokason."

CHAPTER THIRTY-SIX

"Adaptation is one of the things we do best.
We become what life requires of us."

—*Tales of Midgard, Volume 5*

Eight months passed.

Life found a new rhythm, mostly consisting of short sleeps and long days. I woke when Váli woke and slept when he slept. He refused to stay down for more than a few hours at a time, and so I cultivated shadows under my eyes and a yawn on my breath.

Even though I was always tired and adapting to his whims, trying to guess what he might need, even though he ran my life like a tiny, relentless drill sergeant, I loved him. I could watch him for hours, the way his toes curled or how his gaze wandered around the room. And as he got a little less tiny, week after week, month after month, he became more interesting to watch. He was figuring out his body and the world around him. His flame hair was an unruly tuft, the texture as wild as mine, and those emerald eyes grew more curious by the day. There was nothing he didn't want to touch, no bauble he didn't reach for, no hair he didn't want to pull.

It would have been a lonely eight months if it weren't for Idunn. She came nearly every day to check on us, even after things got easier. Sometimes she stayed up with Váli and sent me back to bed, other times she prepared lunch and made sure I ate. It was easier sometimes to tell myself I needed nothing. Váli needed so much. But I did need. And Idunn saved my life every day, making space for me where I could not.

The others came as well sometimes. Hod, Eyvindr, Bragi, Thor, even Lofn when she could. Their visits were briefer, but they brought food and laughter, two of the

205

things I needed most. Thor liked to cradle my boy in one arm, telling him tall tales and tickling him under his chin. There was something in his eyes when he held him, something that looked like a wish.

And so it went. Váli kept my mind occupied, gave me purpose, and most times, that was enough to keep the melancholy from sinking in. Some days were rays of sunshine, and other days, the sight of him brought me to tears, remembering where he had gotten those eyes.

Loki had been gone for more than a year. Maybe the Nornir had it wrong. Maybe he was never coming back. Maybe he was dead.

What would I tell my son when he had the words to ask why he had no Father?

Váli's eyes had fluttered for a while before he stopped fighting sleep. His lips were clamped shut, as if it took all his concentration to dream. I moved him slowly from my arms, loath to rustle him awake, and set him in his crib next to the bed.

A pile of clothing was waiting, so I worked my way through it, hanging and folding, letting my mind drift. I was halfway through when the front door opened.

I kept my voice low, heading toward the bedroom door. "Idunn? Did they have it this time? I think he'll start teething any day, and I—"

It wasn't Idunn.

Loki.

Wild wasn't the word for what he was. His hair was matted, and he'd grown a patchy beard, something I'd never seen on him before. His clothes were the same as when he'd left, but dirtier. And behind him was a gangly grey foal. With eight legs.

I drew closer, in too much shock to form words. He was here. Home. My hand reached for him without my permission, wanting to know if I was dreaming. The thick smell of moss and soil was real, and so was his chest beneath my fingertips. Real.

He *had* come home.

Loki set his hand over mine, such a delicate touch. "Sigyn."

I pushed his hand away. "Where the fuck have you been? *A year*, Loki. Do you have any idea what you put me through?"

"I know—"

"I don't think you do. You sat right there—" I pointed to the kitchen chairs " —and promised me that you'd be here. That you'd love us both and '*have this family together*.'" The words dripped sarcasm. "But you didn't. And I was a fucking *fool*, Loki, defending you to our friends, telling them how you didn't mean to be away, that you wouldn't do something like that. Because I'm an idiot. If it weren't for the Nornir, I'd have thought you were dead, and I don't know what's worse, thinking you're dead or knowing you're a liar."

"Sigyn, listen." His voice was hoarse, unsteady. "I didn't mean for this to happen. You deserve to be angry. But I promise, I didn't want to leave."

"But you did! You left me here! I trusted you!" The tears started, and I couldn't push them back in. I wanted him to see my anger, not how badly I'd missed him.

"Don't you think I wanted to be here? Don't you think I wanted—" Panic spread across his face. "Wait, where's the baby? It didn't...did something happen?"

I rolled my eyes, wrapping my arms around myself. "Nothing happened, and you don't just *get* to see him. Not after everything."

Loki's eyes widened, his mouth agape. "Him? Do we have a boy?"

"Don't change the subject! I'm not finished!"

The foal was picking up speed, spooked further by the fighting. It scampered from corner to corner, in and out of rooms, crashing into the cupboard, then the far end of the room, then the side of the table, nearly a blur. It was so *fast*. And it was tearing the house apart.

"*Skít*. Sleipnir, stop! Calm down!" Loki darted after it, attempting to scoop it up as it flew past him.

In the midst of the chaos, Váli's cries finally reached me. How long had I been screaming over him?

Loki's head whipped around, staring at the bedroom. He snatched up the foal as it passed again, enduring the kicking and thrashing of hooves against his ribs. The crying drew him toward the bedroom.

Part of me wanted to protest, to punish Loki for what he'd done, but I also knew what kind of mother that would make me.

I wanted so badly for Váli to have a father.

Loki rounded the bed, stroking the foal's neck until it calmed. Then he approached the crib and sat down on the floor beside it, peering at Váli. He turned to me, tears in the corners of his eyes. "Can I hold him?"

Something about the way he said it, the way he was asking permission to hold his own son, broke my heart. He was chipping away at my anger. "Alright."

He shuffled the foal in his arms and looked at me expectantly. "If I put him down, he'll run again."

I sat down on the floor, not too close, and held my hands out. Loki hefted the foal into my arms, and I nearly buckled under its weight. It was heavier than a sack of flour. But I settled it against my chest, stroking its mane, its eight thin legs wrapped up in each other.

Loki reached into the crib and picked up Váli. The movement made him open his eyes, and the crying stopped. There was someone new. Loki tucked him into his arms, rocking him and humming, tears slicking his cheeks.

"He's beautiful." He paused, his voice returning as a shamed whisper. "What did you name him?"

"Váli Lokason."

He stopped, staring down at the baby like someone had frozen him in place. There was something in his eyes I couldn't place. A tear fell, splashing on Váli's cheek. The baby squirmed at the sensation, and Loki stirred again, wiping the drop away with a gentle finger. "Hello, Váli. I loved you before I saw you."

I let him have his moment, and then the impatience became too much to bear. "Loki. Why do you have a horse?"

He didn't look at me. "It's...I don't know how to tell you."

"Fine. Where did you go?"

Váli slipped back into sleep, one hand shoved in his mouth. Loki kept watching him, saying nothing. Until he did. "I went to the wall, like I said I would. I thought if I distracted the builder's horse, it would be the easiest way to stop them. So, I shifted into a mare and tempted the horse into leaving. I thought that would be the end of it. Led it away and made it chase me until the deadline had passed." He took a long breath, struggling to finish the story. "The other horse was faster."

He looked at me as if I were supposed to intuit what he meant. I shrugged, growing frustrated. "And then what?"

Loki stretched his neck, delaying the answer. Perhaps putting together the right words. "Sleipnir is my son."

"Who—" But his eyes were locked on the foal in my arms. "Yggdrasil above."

"It takes nearly a year to give birth to a horse." Loki set Váli in his crib and sat back down, facing me. "I lived in the forest. Ate what horses eat. And I was alone the entire time, thinking of you and what you thought of me. Gave birth. Alone. And gods—" He stopped. Took a breath. Hid his face in his hands. "I was so afraid."

My mouth opened to speak, but I had no words. The dappled grey foal in my arms was nuzzling against my chest, its eyes a startling green.

"Say something, please."

The anger that had been building under my skin for the last twelve months evaporated. I had been ready for a hundred excuses, but not this. It had hurt, yes, but it didn't matter. These things couldn't compare.

"Loki, I am so sorry." I reached out and put a hand on his cheek. His face softened, and he nuzzled into my palm, resting his hand over mine. A tear ran down his cheek, but his lips were pulled back in the most hesitant smile.

"I missed you," he whispered against my skin. "Every day."

"If I had known…" I struggled for the words. "The Nornir had said I wouldn't find you. I wouldn't have been looking for a horse. Why didn't you just come home?"

"How?" He leaned against the bed, settling as close to me as he could. "What if I showed up here as a horse, and you didn't know it was me? And even if you did, how could I tell you what happened? I couldn't speak. What would I have said to you if I could?"

I moved closer to him, shifting Sleipnir in my arms. I leaned my head on his shoulder. "You couldn't have…just changed back?"

"It's not that simple, Sig. After…what happened, I stayed in that spot for days. Just hid from everything. And by the time I'd gathered the courage to come home, I knew something was wrong. I *wanted* to shift forms and come back; I knew the promises I was breaking. But this kind of thing doesn't come with rules. I don't know what happens when a mare turns back into a man with a horse in his womb. I thought I was better off late than dead."

I took a deep breath. I didn't know how to piece all these things together. Didn't know the right thing to say, to do. My mind could barely contain it all. "What can I do, Loki?"

Loki leaned his head against mine. "Nothing. This is enough." He pressed a kiss into my hair and chuckled. "Besides, a lifetime of sexual servitude will prepare you for anything."

I darted a glance at him. "That's not funny."

Reaching out to stroke the tip of Sleipnir's nose, a sad smile spread across his face. "Laughing hurts less."

I opened my mouth to speak just as a faint noise penetrated the walls. The force of it shook through me, rattling my bones. Loki stretched his jaw, shuddering. The Gjallarhorn.

We were being summoned.

CHAPTER THIRTY-SEVEN

"When you recognize ill will, speak out against ill will,
And grant no peace to your foes."

—*Hávamál 127*

Defending Loki at Gladsheim was a tradition I hadn't missed. When we arrived, half the gods were already seated on the dais. Idunn bolted out of her seat and down the steps. She flew towards Loki, her lips quivering, and he opened his arms to receive her. He held her against him, Váli snuggled between them in his cloth carrier.

"You're home. Finally." She leaned back to take in the state of him, still dishevelled and mossy, but before she could ask, Odin interrupted.

"Look who's returned at last. Perhaps you could tell us where you've been." Odin leaned forward, looking down on Loki as if examining a spot of dog shit on his boot.

Loki passed Idunn into my arms and stepped toward the dais, the baby still held tightly to his chest. His voice lacked the usual mirth, but none of the defiance. "I sabotaged the wall and kept it from being built, as you asked. The rest is none of your concern."

As if that would be enough to sate their curiosity.

"A lot happened while you were gone." Odin's tone didn't change, but his fingers were digging into the arms of his chair. "Idunn waited hand and foot on your wife. Thor brought her food and drink. Gods have served your family in your absence, and you owe them an explanation. Otherwise...I'm sure I can inspire some cooperation."

His words cracked open an old wound. Certain gods had gone out of their way for Váli and I in the last months. I'd gotten used to a certain measure of support and acceptance, but this was a stark reminder of how fragile that was. Could I have both the love of my family *and* my husband at the same time?

Loki laughed, shrill and biting. Váli let out a whimper, and his father finally broke his gaze with Odin in order to look down and coo at his little boy, letting the child grasp at his fingers. "Your methods haven't changed, *Grimnir*. I know who stepped up for my wife without needing to ask, and I'm grateful to them. And as sure as a bear shits in the woods, I know it wasn't *you*."

"You'll tell us. Now." Odin motioned to my brother.

Thor stepped forward, hammer in hand. "Please, Loki. Just do as he says." There was hesitation in his voice, but Thor was well trained. If Odin said swing, he would swing.

Loki looked at me, nodding to the baby in his arms. I moved to him and started to release the carrier, taking Váli from him. We both knew the price of keeping silent and the odds of walking away whole.

"Are you sure?" I had to hold Váli tightly. He was reaching for his father, his eyes watering.

Loki kissed his son's head. "What choice do we have?"

I nodded, and Loki let out a sharp whistle.

The steady clomping of horses echoed through the hall and into the chamber, but when they rounded the corner, there was only a single tiny foal with eight legs, a broken tether around his neck. Sleipnir dashed toward us, and Loki bent down to let him nuzzle into his side. A pair of Odin's guards stumbled into the chamber, winded from chasing a horse who couldn't be caught.

Odin was out of his seat and down the stairs like a child promised gifts, eager to get a closer look. "That thing moves like lightning! Where did you get it?"

"His name is Sleipnir." Slowly, Loki unravelled the story of how he'd lured the horse away from the wall. As he spoke, Idunn settled onto the floor to scratch behind Sleipnir's ears. The room listened in silence as Loki told them about the plan and the horse. His voice started faltering toward the end. He looked away as he told them—somewhat vaguely—of how the foal came to be.

Odin stared into Loki's face with his single intimidating eye, trying to judge the sincerity of his words. "You mean to tell me that you fucked a horse and gave birth to a foal?"

Loki's face was red, but whether in embarrassment or in anger, I wasn't sure. "Yes."

Odin burst into laughter, and the rest followed suit. Their mockery was deafening. I wanted to crawl into a corner and hide. I hadn't had five minutes alone with my husband to deal with any of this, and they were already laughing at us.

Sleipnir squirmed, pushing himself further into Idunn's arms, and bless her, she wiped away her tears and held him tighter. Then Váli began to cry.

Loki's lips pulled back into a snarl. He marched past Odin, pointing at Freya, who was bent over wheezing with laughter. "You!" he shouted, trying to be heard over the chaos. "You of all people? If it weren't for me, you'd be living out your days in a mountain keep, chained to a Jotun's bed!"

"No one can make me do anything, Liesmith." Freya sat back, waving a hand smugly. "I can save myself."

"But you *fucking didn't.*" Loki turned back to Odin. "The realms are still here because the gods still control the sun and moon. *I* did that. And it cost me things you can never repay, all for your stupid fucking wall!"

Odin was still doubled over, laughing so hard that a tear rolled from his eye. "I don't know, Loki. By the sounds of it, that horse really took you for a ride!"

The room roared again.

"Enough!" I was sick to death of this. "Why do you insist on shaming us? We've done everything you've asked, and every time, it rips us apart. None of this would've happened if you hadn't sent Loki off to do *your* dirty work! All for a choice *you* made. You can't keep doing this to us!"

Odin dried the tears from his eye, and with it, any mirth in his face. The godliness crept back into his features, the stern intensity that so many of us had always feared. "If it were solely up to me, you'd be locked in a room for safekeeping, and Loki would be strung up in the branches of Yggdrasil until his decaying body fell apart." He gestured to his wife, who sat up on the dais, stiff as a statue. "But Frigg has told me that would be unwise. So, it's best that you watch your step. You're in no place to make demands."

I swallowed hard. Váli was still wailing, face pressed into my chest. I couldn't make myself the target of anyone's rage, not with him at risk.

My father turned and climbed the steps once more, returning to recline on his throne. "But that horse…I could use a horse like that. After it's reared and old enough to be ridden, the stables will come for it. We could use that kind of speed. Maybe it'll be my mount." He waved his hand, dismissing us. "Go. We'll call for you when you're needed."

Loki's whole body arched forward as if he were one breath away from tearing out Odin's throat. "If you lay a hand on my son, it'll be the last thing you touch."

But all it elicited from Odin was a laugh. "You're not the first person to make that threat, nor will you be the last. Leave."

The piercing stares and the sudden, echoing quiet was more than I could bear. I put my hand on Loki's back and motioned for him to follow. He resisted at first, looking for something more to say, something more to push back with. And then he sighed, shoulders drooping. He collected Sleipnir from Idunn, squeezing her hand in silent gratitude. And we left, the judgement of the gods searing holes in our backs.

There had been many painful moments since Loki had disappeared, but I had gotten used to it. Having him under my roof again hurt in a different way. There was a quiet, an unease that had never been there before. Some of it was because the others had laughed us out of the room, that much I knew. And the rest was about so much that was left unsaid. A year's worth of horrors and loneliness to sort through.

I paid close attention to the things he did, the way he moved. The familiarity with which he opened the door, the casual way he kicked off his boots, letting them fall crooked on the floor. As if he had never left. He said nothing as he went to the kitchen and looked for something he couldn't find, eventually emerging with a cup. I'd moved them since he disappeared. He got himself some water, and his eyes fell on me as he drank. Watching me as I watched him.

He put the cup down and looked around, as if searching for something to say. "It's strange. It's almost like nothing has changed here."

"And yet so much has." I shifted Váli in my arms. "What now?"

Loki ducked his face towards his arm, sniffed, and made a face. "A bath, I think."

I followed him into the bathing room, Sleipnir on our heels. My insides were in knots. He was quiet, but he was still himself. Still Loki in the ways he moved and spoke. But everything inside me felt different. I had learned to live a different way, learned to be without him. And he was home, but I didn't know what to do with that or what it meant. How to sort through these complications. What had happened to him. The child he had brought home.

Bending over the bathtub, Loki tapped twice on the spout, whispering runes. The pipes rumbled and water rushed out, the tub heating the water as it pooled inside. Sleipnir butted his head into Loki's leg.

"Hey." He knelt down and nuzzled his face into the foal's mane. "None of that."

I set Váli into the basket near the hearth, where he busied himself eating his hand. I went to the window and stared out, the sun beginning to set.

After a moment, I heard the ruffle of heavy cloth hitting the floor. I glanced back. His cloak lay on the ground. He was stripping away the damp, dirty clothes, leaving them in a pile next to the tub. Sleipnir jumped and danced on top of them, a new toy to play with.

Loki dipped his fingers in the water. It must've passed the test, because he tapped the spout again, and the water stopped. He pulled at the tie that kept his trousers closed and I looked away, not sure if I was allowed to look anymore. He'd been gone so long that he felt like a foreign land.

I wasn't the woman he'd left. Who had *he* become in that time?

I listened to the moving water, the sound of him settling into the tub. When the water calmed, I dragged a stool close by and sat down. "I don't know what to say now."

"For once, that makes two of us." Loki dipped his head under the water and surfaced again. It barely shook any of the grime from him or the knots from his hair. He picked at the tangled strands with his fingers, trying to rip one piece from the grip of the other.

I took the hair out of his hands and reached for the soap. The one he liked best, that I'd kept by the bath even though he was gone.

And I said the sure thing that kept bubbling to the surface. "I did miss you."

The slightest hint of a smile appeared. "I know."

We sat in silence. I worked the horrific knots out of his hair while he lathered the grime from his body. The water was dark by the time he was done, and his skin was back to that snowy-white. He got up, splashing water out of the bath. His back was turned, so I watched him as he dried off. The curves and lines of him. There was such *confusion* in me. Old anger and deep sadness, relief and discomfort, all these things fighting for air.

He wrapped the towel around his waist, and his gaze went to Váli, asleep in his basket, then to Sleipnir, curled up on his dirty cloak. He stepped gingerly toward the basket. His fingers lingered above Váli as if he thought the boy might break if he touched him. At last, he picked him up, cradling him against his bare chest.

"Would you..." He didn't finish, but I understood. I bent down and hefted Sleipnir into my arms. He squirmed, then fell back asleep like an enormous snoring stone.

Loki shuffled around the room, readying for bed, barely taking his eyes off his son. I peeled back the bedsheets and placed Sleipnir on the mattress before changing into my nightdress. I slid into bed and Loki stood on his side, Váli in his arms, hesitating.

"If you want me to sleep in the other bed..."

"No. You belong here."

I'd spent so long without his heat to keep me warm through the night and his arms to wake up in. Having him next to me, in a place that had been a void for so long, felt surreal.

Loki put his hand on mine, pulling me out of my thoughts. He looked me in the eyes, holding my gaze. "What happened isn't just about me. You were here with no explanation. I know what people must have said. I'm sorry that it seemed like I left."

Staring into my lap, I sighed. "It was hard, Loki. You made all these promises, and it hurt to do this alone. I wanted you here, and I know why you couldn't be, and it's horrible. I just...I still feel this frustration. So many things keep being out of my reach.

It was devastating to think I couldn't have you either."

He squeezed my hand. "You're right. I wanted to be here, and if it were the other way around, I'd have been lost without you. I was, honestly. I didn't mean to hurt you—"

"It wasn't you—"

"Please. I know, we both know. But it doesn't mean you weren't hurting. Tell me what I can do."

I looked up at him. He was looking at me so intently, so full of love and concern. Asking what *I* needed in the face of all he had dealt with. I took a deep breath, searching for an answer. "Time, I think. I feel so much. And I want you here, I want you home with me. It's just so much. I need time to think things through, to come to terms with it. I'd moved on, in a way. Enough to keep living without you. And now you're back and I—Among other things I'm a step-mother to a horse. I need you to understand."

Loki looked down at Váli, nestled in the crook of his arm. "I understand. Our life together kept turning without me. I missed so much, and now I have to find a place to fit in all this." He craned his neck forward to catch my gaze, pushing a piece of hair away from my face so I could see him. "I know you're afraid to lose this, but I'm not going anywhere again, Sigyn. I can wait for you. We have an eternity to make this right."

CHAPTER THIRTY-EIGHT

"When he returned to Asgard, Loki came with an eight-legged foal in tow. That foal was named Sleipnir and was graciously gifted to the Allfather."

—*Asgard Historical Record, Volume 17*

L oki's presence changed everything. Life stopped being quite so difficult. I was no longer the only person to get up when Váli cried in the night, and sometimes I woke in the morning to find them curled up together in the spare bedroom, still asleep. He went to the market and did the laundry and cooked. Suddenly, I had some freedom. To sleep, to visit, to read.

He was everything he had promised he'd be.

And then there was Sleipnir. Neither one of us knew precisely what to do with a baby horse, and especially one that clearly had seidr in his veins. So we did what felt right. We cleared an unused room and made it into a stable, more or less. We tore a hole in the wall and made a barn door to the outside. Filled the room with hay and oats. I felt clueless, so I did the only thing I thought I could; I offered love and affection. Loki patiently trained him not to run indoors and to clomp at the door when he needed to go out.

And every once in a while, I caught the two of them whinnying and huffing, but when I asked Loki about it, he just blushed and asked me not to tell anyone.

It was good. Even with the lingering tension, the hesitation that was under every action between us, life became steady. Normal. We were confused together, tired together, struggling together. And that was all I had ever wanted.

I knocked on the door. "Are you almost done? I don't want to be late."

Loki had sequestered himself inside his old room nearly an hour ago and hadn't let me in since. "Don't come in! You're going to ruin it." The voice that came back seemed softer than usual. Or perhaps I was imagining it.

I shrugged and went back to the bedroom. It was Midsommerblot and the city was buzzing with anticipation. As per tradition, everyone had been allowed to sleep late in order to stay awake for the few hours of twilight we'd get around midnight before the sun rose again. The longest day of the year, a cause for celebration. There would be food and drink, dancing and costumes. And every year, I tried very hard to make the best of it. It was my favourite day, and also, the very worst.

My costume was a point of pride. I'd been wearing it every year for decades, adding new pieces, thinking that the next one would make it complete, but every year I managed to add or replace something. This time, I'd found a bone-white antler to secure in my hair, curling down against the side of my cheek. The dress was made of airy, black Vanir gossamer that trailed over my skin, brushing against the ground. A mantle of raven feathers hung over my chest. A waterfall of fine gold chains dangled from my hip, lying delicately over the length of my dress. It was perfect.

A pot of white clay sat open on the dresser, and I brought it to the mirror to finish the look. One thin line across my eyes, from temple to temple, and one thin line from the bottom of my lip and down my neck, into the curve between my breasts. Red for my lips, kohl under my eyes.

A jingle drew my attention as Sleipnir clomped around the side of the bed. We'd tied a pair of fake Valkyrie wings to his back, and the gold chains around his neck shook when he walked. Váli was wrapped in a coat trimmed in white fox fur, sitting on the floor, reaching for Sleipnir whenever he came close enough. We'd hired a sitter to stay with the children for the night, but we couldn't help ourselves.

A shadow appeared in the doorway. I turned, and my mouth fell open.

Loki had shifted into the shape of a woman. Her hair was loose over her shoulders, flowing freely. Peacock-blue silk draped over both her arms, leaving her shoulders bare and gifting me with a glimpse of the tops of her breasts. Gold plating covered her midriff like armour, the pieces connected but pliable as she walked. The silk gown ran to the floor, and on top of it was a train of peacock feathers that bloomed out from her waist and over her dress, trailing a few steps behind her.

She was grinning ear to ear, the emerald of her eyes shining, lined in deep, smoky kohl. "Well, what do you think?"

I cleared my throat and forced myself to say something. "Where did you get that?"

"I've had it since before the exile. It's been stuffed in a trunk for a century. I snuck it out to a tailor and had them touch it up. Do you like it?" Her hands ran along her waist, picking at the feathers nervously.

I barely registered moving closer. She was so beautiful, so stunning that I lost sight of the hesitation I'd been feeling for so long. All I could imagine was the taste of her lips and how she would look underneath when I tore the silk from her body.

But something held me back. The one open wound on my heart, that last worry that I would give myself back to her only to have something else get in our way. I took a deep breath. "You look amazing. I've never seen anything like it."

Loki's reaction was measured. Disappointed. She'd been holding her breath as I approached, and she released it all at once. She straightened one of the feathers in my mantle, the smile not reaching her eyes. "And you look ethereal, darling."

A knocking sounded at the door. The sitter. The moment shattered, both of us recoiling with the noise. I swallowed the feelings down. "We should go."

Loki swept her peacock-feather dress train up and hooked the end over her arm, something more reasonable to walk in, then she kissed the boys farewell as I went to the door. A few minutes later, we were out in the bustling streets.

Asgard was packed. Every market and side street were full, a good portion of them making their way upward, toward the Bifrost. The city was alive, vibrating with anticipation. Mead was flowing everywhere we looked, and each block was teeming with people dressed as half-beasts, crowded around casks of drink and cuts of meat ready for roasting, each group singing a different song.

"Happy Midsommerblot!" a young woman called as we passed. I called back, and every few minutes came another well-wisher.

Loki leaned toward me, her hair brushing my cheek. "Ymir's breath, I missed this."

"Did you still feel it in exile?"

"Yes, but it's not the same. Some years, I went down to Midgard to be in the middle of it. Other years, I just sat in my cabin with a bottle of wine and waited. There's nothing quite like feeling full of love and being absolutely alone."

Bitterness coiled in me. I wouldn't know. I'd never been given the chance. It was difficult for anyone to pray to me if they didn't know I existed.

We followed the masses to the edge of the city, where the land broke off and left nothing but sky. It was a clearing, and in the middle was an enormous unlit pyre, surrounded by people. It was made of freshly hewn wood, nearly as tall as two people, and in the spaces between the wood were offerings that the people of Asgard had made: trinkets, food, rune inscriptions, carvings.

The Goddess of Nothing At All

There were citizens of Asgard everywhere, but closest to the pyre were the gods. Like us, they wore intricate costumes. Odin was dressed as himself but with more gold. Freya had painted herself with runes and blood, and her brother was wearing bright Elven clothing. Most of them were gathered near the unlit pyre, but our people were at the cliff's edge.

Eyvindr waved to us as we approached, and then someone stepped in our way, shouldering Loki as she passed.

Loki opened her mouth to snap at them, but the anger turned to a patient seething as she realized it had been Heimdall. "Well. If it isn't the bridge troll. Don't you have something better to do than pick on ladies?"

Heimdall glared at her but didn't say a word. Instead, he looked at me. "Sister. Happy Midsommerblot."

Loki scoffed and strode away.

"Don't think you can act so callously towards Loki and expect me to return that with kindness." I stared him down.

"You could wait until the ritual starts and push him off the edge. No one would know." He actually smirked. "It would save us a lot of effort."

Aghast, I picked up my skirts and hurried after Loki.

"Ah, here she comes." Loki held her hand out to welcome me. She'd already been in the middle of conversation with Hod and Eyvindr, their arms linked as always.

"It's good to have you here. You're hardly in Valhalla anymore." Hod adjusted the collar of his formal tunic, the embroidery telling a story that wrapped around him like a scroll.

Loki smirked. "If I'm home with the boys, no one can have me beheaded."

"You could visit us. We can always use the company." Eyvindr was wearing what I had once made the mistake of referring to as a dress but was actually traditional clothing from his birthplace in Midgard. Long and red, he'd embroidered it himself, covering it with gold dragons and birds, patterns I'd never seen in Asgard.

"We will, I swear. It's not that we don't want to. We just use all our quiet hours to sleep," I laughed. Something caught my eye. "Oh. Look, it's starting."

Eyvindr gave Hod a pat on the arm. "Should I tell you what's happening?"

Hod smiled. "I'd like that."

Eyvindr spoke loud enough for us to hear, even though the story was only for Hod. I stared out over Midgard as he spoke. "The sun is almost gone. It won't be full dark, of course, not for many days. Midgard is below. The forests and plains and rocks seem like specks, hardly big enough to see. It's hard to see much, but there's one tiny light, so small it looks like a star. And now another. It's slow but there are fires starting all over Midgard. Some of them must be the size of houses."

"You always make it sound so beautiful." Hod gave him a look of appreciation.

"It is," Eyvindr said. "But it's just beginning. Do you feel it?"

Hod nodded.

A deep pit welled itself into my stomach. This was the worst part. Midsommar wasn't just the longest day of the year. It was a night of celebration in Midgard, a day for prayer and offerings. Sacrifices so numerous that the gods could feel it, worship made manifest. But I wasn't a god, not officially. I would watch everyone I loved be a part of something I couldn't touch, just like every year before. And then I pushed it down and pretended to be just as elated as everyone else, hoping that I could calm the ache.

I looked down the line of gods that had gathered at the edge of the realm. Each of them was reacting in turn as the invisible current slipped under their skin. Their faces still visible in the dying light, moved to tears and laughter, overcome by the rush.

Loki drew in a sharp breath as the feeling hit her. Her eyes fluttered, and she steadied herself. Her hand was on her chest, her breath coming faster now.

They were all the same, every god. Enveloped by this bliss. And there was nothing I could do to keep the misery from my face.

"Sigyn." Loki drew closer to me, leaning her head in for privacy. "What's wrong?"

My lips quivered, and I tried to hold the emotions back. "This isn't for me. I'm not a goddess."

Her lips parted and a sadness swept over her features. "Oh."

I swallowed, a tear running down my face. "It's fine. Maybe someday I'll know what it's like."

Loki took my hands and pulled them up against her chest. She must have been feeling the bliss of the worship; this was the boldest move she'd made since coming home. Then she tipped her forehead against mine, her lips so near, and asked, "Would you like me to show you?"

There was a moment of hesitation. I wanted to tell her no; I didn't need the pity. I wanted to hold on to that last shred of anger that had been protecting me, keeping me closed to her. But I wanted to know so badly.

I nodded.

A tiny smile played on her lips, and she closed her eyes. Her hands grew warm in mine, and a low hum filled my fingertips. It travelled up, making the hair on my arms stand on end. My heart started to flutter, and my vision blurred. Everything I'd been harbouring in my heart floated away. Then there was something else. Something faint.

Prayers.

I'm so lost.

I know I'm not like everyone else.

The Goddess of Nothing At All

You're the reason I know who I am.

I wish I could tell someone.

If only they would let me love him.

This isn't the life I wanted.

You saved me.

Thank you.

I gripped her hands tighter, overwhelmed by the emotion in their voices. The pain, the grief, the joy. The people of Midgard, reaching out to my Loki for guidance and shelter.

"Loki, I…" But there were no words.

She opened her eyes. "There aren't many of them, not like Thor or Odin have. But a century in exile is a lot of time to do a little bit of good. And they're enough for me."

Watching me for a moment, her eyes seemed a little out of focus. Dreamy. Then she let go of my hands and held my face in her palms. She kissed me, and the world melted away. The worship poured into me until I felt like I would float off, warm and happy, into the great unknown. It slowly settled into every bit of me, a coursing static, and I could feel her lips again, soft against mine. Feel the little ridge where the deepest scar was.

She still remembered how to kiss me to take my breath away.

She spoke against my mouth. "Sigyn, you must be a goddess, because I worship every inch of you. You're the only thing I'm devoted to. You're worth more to me than every sunrise, every sunset, every prayer. You're kind, and you love me, and I don't deserve any of it. You're the guiding star I see by. And I need you more than I'll ever need anything for the rest of my life. I'm here with you, and you'll never be alone again."

I'd started crying the moment her sermon began. I tried to wipe away the tears without smudging my face too badly. I said the only thing I could manage, an understatement. "You're sweet, Loki."

Her thumb brushed my cheek. "How do you feel?"

I pursed my lips, searching for the words. "Loved."

A smile grew on her face. "You'll always be loved."

I reached up and set my palm on her face. She leaned into it, and her expression relaxed. Like a weight had disappeared.

Odin's voice rose over the crowd. "If you fools don't come over here, we can't light this fire." He was waving the gods over, drawing them away from the ledge. "Let's go, come on, before someone falls off."

I wanted to stay where I was, wrapped in Loki's arms. I'd been keeping her a breath away for so long, and all I wanted was another kiss. But she took my hand and pulled me towards the pyre, and I had to let it go.

"None of you like my speeches, I know, but I'm the Allfather, and I'll say what I want." Odin's tone earned him a spattering of hearty laughter. "Each of you has a duty, a responsibility to maintain. Some more than others. You're the gods of War and Peace, Health and Hearth, Sex and Prosperity. The people of Midgard ask you for help, for the tools to help themselves, and for guidance. They pray to you, make sacrifices to you, in order to be served by you. In turn, we rely on their continued faith in us. Never forget that. Do right by them. Earn their loyalty. Now light the damn thing."

A cheer rose up. Loki nudged me, and we both summoned up a rune for wildfire and threw them onto the pyre along with the other gods who knew how. It lit quickly, heat bursting from flames that flickered in blood-red, yellow, violet, lavender, and teal. The offerings disappeared into the fire, and more of the static crackled forth from it, dancing across my skin.

Cheers rose up from the crowd. The formality was wearing away. I stared up at the fire, seeing it for the first time as the true gods saw it, dancing with wisps of something intangible, each trinket that caught releasing another curl of worship. The air was full of it.

Loki snared my attention away, her thumb stroking my face. Everything was so hazy. The fire danced in her eyes, and I was so very aware of how beautiful she was. How beautifully she'd fit back into our lives.

I ran my hand into her hair and pulled her down to kiss me. Her hands found my waist, and then one was travelling up my side, pressing me against her body. Startled, I gasped against her lips, and she made a noise that sent a thrill through me.

The warmth of the moment was swallowed by the slow thunder of drumming. With it came a low growl, the voice of a man as ancient as Asgard itself, far older than either of us. He'd been one of the first to join the gods in Valhalla. The jaw of a wolf obscured his face, draping down over his shoulders, the fire casting shadows over his beastly form. He growled in words no longer heard in Midgard, old and without time. The stomping of his feet cast dust into the air. The music changed, intensifying. Those in the crowd who knew the chant sang along with him, the sound thickening. The music and the air were the same, inescapable. Entrancing. Primitive.

This was the real celebration.

Loki took my hand and began to sway. The crowd around us was already moving, bodies writhing and dancing to the thick, dark drumming. I followed Loki, letting the music wash over me. Letting this bliss she'd given me guide my body.

I don't know how long we danced. The fire was never allowed to go out, wood piled on every time it got too dim. Shadows moved around us, antlers, teeth, feathers, all of us more animal than man. Her shoes discarded, Loki bounced on her heels to the beat of the drum, the feathers of her dress shimmering around her. I lost myself in the rhythm as it changed and became something new again and again, moving my feet as if they didn't belong to me. And then a hand on my shoulder brought me back.

It was Thor, his eyes as wide as a full moon. "Sigyn! Hey! I have to tell you something. Siggy-Sigyn. Sif is going to have a baby!"

I stopped dancing, and the world kept moving around me. I hugged him to keep my balance. "That's wonderful!"

"Congratulations, friend." Loki slapped him on the back. "Maybe a son for Váli to play with."

Thor laughed at nothing. "Maybe! I've always wanted a son." He kissed me on the head. "You wait *right* here; I'm coming back later. I have to tell the others!" He didn't wait for an answer, simply danced away to the next in line.

I sighed, wiping the sweat from my brow and falling easily into Loki's arms. Her lips trailed up my neck, and I giggled, unable to keep steady under her touch.

She kissed my earlobe. "I need you."

I clung to her, biting my lip. "Loki! You can't just say that."

"I don't plan to just *say* it." Her hand skimmed the side of my breast, and I nearly crumbled.

The smouldering look in her eyes was inviting, but the night was hardly over. "I've never left this early before."

Loki pulled me close, her hips against mine. "You've never had my tongue to look forward to."

She leaned in and kissed me, leaving me shivering.

A grin crept across my lips. "I suppose we really should check on the boys."

"We really should."

It was easy to slip away, back into the city. There were dozens of small pyres all over the place, each hosting a celebration in the ways of their Midgard communities. The city was full of music, the song of one gathering drowning out the next. Around one fire the people sang the hundred names of Odin: *Hangi, Grimnir, Ofnir, Sigfodr.* Another sang rune songs into the sky. It was more beautiful than I could put to words.

When we escaped the crowds and were back on our relatively peaceful path home, Loki linked her spare arm in mine. "Thor has it wrong."

I looked at her, still feeling drunk on all this worship. "Has what wrong?"

"A son is wonderful, but I've always wanted a daughter."

"That's sweet, but that's not what the Nornir gave you."

"No. But there's still time."

I stopped, bringing her to a halt as well. "Say what you mean, Loki."

She stumbled over her words, her silver tongue suddenly missing. "I know I wasn't here, and I can't go back and fix it, but I don't want that to have been my only chance. I want to try again. Another baby for our family. I would never let that happen again, and it's not for me to decide but—"

"Loki." I put my hand on her cheek. "Yes."

"Really?"

"I asked for time, and you gave it to me." I took a long breath, letting the words spill out before the walls came back up. "You love us, and you'd do anything for us. And I don't want that to be the only version of this story either. If you'd been here, we'd probably have already decided on another child. Don't you think?"

She nodded, saying nothing. Like she was afraid any sudden movement would ruin it.

"So then yes, Loki. I will have this family with you."

A relieved smile burst onto her face, and she looked away. "You must be out of your mind."

I took her hand and pulled her toward the house, the spark still alive and burning under my skin. "Aren't we all?"

We did our best to behave as we paid the sitter and let her leave. The boys were snug in their beds, and the moment the front door locked, Loki pressed me against the wood. She trailed soft kisses along my neck, up the curve of my jaw. With all the worship thrumming under my skin, my body was threatening to melt away under her touch.

But there were too many things in the way. She unclasped the peacock feather trail and let it fall to the floor next to the table. We took care with the baubles on each other's costumes, unclipping the antler from my hair and the gold plating from her waist. Each piece was delicately put aside until we were both down to the last bits of clothing. Then her hands were on me again.

I'd missed how she knew expertly where to touch me.

I pushed her up against the counter. Loki looked at me, startled yet very approving. My hands ran against the satin of her shift, pushing it up her thighs. She bit her lip, and her head lolled back. I slid my hands around to grip her ass, and she held onto the counter for balance. Kisses. One after the other, I trailed them down her neck. I bent, placing them on her satin-covered belly, down until I was on my knees in front of her, kissing her thighs.

She slid her fingers into my hair, and I looked up, a grin on my face, and whispered, "It's my turn to worship you."

CHAPTER THIRTY-NINE

"We don't get given a lot of second chances in this life. My advice? Don't fuck it up."

—*Tales of Midgard, Volume 18*

12 Months Later

" This is it," Eir said. "One more push."

I couldn't. I needed to catch my breath, to stop the pain. Tears streamed down my cheeks. Somehow, I'd forgotten how truly horrific childbirth had been.

Loki pressed kisses into my shoulder, holding my weight on one side, while Idunn held the other. "You can do this. You're so close, darling."

I nodded, unable to choke out anything to say. I took a deep breath and pushed. Just like when Váli was born, a celebration swelled on the other side of the door as my family waited on the birth of our new baby. They roared when I did, a war cry shared between us. I pushed and breathed and cried until I thought I would carry on like that forever. And then it was done.

Eir swept the baby up into her arms. She wiped the fluid from the child's face and waited. No one spoke. I'd never heard such silence in my life.

And then the baby cried.

I fell onto my bottom, laughing with relief.

"You did it." Loki took my head in his hands and kissed me. "You're incredible."

"I'm tired and disgusting." I wiped the sweat from my forehead with the back of my hand.

Idunn reached over and pulled a bowl of water closer. She gave me a smile and handed the bowl to Loki. "You're still incredible," she said.

While Idunn went to help Eir with the baby, Loki dabbed the cloth against my face.

I was so warm that the water felt chilled. He slid the cloth down my cheek, then along the line of my chin. He was so gentle that I could've fallen asleep while he worked.

A smirk slid its way onto his face. "So. How soon would you like to have another?"

I groaned, slapping at his hand with what little energy I could muster. "Never. I'm never letting you do this to me again."

He put on that look of false offence that he was so good at. "Me? Do this to you? These things take effort from both sides, you know. You were there; you should remember."

That was enough to make me crack a smile.

Idunn came back and helped Loki get me into bed. My eyes were already fluttering shut, but I wasn't going to sleep without seeing my baby. Eir came to the bed, the tiny bundle in her arms. "A boy. Congratulations."

She passed the baby to me, and I nearly sobbed just looking at him. He was wrapped up in a tiny blanket, his little round face sticking out. The wisp of hair on his head was brown, and his skin was like fresh snow.

Loki crawled into bed next to me, leaning over us. "He's so beautiful. And wrinkly."

I smiled up at Loki and shuffled the baby into his arms. "Hold his head. Like this, yes."

Loki held him so gently as if he were glass and might shatter with a breath. I laid myself down in the sheets, my head against his hip, and drifted off to sleep to the sweet murmur of Loki making promises to our son.

We took our time finding a name for him. We'd thought of many, but now that he was here, none of them seemed to fit. We poured over books and listed the names of distant relatives, hoping to spark an idea. Eventually, I found myself staring into his tiny face, hoping he might reveal his own name if I looked hard enough.

And then on the fifth day, we found it, tucked in the back of some ancient textbook. Narvi Lokason was named by his father, surrounded by our family and friends. The evening was full of food and drink and merriment, made more beautiful in light of past pains. Loki took in every moment as if nothing else in the world had brought him more joy. And perhaps nothing had.

It would be a lie to say that everything fell into place after that. It didn't. We struggled with having two young boys and a spirited pony. Narvi fussed through the day in a way Váli never had. He had an incessant need for physical affection, which was endearing when it was suitable and irritating when other things demanded our attention. And demand they did.

The Goddess of Nothing At All

Sleipnir needed to be groomed and tended and taken out to run and frolic. He could be destructive if the mood suited him, and it took a great deal of expertise from one of Asgard's best horse breeders to teach Sleipnir the things a horse should know. His needs were entirely different from the boys.

Váli couldn't be set within arm's length of his brother, otherwise he'd begin to yank at his hair or limbs. Loki insisted he was just curious about his new brother, but I saw the mischievous look in Váli's eyes. He couldn't even stand to let Narvi sleep. In order to keep the peace, we often kept the baby strapped to one of our chests, where he could coo and drool away from the reach of Váli's eager hands.

They slept in shifts, meaning we did as well. Sometimes, Loki would wake for the day as I was crawling into bed. I stopped living by the illusion that the day began with the sun and instead let the beginning of the day come whenever it had to. Often, it began at noon and ended in the early hours of the morning. More than once, we came close to putting the boys to sleep with runes, but thank the Nornir Idunn was happy to step in before it came to it.

One day passed and then the next and the next. One morning I looked up, and summer was gone. By the time we got the boys sleeping on the same schedule, the snow had begun again.

Despite the exhaustion and the bickering that seemed to occur daily, Loki thrived as a father. He tended to the boys and to Sleipnir, giving them as much of his time as he could stand to give. He still ran errands and attended to the odd task from Odin and took up the wolf's share of the cooking. Best of all, his busy schedule kept him from getting himself into any real trouble. Sure, he was caught cheating at a round of dice or committing some small prank in Valhalla, but I was thankful that he'd stopped coming home bleeding.

And me? I was tired, but I was happy.

Other babies were conceived and born as ours grew; Sif gave birth to a girl named Thrud, and Thor's mistress surprised everyone by showing up in Asgard with a pair of half-grown boys, Magni and Módi. That left Thor sleeping in our spare bedroom for a while. Freya, never one to be left behind, had twin girls, Hnoss and Gersemi. Time passed as the children grew up together, though some gods were happier about that than others. Narvi was too sweet for their war games, and Váli sent most of them home crying. Not to mention a nearly full-grown horse to keep them company.

I blinked, and four years disappeared in front of my eyes. Gone, just like that.

CHAPTER FORTY

"Very little about Loki was peaceful for long. More often than not, he was causing trouble, picking fights over something as small as a game of dice. Like he couldn't help himself."

—*God of Lies Revealed*

I peeked out the window. The boys were shrieking, chasing each other in front of our hall. Narvi had a handful of worms that Váli wanted nothing to do with. Sleipnir was lying on the grass, curled up more like a cat than a horse, keeping subtle watch over his brothers. Six years for a boy was enough for games and make-believe, but for a horse…He was nearly grown, and sometimes wiser than the rest of us.

Movement in the distance caught my eye. Loki was home, walking with the kind of easy confidence that had captured my attention all those years ago.

Gods, I loved him.

The boys ran to their father, stumbling over each other for affection. He bent down and hoisted them into his arms, attempting to haul them both to the front door.

"Father, look. These worms have no eyes." Narvi held them up for him to see.

Loki made a face, craning his neck away from them. "No, I suppose they don't."

Váli knocked Narvi's hand to the side and the worms spilt onto the ground. "Hey!" Narvi pouted as Loki shook the stray worms from his leg.

"The worms are gross like you." Váli stuck his tongue out at his brother.

"You're gross, not me." The two started to swat at each other.

"Ymir's breath, enough! You're both gross." Loki flashed them a grin and a wink that made them laugh. "Where's your mother?" His boots hit the wooden deck, slow and heavy with the weight of his sons.

I opened the door. "Right here. Where are my carrots?"

Loki wiggled his hip. "In the satchel. Come boys, down you go." He set them down and they ran off, back outside. He huffed and stretched out his back. "I'm afraid I'm becoming an old man."

I took the carrots from him and leaned in to give him a long kiss. "Let's hope not. I still need your stamina for a few more years."

"Is that so?" He laughed and pulled a few other necessities from his bag, then leaned on the counter. His gaze went to the window, and the smile faded. He stared at the boys as they played, his thoughts a thousand miles away.

I wrapped my arms around his waist, pressing my cheek into his back. "What's wrong?"

He straightened and pulled me into his arms. "I think we should enlist Váli in the einherjar."

"What?" I pulled back, straining his hold on me. "Why?"

"He's wild, Sig. Some of the tricks he plays are innocent enough; I still haven't found that left boot. But yesterday I caught him trying to talk Narvi into climbing onto the roof."

"Why didn't you tell me?" I pried his hands away and went to the door, watching Váli.

"Because I hate to see you worry. I already spoke to Tyr, and he'll train Váli himself if we want it."

"He's only six, Loki!" I gestured out the door, unable to believe what I was hearing. "You can't send him off to learn to fight and kill at *six*."

"He's been picking at his brother since Narvi was born."

I scoffed. "Váli loves Narvi. He punched Magni in the nose last week for calling Narvi a Jotun frost-skin."

Loki bristled at the slur. "Exactly, Sig. When do we say enough is enough? When he breaks someone's arm?" He sat at the table, elbows on his knees, watching me. "Nothing we've done has worked. This isn't a bit of mischief anymore. He needs a firmer hand. I don't know what else to do."

The comment stirred my anger. "Are you saying we didn't do a good enough job?"

"I'm saying that we need help." Loki looked me in the eyes. "He's reckless, and everyone knows it. He won't have the freedom to make the same mistakes as other children. You hear what they call him now. Tricksterson. Little Liesmith. If he keeps this up, the names will stick. We need to stem it now."

I let his words settle. "You're afraid he'll turn out like you."

His gaze fell away, and he didn't answer.

"And what if this isn't what *he* wants?"

"If he learns the discipline it takes to be an einherjar, it could open up a lot of opportunities for him. It might be the single best chance I can give him. You have no title for him to hide under, and there's no place here for another God of Lies."

His words stung. "I've been a little preoccupied, raising three children."

He stood immediately and pulled me into his arms. "I'm sorry. You know that's not what I mean by it."

I sighed into his chest, still irritated. "I know."

A wailing cry rose from outside. Narvi was sitting on the ground, his hair covered in dirt, pulling a worm out of his mouth. Váli stood above him, his hands caked in brown, the slyest grin on his face.

Loki just looked at me.

"Fine."

Einherjar trained in sleet and snow and rain and fog. Ragnarok wouldn't care about the weather, Tyr told them. They'd just have to learn to like it.

But I was no einherji, and I didn't feel compelled to like it at all. Váli had been training for weeks, and there had been more rain than sun in that time. One of us had braved it every day to go with him. Neither Loki nor I trusted the city enough to send him alone, especially with a name like Lokason. But Loki was off on some errand to Vanaheim, and it was still my turn to be wet.

The dirt had turned to mud by the time the boys and I arrived, water dripping from our cloaks. Tyr was waiting for him, a wooden sword in his hand. The God of War was no small man. He wore a stern scowl under a fierce black beard and moustache, with harsh eyes and crisp, leathery skin from spending all his days outside, training the einherjar. He wore the same simple armour as everyone else, though his was dyed a dark blue.

Váli had been terrified of Tyr since the beginning, but so was everyone else. I reminded him that he was lucky to be given such devoted attention by a God of War. Any einherjar would kill for that kind of training. What he didn't know was how much Loki had bargained in gold, mead, and future favours to Tyr in order to fix that position for him. Hopefully, he'd warm up to his new mentor.

"Don't be a fool, boy." Tyr's voice was cold and deep. Wood cracked against wood, Tyr parrying the boy's strike. "Where's your skill? Have you held a sword before?"

Váli huffed and puffed, his knuckles white around the wooden sword hilt. "I'm not stupid."

"Show me." Tyr braced his feet in the mud.

The Goddess of Nothing At All

Watching them from the other side of the fence made me restless. I'd spent my youth out here, watching the einherjar hack each other to pieces, but it was another thing for it to be *my* boy. But Váli was surprising everyone. Every day, he walked away frustrated and enraged and covered in dirt, and each morning he sprang out of bed looking for more. He had passion for it and worked like he had something to prove.

Váli leapt forward, putting all his force behind a single blow. Tyr sidestepped his attack and slapped him on the back with his wooden sword. Váli swung back around, his boots slipping in the mud, screaming a tiny battle cry.

"Come on brother! You can do it!" Narvi hopped up and down on the rail of the fence, fist in the air. He turned to look at me. "I don't want to be a warrior."

I ruffled his hair. "You don't have to be."

"But if I could do seidr, no one could stop me and Váli. We'd be hero brothers."

Seidr. A thing Loki and I had talked about endlessly. When the time came, when one of them asked, what would we say? Loki was torn. He didn't want his sons living with what he did. But how could we tell them no if they wanted to learn? How could we explain what had happened to their father and forbid them to practice what he so openly flaunted?

"Narvi, sweetheart." I made sure I had his attention before continuing. "I'm going to ask you something very important, and I want you to think about it before you answer. Sometimes people say mean things about our family, and sometimes those things are about your father and how he uses seidr. You understand that, yes?"

He nodded, a stillness settling over him as he listened.

"If you decide to learn seidr, they may say some really mean things about you too." I pushed a piece of his hair behind his ear. "I love you dearly, and I don't want people to have more reasons to be cruel to you."

There was pain in his eyes as he shrugged. "It's alright, Mama. I'm used to it."

That casual acceptance… My heart broke. What life was I giving him if cruelty was the norm? No matter how safe I made my home for him, I would never be able to control what happened outside of it. My chest felt hollowed out. What point was there to being a mother if I couldn't protect him?

Perhaps the best I could do was help him protect himself.

I sighed. "If I said yes, would you use it responsibly? You could never use it against anyone else unless it's to keep yourself safe."

Narvi nodded so hard I feared his head might pop off. "Pinky swear."

"Alright, if you're sure." I would smooth it over with Loki later. He of all people should understand. "Do you want your father to teach you?"

Narvi shook his head. "No. Well, maybe sometimes. I don't want to hurt anyone.

I'd be a healer like you."

Tears welled up in my eyes. I sniffed, blinking them away. "We could start tomorrow, if that's what you'd like."

"Start what?" The familiar voice came from behind me, bringing a smile to my lips.

"Father, you're back!" Narvi turned around on the fence and reached out. Loki stepped into his embrace and hoisted him into his arms. His father ruffled his hair, knocking his hood down. "Mother's going to teach me to be a healer, cause she's the best völva in Asgard."

"Is that so?" Loki turned his smile at me, and I warmed inside. Rain dripped down his uncovered head, soaking into the thickly braided tail in his hair. He flipped Narvi over, holding him upside down by his ankles. "I thought you said *I* was the best völva in Asgard."

"You're both the best!" Narvi laughed, his long hair sweeping against the ground as he hung helpless.

I poked the boy in the belly. "And you're sucking up to your father."

Loki righted Narvi and set him back on the fence. He kissed me on the cheek. "Have I missed anything? Is he a righteous hero yet?"

I put my arm around him. "It's incredible. He's too tired to raid the kitchen most nights and too busy to convince Narvi to do anything foolish."

Loki chuckled. "Give it time. He'll be back to his old tricks once it starts getting easier."

"The apple doesn't fall far from Yggdrasil, my love." I took his face in my hands, pulling him down for a kiss. I'd missed his lips.

"No?" Loki asked between kisses. "I don't know—what you mean." His tongue snuck a tiny lick onto the edge of my lip, stirring my body.

Narvi made a retching noise. "You're gross."

A battle cry came from the other side of the fence. We looked up in time to see Váli slide into the mud, his sword gone from his hand. Tyr pinned him to the ground with his foot, his wooden blade at the boy's throat.

"Again," Tyr commanded.

Váli looked toward us. The anger turned to surprise. "Father!"

Tyr removed his boot from his chest and hauled Váli up by his collar, setting him on his feet. "Drink something and be ready to fight again. Go."

Váli scooped up his sword and rushed toward us, covered head to toe in mud. He vaulted himself over the fence and sat down next to Narvi. "Did you see me? I'm getting good."

"You'll soon be mightier than the Allfather himself." Loki pinched Váli's chin, wiping the mud from the boy's cheeks.

"Father," Váli moaned, wriggling away from his grip. "Leave me alone."

"What's this? Too good to be seen with your old man? What a shame; I'll have to make a scene." Despite all the mud, Loki pulled Váli in for a dramatic hug, lifting him off the fence. "You're just so adorable, my precious little man. How I love you!"

"Ah, just who I was looking for."

We all turned. Odin strode toward us, rain slicking down his decorative gold and grey armour. One of his ravens cawed from his shoulder and flew off as he approached.

Loki put Váli on his feet and stepped in front of him. "*Grimnir.* What brings you out in this weather?"

Odin put his hands on the fence and gazed out at all his einherjar, fighting and slicking the ground with each other's blood. "I hear the horse is ready for riding."

Loki tensed beside me, and as he stepped forward, I pressed a hand against his chest, holding him back. "Father, you can't take Sleipnir. He's not just a horse."

"You're right, he's not." Odin turned his head, so he could see us all with that one eye. "He's faster than any other beast in our stables and faster than those cats Freya keeps. Sleipnir could be the difference between victory and failure in the battles to come. There are bandits on the roads to Vanaheim again. We could get news to the city without a chance of it being intercepted. Who can shoot an arrow as fast as Sleipnir can run?"

"No." Loki's chest heaved under my hand, deep, tempered breaths. "You can't just take my son as your pack horse. I won't let you."

"Yeah!" Váli leapt out from behind Loki's legs, his wooden sword pointed at Odin. "That's my brother. He stays with us!"

"Váli, no." I knelt down to look him in the eyes, brushing a loose curl from his face. "We're going to handle this, alright? Don't you worry. Go back to your training, please." I hauled him up and over the fence, nudging him forward. He looked back, considering his options, then trudged back to Tyr.

I pulled Narvi into my arms, eyes on Odin. "There has to be another way."

"Sleipnir is coming with me, one way or the other. If you bring him willingly, your family will have full access to the stables whenever you want it. If you don't, you'll never be let within an acre of him. I would think this would be an easy choice."

"You can't have him." Loki's knife was at Odin's throat before I could stop it, the point tucked under his chin. "I could kill you here, and the realms would be better for it."

The skirmishing quieted around us, all eyes on the would-be killers of Odin, an army of einherjar inching closer. Narvi whimpered, tucking his head into my chest. I held him to me, as tightly as I could. "Loki."

"You pretend to be almighty and benevolent, but you and I know better, don't we? We know the blood you've soaked me in." Loki pushed the dagger up, and Odin raised his head, a drop of red running down the blade. "Why don't we end it right now, hmm? What do you think, *Hangi?*"

Odin's smile was as dark and foreboding as I'd ever seen it. "Would you kill me in front of your children? Their grandfather? Then they'd really know who you are."

"I'd be doing them a favour," Loki hissed.

The einherjar were nearly at the fence. Tyr had his hands clenched on Váli's shoulders, like a warning. I reached out, heart racing, and put my hand on Loki. "Don't."

He didn't turn to look at me. "Why not, Sig? What good has he ever done you? You have no idea what he's done. What he hides."

"If you kill him," I spoke slowly, trying to keep him calm, "they'll kill us all."

"What price will you pay today, Loki?" The blade bit into Odin as he spoke, but he barely winced. "One horse or your whole family?"

"You're a fucking *monster.*"

"Loki. Please, let's go home."

I could barely breathe. Loki was going to do it. We were going to die. It was now or never.

I took a deep breath and whispered a light variant on the sleep runes.

The blade fell away as his arm sagged, Loki's whole body slumping into half slumber. He stumbled back, and I put my arm out to catch him. He blinked heavily, trying to fight what I'd done.

Narvi reached up from my arms and put his hands on Loki's cheeks. Both of their eyes were red with tears. "It's alright, Father. We'll go home now, okay?"

Loki nodded, kissing one of Narvi's hands. "We'll go home." He met my eyes and straightened out, doing a horrible job of looking composed. "Come on, Váli." He waved the boy over.

Tyr let go of his shoulders, and Váli darted to us, hopping nimbly up the fence, and reached for Loki's hand. They took the first wobbling steps forward, away from Odin. Narvi and I followed, the four of us pushing past the seething wall of einherjar that had gathered around us.

CHAPTER FORTY-ONE

"Sleipnir is a horse of the very highest order.
He can run faster than anything else, and
because he is best, he belongs to Odin."

—*Gylfaginning*

I put the boys to bed alone. They had questions. So many questions. Narvi had heard Odin accuse his father of horrors, and Váli had heard nothing. And I had no idea what I didn't know, but I did the best I could.

Your father isn't a bad man.

The world is hard, Narvi. Sometimes, we have to kill.

Everyone in the realms makes mistakes and bad choices. Me. Your father. Odin.

Everything will be fine. I promise.

When they finally dozed off, I closed the door behind them and tiptoed across the hall. Sleipnir's door was closed, so I put my ear to the wood and listened.

Singing, soft and low.

I cracked open the door, peeking through the slit. The floor was covered in straw, and a mattress had been laid out in the corner. That was where Sleipnir was curled up, right next to Loki.

There was a half-empty bottle of Elven wine next to Loki's leg, and he was sitting with his back against the wall, eyes closed, neck craned up at the ceiling. Singing. Crying.

Not daring to move, I watched. His hand ran blindly across Sleipnir's neck, back and forth, as the horse slept. Had he told him?

The song ended, and Loki was quiet for a moment before he opened his eyes to find me crying along with him from the doorway. He sniffed and wiped his face on his

235

sleeve. "How long have you been there?"

"I didn't see a thing." I gave him a weak smile, and he returned it, appreciative of the little lie. "Can I join you?"

He nodded, turning his attention back to Sleipnir, parting the front of his mane into three sections. I sat down next to him, silent as he nimbly worked the hair into a thick braid.

"It's strange, being something's mother." He moved on to a new braid, working his way from Sleipnir's ear down his neck. "When you were pregnant with Váli, I knew I would do anything for him. I'd kill for him and for Narvi. But I feel it in my bones with Sleipnir. I almost did today."

I nodded. I couldn't really be angry with him. I knew what I would have done.

"I don't think I have a choice." A sob hitched in his throat. He took a deep breath and waited until it subsided. "If I just *give him* to Odin, he'll be ridden like some common horse. I could take him to the forest and let him run far from here. A free life. But it would kill me to never see him again."

I leaned against his shoulder, resting my head on his. "Sleipnir isn't like other horses, Loki. He knows his way home, and he'd never agree to stay away. And if he did? What happens when a poacher stumbles on him? They'd find a way to catch him and sell him to the highest bidder."

Loki pursed his lips at the thought, thumbing the corner of Sleipnir's ear. The room grew quiet. The night that spilt in through the open window was full of small noises, the chirping of insects and the scurrying of animals. The wind rustled the leaves outside, and it was very nearly peaceful.

When Loki finally spoke, his voice was nothing but a whisper. "Then what can I do?"

"I think you know."

He said nothing.

"There are good things about the stables. He'll have the chance to be part of something bigger. He'll be infamous, the fastest and the bravest. If he's revered by Odin, the stable hands will have no choice but to be kind to him, and if any of them step out of line, you're right here to remind them of their place."

He looked back at me, a sad smile on his lips. "You make it sound like some grand adventure."

I ran my hand through his hair, smiling back. "Isn't it, though? It's not what you wanted, and it's too early, I know. But we let our children go eventually. Leaving could mean a lot for him. He may even meet another beautiful horse to love."

Loki exhaled, long and slow, staring up at the ceiling. "If it's the right thing to do, why does it hurt so much?" He burst into sobs, and I pulled him toward me, holding him against my chest as he cried.

We stayed up all night, watching Sleipnir sleep. We finished the bottle of wine and held each other as the dark turned to light. The door creaked open, and Narvi's sleepy face peered in. I waved him over, and Váli followed behind. They came to us, still half asleep, and curled up next to Sleipnir. He stirred and shook his head, and his eyes told me he knew something wasn't right.

And so, Loki told the children what had to happen. There were tears and screams and frustration. Váli stormed out, while Narvi found a corner to withdraw into. There was so much devastation. And none of it was fair, none of it was okay. But Sleipnir wasn't mine the way he was Loki's, and I put my feelings aside. I needed to be the rock this time.

Sleipnir protested in the ways he could, stomping around the room, pushing at the door to the outside. Wanting to run from it. Loki pressed his tear-slicked face into Sleipnir's nose and spoke in that strange way that only they knew. I don't know what happened, what was said. But after a while, Sleipnir conceded. Had Loki told him the consequences of staying? What Odin might do? Part of me wanted to know, and the rest of me couldn't bear it. It was so cruel to make him choose.

We brushed Sleipnir's coat, and Loki finished his mane. Narvi told him stories as he nuzzled into his shoulder. Even Váli came back when he was ready.

Then we opened the door to the outside and walked Sleipnir out. He nudged Loki with his nose, and Loki sighed. "Don't make this harder, please. Be brave, for me."

Sleipnir huffed and shuffled his hooves, pushing Loki out of the way. The pain on Loki's face broke my heart.

The boys made to follow, and I stopped them. "You can visit him soon, I promise. But your father needs to do this alone." And so, we watched them walk away, then went inside to pick at a solemn breakfast.

Loki didn't return until long after sundown. He had blood on his knuckles. When I pressed him for an answer, all he said was, "The stable hands fell out of line. They won't again."

CHAPTER FORTY-TWO

"From his weapons in open country
a man must move less than a pace;
no man knows for sure, when he's out on a trip,
when he might have need of his spear."

—*Hávamál 38*

We managed to avoid Valhalla quite consistently for months. Loki refused to be caught in the same room as Odin, and I wasn't about to argue with that logic. But when Yule rolled around, neither of us could justify making the boys miss out because we wanted to lick our wounds. We could handle one night. For them.

Valhalla was adorned with Yule decorations. Entire fir trees had been hewn and brought inside to cover in delicate chains and baubles of gold and silver. Einherjar ran about with the hides of rams and goats on their backs, the horns sitting on their heads like crowns. The city had been full of them as well, singing as they danced and drank their way from home to home. I couldn't help but smile; Loki and I had both pranced around in this hall in our own times, with horned costumes on our heads and Yule cake in our bellies. Now our sons would do the same.

"Alright, go on you two." Loki nudged Narvi forward, tipping his goat hide to the side a little. Narvi straightened it and hesitated, looking back up at his father. Then Váli pulled on his arm and dragged him out to play. They ran off together and joined the crowd, dancing to the drums.

Loki and I made our way up to our seats at the head table. There were eyes on us, and I didn't much like it. I groaned. "Can't we just get drunk and kiss in the shadows like our first Yule together?"

He laughed. "I don't think you remember that the same way I do. You spent the whole time looking around corners because you were terrified of getting caught."

"And yet I'd still find it more relaxing than this."

Loki nodded to the empty centre seat as we approached. "It seems old *Grimnir* is missing."

Our chairs were still there, practically growing cobwebs from disuse. We sat down. "I'm sure he'll be along. Odin would never miss an opportunity to act the hero."

And as if I'd summoned him with the very thought, Odin strode through the doors. He was decked in a cloak of blood-red fabric, trimmed with white fox fur, his usual Yule attire. But beside him was a young man, too pale and tall to be anything but Jotun.

Loki looked from the young man and back to me, a question on his face. I shook my head. I'd never seen him before.

The room caught sight of them, and the mirth gradually changed to whispers and curiosity. The attention was just what Odin was after. He made his way to his seat at the head table.

"Another day of good Yule to you all! I hope the last five have treated you kindly. You'll have drunk my casks dry by the time it comes to an end, and we'll all be better for it. But I see you have a question for me, yes? *Who is the boy?*"

Loki leaned over and whispered in my ear. "Your father is so *dramatic*."

Odin slung his arm around the young man's shoulder. He couldn't have been more than 16. There was something about him that reminded me of stone, the hard lines of his face and the apparent inability for joy. He was already taller than the Allfather and was well on his way to becoming a giant among the Aesir.

"As you all well know, it has been foretold that I will die at the battle of Ragnarok." The crowd began to boo and cry out, but Odin hushed them. "Yes, be that as it may, it's still true. But I have good news. Another prophecy has spoken of this young man. His name is Vidar, and he is my son. When I meet my fate, he will be the one to kill the wolf and avenge me."

The einherjar cheered, raising their horns and toasting their god. But the head table was silent. I looked, scanning their reactions. It seemed no one knew how to take the news of a new brother, except for Baldur, who had the presence of mind to set his hand on his mother's shoulder. Frigg stared into the crowd, stoic and distant as ever.

"Come now. Let's celebrate his arrival properly." Odin beckoned a man forward with a wave of his hand. He approached the head table with a bleating goat struggling against a leash, which he passed to Odin.

The Allfather stroked its head, trying to keep it docile, but we all knew what was coming. "Each Yule we celebrate the end of the long, sunless days and the slow return of summer. We praise Sol and Mani, the gods who have sacrificed their place among us to pull the sun and moon across the sky and keep them safe from the wolves who wish to destroy them. We give thanks to Yggdrasil as She holds the realms together. May She continue to shade us in our time of need." He turned to Vidar and held the goat out for him to take. "It's your first Yule among the gods, and you should do the honours."

Loki leaned in to whisper in my ear, biting sarcasm on his voice. "I see we're honouring Jotnar half-breeds now. Wonder what that would've been like."

I spotted the boys rushing toward the head table. I hauled Váli up onto my lap, and Narvi crawled onto Loki's. It was the perfect excuse to look away. I'd never liked that part of Yule. Ritual sacrifice never helped me keep my meal down. Thankfully, it was over quickly.

And then, the same as every year before, Odin walked in front of the table and blessed the gods one by one. When he reached us, he dipped his fingers in the bowl and touched them to my forehead, drawing a line of blood down to the tip of my nose. It was still hot. He did the same to Loki, and each of the boys.

"Good to see you both. Finally." Odin gave us a crooked smile. "I've been waiting for you to come back."

"Why?" Loki's voice was smooth and venomous. "So you can take something else from us?"

"I've heard your visits to the stables have been going well." Odin looked at his grandchildren. Váli was sneering openly, but Narvi loved the attention. "Do you like to visit Sleipnir?"

Narvi nodded. "He has pretty armour now, and he's always shiny."

"You see," Odin said, turning his attention to us. "We take good care of him. But Loki, I want to make up for all this. It's been trying on you, I'm sure. As soon as the thaw comes, let's go down to Midgard together. Visit the people, get reacquainted. All this pettiness can't go on until Ragnarok."

Loki raised an eyebrow. "You'd know better than I would."

Odin's unnerving smile widened, his teeth showing. "I doubt that."

"Father." I nodded down the table. "I think the others are waiting for their blessings."

"Of course. We'll make the plans another time." And then he moved on.

Once he was out of earshot, Loki turned his head to me, wide-eyed. "What was that?"

I struggled for words. "I don't like it."

"Father." Narvi tugged at Loki's shirt. "I'm hungry."

"Alright, let's get your bellies full. Your mother and I will discuss things later, hmm? Away from prying ears, isn't that right?" Loki pinched Narvi's sides, tickling him until he burst into laughter and toppled his own goat horns off.

And he was right. We were going to talk about it.

CHAPTER FORTY-THREE

*"If you've a friend you fully trust, visit them often, for weeds
and wild long grass will grow on a track that lies untrodden."*

—*Hávamál 119*

The trip came up at breakfast the next day. And again at the market the week after. And again after we'd shared a bottle of wine and a roll in the sheets. It came up for months. By the time the thaw came, we still had no answer. You didn't just say no to Odin.

So, when the invitation came, Loki packed his satchel, aired out his bedroll, and left.

The front door opened and shut again.

"Hello?" I sat up in the bath, sloshing water over the edge. The boys were already asleep, and Váli was stealthier than that when he was raiding the pantry.

"It's just me."

Relief settled over me. Loki was home. I wrung out my hair and got out of the bath to dry off. He came to me though, opening the door and raising an entertained eyebrow at my nakedness.

"This is definitely my favourite way to be welcomed." He took my face in his hands and kissed me, but I startled at the touch.

"Loki!" I pulled his hands away and turned them palms up. They were calloused and damaged, pink around the wounds like they'd been on the mend for a few days. "What happened?"

His shoulders sagged. "It was a lousy trip."

I gathered all my supplies and made him come to the table. As he told me the

242

story, I cleaned and sterilized the wounds. He clearly had still learned nothing from me. If he had, he'd have healed them himself.

"—but your father likes to keep up the facade that we're wandering beggars, so we had no rations on us and not a village in sight. But there was a herd of oxen, and I said I wasn't going another step without something to eat—Ah that burns! Easy darling— And it was a hel of a time sneaking up on it and slitting its throat, but we made a fire and started to cook it. But Sig, it doesn't cook! The fire wasn't even hot! And as we're at each other's throats over whose fault it was, this *eagle* starts laughing from the trees!"

"An eagle?" I turned my focus to runes to heal his hands, trying to listen at the same time.

"An eagle. It was huge! Three times as big as it should've been. And it says to us, 'If you promise me a piece of that ox, I'll let it cook.' And we were starving so of course we said yes. And the godsforsaken eagle takes all but one back leg for itself! I was so fucking angry that I started beating it with a tree branch, trying to get our food back, and the fucking eagle grabs the stick and flies off with me attached! I couldn't let go because I thought I'd break every bone in my body when I landed. It took me so high that there was hardly any air to breathe. Eventually, it got tired of me and put me back down, but my hands were a mess for days from hanging onto that stick."

But they weren't anymore. The runes had healed the damage, and other than a few faint silver lines, they looked as good as new.

"I don't understand how you can end up in trouble no matter where you go, Loki. I'm surprised you don't get attacked by wolves every time you go to the market."

He tilted his head just slightly and bit his lip. "You wouldn't know what to do with yourself if I were boring." He leaned in and stole a kiss. "It's half the appeal."

I pursed my lips, trying not to smile. "You smell like you haven't had a bath in two weeks."

"Well why don't we do something about that?"

"Aunt Idunn, can I have some? I'm hungry."

Narvi huddled closer to Idunn, curling against her side. She gave him a warm smile. "Of course."

A leg of rabbit was put on the grill for Narvi, and a few extras besides. Idunn had invited us to her home for an evening around the fire. The weather had been cool, the kind of damp cold that gets under your skin and into your bones, but tucked together around the roaring flame—in natural reds and oranges for once—and wrapped in our cloaks, we were cosy.

Loki, Váli, and I were working on the soup, and there was still half a pot left.

Váli was sitting on the ground, as close to the fire as he could get without singeing his eyebrows off. I tipped my bowl to my lips, savouring the hot broth. Loki's eye caught mine, and we both smiled. This was good. Things were so very good.

"Will Bragi come home soon?" Loki stood and took another ladle of soup from the pot. I pulled his cloak back, concerned the whole thing might catch fire. He only smirked.

"Not yet. He was talking about making a trip as far north as he could go. He doesn't make a trip like that very often, so he takes his time coming back." Idunn flipped the meat on the grill with a pair of iron tongs, and the grease sizzled and popped in the fire.

"Are you afraid when Uncle Bragi isn't home?" Váli eyed her curiously.

"Oh no," she chuckled. "I'm not afraid. I have all my very best friends here when my husband isn't home. They take care of me."

"Aunt Sif yells at Uncle Thor sometimes when he talks about going away. Do you get angry too?"

I gave Váli a tap on the shoulder. He didn't always know when to stop asking questions.

But it didn't bother Idunn in the slightest. "It doesn't matter how long or how often Bragi is away. He brings his poetry to the world, and that's part of what he is. I knew that when I married him. Even though I miss him, I know he'll always come back to me. I trust him, and I'm not jealous that he loves his work. But everyone is different. We all need a different kind of love."

"When either your Father or I go away, we feel the same as Idunn. We miss each other, but we trust each other too," I said. Váli turned to me. "If your father were gone as often as Bragi, I'd be very sad, but that's why Idunn and Bragi are perfect for each other. They love each other the way they are."

Váli let out a satisfied harrumph and turned back to the fire, mulling it over.

When the food was ready, Idunn deposited a piece in each of our bowls, and we gingerly picked at the fire-hot meat. Afterward came hot mulled apple cider, which we drank until our bellies were bursting and our bodies were warm. The boys played dice games near the fire while the adults talked, and eventually, the two of them were slumped up against the wooden benches, half asleep.

Loki leaned over and planted a kiss on my cheek. "I'll bring the boys home. You should stay."

I tilted my head. "Are you sure?"

"Of course. I insist."

I glanced down at Váli and Narvi again, then to Idunn. They clawed at my heart in both directions. "But what if you need me to get them to sleep?"

"I won't. I'll carry Narvi, and when was the last time Váli let us put him to bed? It's a perfect night. Be here." He slid a thumb over my chin.

"Alright." I kissed him and stood to help him gather Narvi up. Váli was still awake enough to walk. I ruffled his hair. "Be good for your father."

"Yes, Mother. Goodnight."

I watched them for a moment as they walked down the path and disappeared into the trees. My beautiful little family. When I turned back, Idunn had pulled a bottle of spiced mead from between the wooden benches. She waggled an eyebrow, all mischief in her eyes.

We pulled a blanket over our shoulders and sat snuggled against each other, the fire crackling in front of us, and passed the bottle back and forth, not bothering to dirty a cup.

She turned to look at me, all seriousness. "It's been a while since we could talk alone. So just between us…are you still happy?"

The question took me aback. "Of course I am. Why would you ask that?"

The easy look returned. "Because I've been married for a long time. We'll never have children, so that's different from you, but I do know about love. It comes in waves. Some days you like them a little less, some days a little more. Sometimes you have to choose to love them, and sometimes they make it so hard to. Sometimes you just don't feel *in love*. Are you still in love with Loki?"

I blushed. "I am today. I know what you mean, though. When he came back with Sleipnir, I wasn't. I loved him, but it was buried beneath all that pain. It feels horrible to admit it, but there are days that he aggravates me so much, I want to rip my hair out and send him away. But it always goes away, and things get better, and I feel in love again. It's not what the love stories talk about. Not at all."

"No, it never is." Idunn took another drink. "Sometimes, when Bragi stays away too long, I do get angry. Not each time, not predictably. But he and I aren't perfect. No one is. You just choose love, every time. That's all you can do."

I took the bottle from her and drank. "You give good advice."

She wrapped her arm around my shoulder. "That's because I love you. You and Loki and Narvi and Váli. You're my family, and I want to know you're okay."

"We are. I promise. And I love you too. You're the only person in the entire world silly enough to still be friends with us after all this."

She laughed, her voice a light song on the air. "I couldn't imagine being anywhere else. Now, let's finish up the rest of this food before the wine goes straight to our heads."

CHAPTER FORTY-FOUR

*"No matter where I am in the realms, no matter how far
from home, I carry you with me. Every night spent telling
stories around the fire, I imagine you there with me. Always."*

—*Bragi - Letter to Idunn*

I dunn became hard to track down after that. When Loki and I decided to brave
Valhalla, she never appeared. When I went to her home, she was never there. After
a few failed attempts, I started slipping notes under her door, asking her to come
around, but she never did.

Two weeks passed like that. I couldn't remember the last time I'd spent two weeks
without her.

"I'm really worried, Loki. It's not like her."

"I don't know, Sig." Loki was busy making lunch, slices of bread set out to go with
venison stew. "You said yourself that she admitted to not *always* loving that Bragi was
away. Could she have gone down to Midgard to join him?"

I leaned on the counter and peered out the window. It was never like her to go far.
She had apples to harvest, even in winter—god-like trees do what they like—and she
wasn't an enthusiastic adventurer like Bragi. Never had been. But maybe.

"And no one else seems worried." He gave the stew a stir. "If something was
wrong, Odin of all people should know."

"I don't think anyone cares about her the way we do." I turned from the window,
staring at the swirls in the wooden countertop.

"What? Of course they do. Who wouldn't like her?"

"She's important and her apples keep the gods healthy, but it doesn't mean they want to spend time with her. Be her friend. She's too kind for some of them. Outside of his own interests, I don't think my father would notice she was alive."

Loki came to me, pressing a kiss into the top of my head. "I think you're being a bit pessimistic."

"Maybe." I folded my arms over my chest, holding back the worried tears. Loki was completely calm. Why was I so sure something was wrong?

He took my face in his hands. "Of course, you're worried. It wasn't very thoughtful of her to leave without saying anything, wherever she went. Do you want me to go look? I can go right now if it'll ease your mind."

I nodded. "Would you? I can't stop thinking about it."

He kissed my forehead. "Anything for you, my love."

When he came back, he had a piece of parchment in his hand. He gave it to me. A note.

> *Dearest visitor. I've taken a small break from my duties and*
> *gone down to enjoy Midgard with my husband. We'll return*
> *together shortly. See you soon!*

> *Idunn*

"I found it on the ground near the steps. It must have been pinned to the door, but the wind pulled it off." He rubbed my shoulder. "Nothing to worry about."

I took my first deep breath since he'd gone to look. She was safe. She was fine. I'd been bothered over nothing. I wiped the tears from my cheeks, and it was then that I noticed the lines in the backs of my hands. The age of them.

Loki saw me looking and fished something from the inside pocket of his cloak. A pair of golden apples. "I may have also stolen these. I'm too vain to wait for her to come back."

I laughed. I was too, though it wasn't a pretty thing to admit. So, we cut the apples into slices and called the boys to lunch. We ate them with the stew, the four of us laughing and warm and content, bits of life breathing back into Loki and me. The weight of worry finally missing from my chest.

And then Bragi came home. Idunn wasn't with him.

CHAPTER FORTY-FIVE

"Eternal youth isn't something I intend to share with the nine realms. Bind the apples to Bragi's new wife and make sure no one but her can pick them. Maybe the responsibility will make her stop crying."

—*Odin - Note to Freya*

"They were all shoved under the door." Bragi threw the handful of notes on the table, nearly all of them from me. "There's rotted food and milk so old I could barely recognize it. How long has she been gone?"

"Weeks." I choked back the bile rising in my throat. "We thought she was with you. The note on the door said she'd gone to Midgard."

Bragi pushed his hair back, eyes wide and wild. "What note?"

Loki tapped his fingers on his arm, lips pursed. "When I went to the cabin, there was a note from Idunn that said she'd gone to find you."

"Why would she do that?" There was an edge to his voice, panic sitting so close to the surface. "She'd have no idea what town I was in or what road I'd be on. She's not a diviner! It makes no sense. How could you have believed that?"

"I had nothing else to go by, Bragi. I—"

Bragi slammed his fist on the table, knocking over a pile of my books. I couldn't ever remember him getting angry. "You know her better than this, Sigyn! I don't understand how you could let her be missing for *weeks* and think nothing was wrong."

I swallowed. "Eight weeks."

"*Eight?*" He turned and walked a few paces away, his palms over his face. "She could be dead, Sigyn."

"Hey now." Loki put his arm around my back. "Before you decide one of us is a murderer, why don't we start by looking for her?"

"You should have been looking for her already!" Bragi picked up the closest thing to him, a wooden plate, and threw it across the room. There were tears in Bragi's eyes, and his breathing was ragged. Beneath all the anger, he was petrified. "When I leave, I trust that Idunn is safe because she has people around who love her. I thought she'd be safe with you, and you didn't even notice she was gone."

"That's not fair. We thought—"

"Alright, that's enough." Loki went to the door and pulled on his boots. "Standing here solves nothing—"

"Well, it's suited everyone just fine for the last *two fucking months*!" Bragi tipped his head back and took a deep breath. All this anger that he never used, but that he had surely learned from our family, just like I had. Then the desperation started to bleed through. "I don't understand. I just don't. How could no one be looking for her?"

Because like me, we'd all been wrapped up in our own lives, too busy to look any harder at the lie. I'd just accepted it. Loki had brought home that note. A note I hadn't seen. If she hadn't written it, who had?

I looked up, watching Loki as he secured his cloak around his shoulders.

"I'll tell Hod to keep the boys at study until we come get them, all night if needed. Then I'll go to Odin and have them put out the word." Loki turned to me. "Sig, try Freya. Maybe she can help."

I nodded, doubts writhing in my mind. I shook myself and closed the door on them. There wasn't time for misguided worry.

Bragi opened the door and stood for a moment, the wind whipping at his cloak. "You had better find her. I swear, if she's missing and—" His voice cracked. "She is everything to me." Then he disappeared out the door and into the city.

When Loki had told me about the note, I'd been relieved. I'd taken it at face value, and so had the rest of the gods. It was inconvenient, growing older as we all waited for Idunn to come back, but there was nothing to be done. Without the apples, they'd been growing a little weaker every day. We'd all trusted that she'd be back soon.

Freya was no exception. As I explained to her what I knew, I noticed the furrows in her forehead and around her mouth. The way her eyes seemed to sit in hollows. She seemed thinner. She hadn't worn metal armour in weeks, keeping only to dresses and thin leather when the occasion arose.

No one had asked Loki and I why we hadn't faded quite as quickly. Silver had sprung up at the roots of his hair, and the lines in both our faces had begun to deepen.

It wouldn't be long before time caught up with us as well. But Loki had warned me not to tell anyone about the extra apples. Jealousy makes good gods do very bad things.

"So all this time—" Freya's voice was raspy, like she'd been smoking a pipe all her life. "—the note was a fake, and she's missing? You lied?"

"No! We don't know where she is. She might have gone looking for Bragi and never found him. The note said—"

"And where did the note come from exactly?"

"I found it on her cabin door." This lie, the only one, was necessary. No matter what doubts had crept into my mind, I wasn't going to implicate Loki in this. It was too dangerous, and I knew that I had to be wrong. "It was her writing."

"Runes aren't hard to fake, Sigyn. It's all straight lines and hard angles. I could write like her if I tried." Freya opened the door to her student's study hall and peeked in. They were still quiet. She closed it. "There's been nothing found on the way to Midgard?"

I shook my head. "We've just started looking."

She sighed and stared at her hands. The skin was thinner, boney edges poking through. "I won't do the divination myself. I can only do so much in a day now. I get tired. It'll be good practice for the students."

I followed Freya into the room. The heads of eight female völur looked up, eyes on their goddess, books in their laps.

"Stop what you're doing. We're putting you to the test. Go fetch the rabbits."

Their response was immediate. They were up and gone, and when they returned a few minutes later, it was without their red silk robes and each with a rabbit wriggling in their arms.

Freya and I sat as the eight of them made their sacrifices and painted the blood on their skin. Their lips moved quietly, in near unison. Some slipped under more quickly than others. And then they were all gone, their bodies sitting perfectly still, waiting for their souls to return.

It was more interesting watching them come back. They returned to themselves slowly, one by one. Sometimes, it would be minutes between, sometimes only seconds. No one spoke until all eight were back in the room.

"Where is Idunn?" Freya asked.

"In the north," said one.

"In a cold keep," said another.

"Jotunheim."

"Is she alive?" Freya's knuckles were white, worrying one hand into the other.

"The Nornir say yes," said a woman in the back.

The rest echoed her response; *yes, yes.*

I couldn't hold my tongue. "Did they tell you what happened to her?"

"A forest."

"An eagle, bigger than a bear. It took her."

"To Jotunheim."

"Someone was with her. Someone betrayed her."

I sat forward, a knife twisting in my gut. "Who? Who betrayed her?"

There was silence and a look of shame on their faces. Only one dared to speak up. "It's difficult to know. There were enchantments to keep them from being seen. But..." She took a deep breath. "They had red hair. Tall. This much I know."

Freya stiffened beside me, drawing a breath so long that I thought her lungs might burst. She exhaled. "Thank you, ladies. Well done. Take your things and go."

She said nothing as she waited for them to wrap themselves in their robes and take their bloody messes with them. When the room was empty, there was still a spatter of red across the stone.

"I know what you think—"

"Do you?" Freya snapped. "Because right now, I'm wondering if you helped him."

"He hasn't done anything! Why would he? Idunn is a sister to him."

Freya straightened out, her body cracking and popping. "He doesn't love anyone more than he loves himself." She pried the door open and left it open for me to follow.

We found Loki where he said he'd be, with Odin.

There were others there as well. Baldur, Thor, Sif, Bragi, Frey. They'd all seen better days. Though the gods sat on the Gladsheim thrones, they looked small. Lacking.

The only ones standing at the foot of the dais were Loki and—

"Heimdall?" Freya approached him, arms crossed over her chest, doing her best to look stern and strong, despite the frailty that had seeped into her bones. "If you're here, we must really be in trouble."

"You are." Heimdall's skin was leathery, too many centuries of sun catching up with him. He grinned at Freya, and I thought the corners of his lips might rip. "But more than anything, I wanted to be here to witness this."

"Witness what?" Odin shifted in his seat, straightening his clothing. They were too large for him. Frigg had grown skeleton-thin, but he had shrunk in all manners, a thin old man playing at being a god.

Loki pulled me aside as Freya started to tell them what she'd seen. "You look worried. Are you alright?" He brushed back a loose piece of my hair.

I shook my head and pulled him close, stealing a kiss as an excuse to speak quietly. "Loki, you need to go. I know it wasn't you, but she thinks it was. You should hide until this is all over and—"

"—and they saw a tall man with red hair helping an enormous eagle take Idunn."

I turned, keeping myself between them and my husband. "What you're saying is insane. As if you can identify someone on their hair alone. Ymir's breath, *Thor* has red hair. Who says it wasn't him?"

Freya had already taken the dagger from her belt. "Whoever it was cloaked themselves with seidr. Do you think Thor is intelligent enough to think of that, let alone cast the runes?"

"Wait just a minute!" Thor straightened in his chair. "How dare you."

"Shut up." Odin kept his eye on Loki. "And what do you say for yourself, Liesmith?"

"I didn't do it." He didn't elaborate, so I did.

"Idunn is part of our family. She's our best friend and an aunt to our children. Why would we do anything to jeopardize her safety?" I was seething. I was tired of being the target of their accusations.

"Except that he did." All eyes went to Heimdall, the silence echoing through the room. "I've sworn to keep my nose out of things, just to watch and to intervene only when I absolutely must. But you've already found your answer. It was him."

Loki stepped from around me, heading for Heimdall. "You're insane—"

"I saw you. First in Midgard with Odin. You went to camp, and the eagle stole your dinner, yes? Hoisted you into the air and left your hands in shreds when he let you back down. But how did you get free, Loki? Tell them what you bargained."

I pulled Loki back, trying to keep him from ripping Heimdall's face off. He was snarling. "I didn't bargain anything. He dropped me and I lived."

"That eagle had you in the clouds." Odin rose from his seat and came down the steps, leaning on his spear for support. "If it had wanted you dead, it would have dropped you from there. But it didn't. It came back down. What did you bargain, Loki?"

After dragging his hand down his face, Loki groaned. "I can't make you believe me, but that's the truth. There's nothing else to tell!"

"Guards." Odin waved a hand, and his einherjar were on Loki in an instant, tearing him from my grasp. He started to whisper runes until one clasped his jaw shut. They bound his hands. He tried, but in all honesty, Loki was older than he once was. Slower. Weaker. And the einherjar were an unageing snapshot in time, solid ghosts. They won before it had started.

By the time I'd summoned up a crackle of lightning in my hand, another of the guards had found his way behind me. He struck me in the head, and the world dimmed. I fell to the floor, everything spinning.

I blinked the haze back as they pulled me up and covered my mouth.

The Goddess of Nothing At All

What a pair we were: husband and wife, bound and gagged.

Heimdall smiled as the guards pinned Loki to his knees. "I saw you with Idunn that last day. You'd slathered yourself in enchantments to keep our prying eyes off, but I knew. It was you, clear as day. You laughed and joked and charmed her and took her out to the woods across from the city. Took her to your old cabin. And after a while, the eagle came. It flew into the clearing and left with Idunn, flying toward Jotunheim." He crouched down in front of Loki. "I'm not sure what's more disgusting. That you're capable of that kind of betrayal, or that you passed by the market for fresh lamb shanks on the way home."

No. That sinking feeling I'd been fighting all day. That thing I hadn't wanted to believe, couldn't bear to look at.

He couldn't.

He would never.

Odin waved a hand. "Let him speak."

The guard let go of Loki's jaw, and immediately the runes were on Loki's lips. Odin snapped his finger, and the guard punched Loki in the face, stopping the whispers before they could become anything.

"You have one chance to defend yourself, Liesmith. Use it wisely." Odin shifted his feet, leaning on the spear as if it were the only thing keeping him standing.

"Husband." Frigg tiptoed down the stairs, her frost blue skirts dragging behind her like mist. "This day changes everything."

Odin looked at her. "Stay the course? Or turn away?"

Frigg turned her head and looked directly into my eyes. "This must happen."

Panic streaked through my body. I struggled against the man holding me, trying to pry my wrists from his grasp. What must happen?

"Who is the eagle?" Odin asked, trying to mask the weakness in his voice.

"It was trying to kill me, so I never thought to ask—" Loki's grin was met with a fist. He spat blood across the stone. "Oh, I have missed this. Nothing like a good beating to get a man all riled up."

"Please." Bragi approached Odin and put a gentle hand on his shoulder. "We're wasting time. My wife is alive, out there somewhere, waiting for us." Tears rolled down his cheeks.

Freya turned to Loki. "He's right; let's speed this up. Tell me exactly where Idunn is, or I'll burn you alive."

Loki licked the blood from his lips. "I can't tell you what I don't know."

"You always know something." She held out her hand a few inches from his chest. As she whispered, a crackle of lightning jumped from finger to finger as if it were alive.

And then she pressed it against his chest.

Loki seized against her touch, back arched and eyes wide. He choked on the scream, the sound bubbling in his throat. The current ran under his skin, charring his clothing at the point of contact.

I swung my legs, trying to hit the guard, strike him where it counts. He cursed at me and pulled my jaw back, trying to snap my head from my neck. I had to stand on my toes to dull the ache.

Freya pulled her hand away, and Loki's seizing slowed. He slumped forward, panting and shaking. Between pained breaths, he managed a single word. "Again."

Her hand connected, and the smell of burnt hair was overwhelming. She was killing him, and she was smiling while she did it.

She released him. "Who is the eagle?"

"Go to Hel." He spat on her boots.

The strength was leaving Freya. She wobbled, moving her feet to stand more steadily. Normally, she could keep something like this up for a few hours, but already she was dwindling. And so she looked at me.

"I suppose if you won't talk, perhaps your wife will. Forever your dutiful accomplice." She reached toward me, her sparking fingertips hovering over my chest.

"No." Loki stopped struggling. The defiance in his eyes turned cold, empty. "She doesn't know anything. Not now, not ever."

Freya wiggled her fingers over my skin for him to see. "Then tell me what you know."

Pressing my toes into the floor was the most I could do, trying to force the guard and I back, away from her hand. He was an einherji; he'd be fine. I wasn't ready to die, not at her hands, and especially when we were innocent.

"The eagle is Thjazi of Jotunheim. He took Idunn." Loki stared at the floor, his head drooped in resignation.

No.

"Thjazi." Odin turned over the news, scratching his coarse, brittle beard.

The guard made the mistake of loosening his grip on my neck. I drove my heel into his foot and startled him. One bite into his hand had him threatening me again, until Freya intervened.

"Let her go. It'll be more entertaining."

The guard did as he was told.

"Tell them you don't know anything, Loki." But he wouldn't look at me. "Loki!"

He took a deep breath and then another. "I'm sorry."

"No." Tears welled in my eyes. It was hard to breathe, like someone was squeezing my lungs. "You wouldn't. Not this! Loki, please!"

"I had to."

A scream ripped through me. I pushed him, toppling him backwards and out of the grip of the guards. On top of him. Pounding my fist into his chest. He tried to catch my arms, but I fought him, thrashing and clawing until there was blood under my nails and he had stopped trying. He didn't hit me back, but he'd already ripped my heart out. He smelled like burnt flesh and shame, and I wanted him to feel the gaping, searing hole he'd torn in me.

He took each blow until the fight went out of me. Then I sat on his chest and sobbed. "How could you?"

Someone pulled me away, aiming to hold me down, but it wasn't needed. I was a void. People spoke around me, but the words couldn't hold my attention. I tried to grasp for something that made sense. Idunn was gone. My husband had orchestrated it all. Had he ever loved her? Did he love me? Did he know how to love? I couldn't linger on any single thought. Any one of them was enough to shatter me.

"Loki's collusion with a known enemy of Asgard shouldn't surprise any of you." Freya made her way up to her seat, one wary step at a time. She nearly collapsed into it. "He should be killed now."

"What about my wife?" Bragi had slunk down onto the stairs, head in hands.

"Justice can wait," Frigg said. "We must bring Idunn home before we're all too withered and weak to do anything about it."

"It's nearly true already." Thor's words slurred as one of the help filled his horn with dark ale. His arms had become loose bags of sagging skin, the muscle wasted away. "I can hardly lift Mjolnir anymore. Look at me. What good am I to the realms like this?"

"You're better off sober than drunk," Odin chided. "If any of the gods appear at Thjazi's doorstep looking like a bag of bones, they'll laugh us out of Jotunheim. Someone else has to go."

I shook myself and sat up. "I'll go."

"Why?" Bragi's voice was weak at first, but rage flooded in. "Why would I ever let you near her again when you *let* this happen—"

"Quiet," Odin cut Bragi off before another fight could begin. "Perhaps, Sigyn, but what chance does a healer stand against an entire keep? What could you possibly do?" Odin glanced up and stared at the wall, lost in thought. He stayed like that for a very long time. One of his ravens cawed from its perch above his head. The second was missing. "Sorry. I've lost my place. What was I saying? Yes, yes, Thjazi. No, someone else must go."

"I can do it," I pleaded. "I'm not just a healer. I've been studying disenchanting and elemental seidr for *years*, and I know enough—"

"I'll get her." Loki pushed himself upward, gritting his teeth as he moved his bruised and charred body. He wiped his face with his sleeve, smearing the blood that dripped from his nose. "No one needs to sacrifice anything for me."

"What makes you think you'll live long enough?" Freya snapped, leaning forward in her seat.

Loki struggled to his feet. "Unlike you, I can manage more than a few runes before I need to lie down, and if I have your falcon cloak, I'll have enough seidr to get into the keep and bring Idunn home."

Odin looked to Frigg.

She nodded. "It's the clearest path ahead of us."

"Fine," Odin said. "Freya, have someone get the cloak from your keep."

Freya shook her head. "I don't trust him."

"No one in this hall is stupid enough to trust him." Odin looked down at Loki. "But if you deceive us. If you don't return here with Idunn, your children will be punished in your place."

"What?" I strode towards Odin, blocked at the last moment by a guard. "You can't. They haven't done anything!"

"Neither has Idunn." Bragi rose to his feet and came within a breath of me. "I've never wanted violence for anyone, but for you? You and this *piece of shit* you call a husband? I would see you bled out and hung from the rafters for what you've done to her."

I glanced around the hall, eyes travelling from face to face. Sullen, angry, horrified. I hadn't known. Hadn't touched her.

But that didn't matter.

I had no allies left in the room.

CHAPTER FORTY-SIX

*"Valuing his own life over all others, Loki made a deal
with Thjazi. He brought Idunn and her apples to the
woods. The eagle swept her away, dooming the gods to a
slow, inevitable decay."*

—*Asgard Historical Record, Volume 24*

It took them three hours by horseback to fetch the falcon cloak. Three hours in
which I sat on the cold stone floor, legs pulled up to my chest, waiting. Mulling
over every moment of our life together, looking for the smallest inconsistencies, the
tiniest cracks.

Loki was a liar. I wasn't stupid. I had just always thought that I was different
somehow. Exempt. That my love for him, that all the years of devotion, would protect
me from it. Because how can you be so heart-shatteringly in love with someone and
still burn them to cinders?

The guards were hovering over Loki. His hands had been bound behind him and
they'd stuffed a gag in his mouth to keep him from whispering. And for the first time, I
felt no pity for him.

I felt for Bragi, though. Sif had gone to sit with him, her arm around his back.
Two souls in the long line of people that Loki had hurt.

So much of it had felt justified. In line with my own bitterness. It was different
when it was you he'd torn apart.

Things moved quickly when the cloak arrived. They took the shackles from Loki's
wrists and gave him back his voice, getting him ready to leave.

"You'll bring Idunn back alive." Odin's gaze was locked on Loki, as formidable as his frailness allowed. "No deviations, no exceptions. This is the only result that spares your family. Do you understand?"

Loki rubbed the red lines on his wrists. "Make sure the trap is ready, and I'll have Idunn home safely."

The guard passed him the cloak. Loki wrapped it around his shoulders, the feathers nearly dragging on the floor. And then he turned to me.

I stood as he approached, determined to hold my ground even though every part of me yearned to run. The blood was still on his face, and a line of scratches ran across his jaw. I'd already picked his skin out from under my nails.

"Sigyn. I…I'm going." He just stood there, waiting for some kind of reaction. "Good."

He bit back his lip, his brow furrowed. "I want to explain. And I can't now, but when I come back, if you'll just…" He reached out and cupped my cheek.

The touch seared me. I batted his hand away. "Don't. Just leave."

For a moment, something broke in him. The pain in his eyes, the desperate inhale of breath. And then it smoothed over like river-worn stone. The coldness he reserved for everyone he loathed. The mask he hid behind.

He left.

CHAPTER FORTY-SEVEN

"No man should ever reproach
another man for his love;
they often snare the wise,
what cannot catch the fool:
the loveliest looks of all."

—*Hávamál 93*

"Mama?" Narvi looked up at me as I piled his arms with firewood. "Everyone is talking about Father. What did he do?"

I loaded Váli's arms and then my own. "It's difficult to explain."

"Someone said he kidnapped Aunt Idunn. They're saying he's evil." Váli clambered to keep up with me as I strode toward Asgard's wall. Around us, dozens of others were doing the same, stacking wood against the inside of the stone. This far away from the city centre, there were trees to be cut for wood and farms to borrow from. Debts could be repaid later; who knew how much time it would take for Loki to fly to Jotunheim and back? Night was falling, and the logs and kindling were already piled like a snowdrift, as tall as we could manage.

I let my armload fall and helped the boys empty theirs. Then I knelt down in front of them. "Your father isn't evil. He's like you and me. We make choices, and some of them are better than others. Your father made a very terrible choice."

Váli kicked a rock. "But it's real? He did it?"

I took a deep breath. A large part of me wanted to lie, to spare them, but they were bound to spend the rest of their lives listening to stories of this day from lips more cruel than mine. "It's true. I wish it wasn't. Your father didn't take Idunn, but he helped the person who did, and that's just as bad."

Narvi pouted, looking around. "Everyone hates him."

Pulling him into my arms, I spoke gently into the top of his head. "I know. Sometimes people do unforgivable things, and anger is all there is to feel."

"Are you mad at him?" There was venom in Váli's voice that I didn't recognize. Everything about him seemed hard, his lips pursed and his shoulders tight.

I made room for him in my arms as well. My own fury was all-encompassing, burrowed in my gut and burning a hole in me. So I chose my words carefully. "Yes. But we'll get through tonight, and then we'll get through tomorrow, alright? I love you both, and your father loves you, and nothing will change that—"

"Tired already? Shouldn't you be more eager to prove yourself?"

I sighed. Freya was the last thing I needed.

I stood up to face her. "Please, leave us alone. Wasn't this enough of a comeuppance for you?"

She put her hands on her hips. Some of her vigour had returned, likely through some act of seidr her students had concocted. She was still as old and grey, but alive enough to be an annoyance. "It is a bit satisfying, I'll admit. You had so many chances to walk away, but you didn't. We told you over and over."

"Freya, for a Goddess of Love, you seem to lack a fundamental understanding of it." I really wanted to refrain from saying caustic things, but gods help me, I couldn't keep my mouth shut.

She laughed. "Do you call what he does *love*? Is that what makes a man betray his oldest, most loyal supporter? Have you still not managed to comprehend that what he feels for you is convenience? He *loves* that you're accommodating. He *loves* that you're an easy place to stick his prick once in a fortnight—"

"Freya!" I pulled Narvi to my side, where he whimpered against my leg. "Can you at least wait until my children aren't listening?"

Váli stepped toward her, fists balled at his sides. "Don't talk about my parents like that."

She laughed and ruffled Váli's hair. "You'll be fierce someday. Maybe even convincing. But not yet." She skirted past him, looking me in the eyes. "Sigyn, hate me all you want. You might think I've been mean, but I've tried to make you see him for what he is. This is your chance to leave. To change things. You don't need to clean up after him anymore. You've lost everything because of him."

"How can I lose everything when none of you let me have anything?" I pressed toward her, my face as close to hers as I dared. "What I do is none of your business. Leave us *alone*."

The Goddess of Nothing At All

She threw up her hands and turned to leave. "Alright." But before she'd gone more than a few paces, she yelled over her shoulder, "Better move faster. You'll need to save him again tonight."

A line of völur stood inside the wall of Asgard, watching the sky. Word had spread, and the people of the city had gathered behind them, parents holding their children, couples consoling each other with silent gestures. The only sound was the brush of the wind through the trees and the crackle of the torches that lit the night. Everyone knew what was at stake if Idunn didn't come home.

The city was waiting.

A shriek sounded in the distance, and the völur came to life.

"Ready, ladies!" Freya swung her sword into the air, holding it for all to see. "Wait for them!"

I held Narvi and Váli to my sides, drawing long, deep breaths. I didn't want to blink, didn't want to move a muscle. Even after what he'd done, I needed to see him come back.

A small eternity passed.

A falcon bolted past the stone wall, a flash of feathers in the dark.

"Now!"

The völur reacted as one, their lips moving, hands outstretched. The wood caught, exploding skyward in brilliant colours, as varied and beautiful as the Bifrost itself. The wildfire burst past the edge of the wall, illuminating the dark. Something else flew through the flame.

An enormous bird screamed out, its body engulfed. It crashed to the ground, dragging rock and dirt with it, thrashing to put out the fire. Its voice was torn between the cry of an eagle and that of a man.

I pulled the boys closer, trying to shield them from the sight.

The city looked on, waiting for the bird to be still. And then it was.

I knelt down. "Are you alright?"

Narvi was crying, but he nodded. Váli was peering around my shoulder, his eyes glued to the einherjar approaching the charred, flaming mass. The air reeked of burnt game and cooked human flesh.

Freya strode past us, away from the fire. Toward a lone falcon sitting on the ground.

"Come on." I herded the boys forward and followed her. She stopped a few paces from the falcon and so did we. She looked at me and I knew she was thinking the same thing.

Where was Idunn?

261

The falcon shook itself and hopped forward on one foot, an acorn held tightly in the other. It put the acorn down and backed away. Whatever he had done was fading, the air in front of me distorting. I blinked, and when I looked back, Idunn was lying on the ground.

She was curled into a ball, her dress filthy and her once-beautiful hair matted like old sheep's wool. Where she'd once been supple, her skin clung to her bones, and her cheeks were sallow. She wasn't old like us. She was broken, half-starved, abused. Shaking like a leaf in the storm.

I rushed forward, sinking to the ground next to her. I tried to gather her into my arms, but the look on her face made me recoil. Tears were running down her cheeks, disgust and fear in her eyes. She was cowering. From me.

Her voice was a rasping whisper. "Don't touch me."

Unable to look away, I sobbed into my hands. "I'm so sorry. I promise you, I didn't know! He never told me. I didn't know."

"I should have." She shifted away, her words distant and disjointed. "I should've listened. I didn't want to believe. I trusted that he was good inside. That he loved me. What makes you any different? Stupid, so stupid." She looked above my head, her eyes narrowed in defiance. "They were right. There was never anything good in you."

I turned. Loki stood behind me. His hair whipped in the wind, blending with the flames at his back. His expression was hard, unreadable.

"Idunn!" Bragi ran toward us, dropping to his knees when he reached his wife. He swept Idunn into his arms, and he whispered into the crook of her neck, both of them sobbing.

All their attention was on each other, and we were forgotten.

And I knew. It wasn't just the betrayal or whatever had gone on in that Jotun keep. It was all the doubts that she had ever had about him, coiled into a bitter mass of hate and shame. She'd had spent months toiling over the same things I had wondered about Loki in the last hours. Who he really was. What was real. If anything had ever been true. She was right to hate me. I should have known better.

And now I'd lost her.

I wiped the tears from my cheeks. It was getting too crowded. The other gods were gathering, and too many eyes were already on me. On Loki. I needed to get my boys somewhere safer.

"Váli, Narvi, it's time to go." I took each of their hands and strode up the path as fast as they could manage. They were both quiet and that, I think, was worse than the questions.

Crunching stone rose up behind us. I tried to ignore it, but it was catching up. I let go of Váli's hand and whipped around, ready to fight whoever had come for trouble.

"Sigyn."

My hand twitched, my mind teetering on the decision to set him alight. He deserved it. "What do you want, Loki?"

"I want to explain." He came closer, palms out, begging. "Please, darling. Just let me tell you what happened."

"No. There's nothing to say." I stepped forward, wanting to keep the boys away from whatever came next.

Loki stopped just in front of me and reached for my hand. Repressing the scream in my chest, I pushed him backwards. "You don't get to lay your hands on me." I glared, waiting for him to try and defend himself. To apologize. To tell me that none of it was true, that it had all been a horrible nightmare.

When he spoke, his voice was a desperate whisper. "Sigyn…"

"Váli, take your brother home." I pulled the dagger from my belt and pressed the hilt into his hand. "If anyone stops you, take their eyes. Don't stop running until you're home, and open the door for no one."

He took the blade in one hand and his brother's arm in the other. I kept my eyes on them as they ran, until they were out of sight.

"I wasn't going to hurt them. You *must* know that."

"You already did." I turned back to him, stepping forward until I was pressing in on him, pushing him back. "You don't need to lay a hand on us to rip us apart."

"I didn't—Please listen!" The pain on his face was so evident, and yesterday, it would have worked. I'd have believed it.

"Why? How could you do this?" I pushed him again. "You've destroyed everything. Not having Idunn would've killed us all, every god in one fell swoop. Me. You. Eventually your children. How was that plan supposed to resolve itself, hmm? And now everyone knows. No one in Asgard will ever trust you again." I jabbed my finger into his chest. "And Idunn. She was my best friend. *Your* best friend. Did you see her? She'll *never* be the same. And *you* did that to her."

"I didn't have a choice." Loki's back hit the wall of a house, stopping his retreat. "When Thjazi had me captive, he told me he'd let me live if I brought Idunn to him. And if I didn't, he'd drop me from a thousand feet up. If I didn't deliver, he'd come after *you.* What was I supposed to do?"

"He's one Jotun, Loki!" People were watching, but I didn't care. I kept screaming. "We could've done something if you'd just told me! We could've dealt with it together! We're a city of gods and völur and einherjar. We could've done something!"

Loki's lips turned to a snarl. "Who is 'we'? Freya, who would love to see me skinned and beaten? Heimdall, who sees everything and does nothing? Your father, who threatens our kids to keep me in line? Who would believe me, Sigyn? Who would help me?"

I grabbed him by the jaw and held his gaze to mine, as if I could finally get through to him. "I would've helped you!"

He stared at me, prying my fingers off his face. He held my arm like a threat. "It's not that simple."

"Of course." I yanked myself from his grip, rubbing the dull pain from my wrist. "You had to do it alone because you're Loki and the realms are against you. You're at war with everyone, including yourself! I've stood by you at every turn, and you repay me with deceit. You always find trouble; I can live with that. You lie to others, but we're supposed to be different! How am I ever going to trust you again? I've forgiven so much of what you've done, Loki. How am I supposed to forgive this?"

"I was trying to protect you. That's what I've always tried to do. You have no idea what's happening in these walls, the things your father isn't telling you—"

"What, Loki?" I threw my hands in the air. "What isn't my father telling me? And how exactly would you know? What else have you been hiding from me?"

Loki's mouth snapped shut, his teeth gritted in frustration. "It wouldn't do any good—I can't just—" He ran his hands down his face, speaking into his palms. "Even if you knew, it wouldn't do any good. Maybe it's not even real, and maybe we can't stop it. Gods, Sigyn, you don't understand!"

"You're right, Loki." I threw my hands up, finished. The pain he'd already inflicted was enough for a lifetime. "I don't. How the fuck could I? I'm here, day in and day out, sticking up for you. Protecting you. And you're keeping secrets I can't pry out of you. How could I ever understand? You won't let me. I'm just your moronic wife, too simple to understand complicated, tortured Loki." I gave him one last push into the wall and turned away, back up the path toward home.

His footsteps didn't follow.

CHAPTER FORTY-EIGHT

"Thjazi was killed, and Idunn was returned to her husband.
The city was quickly put back in order. Despite the discord,
everything returned to the way it had once been."

—*Asgard Historical Record, Volume 25*

I f it had just been Loki and I, it would've been an easier choice.
It was tempting to toss him out. Just change the locks and banish him for good. But we had two children. I couldn't look at him, but did that mean that Váli and Narvi were better off without a father? One didn't seem to equal the other. We'd never planned for something like this. We'd been in love; why would we have been ready for anything but love?

It wasn't me who'd chosen to throw it all away.

The gods asked me to weigh in on a closed-door trial to decide how Loki would be punished. They had shouted at each other over whether he should be allowed to live or die. They asked me, and I told them I didn't know. And that was true. I loved him too much to see him die, but he had done something I would have dismembered anyone else for doing. Ultimately, it was agreed that for better or worse, he was one of the Aesir; if the realms saw division, if they saw a god killed, it would create an opening. A certainty that the gods' reign could end—and at each other's hands no less.

They'd asked if I'd wanted a divorce.

I told them I didn't know.

And while they talked about punishments, I remembered having promised them, once, that I could keep Loki out of trouble.

What a silly, ignorant thought.

265

They stopped speaking to me after that. That day and every day after.

Loki was stripped of his right to be present in Gladsheim—not that either of us had had a seat—and forced to do menial labour in the kitchens: scrub the pots and pans, clean the caked-on grease from the roasting grates, wash the flour from the aprons. There was seidr for these things, of course there was; it was too large an army to clean up after by hand. But Loki wasn't given such a luxury. He was to grind his fingers down to the bone serving his people. Any instance he was caught cheating, he would be given another day of work. Doubtless, he would still try.

With my own pots clean, I looked out the window. Loki was outside, sitting on a chair he had hauled outside, picking at his dinner. His bowl was on his lap, carefully balanced. His hands were wrapped in thin bandages, and there was a stiffness to them that gave him trouble with the bowl and the spoon.

Good.

"Mama, I'm finished. Is Father coming inside this time?" Narvi brought his bowl to the counter and put it next to the washing basin.

"No, darling, I don't think so." I had banished him out there days ago. Just having him inside stripped me of my appetite. But I couldn't tell Narvi that. It would break his heart.

"I miss being together at supper. Father was funny. Now it's just quiet."

I dried my hands on my skirts and bent down. "I know, I'm sorry. I'll try to be funnier, I promise. I could help you work on your energy channelling tonight if you want?"

Narvi swayed on his heel, looking at the floor. "I want Father to do it."

I swept his hair back from his forehead. It was getting so long. "Of course. You can still ask him anything you want. Things are odd, I know, but nothing between you and your father has changed."

"I guess that means he's coming in?" Váli was scraping out the last of his stew, eyes trained on the table.

"I'll get him, yes."

He hauled himself out of his chair and slammed down his cup. "Fuck him."

"Váli! He's your father, and you still need to treat him with respect." I stared him down, hands on my hips.

Váli looked me in the eyes. "No, I don't. And you can't make me talk to him." With that, he stormed off to his room, the slam of his door shaking the pots hanging on the walls.

I took a deep breath and released it, then turned back to Narvi. "Go on, get your things. I'll talk to him."

His smile spread from ear to ear, and he sprang toward his room like a deer.

266

The Goddess of Nothing At All

I pulled on my shoes and summoned all my patience before going outside.

Loki's head didn't move up at the sound of the gravel, but his eyes shifted, confirming it was me. He dropped his spoon back into his nearly empty bowl and waited.

"Your son wants to spend time with you." I crossed my arms over my chest, keeping enough of a distance that there was no danger of him reaching out to touch me.

"Which one?"

"Narvi."

"Váli still wants me dead, I suppose."

I huffed. "And whose fault is that?"

"Please." Loki held up a bandaged hand. Tiny specks of blood had seeped through in places. "I'm exhausted. I don't want to fight with you. If you'll let me come in, I'll sit with him."

I nodded my head toward the door. "Go on."

Loki rose and walked past me, bowl in hand.

I took care of the last of the washing, listening to Loki and Narvi talk at the table over a book of Narvi's notes. Hod had sent him home from the archives with some reading about basic runes, and he was barely stopping to breathe as he showed them to his father.

All seemed well, so when the washing was done, I went to the bedroom to give them some space. I left the door open just a crack, enough to see out of, and went about reorganizing the room.

I'd packed Loki up and moved him to another bedroom, but there were still so many of his things tucked in the corners. I pulled a pair of his trousers from under the bed and crumpled them into a ball, the start of a pile I'd rather burn than give back. It would feel more comfortable when it was gone, I told myself. Then I could stop crying myself to sleep in a bed that was too big for me alone.

I hadn't washed the sheets yet. They still smelled like him.

"You're learning so quickly. I'm proud of you."

I tiptoed back to the door and peeked through. Loki was leaning over Narvi and the book, the two of them tucked close together. Loki turned the page, and Narvi reached out to take his hands. Even from my hiding place, it was plain to see how delicately he was holding them.

"Does it hurt?" Narvi asked.

Loki shook his head. "I'm alright."

"But you're bleeding." Narvi turned them palm up. He found the tail of the bandage and started to pull it back.

I already knew what was underneath. They were red and calloused, the flesh between his fingers dry and cracked, broken open along the lines of his palms. The

267

others thought it was good for a laugh, talking about Loki the scullery maid, but in reality, it was an indirect form of torture.

Loki kissed his son's temple. "It looks worse than it is."

Narvi unbandaged his other hand, and Loki's face twitched despite his effort to keep the pain from showing. Narvi's hands were small underneath his father's. His lips began to move, and his father's brow furrowed. Knowing better than to interrupt, Loki waited.

A moment later, his jaw dropped.

Narvi was healing him.

It didn't last long. It was the first time he'd used runes in front of either of us, and seidr took years to master. But—

"You did it." Loki held up his hands and turned them around. "Ymir's breath, look how well you've done."

From the door, I could see that some of the wounds were closed. The skin was still pink and raw, but it looked as if he'd been resting them for days.

Loki pulled Narvi in for a hug, holding him as tightly as he could. "You're going to be so strong." He released him and put his hand on Narvi's cheek. "But you can't do that. They'll know, and it'll be worse for me."

Narvi frowned. "But it's the right thing to do."

"Maybe. But you can't get into trouble because of me."

"It could be our secret. I could help you." Narvi squirmed closer. "I won't tell. I'll just do it a little. For practice."

Loki's lips pursed, staring his pleading son in the eyes. "Just a little. Sometimes." He kissed him on the forehead. "I love you more than life itself."

I stepped away from the door.

My sweet boy with the kindest, most generous heart. Even for those who didn't deserve it. Would he be able to remain so good when there was so much evil all around?

CHAPTER FORTY-NINE

"The trouble with having prophecies is that it colours everything. There's not a Jotun in the realms that can step inside Asgard without the assumption that they're here to ransack the place."

—Laufey - Asgard Historical Record, Volume 2

A summons arrived for us the next evening, strapped to the leg of one of Odin's ravens, and with it was a threat. Come to Valhalla or else.

What awaited us was a feast. An excess of the finest foods laid out as far as the eye could see, despite it not being an official feast day. If anyone else thought it was odd, they weren't about to complain.

At the head table, next to Odin, was an unfamiliar Jotun. She towered over him even while she was sitting. Hel, she even made Thor seem small. Her face was severe, and she was so pale, she was nearly translucent, her skin covered in long, swirling tattoos. The blue ink of the tattoos disappeared under her leather armour, up the length of her arms, and all the way to the tip of her chin.

Never in my life would I want that woman's scorn set on me.

There were two empty chairs at the far end of the table, so we took them. No one had bothered to put up seats for the boys, however. Narvi crawled up on Loki's knee, and Váli, too proud for something like that, stood at the end and stole food off my plate. It was a long, uncomfortable meal.

After the meal, Odin stood. "I'm sure you've noticed that we have a guest tonight. She is Skadi, daughter of Thjazi, the rightful heir of his keep and leader of her family in his stead. She has come—"

"I have come—" Skadi stood, stealing the room's attention. She leaned against the table, her palms resting on its top. "—to seek retribution. One of your own came into my father's keep, lured him to Asgard, and is responsible for his death."

Odin cleared his throat. "Thjazi also kidnapped Idunn and kept her against her will, which was the reason that Asgard interfered in the first place."

"Her presence at the keep was entirely in line with the bargain that Loki made with my father." Skadi's eyes travelled down the table towards us, and a chill ran down my spine.

Loki muttered something under his breath and looked away, entirely too focused on helping distract Narvi with food.

"Asgard took back its property and that is final." Odin waved a hand.

Skadi slammed her hand on the table, shaking everything on it. "And none of you died for it. My father was killed deliberately and by your hands. If you won't give me the recompense that I'm owed for his death, I'll return to Jotunheim and rally every one of my people against your city. We'll see how you stand up to that."

Odin sighed. "There's no need for a war."

"No," Skadi said, a grin splitting her face. "You wouldn't want a war with us. Because one day, you'll get one, and you know as well as *everyone else* that one of those wars will end you. So. What will you give me?"

The room was deathly silent. Every last einherjar had stopped eating, every Valkyrie was standing still to watch. One Jotun against the Allfather.

Odin took a drink, biding his time. He wiped his lips with the back of his hand. "As our messenger would have told you, we were able to recover your father's body after his death. He remained more or less...intact. He's been preserved with seidr by the infirmary as requested, and now that you've come to claim him, we'll provide him with a proper funeral pyre."

Skadi pushed back the thick locks of hair on her head. They fell back down in a cascade of white, glinting with silver beads and sharp canine teeth. "Not even close to enough. What else?"

Tapping his fingers on the table, Odin continued. "To ensure his memory lives on for your kin, I'll arrange for his eyes to become part of the night sky. Stars." Odin waved a hand for a refill of his drink. "And if memory serves me, you lack a husband. You could remain the sole ruler of your keep, or we could help you to select someone suitable."

Frigg looked up at Skadi. "Depending on who you choose, your marriage would bestow a place of status in Asgard. Perhaps even the title of goddess on you and any children that may come from your union."

Her eyebrow raised. "Finally, something that sounds appealing." She looked up and down the table. "Hmm. I'd insist on a woman, but your ladies are too brittle for my taste." Her eyes stopped on Baldur. "But this one seems like he could gallop at a decent pace."

"Unfortunately, Baldur is already spoken for."

"I'll have him or nothing." Skadi crossed her arms over her chest, looking down at Odin like she might take his head off for the fun of it.

Frigg stood and put her hand on Skadi's shoulder, something I would never have dared to do. "If you insist on a chance at having Baldur as a husband, we can find a more impartial way to choose. Our other eligible men will line up, and you can choose them by their feet alone. Surely, you'll be able to pick Baldur out from the rest, since he's by far the most beautiful."

Skadi mulled it over, a look on her face that said she wasn't taking it at all seriously. "Why not? It's not every day you get to prove that the gods are fools."

Odin started to sit down, but Skadi pushed back his seat with her foot. "We're not done. The death of my father has been a burden on my spirit. Immortalize my father, get me a husband, and make me laugh. Then I'll consider this debt repaid."

Odin scanned the room. "And how would we do that?"

Skadi sat down, kicking her boots up onto the table. She ripped the meat from a leg of boar, chewing slowly. "I already have something in mind. Bring me Loki Laufeyjarson, father-slayer and traitor to his people."

A murmur rose in the hall. I looked at Loki. His face was grim as he kissed the top of Narvi's head, then his eyes met mine. I held out my hands to take Narvi from him, but the boy clung to Loki's tunic, whimpering.

"Come now," Loki whispered, prying Narvi's fingers away. I wrapped my arms around Narvi and dragged Váli closer to me.

Loki made his way around the table to stand in front of Skadi. Without a hint of guilt or weakness, he looked up at her.

"Make me laugh, *fathur-morthingr*." Skadi took another bite, watching him with a sly grin on her lips.

Loki's face tightened, his arms crossed over his chest. "There once was a skald and a beggar—"

"No." Skadi threw the meaty femur at him. It bounced off his chest and clattered to the floor. "No jokes."

He drew in a long breath, his fingers digging into his palms. "Then what do you want from me?"

She didn't need to think it over. "Bring me a goat and a rope."

271

The room waited a small eternity in silence as the rope and the goat were found and brought to the front.

"Now," she commanded. "Tie his cock to the goat. I want to hear him scream."

The hall burst into chaos. Some were calling out in encouragement, while others seemed to think she had gone too far.

"Perhaps we'll attach the goat to *your* balls," Loki snapped. "They must be as large as boulders to demand something like that."

"They certainly out-measure yours, little traitor." She stared down at him, as casually as if she had asked him for a horn of mead. "You wouldn't want to start a war, would you?"

Odin glared down at Loki. "Do as she says."

"Mama." Narvi curled up against my chest, whimpering.

I hushed him. "Get down. We're going to take a walk in the garden, alright?" I nudged Narvi to his feet and took his hand. I offered the other hand to Váli, but he refused, his face full of shame. He took off ahead of us, bursting out the doors before we were halfway there. I tried not to listen to the bartering and bickering behind me, to the eventual capitulation and defiant acceptance of what was coming.

Váli only stopped when we were well into the garden, where the noise of Valhalla became more of a hum. He dropped onto his bottom on the grass. I sat down next to him.

"Would you like to hear a story?" I pulled them both against me.

Narvi nodded, sniffing back tears. Váli was silent, staring out ahead.

"In the time before time, there were only two realms. On one side sat the flaming, volcanic realm of Muspelheim and on the other was the frozen wasteland of Niflheim." I stroked their hair, speaking in a low, calm voice. "In the middle was Ginnungagap, the great void. One day, the ice and the flame drew together, and from it grew the largest of all giants, Ymir. But Ymir, he was a sleepy creature. While he slept, he started to sweat. The first Jotun was born from the sweat under his arms, one man and one woman. Your very oldest ancestors."

A scream rose up from the hall behind us. It was drowned quickly with cacophonous laughter.

I hugged the boys as tightly as I could. "Ymir slept on and while he slept, the ancient cow Audhumla fed him with her milk. What Audhumla liked most of all was salt, and there was salt in the ice, so she began to lick and lick and three days later, she found a man inside. His name was Buri, and he was the grandfather of Odin…"

Dusk had already come and gone when a hand came to rest on my shoulder. Loki sat down across from me, his eye purple and his lip split. His gaze went to the boys, who'd fallen asleep against me.

"It's done," he whispered.

"Good. Has she chosen a husband?"

"Njord." He stared down at his lap as he picked the raw skin from his thumb. The corner of his lip turned up. "Freya's not impressed with her new step-mother."

I managed a smile as well. "She seems destined to have Jotun blood in her family."

Loki didn't reply. He just stared at the hall behind me.

"It's time to go." I scooped Narvi into my arms. "Can you—"

"I have him." Loki hoisted Váli up, propping him against his chest. As I passed, he reached out for me, stopping me in my tracks. There was something odd in his eyes. Impatient. "Does any of this mean anything to you?"

"Why would it? You made penance to Skadi, not to me. I'm just as lonely as yesterday. Just as broken." I turned from him and walked away.

CHAPTER FIFTY

*"After all those years, after the pain and anguish,
there he was. Looking at her like she was the only thing
he'd thought about since he'd left home.
Maybe he was her destiny after all."*

—*Other Shores*, Erna Bjorndottir

More Than A Year Later

I'd tried to read. Really, I had.

Once upon a time, I'd enjoyed those types of books. The romantic sagas of wild, driven lovers, the kind that could leave a girl pining for a properly torrid affair. But now…I'd spent most of the late hours trying to read the same pages over and over, never managing to get very far. Who would tell these poor lovers that love comes to nothing? That there is so much sorrow in their happily ever after?

I drank back the last of my overly large glass of wine and put it back on the dining table. A glance out the window told me how late it was. The boys had been in bed for hours, and it was always the quiet solitude of night that drove me to indulge in a drink to soften my bitter edges.

With a sigh, I closed the book without marking the page. What was the point?

I reached across the table to the cloth bag that had appeared on my step this morning, as it did every month. I pulled on the corner until one of the two apples rolled out, gold and fresh. Each time they arrived, I avoided them. They were necessary, yes, but each time was another reminder of what I had lost. How alone I was.

I'd seen her at a distance. Idunn was better, but something about her had wilted. She frightened more easily, smiled a little less. I wanted to have heard something in passing, to know how she was, but there were no allies to pass us rumours. Not anymore.

The Goddess of Nothing At All

The first bite of the apple was bitter. Just touching it to my lips made me nauseous, but I forced it down. Throwing it up wasn't an option; I didn't have the guts to go ask for another.

A rustle sounded from outside. Then boots on the step. I didn't bother to turn to the door. No one came here that didn't live here. Instead, I stared across the table, into the crackling fire, and poured the last of the bottle of wine. It felt like I'd need it.

The door opened and closed again. His boots made a final clunk as he took them off. I only looked up when he put his travelling bag on the table.

"It's late." I took a sip, trying to resist the urge to drink it all at once.

"It's bad weather." He brushed the last of the snow in his hair into the washing basin.

Neither of us spoke as he rustled through his bag, pulling out leftover rations and setting them on the table. Once he was done, he went to warm himself by the fire.

"Narvi asked after you today." Another sip. "He came into the room dressed in his travelling gear and cried that he wanted to live with you in the woods."

Loki turned his head, looking toward me but not at me. "And what did you say?"

"I told him that you live here and so does he. But that wasn't good enough. He wants to be with you all the time." I put the wine down and pushed it away, an attempt at moderation. "He cried himself to sleep again."

Turning to lean against the mantle, Loki scratched at his chin. "I didn't put this idea in his head if that's what you're thinking. The boys are better off here."

"They are. Only the Nornir know what you're doing out there. But he's desperate for your affection."

Loki threw his hand up. "And I give it to him. I spend every moment with him because the rest of you won't speak to me. The last time I asked Váli to go hunting, he threatened me with a knife. So how better should I divide my time?"

I pushed my chair back and got up. "The more time you spend with Narvi while you're home, the harder it is for him when you leave. How is he supposed to feel about that?"

"I don't know! I—"

"Quiet!" I hissed. "You're going to wake them."

He lowered his voice and came to the table, his hands on the back of a chair. "What do you want me to do, Sigyn? It's been more than a year, and you still want nothing to do with me. Why would I want to be stuck here every day while you stare holes in the back of my skull because I have the audacity to exist?"

My mouth was dry, but I could feel the warmth and haze of alcohol spreading out across my body. More wine was a bad idea. "This isn't about me. It's about your son. He wants you here."

Leaning heavily on the chair, Loki took a deep breath. His hair fanned out, hiding his face. "The nights I spend at the old cabin are because you don't want me in this house. I started going further because the place barely has four walls and a roof, and it kills me to be there alone. At least when I'm out in the realms, I'm not thinking about this."

That was enough to have me reaching for the glass. I tipped it back and swallowed it all.

"Will you stop that?" Loki's eyes were on me. "I'm trying to talk to you, and you're getting drunk."

I set the glass on the table with a flourish. "Unlike you, I can't just run away from our life. I have the boys to raise. I have to stay here in this city where they spit at my feet in the market and stare daggers at me in Valhalla. Seeing Idunn *anywhere* is like having my chest ripped open because I want so badly to have one *single* friend. So this—" I pointed at the wine bottle "—is how *I* forget."

Loki pursed his lips and took a breath. "Fair enough."

"Why are you so calm?" I rounded the table, slowly closing in on him. "Why does nothing bother you?"

He straightened out, stepping away from the chair. "Everything bothers me, but I don't get to do anything about it. I have to live with what I did and suffer the consequences, just like you wanted."

"What I wanted? What I *wanted* was a happy life." The words came without hesitation. My limbs were loose and so was my tongue. I stepped closer. "You took that from me. I wanted us to live forever, watching the boys grow into accomplished gods. To watch them have kids. To wake up next to you over and over, and to kiss you to sleep every night. To walk proudly with you. Not to feel this cold fucking loneliness that you've left me with."

His face shifted into a look of pure scorn. "Someday, Sigyn, you're going to have to accept your part in this. You *choose* to stay angry."

I grabbed him by the tunic and pushed him up against the mantle.

Loki stumbled, eyes darting to the fire near his feet. "*Skít*, Sig. What are you doing?"

Tears blurred my vision. I pushed him again, keeping his back against the stone. "Do you have any idea how horrible it is to still care about you and still want you, even though you betrayed me?" I leaned forward, the tears escaping down my cheeks, my face close to his, my teeth bared in a snarl. "It's torture."

Loki opened his mouth to say something but thought better of it. Instead, his hand found my cheek, his thumb wiping away the tears. Like an old habit.

I kissed him. It was wrong, but I did it anyway.

He startled, but I pulled him back down, a handful of his hair in my fist. He growled in protest, but his lips found mine all the same. Hands gripping my face, his tongue darted against mine as he backed us away from the fire and into the table.

If I stopped to think, I'd have been ashamed, so I didn't. I balled his tunic up in my hand and pulled him toward me until I was propped on the table, with him between my legs. My hands dove under his tunic, gliding across the once-familiar terrain of his stomach. His body was just like before, but I wasn't. We weren't.

I dragged my nails down his chest. I wanted him to hurt.

It drew a hiss from him, but he pressed on, leaning in to bite into my shoulder in return. Not hard enough to break skin, but hard all the same.

This wasn't the way we had done things. This wasn't for love.

The frantic press of his hands drove all sense from me. They ran over every inch of me, like I was a craving he was giving into. One hand strayed, pushing my dress up to my thighs and searching beneath. I pressed against him, willing him to find me. There hadn't been anyone since him, and I yearned for it.

Instead, he pulled me up, my legs wrapped around his hips. He carried me into the bedroom as I nipped at his ear, paying attention to the places I knew drove him wild. He closed the door behind us and threw me onto the bed. He was angry too.

Good.

The wind had picked up outside. It tore against the hall, inconsistent bursts battering the walls. It was cold, and my skin was slick with sweat, but it wasn't enough for us to touch.

He had known exactly what to do. How to touch me, like he'd never forgotten the shape of me. There was still that smell of cinders about him and a hint of sweetness on his lips. He'd felt hard and lean and strong, and I'd wanted all of it. But now that it was done, I had to force myself to look proud. The anger and lust had faded, and the only thing left was the gaping loneliness that had been swimming underneath.

Loki was sitting against the headboard, furs pulled up over his legs, quiet.

I refused to move, lying bare and tempting, staring at him. No matter how deep the chill went in my bones, I wanted him to move first.

"Did that help somehow?" His voice was little more than a whisper.

I tucked my arm under my head. "It was good, if that's what you're asking."

"You know I'm not." He looked at me and I was suddenly sure that this little tryst had taken all the fury from my body and poured it into him.

Taking a deep breath to stifle the guilt, I propped myself up on the mattress. "I'm not sure."

Loki touched the long red welts on his chest. He flinched.

I shuffled toward him on my knees. "Let me heal it—"

"No." He got up and fished around under the bed for his trousers. He pulled them on. "I think I'll keep them. As a reminder."

I knelt on the bed, watching him look for the rest of his clothes. "What do you mean?"

"This was a mistake. It's too late, Sigyn. There's no going back."

I got up, pulling a sheet around my body against the cold. "Of course there isn't. Gods, I can't even look at you some days. I don't know, I—don't you ever want to go back? Don't you ever get tired of this? I'm tired and confused and just…maybe there's *something* we can fix."

"Fix? Is that what you call fixed?" He gestured to his chest again before he pulled his tunic back on. "That woman tonight? That wasn't Sigyn. I don't know where she's gone, but she's not here."

The words hit me like a slap. "If I'm someone different, who do you think made me that way?"

"You did." He opened the bedroom door and stormed toward his cloak hanging on the wall. "I gave you a good excuse, and you rose to the occasion."

"How dare you." I pulled the sheet tighter around my chest, fearing what the boys might see if they woke. "How can you say that?"

He pulled his cloak over his shoulders and forced his feet into his boots. "The woman I married stood by me through everything. She was gentle and compassionate. She never hurt anyone else. She was better than me, and no one knew why she loved me, but she did." He looked me in the eyes. "You aren't her."

The anger sparked again, new and overwhelming.

I reached for the first thing I could find.

CHAPTER FIFTY-ONE

*"Some tortures we must inflict on ourselves over and over,
because it's the only thing we deserve."*

—*Tales of Midgard, Volume 4*

Eight Years Later

The wooden bowl flew across the room, sending discarded leftovers flying against the walls and the door. I'd missed him, for the most part, but it still felt satisfying.

Loki shook the food from his boot and pulled his cloak over his shoulders.

"You're just going to leave then? Again?" My nightdress was askew over my body, my hair a mess. He looked up but didn't answer. He was perfectly accustomed to this crooked old tradition of ours. We'd fall into bed together, and then he'd leave, and we'd gradually forget, until a few months later when it all happened again. Pushing and pulling and never letting go.

"If you disappear without saying goodbye to Narvi again, you'll break his heart." My lips trembled as I spoke. It was true, but it wasn't the only reason.

Loki sighed and swung his pack over his shoulder, muttering something under his breath in Jotun before he looked up at me. "Narvi's fifteen, Sigyn. He's not a child anymore."

A scream was building in my chest. "Just go! Get out!"

He didn't need to be told again. He walked out the door and into the darkness, letting it slam behind him.

I grabbed a cup from the table and went to fill it from the cask of mead in the corner. My hands were shaking. I drank it down and filled it again before collapsing into the seat at the table, sloshing mead onto the wood. Not knowing what else to do, I laid my head on my arms and sobbed.

I never learned. We'd done this dance so many times. It wasn't hope that brought me to bed with him, not exactly. It was the solitude. Nothing had been easy, not for so very long. The entire city had shut us out, gods and all. Tyr kept Váli in the einherjar because he was strong, and Hod kept Narvi in class because he was brilliant, but those were the only kindnesses they gave us. And no one had stepped up to be a boon to *me*. I was tired and alone, and there were days when Loki would stroll back into the house as beautiful as the day I met him and the loneliness would burn more than the last time he hurt me. One weak moment, that's all it took. One slow kiss, and I melted for him. We fell into that bed of lies together, searching for whatever it was we needed and finding nothing.

All this time, and I was still a fool.

I'd been stretched out over the table for a long while when the front door opened again.

Váli stepped into the food that was strewn across the floor. "What the hel happened here?" He looked at me, and I knew what he saw. A mess of hair and charcoal and clothing.

Embarrassed at the state of myself, I straightened out my nightdress and wiped the tears from my eyes. "You're out late."

"I am."

Váli sat down next to me and stole what was left of my drink. He'd become a man in every sense. At seventeen, he was cut like an einherji twice his age with cheekbones sharp as axes. He'd curled his mess of red hair into an unruly knot on the back of his head, strands of it hanging in his face. He was rough, covered in stubble and sporting a roguish smile that could melt hearts. Ladies eyed him everywhere we went. To them, he looked like a taste of danger, handsome and wild, but anyone who knew him as Lokason kept their distance.

He also smelled like a brewery.

"I see we're both awake for the same reasons." I watched him drink down the last of my mead, the black ink of his knotted tattoos disappearing under his right sleeve. Last year, he'd decided he would learn to be an *úlfhethnar*, a wolfhide. He'd spent six months learning to take the shape of a wolf, and his tattoos were his badge of completion, each swirl and rune etched with seidr that would ease his transformation to wolf and back again.

He shook his head. "Oh no, I'm not drunk for nearly the same reason you are." He leaned on the table and stared at me with his father's eyes. I looked away. "Look at you. You're sitting here in your nightdress crying into your cup *again*. He's not worth this.

Why do you do this to yourself?"

I blushed, angry with his mostly accurate perception. "And how do you know what I'm crying over?"

Váli rolled his eyes, gesturing around the room. "His stuff is gone, for a start. Narvi and I *left* because we could hear you getting up to things again. You're not exactly subtle."

I buried my face in my hands. "Yggdrasil shade me, I'm so sorry. Where's your brother?"

He huffed, a snarky laugh. "I left him at the pub with Gersemi. Freya's away again, and she's taking advantage of it. Scandalous, socializing with the likes of us."

"Good. At least if someone picks a fight, Narvi has someone there who knows how to use a knife."

Váli looked me over, brow furrowed in pity. He put his arm around me and pulled me into a hug. "You know I just want to see you happy, right?"

I sniffed and wiped the stray tears away. "I'm your mother. Let me worry about you instead."

He grew quiet, withdrawing his arm. Staring at the table, he started to fidget with the empty cup, spinning it on its side.

Leaning in, I nudged his shoulder. "Váli, *is* there something to worry about?"

"It's nothing." He stood immediately, taking the cup with him to fetch more mead.

I waited, but he kept his back to me. "You've always been honest to a fault, Váli. Don't start lying to me now."

His shoulders slumped. He paused, then came back to sit down. There was no coy smile, none of his usual sarcasm or bitter humour. "I can't tell you."

I leaned forward, forcing him to look me in the eyes. "You can tell me anything. Always."

He sighed. "If I do, you can't tell anyone else. Especially not Loki."

I cupped his face in my hand, the stubble of his patchy beard poking into my skin. "It's just you and me. I'd never betray your trust."

He pulled away from me and drank again, staring at the tabletop. "There are things that I know. I wish I didn't. Things about you and Loki." He paused, like he didn't know how to choke out the words. "I know that he used to change shape and be a woman. For bed."

"Oh?" I stumbled, trying to think of something to say. I'd already discussed my sex life enough for one day. "No, no. You're mistaken, I—"

He rolled his eyes. "Please, Mother. I saw it with my own eyes. Those times I raided the cellar at night? You didn't always catch me. Once, I hid under the table because someone was coming, and out walked a half-naked woman. She had that same red hair, same scars. Same smug bastard. I'm not a moron."

I blushed, hiding my mouth behind my hand. "Váli. I—"

He shook his head, waving his hand. "Don't you dare tell me. The shapeshifting I was used to, but the rest is more than I need to think about." He looked up at the ceiling, struggling to find words. "I just...maybe you can help me understand something."

"I'll always help you if I can."

He drank again. "My training is my life. It's what I was meant to do; I know that. I get to be Váli the einherji, not Váli Lokason. Not Trickster-spawn, not Son of Lies. Just me. It's mine, and I've earned it. I've moved up the ranks on my own, gotten my wolfhide on my own. But I think I need to quit." He looked at me, gauging my reaction. I waited, and he continued. "The longer I stay, the worse it gets. This thing... I've tried to stop it, but I can't. It keeps me awake at night and steals my focus all day. I can't keep going like this."

He was being far too cryptic. I couldn't decipher what he meant. "What's haunting you?"

Váli took a deep breath, tapping on the rim of his cup. He was shaking, and for a moment, I thought he might not tell me at all. "There's this einherji. I've been training him. And it's not just him, but it's...When we spar, I notice things. The way he smells. The way he looks and moves. I think of things I shouldn't." Váli looked away. "Sometimes, I think about kissing him."

I pursed my lips, his words washing over me with a sudden all-encompassing clarity. The girls he'd taken no interest in, the brooding, the avoidance of any talk of marriage or relationships.

Before I could find the right words, he burst into tears, collapsing into his hands. "Mama, what's wrong with me?"

I leaned over him and wrapped my arms around his shaking body. My head resting on his shoulder, I whispered to him. "Oh, Váli. It's alright, I have you." I waited, letting him cry out the worst of it. "There is nothing wrong with you."

"There is!" He curled his fingers into his hair, nails digging in.

"Listen to me." I sat up and pulled him with me.

He fought me off, glaring at me with bloodshot eyes. "You and I both know what people in this city think. The worst thing you can be is a man who doesn't act like one. The things they say about Loki! That he's *argr*, that he sleeps with beasts and lets men use him. They used to tell me that every single day, made sure I knew it, until I beat one of them so badly, he didn't wake up until resurrections the next day. Then they stopped. And it's not fair because women can be with women, but if I—I am not *argr*. I am not my *father*—" The words caught in his throat. "I can't be this. I can't. How do I stop?"

The Goddess of Nothing At All

I held him tight, his pain tearing me open at the seams, taking all my effort to choke it down. "Váli, you listen to me. There is nothing wrong with you. The people here, they fear what they can't understand, and they always have. It doesn't matter. Let them be afraid; you don't need them."

"It matters! How will I keep the respect of the einherjar if they think I'm letting someone make a woman out of me? How am I supposed to take a wife that I don't want just to convince everyone else that I'm *normal*? How am I supposed to pretend to be something I'm not?"

His questions were so difficult. What could I tell him that wasn't a lie? "I don't know. I don't have the answers." I took his hands. "I promise you this; when you find a man who loves you, the two of you will always be welcome under my roof. You told me because you knew I'd understand. I promise you, I do. A long time ago I fell in love with a Valkyrie, and a lot of people didn't want to see us happy. And it's not the same, I know, but you're not strange. Your father once told me that people like me—like us—are more common in these realms than we think. He and I protected each other. We'll protect you. You're just like us."

"I am *not* like Loki, and I don't want to know anything about him." Váli snarled, the way he always did when the subject came up. He watched me for a moment, trying to breathe. "I—I don't know what to do."

I pushed one of his stray ringlets behind his ear. "You live your life. There are ways to know without speaking. That's how I knew, when Alruna and I found each other. Someday, a man will look at you, and you'll see it in his eyes or by the way he talks and acts. You'll be subtle and patient until you're sure, and then you'll make small hints until he makes himself clear. You'll keep your head down, laugh along with all the horrible things people say, and you'll bring all that rage and injustice back here where you can curse their ignorance in safety. I can't fight this battle for you, but I can give you a home that loves you as you are, the same thing I tried to give your father."

Váli sat back, slowly beginning to return to some semblance of calm. "Is that why Loki still has so much sway with you? Because you have this in common?"

I sighed. "Your father was my world, Váli. We were so much for each other. When it's your turn, you'll understand."

We sat in silence for a while, listening to the crackle of the wood in the fireplace. A long time had passed by the time he chose to speak again.

"So." He turned to me, unable to keep a straight face. "Does that mean I can bring home any man? As many as I please?"

I shook my finger at him. "Don't go turning this house into a brothel. You've got a baby brother to think of. Now get us a drink. It's time I told you about Alruna and I."

CHAPTER FIFTY-TWO

*"Ragnarok won't come as a great, dramatic burst. No, I
believe it will arrive as a series of small moments, a collection
of choices that will become an unstoppable force. We won't
even hear it when it comes knocking."*

—Unnamed Scholar, Prophetic Musings

"You could add Fehu to the string of runes, right at the end, and that should create a stronger effect." Loki scribbled out the new bits in Narvi's notebook.

Narvi leaned in, scratching his nose, leaving a spot of charcoal behind. "But couldn't that backfire? It's also used in fertility seidr."

Loki pointed to one of the runes further back. "It shouldn't, not with Nauthiz there to indicate constraint."

I reached around Váli to take his empty plate, the last remnants of dinner. "What are you working on?"

Narvi's face was alight when he looked up. "Communication with animals. It would give Váli and I a big advantage if we could speak while he's in his wolf form. I looked, but there's nothing successful in the archives." He pointed to a pile of books. "I read through all the old attempts, and we're trying to find where they went wrong."

"That's incredible." I looked to Loki. "Can it be done?"

He folded his arms over his chest and leaned back. "It's not impossible. He's been trying it with Sleipnir since I can at least act as a control, so we know if the communication is correct or not. The trouble is that we either need to translate the speech patterns of the animal or be able to communicate mind to mind. He'll be a genius if he cracks it." He ruffled Narvi's hair.

"Well, don't give up. I want my sons to be so undeniably amazing that they lay gold at your feet wherever you go."

"That'll be difficult." Váli put his feet up on the table and slid a whetstone against the blade of a hatchet, one piece in his vast array of weapons.

Loki blinked slowly, drawing a long breath. "Why's that?"

"Your reputation precedes us." Váli didn't raise his head, but the corners of his mouth were turned up in a little smirk.

I didn't correct him.

A knock sounded at the door. I looked to Váli, who shook his head. So did the rest. No one ever came to our hall, and certainly not in the middle of the evening.

As I made my way to the door, Váli stood, hatchet in hand. Loki's arm was around Narvi's back. They were as ready as they could be for whoever had come looking for trouble. I made time for a quiet hope that it was Gersemi or one of the einherjar looking for Váli, anything that didn't end in blood.

I opened the door.

A woman was on the other side, the hood of her cloak drawn up around her head to keep off the pattering rain. She was taller than I was and built sturdier. Jotun. There was a travel sack on her shoulder and the head of a snake was peering out from inside her hood, its tongue flicking at the air. Beside her was a young girl, draped in her own cloak, cradling a tiny white and grey wolf pup in her arms. Half her face was hidden. One emerald eye peered out, and something about it chilled me to the bone.

"I'm sorry." I tore my gaze away from the child, looking back at this woman. "I think you're in the wrong place."

"No, I'm not. Where is he?" Her voice was rugged, confident.

A chair scraped back and clattered to the floor behind me. Loki pushed me out of the way. He was ushering them inside before I could protest, checking the street for anyone else.

Once the door was shut behind them, he cornered the woman. "What are you doing here?"

My eyes darted to Váli. His knuckles were white around his hatchet. I held up a hand to still him and pointed at his brother. *Protect Narvi.*

"I had no choice." The woman pulled back her hood. Her hair was threaded into long locks, immaculately kept. Her eyes were so brown they were nearly black. "They know. They found us."

"*Skit.* Alright." Loki pulled his hands down his face, eyes wild with panic. "Alright."

"Yes, hello. I don't know you." I went to stand near them, forcing my way into the conversation. "What's going on?"

The woman looked down at me with such disdain that I almost backed away. "No, I don't suppose he would've told you."

"Angrboda, don't." Loki took me aside, his hands on my shoulders. "This was never supposed to happen. You were never supposed to know and now… they're in trouble, and I'm begging you to understand."

I shook my head, resisting every urge to push him away. "Understand what?"

Fear passed over his face. He took a deep breath and let it spill out. "This is my family. My other family."

The noise that ensued was all encompassing. Váli lobbed threats at Loki and his—what? His other wife?—Angrboda was egging him on while Narvi held the two apart. The wolf pup started howling. The child was yelling at everyone else and I—

I punched Loki so hard his knees buckled.

"You kept this from me?" I screamed at him, needing every ounce of my effort not to beat him to death. "You were with someone else, and you *lied* to me? You have a child with her and—"

"Three children." Angrboda turned her attention away from Váli's insults. "I hope it stings, goddess—"

"And I'm supposed to call you *Father,* you worthless sack of—"

"Stop, everyone! Please! If you just listen—"

"What right did you have to know anything? You never—"

"*ENOUGH.*"

The room fell silent, the word ringing out, a foreign thought inside our heads. A chill fell over the room, covering me in gooseflesh.

"You're acting like children." The girl was still, watching us, her voice as cold as winter.

Váli scoffed. "What are you, seven? What are you going to do about it?"

"Whatever I want." She pulled her hood down, and my stomach rolled. The right side of her face was mottled blue, like week-old corpse skin. The flesh around her right eye was sunken in, exposing the round whiteness of it. Her lips ended just past the middle, pulled back to show her teeth. She pulled off her gloves, revealing the same rotted blue on her right hand. With a move of her lips, all the shadows in the rooms lengthened and flickered.

Váli had nothing more to say.

"Please." Narvi slowly put his arms down, testing Váli and Angrboda to see if they'd strike at each other. "She's right. If you just stop, we can talk about this."

The screaming was over, but we were all coiled and ready to spring at the first sign of danger. My eyes flitted to each of them in turn, waiting for someone to make a move.

"Fine." The girl made her way to a chair and climbed up, standing on it to make herself tall. "Mother is too proud to ask, but I am not ready to die. If Odin finds my brothers and I, he may kill us. Or something worse. So, stepmother, I formally request refuge for us in your home."

"Hel, get down—"

Hel interrupted her mother. "I will not. This is stupid, and I'm not leaving."

"Why would the Allfather want to kill you?" Narvi took a step closer to Hel, nearly eye-level with her.

"He thinks we're fated to destroy what he's built," she answered.

"Where are your brothers?" I stretched out my tense fingers, cracking the knuckles. "Did you leave them somewhere safe?"

Hel pulled the wolf pup out of the neck of her dress where she'd stowed him, holding him out towards us. He was cowering. "This is my brother. And so is he." She pointed to the snake coiling itself down Angrboda's body, heading for the floor.

I looked to Váli. He shrugged. The child could have her games, but this was serious. We were a breath away from having daggers at each other's throats. "Little one. You have beautiful pets, but where are your brothers?"

Loki picked himself up off the floor and went to Hel's side. He ran a hand down her long, silken black hair and held her against his side. His eyes caught mine. "She's telling the truth."

"You finally have lost your mind, haven't you?" Váli laughed, tucking his hatchet back into his belt. "I mean, we all knew it was coming, but I'm glad I got to witness it."

"Your father said you had a mouth, but I'd be happy to close it for you." Angrboda crossed her arms, starting at Váli.

"Please." I gestured for them to stop, taking an impatient breath. "Someone, tell me what's happening."

Angrboda turned to me. "Loki and I created three of the most powerful children these realms will ever see. They'll tear through Odin and his spawn one by one until no one is left to hold the rest of us hostage. They'll change everything."

Loki took the pup from Hel's hands and held him gently against his chest. "Fenrir is only four months old. He still stumbles when he walks." He gestured to my feet, where the snake was passing by. I jumped back. "Jormungandr is three."

I watched the snake slide toward the table, where a stray piece of meat had fallen. Its tongue flicked at the air and it hissed, "Ssssnack."

Something cracked inside of me. A tiny bit of the normalcy and dignity I'd been holding onto all those years. It snapped off and floated away, like a piece of ice flow headed for sea.

And then Váli started to laugh.

"No. This is too perfect! I can't—" The unhinged laughter continued as he struggled to breathe, let alone speak.

"You won't find it so funny when I cave your face in, boy." Angrboda's cheeks were flushed, her whole body tensed for a fight.

"Can't you see it?" he asked me. "The wolf. The snake. Mother, he brought home Ragnarok."

"No. No, no, that can't be."

"But it is." Angrboda took a step toward me. "You and your father and your whole family have kept the realms in shackles long enough, and now we're going to free it."

Loki stepped between us, pressing Fenrir tightly into Angrboda's hands. "Sigyn is not like her father."

"It doesn't matter," Angrboda hissed. "She's one of them. *Skít, you're* one of them. You're lucky I didn't string you up when I first found you, licking your wounds like a dog. I'm not going to compromise to spare your feelings."

"I am *not* one of them. You came here because you need her." Loki gestured to me. "You want a place to hide the children, then you owe her some respect."

"I don't owe her anything. Not any of these Aesir, not ever."

Váli shoved Angrboda back, pressing himself into her space. "Good, that makes this easy then. Get the fuck out. Why would we ever protect you?"

"Because Odin plans to kill you too."

All eyes turned to Loki.

"What did you say?" I grabbed him by the collar, calling up energy under my skin, ready to burn his skin off. No one threatened my children.

He stared down at me, eyes cold. "Your father will be the end of us. You. Me. Váli."

"How can you know that?" I shook him.

He looked at Narvi, who stood all but helpless in the face of so much turmoil. "Go to your mother's bedroom. Take Váli. There's a floorboard under the bed with the tiny black x on it. Pry it up and bring what's underneath."

Narvi had to drag Váli away from Angrboda, but they went. The bed scraped across the floor, then creaked as they tipped it on its side. I kept Loki in my grip, not willing to lose my chance to hurt him if I needed to as the scratching and screeching of the wood floorboards came from the other room. And then they were back. In Narvi's hands was a cloth bag, drawn closed with a string. He brought it to Loki, who offered it to me.

"I hid it at first because I didn't want to lose you. And then I kept hiding it because I thought I could protect you. Change our paths. But I didn't."

The Goddess of Nothing At All

I pulled the strings. There was years' worth of dust caked on the cloth, and it filled the air as I wiggled the bag open. Inside was a book, old and nondescript. A journal. I opened the cover.

> *The contents of this book are not for the eyes of anyone else. It contains*
> *the prophecy of the seer, transcribed as accurately as I could manage.*
> *No one is to read the contents of this book, not even you.*
> *I'll return for it when it's time.*
>
> —*Odin*

And like that, the memory started to come back in flashes. A locked room. Stealing keys. Sneaking through the archives. Finding this book under the mattress. Our names inside the pages. The full prophecy of Ragnarok.

I flipped to the earmarked page and read it aloud.

> *War bonds twisted*
> *Fetters woven from Váli's entrails*

> *She saw a prisoner bound under the hot springs*
> *A lover of evil, in the likeness of Loki*
> *There sits Sigyn, alongside her husband*
> *And she feels no joy, do you not see?*

Angrboda's smile was wicked. "So. Whose side are you on, goddess?"

CHAPTER FIFTY-THREE

"They learned through prophecies that evil and misfortune
were expected from these children. All of the gods became
aware that harm was on the way, first because of the mother's
nature, but even more so because of the father's."

—*Gylfaginning*

I tossed the sewing kit on the table, next to a pair of Narvi's old clothes. Angrboda was at the far end, continuing to wolf down the food Narvi had brought up from the cellar. Váli and Narvi sat together, pouring over every page of the journal, looking for something, anything that might tell us more.

Loki had taken his other children to his bedroom, eager to get them out of earshot of the conversation we were about to have. Hel had protested, but she'd been yawning, and her fight was short-lived.

When he came back, I was halfway through hemming the bottoms of a pair of old grey trousers. The rune-blessed needle stitched itself through the material again and again, sewing a line that followed my finger.

"What's this?" Loki put his hand on my shoulder, and I flinched away, causing the sewing to veer off in the wrong direction.

I huffed and took the needle in hand, manually stringing it back through to erase the mistakes. "Your daughter's clothes are filthy, and she has no more. Now she'll have something to wear while I wash them."

"Sig, that's—" His voice hitched on the words. He took a breath. "Thank you."

"And why would you do that for scum like us?" Angrboda pushed back her plate, finally finished.

I glared at her. "Because no matter what I decide to do, no matter what you have planned for the realms, Hel is only a child. I still have some compassion."

Loki sat down across from the boys, leaving several seats between him and either Angrboda or I. "Did you find anything?"

"What?" Váli snapped. "Aside from the part that says you'll help destroy the realms?" Narvi read the passage aloud.

> *A vessel journeys from the East, Muspell's troops*
> *will come*
> *Over the waters, while Loki steers.*
> *All the monstrous offspring accompany the ravenous one*
> *The brother of Býleist is among them on the trip.*

"Assuming that they also consider you 'the ravenous one,' you're mentioned three times, twice by association. They're certain you'll be on that boat. So what we know is: Father and Mother will be trapped in a hot spring, where Father will be bound with Váli's entrails." Narvi shuddered. "Father will arrive at Ragnarok by ship to help fight against Asgard. It says the serpent will kill Thor and the wolf will eat Odin but doesn't mention Jormungandr by name. Fenrir is only used to refer to a brood of wolves." He tapped his fingers on the table. "It doesn't mention me at all. I don't know how to feel about that."

Váli leaned his elbows on his knees and looked to me. "So what do we do?"

"Why don't you ask your father?" I snapped. "He's had lots of time to think on it."

"All your wrath aside, I have thought on it." Loki got up and gathered wine and cups enough for everyone. "I thought about it every day, how I could change things, how everything we did might change the outcome. What I could do to protect you. When you got pregnant, and I came home to find out that, of all the names in all the realms, you'd named him Váli...Sig, it tore my heart out. But I couldn't tell you that."

"This has always been the problem with you, Loki." I didn't want to cry; I *wasn't* going to cry. I blinked away the mist and started hemming the second trouser leg, just to focus on something else. "You've never given me the chance to help. To make my own choices. It doesn't matter to you that it was my life. I can't imagine how little respect you must have for me."

"It's not like that. You were one of the only people that trusted me, Sig. I didn't want to lose you. What were you going to think when a prophecy named me 'the bringer of Ragnarok'? I never wanted to be that." He laughed. "And here we are anyway. Like some cosmic joke."

"You manipulated me. Took my memory. Years of our lives built on a lie."

Loki pinched the bridge of his nose. "I did what I thought I needed to. And it was wrong, but we got to have a family and so many good years. Am I supposed to regret that?"

I glared at him. "You're supposed to regret the lie."

"I do, alright?" He looked up, anger in his voice. And then he took a breath. Let it out. There was something buried in the emotion on his face. "I do."

But that wasn't enough. I stopped the needle, folded up the trousers and started adjusting the bottom of a small shirt. "It's strange. It fucking burns, Loki, but it's not all that surprising. The details, yes. But not the betrayal. I'm used to that by now. You should have told me about the prophecy, and you should have told me about her."

"*Her.* Like I'm not right here." Angrboda took a long drink.

"Bo, will you please shut up." Loki glared at her, then put his head in his hands. "I've tried to be diplomatic here, to at least keep you two from killing each other, but honestly, Sigyn, what right did you have to know?"

"*Excuse me?* How dare—"

"You cut me out!" Loki slammed his fist onto the table, shaking the bottles. "We had a life, and you couldn't forgive me. What was I supposed to do? Spend the rest of my eternity sulking behind you like a shadow? It was killing me to be here so close to you, knowing you'd never be mine again."

"You tore this family apart. The least you could have done was make it right."

He threw a hand in the air. "How? Nothing I did made a lick of difference. You weren't going to make space to forgive me, no matter what I did."

I pursed my lips, trying to find something smart and cruel to say. But he wasn't wrong.

"There's something I need to know." Narvi closed the journal and slid it into the middle of the table. His face was hard. Determined. "How did you do it? Are the children...naturally born? Is this something most Jotnar can do?"

"Hardly! If any Jotun could spawn an army blessed with seidr, do you think we'd be living under Odin's thumb?" Angrboda scoffed. "No, what we did was spectacular. Unique."

Loki looked at Narvi. "I was angry when I found Angrboda. Everything I had worked for was gone, and I was trapped in this...darkness. I thought, if all my effort avoiding my fate had been for nothing, why wouldn't I just do it? Just become the thing they wanted. It felt like everything was gone and nothing mattered. So I chose it. Angrboda and I worked with seidr that I hope you'll never touch, and it changed things. It changed the children."

The Goddess of Nothing At All

"Listen to him, sugar-coating this for you." Angrboda leaned in. "We drank and cast runes and fucked and cursed the gods and poured all that rage into these children. We made them, and they will be *glorious*."

I leaned back in my chair, tossing the sewing aside. "Yggdrasil shade me."

"And is that what you still want?" Narvi's face had paled. "To destroy everything?"

Loki shook his head. "I'm not proud of it, Narvi. I'd lost everything, and I was so tired of losing. I became everything you would hate."

A deep pain was furrowed on Narvi's brow. "And what changed that?"

A sad, delicate smile found its way to Loki's face. "You did. You always loved me, no matter what I was or how long I was gone. I would come home, and you'd wake up this small part of me that knew how ashamed you'd be of what I was doing. And it took years, and it was already far too late to go back, but that light in you kept pulling me back. I still don't believe in fate. We can make something of this, something different. Your new siblings, they're here now. Angrboda wants them to live up to the prophecy, but that's not what needs to happen."

"Fucking try and stop me," she barked.

"Bo, they're children, not soldiers. Leave it alone."

"And Hel?" Narvi tapped the cover of the book. "She's not in there, just the place."

"Self-fulfilling prophecy." A proud smile spread across Angrboda's lips. "The book refers to places that belong to Helheim. 'The halls of Hel', 'the paths of Hel.' But it doesn't have to. Not if they're her halls and her paths. She's gifted. They could be hers if she wants them."

"Gifted how? She's disturbing, that's what she is." Váli poured himself a generous cup of wine.

"She's been able to manipulate shadows since she was just a baby." Loki's eyes went to the door of his room, where she was safely tucked away. "She's got seidr in her blood. And she's smart. Pure, cold logic. But she's not evil. She protects her brothers and always argues for fairness even if it's just over sweets." That brought a smile to his face.

"You always wanted a daughter," I said.

He looked up at me, the smallest acknowledgement.

"So now what?" Váli stood up. "There's been all kinds of talking but no one has said anything about what we're going to do."

Now, that was a good question. I had the power to end it all in a moment, to throw them back on the streets with Loki and every last piece of his clothing. Never, ever see any of them again. Surely, Loki would come up with some devious plan to keep them all hidden away. He'd done it this long after all. But should the crimes of their father doom these strange children to whatever death Odin had in mind for them? How would their deaths sit on my conscience?

"I think they should stay here," Narvi said. "It's close to Valhalla, and like Hel said, maybe they won't look here. If Odin were coming, he'd have come by now. Maybe he won't figure it out. I…I don't know what to think, but I don't want to see anyone hurt because we turned them away. They're family, no matter what any of us feel about that."

"And what if Odin *does* find them here?" Váli argued. "What about us? And Mother?"

"Your mother can take care of herself, thank you." I pulled my hair back, fumbling with it as I thought. "If they get caught, they'll drag us down with them no matter how far away they are. The realm will be convinced we were involved, true or not. They stay. Under conditions."

"And what kind of conditions would those be, little goddess?" Angrboda stared me down.

"None of you leave the house. It's a miracle you haven't been spotted already, and there's no guarantee that you'll get that lucky again. We'll provide whatever's needed, and you'll stay inside until we come up with another solution." I sat straight, trying to appear more confident in my decision than I felt. "You will not pick fights with my family, physical or otherwise, and all of you will respect the way we run this household. No snide remarks about parenting, no pitting us against each other. Are we clear?"

"Clear as glass." Angrboda smirked.

"Good." I got up. "I think that's enough trouble for me. Loki can help you find a bed. Gods know he's shared enough of them with you."

I made for my bedroom, not waiting for a response. Another chair scraped against the floor. I nearly had the door open before Loki caught up.

"Sigyn."

"What do you want? I'm tired."

He gestured inside the room. "Just give me a minute. Please."

I let him in and closed the door. He was closer to me than I wanted. "What?"

Loki's face was a confused mix of shame and fumbling gratitude. "This means a lot, what you're doing. None of this is fair to you and no amount of apologies will fix it. But I'm sorry. You deserve better than this." He took my hand.

I let him touch me. Let it crawl up my arm like beetles under my skin. I squeezed his hand back. "No, I don't. If we're all bound to fate, then you and everything you bring with you are *exactly* what I've always deserved. Now get out."

CHAPTER FIFTY-FOUR

"The rules of hnefatafl vary by region, but the goal is simple: capture the king or die trying."

—*Midgard: Culture and Artistic Expression*

The butcher tossed each cloth-wrapped cut of meat onto the counter, one slab at a time. Twelve packages in all; stewing meat, deer steaks, and two full rabbits. Enough to do us for a few meals.

"Thank you." I put the gold on the counter, knowing full well he wouldn't take it from my hand.

The butcher kicked the door to his cool room closed, and the runes around the door jam flickered blue, humming to life. He wiped his hands on his apron and counted out the coin. "You're two pieces short."

Not this again.

"This is what we agreed a minute ago."

He spread out the coins with his red-stained fingers. "Price went up."

"I should string you up from the wall. This is extortion."

"Yup." He leaned against the counter and wiped the back of his hand across his wild beard. "We both know that I'm the last butcher in town that'll sell to you, Wife of Lies. Now shell out the two coins, or go home with nothing."

I reluctantly dug into my coin purse. He was right, and every few weeks he jacked up his prices. Threatening him hadn't worked because he and everyone else knew that I hadn't shown my face in Valhalla in years and that I more or less needed him. I tossed the coins with the others and haphazardly piled the meat into my bag before storming out.

Thankfully, that had been the last stop. I'd already gotten eggs for Jormungandr,

295

a pastry for Hel, and all the odds and ends we'd need to feed the small army we'd acquired. But the meat wouldn't last long, not with eight in the house.

I kept a steady pace through the market, keeping my hood up and my head down. Someone still spat at my shoes as I passed. I spent the rest of the walk home imagining what life would be like if I had just divorced Loki when I had had the chance.

When I arrived at home, I knocked three times, paused, and knocked three more. The key scraped in the lock from inside and an eye peeked through. Loki let me in and locked the door behind me.

"Did you get it all?" He took the bag and set it on the table, unpacking things one by one.

"I think so." I hung my cloak and took the packages of meat from him. "You're going to have to risk going in disguise again, or Váli's going to need to start hunting. If I buy this much from the butcher every few days, he'll either bleed my purse dry or realize we're up to something."

Angrboda came out from the bathing room, fully dressed, her face still flush from the warm water. "She returns."

I fished a bag from the pile of goods and held it out to her. "Your order, your highness."

Delighted, Angrboda held the package up to her nose and inhaled. "I've never loved anything in my life as much as I love Jotun coffee." She put it on the mantle and set to work putting water on to boil.

"You're welcome," I muttered. "And things here?"

"Calm as could be." Loki closed the door to the cellar and went back to the furthest end of the room, where he settled onto the floor among stacks of open books and notes.

Which left Angrboda and I alone.

She was raiding the kitchen for something, and feeling unwilling to help, I took in the scene in front of me.

Hel and Narvi had pulled the chairs out from the study and were playing a game of hnefatafl with Loki's wooden game board. Even from here, it was clear that Hel was struggling, and when Narvi moved his final piece into place, her expression didn't change, but the shadows around the room flickered and bent for just a moment.

On the other side of the room, Váli was getting ready to go back up to the training grounds for the second half of the day, but Fenrir was incessantly following him around, sniffing and yipping. Angrboda had said it was the wolf in Váli, that the pup could smell it on him, like family.

And last, Jormungandr had slithered his way out of the hot bathing room and into Loki's lap, where he curled up against the heat of his legs.

The Goddess of Nothing At All

A cup of dark coffee interrupted my view. Angrboda had her own, and apparently one for me. Curious. "Thank you."

"The kids?" I went to stand nearer, though not too near. "I think…I think they'll be alright. Hel seems versatile, and Narvi doesn't have it in him to hate anyone. Though I'm shocked Váli hasn't gutted Loki in his sleep."

"Frankly, little goddess, I thought that would be you." She returned my glare with a laugh. "Come on. You may not be my type, but you've got a little fire in you. If our roles were reversed, you wouldn't still be breathing." She took a long drink.

"One of the many differences between us, I suppose."

"Were you harbouring some hope of having him back?"

I looked at her. "Isn't that a bit personal?"

She swept a hand out toward the room. "And this isn't? We're all sleeping conveniently under the same roof, all connected by one scrawny man." That grin crept back on her face. "I've always wondered. What's he like when he's here? Is he the same Loki I know?"

"That depends. Now or before?"

"Both. Entertain me."

I sighed, taking a sip of the hot, bitter coffee. "He used to be sweet. Sure, he got us in a lot of trouble, but then he'd come home and do the dishes and read with me in bed. I could rely on him for anything. Now, he's a stranger. Narvi has all his affection, and the rest of us are just here. We exist together; that's all."

She shook her head, lips pursed. "No. Not the Loki I know at all. My Loki is full of rage and passion. Even this is too much. He's just sitting there, reading." She looked directly at me. "I used to know, you know. The times he slept with you. He'd come back dejected and sour. Mope around like everything in his sight was a mistake. Made him unbearable. I was almost jealous."

"I don't see you as the jealous type."

"I protect what's mine. That's not the same as envy." She took a drink. "Honestly, you could take him to bed now, and I'd be more likely to join than fight you off. But that doesn't seem your style."

My face turned red, struggling for something to say.

Angrboda chuckled. "Don't worry. You're too nice for what I'd want to do." With that she walked away, settling in beside Hel's chair to give her a few strategic pointers.

CHAPTER FIFTY-FIVE

*"Shared blood means nothing. There are some people you
would die for. Those people are your true family, a
nd fuck the rest."*

—*Tales of Midgard, Volume 11*

"This place is a cage. You've trapped me in here like an animal for weeks." Angrboda splayed herself over the table, still in the nightdress I'd loaned her for sleeping. Given to her, more like. She could burn it when she was done.

"You can always make yourself useful and help with breakfast." I swept past her chair and laid out the plates.

"I'll go hunting. I'll catch fish with my bare hands. Just let me outside."

"If you get caught, we all suffer. We're pushing our luck staying this long as it is." Loki was tending to the pan over the fire, the smell of bacon wafting up as he turned each piece. "Besides, Váli's been bringing home enough food for everyone."

"Really not the point, Lokes." Angrboda got up and stretched, then went to the counter to dice up some raw rabbit for Fenrir.

The door to Loki's room crept open and Hel wobbled out, rubbing her eyes. She made her way to the hearth and pressed herself against her father. "Morning," she mumbled.

He planted a kiss on her head. "Good morning, dove. I know what you smelled." "Bacon."

"Hop up to the table; it's nearly ready." Loki looked around. "Where are the rest?"

Narvi was curled up in the middle of a scattering of maps in the far corner, Fenrir on his lap. But Váli and Jormungandr still hadn't shown their faces.

"Váli came home late last night. Maybe he's still asleep." I gave a knock, calling

298

through his door. "Breakfast is ready."

A muffled grumble rose from the other side. I shrugged and left well enough alone. It wasn't my problem if he didn't get up. Just more bacon for the rest of us.

Angrboda put the plate of rabbit on the floor and clicked her tongue. Fenrir's ears perked up, and he bounded across the room towards breakfast. Meanwhile, Loki was putting the sizzling pan on a rack in the middle of the table, perfectly placed for each of us to pounce on it.

That was when we heard the scream.

Something hit the floor in Váli's room. Hard. There was a series of thumps, and before any of us could properly react, the door flew open. The screaming continued as a half-clothed bear of a man stumbled out, backing away from the door. His chest heaved, his whole body posed for a fight.

Out slithered Jormungandr, unconcerned with the man waiting for him to attack.

"A snake! There's a huge snake!" He turned to us to point it out, and the fear turned to a cold panic as he realized what he had done. "It's...oh, shit." He shrunk into himself, unable to cover his rather hairy chest with just his hands. Lucky for him, he'd had the sense to keep his trousers on.

Loki tilted his head, an amused smirk on his face. "Hello."

"H-hello, sir. Good morning. I'm so sorry."

"Who is this?" Angrboda had a kitchen knife in her hand, slicked with rabbit blood.

"I don't know." Loki leaned against one of the chair backs, looking more or less as predatory as Angrboda. "She doesn't like strangers, so you should speak quickly."

Narvi came to the table, hardly a care in the world. "It's only Hreidulfr."

"Leave him alone. You're going to scare him away." Váli came out of his room with two shirts in hand and passed one to Hreidulfr, who whipped it over his head in a heartbeat.

"So, I assume this is what I think it is?" I asked, staring pointedly.

"Yes, Mother, it is." He took Hreidulfr by the hand, and the young man's face turned bright red. "Are you finished interrogating him? Or will you let breakfast get cold instead?"

"Oh, I'm never finished." Loki pulled out a chair. "Come, we don't bite. Much."

Hreidulfr, bless him, did his best to look unaffected. He took a seat with Váli tucked closely to him. The rest of us found a place around the table and freed up an extra portion for our new guest. Only Angrboda was left standing.

"Bo. Put the knife down." Loki pushed her plate towards her, trying to tempt her.

"None of us know him. What if he tells someone?" She stretched each of her fingers on the grip of the knife, one by one.

"Have some sense." I gestured to the two lovers. "He's just been caught half-naked coming out of another man's room. We know his secret, and we could take him down with us."

"Mother!" Narvi's jaw was open, letting flies in.

"But that won't happen, will it?" I shovelled my own portion of breakfast onto my plate.

"One of the things you'll learn, Hreidulfr, is that being part of this family is about loyalty. Some of us are better at it than others—" my gaze flicked to Loki—"but the hard truth is that we are all we have. It's a difficult initiation, but we'll keep your confidences in return for the same. None of us fit out there, so we may as well fit together here." I picked up my drink and tapped it against Hreidulfr's cup. "To odd families."

That earned me a smile. Hreidulfr pushed his curly, short-cropped hair back, clearly still nervous. "Indeed, ma'am. You have my word, though I'm not sure what secret I'm keeping for you. Thank you for breakfast."

Seeing she was outnumbered, Angrboda slowly took her seat.

"So," Loki said between bites. "Where did you meet?"

"He's one of the einherjar." Váli reached across the table for bread, taking enough for two. "He's been training in Asgard for a couple of decades now."

"I was nineteen when I died, sir. Been here long enough to see my brothers arrive as old men." His voice had a dialect to it, something rural and traditional.

"And you know who we are?" I took a slow drink.

Hreidulfr nodded. "All due respect, ma'am, I've heard a lot of stories. I don't know what's true and what's not, but my pa always said a man shouldn't believe everything he hears. People say you're evil, but I know Váli isn't, and you all seem nice enough to me." He cleared his throat. "Anyone else would've run me out of town already. I appreciate that you didn't."

An uncontainable grin spread across my lips. "Oh, Váli, I like him."

"You're probably too sweet for this family." Loki pointed down the table with a piece of bread. "But treat my boy well, and you're welcome here. I assume he's been good to you?"

"Yes, sir, Váli is...he's very good to me, sir." He hazarded a glance at Váli and was answered with a kiss on the cheek.

"That's right I am." Váli was actually blushing. Love looked good on him.

"Tell me. How is it that Narvi knows you and we don't?" I got up to stoke the fire and put on a second round of food.

Váli shrugged. "You weren't always home when I brought him around."

"It's good to finally meet you, ma'am. He speaks highly of you."

I ruffled Váli's hair as I passed. "Such a good boy."

"I won't dare ask what he says about me." Loki laughed and reached under the table to scoop Jormungandr up and place him around his neck.

Hreidulfr mumbled awkwardly until Váli spoke over him. "Maybe if you'd do something worth being proud of, I'd have better things to say."

"Whoa." I stepped into Váli's view. "Not today. Neither of you. No egging each other on, no fighting, no knives. I'm having a nice day for once, and neither of you is going to ruin it."

"Yes, darling." Loki was grinning.

"Do not call me that."

But truth be told, it was the best I'd felt in a long time. It was a strange, mottled, misshapen family that I suddenly found myself in, but I wasn't lonely. As frustrating as it was to deal with Angrboda, and as much as I hated watching Loki being warm with someone else, it all felt...companionable at worst. The last two weeks had been a challenge full of wolf howls and bickering and shadows that moved of their own accord, but I'd never once felt alone. We loved our children, and that bound us together.

With something to be joyous over, this new addition to the fold, the entire table almost looked happy.

I was honestly surprised to see Hreidulfr return after training that night. He brought a sack of mixed vegetables to add to supper, and by the time we'd finished eating, he felt familiar, like a piece of the furniture.

"You think he'll stay?" Loki asked, before going back to whispering runes to keep the dishes washing themselves.

Váli and Hreidulfr were on the floor, tossing an old leather ball for Fenrir to play with. He was trying to explain things to Hreidulfr: why Hel was so strange to look at, why there was a snake and a wolf and a second woman. He seemed to be taking it with an odd sort of stride. As if he were happy just to hear Váli speak.

"He hasn't run yet." I wiped down a splash of water on the counter. "Váli needs someone. He's never brought home a friend. Even with all those einherjar, I don't think he has one."

Loki's lips pursed. "The boy could use a fresh start. Somewhere he can lie about his name."

"Maybe."

Loki turned, letting the dishes fall still. "Sig, you know I've been trying to find a place for them to go. It's only a matter of time before Frigg has a premonition and sends Odin in this direction. And I think you should come with us." He held up a hand as I started to speak. "Just wait, please. There's nothing for any of us here. We could take both the families and run. No more talk of fate, no more gods, no more watching our backs. Build a home on a lake in Jotunheim and just *live*. Don't you want that kind of freedom?"

I thought about it a moment, then shook my head. "We wouldn't make it three months without the apples."

"I'm working on that. I just have to be a very good thief, that's all. If we could solve it, would you come? Be a family with us?"

I sighed. "Do you have any idea what you're asking me? To go off on the run with you and your mistress, like that's supposed to be the end of some romantic story? You cheated, Loki."

"It's not that simple, and you know that. We were as good as separated." His eyes narrowed, staring me down. "Why didn't you ask for a divorce?"

I took a moment, staring at the wall, trying to find the right words. "It wasn't that easy for me. At first it was for the children, and then I was too embarrassed, too hurt. And then it didn't really matter."

He pointed to my hand. "You're still wearing the ring."

"I couldn't decide if I should keep it on or take it off. So, I didn't decide anything and here it still is."

"Do you still want us to be together?"

I glanced across the room, making sure Angrboda wasn't close by. "I don't know. No. But not no. You destroyed our lives so thoroughly that I don't get to move on. I don't have other options but you." I braced myself against the counter, staring down at the knots in the wood so I didn't need to look him in the eyes. "If I were to say yes and we left, how would—"

Fenrir started to howl.

"Nothing's wrong, Fen." Váli scooped him up. "Quit that."

But Fenrir scrambled out of his grasp and ran to the door, sniffing and pawing at the gap at the floor.

I looked out the kitchen window. Twenty einherjar were nearly on our doorstep, Odin leading the pack.

I turned to Loki. "They're here. Hide them."

"Bo, get the kids!" Loki ran to the door and grabbed Fenrir, holding his hand over the pup's tiny jaw to keep him from howling. "Hreidulfr, get out of here. Through Sleipnir's old room, here. There's a door to the outside. Go!"

Each of us was moving, but there wasn't enough time. Váli had just closed the bedroom door on Hreidulfr when the einherjar burst through the front. Angrboda had Hel in her arms and Jormungandr around her neck, dagger held forward.

"Stay away, hangman," she hissed.

Váli stepped up beside me, already removing his shirt, the rune tattoos on his chest beginning to shimmer.

The einherjar made way for Odin. He took us in, trembling and ready to fight, and entwined his fingers like an impatient father. "Come quietly."

"What, and no one gets hurt?" Loki spat. He'd grabbed the poker from the hearth and held it at arm's length, Fenrir tucked against his chest.

Odin shrugged. "I didn't say that. Take them."

The einherjar flooded into the room, knocking over everything in their path. I grabbed a kitchen knife and swung at the nearest, drawing a gash on her arm. Whispering the runes for lightning, I touched my hand to her face and sent her writhing to the floor. One down.

A deep howl pierced the room as Váli changed shape, the rest of his clothing ripping from his body. Fur sprung up, and bones cracked as he shifted. His wolf form was dark grey and emerald-eyed, and he was massive. Immediately, he sprung forward and knocked over a pair of soldiers, ripping one of their throats out.

Teal flame shot across the room and a tiny, shrill howl pierced the cries. Narvi was yelling, begging everyone to stop and see reason. Angrboda removed her dagger from someone's eye and swung for the next, wild with rage.

The shadows began to move.

One by one, the black shapes peeled off the walls, standing on their own crooked legs. They were flat as paper, hunched and broken in strange places. Heads with no necks. Long, creeping torsos that made them taller than anyone in the room. Each of them moved like oil toward their owners until they were on top of them, seeping down over them as if the einherjar had rolled in tar. Their screams were deafening.

Hel stood on the table, her tiny arms outstretched, lips moving in rune whispers.

I tried to take advantage of the distraction, but a flash of light burst from Odin's palm, flooding the room. It was blinding, nothing but white. Spots of black ran in my vision, and then the shapes of the einherjar, the table, my kitchen, slowly came back. When I could see, the shadows were gone, slunk back into place at their owner's feet.

"Get the girl!" Odin's voice stirred the soldiers back into motion, each of them squinting and rubbing their eyes, trying to get their grasp back on the room.

Hel. She had fallen back onto the table, hands over her eyes.

I rushed toward her, climbing over the limp body of one of the einherjar to step onto the table. I scooped her up and tucked her against me, leaping from the table. If I could get her out the door in Sleipnir's room, out into the city—

Something bit into my leg like it was butter. Pain shot up my calf and it gave out beneath me, toppling Hel and me to the floor. I barely felt the impact, only the searing burn of my leg. My dress had come up around my thighs and a bright streak of red tore through the back of my calf. Deep. A sword. My stomach lurched, more pain than I could bear. But I managed to roll on top of Hel, shielding her from everything above us.

"Sigyn!" Loki was close, but I couldn't wait, couldn't look for him. We needed to hide.

"I'll keep you safe. Crawl to the room." My words were a hiss, barely a whisper, but Hel nodded, tears streaking her face. We began to inch away, dragging my leg behind me.

Someone grabbed me by the arm and hauled me up, away from Hel.

"No! Let me go! She's just a child—don't fucking touch her!" I tried to fight, but I couldn't put weight on my lame leg. Then another had me, pressing my jaw together until my teeth hurt. A muzzle was wrapped around my face, to keep my mouth from moving. Every breath I took was steeped in old leather and sweat.

The fight was over. They'd brought enough muzzles for all of us. Loki and Angrboda were still thrashing against their captors. My boys were unconscious, splayed out on the floor. Hel's hands had been bound behind her, a leash clamped around her neck. There were two cages, one for Jormungandr and another for Fenrir.

Odin loomed over us, hands behind his back. He was proud of himself. My father, my captor. He laughed. "Did you think this would end any other way? That you could hide from us? There is nowhere that we can't find you." He waved a hand. "Take them to the dungeons."

The einherjar at my back pushed me to walk and I fell, the muscle in my leg refusing to work. I was sitting in my own blood, my hands covered in it. I blinked, trying to force back the darkness that was looming at the edges of my vision. Another attempt to drag me up only shot a flash of pain through my body.

The light in the world flickered and went dark.

CHAPTER FIFTY-SIX

*"The portents of Ragnarok were found deep in the
woods, hidden by their Jotnar parents. Their capture was
easy and without incident, and the city has nothing
more to fear from them."*

—*Public Notice*

I knew something was wrong before I opened my eyes. The smell. A thick mildew,
like an abandoned cave, and underneath it was sweat and human waste.

Fingers stroked the top of my head, a gentle caress. I rolled over. My muscles
ached and the floor beneath me was hard, only thinly lined with dirty straw. Narvi
smiled down at me, my head on his lap. His face had started to bruise.

"Good, finally." He looked away, through the bars that separated our cell from the
one next to us. "She's awake."

"Sig." Loki pressed himself against the other side of the black steel bars. "Are
you alright?"

I shivered, the damp cold having already made its way into my bones. I'd certainly
had better days, but it was all aches, not the burning of an open wound. I pulled my
dress up. My calf was intact, a thin pink scar where the gash had been. Someone had
healed it.

I looked at Narvi. "Did you do that?"

He shook his head. "The dungeon is warded against seidr. I can't cast anything.
Someone must have done it before they threw us in."

"Is everyone here?" I struggled to sit up, taking in the dark, putrid room. It was
dimly lit by a pair of torches, condensation dripping down the walls. At the far end of

305

Loki's cell was Angrboda, curled up in the corner, head hidden in her arms.

"I'm here." Váli was in another cell past Loki's. They'd given him a blanket to cover himself, but that was all. His skin was littered with small wounds, but he seemed alright.

Loki stared at the ground. "They took the children."

"I don't understand why they wouldn't just listen." Narvi touched the purple and yellow bruise around his eye, wincing. "We could have talked it out."

"When have you known your grandfather to listen to anything?" Loki leaned his back against the bars, facing away from us, but still close. His voice came back as a whisper. "He's going to kill them."

Narvi reached through the bars to touch his father's arm, his face twisted with grief. "You don't know that. There's still time. We can find a way to compromise."

No one had the heart to tell him he was being naive.

Not long after, the iron door to the dungeon scraped open, dragging across the stone. Einherjar poured in, two for each of us.

"Those two last," one said, pointing to the cell with Angrboda and Loki. "They're dangerous."

Our cell opened. Four einherjar came in, pulling us up and strapping our hands into iron cuffs and putting the muzzles back onto our faces. Narvi kept his eyes down, and I waited for one of them to step out of line, just once. I was no warrior, but they'd leave with a black eye. They went for Váli next.

And against everything I'd seen from her, Angrboda didn't fight the einherjar. They had to drag her from the floor and force her to her feet like a ragdoll. Her steps were stumbling, automatic, like she was barely there at all.

They took us through the corridors of the dungeon, up the stairs, and back into fresh air. I could still close my eyes and navigate every corridor of Odin's halls, even though I could barely remember the last time I'd stepped foot inside. They were taking us to Gladsheim.

Everyone was there when we arrived, all the gods staring at us from on high. Only Idunn's seat was empty.

At the base of the dais were three cages. One for a snake, one for a wolf cub, and one for a little girl.

Angrboda came to life at once, tearing herself free from the grip of her captors and racing forward. She nearly made it to the cages, but one of the einherjar caught her by the hair and pulled her back down. She hit the floor, muffled cries bursting out from her leather muzzle.

Hel grabbed the bars on her cage, her mouth bound, tears rolling down her cheeks as they dragged her mother back into line with us.

"Welcome," Odin said, far too jovially. "I'm sure you'll want me to get right to the point, so please, have a seat."

The einherjar pushed us down in front of the dais, forcing all of us onto our knees. Odin sat back in his throne. "You're here today charged with the crimes of treason against Asgard and the nine, conspiracy to invoke Ragnarok, and, at the very least, aiding and abetting. The einherjar will remove your bindings since we've temporarily warded Gladsheim against runes. I want to hear what you have to say for yourselves."

He waved his hand, and the soldiers behind us began to unbuckle the straps of our muzzles. I needed to think quickly. Loki and Angrboda knelt on one side of me, Narvi and Váli on the other. What could I do to save us?

As soon as her muzzle came free, Angrboda was screaming. "You fucking monster; I'll kill you!" Angrboda spat on the floor. "I'll rip off every last fucking piece of you!"

"You'll be lucky to see tomorrow." Thor leaned forward, the fingers of one hand reaching for the handle of Mjolnir, which sat on the floor beside him. "Shut her up."

The einherji cuffed her in the face, toppling her to the ground. Angrboda struggled up and spat again. Blood spattered onto the stone, and one of her teeth came with it.

"You've spent too much time thinking about fate, Odin." Loki looked up at him, pleading. "They're just children. None of them *have* to do anything. Please, let us prove it."

"Your paramour has other ideas about that." Odin accepted a cup of drink from one of the servants and paused to take a sip. "She'd like to see us all dead at their hands."

"You're fucking right I would." Angrboda snarled.

"It doesn't matter what she wants," Loki said. "They have minds and lives of their own. It's going to be their decisions that make their future, unless you give them no choice at all. If you kill them—"

"I don't plan to kill them." Odin smirked. "Just remove their chance of survival. Semantics, I know."

His tone curdled something in my stomach. "What are you going to do?"

"Why do you care?" Odin asked. "It's curious, isn't it? That you'd hide and help the woman who birthed your husband's bastard children."

And I just did it. After years of trying to be Loki's saviour, rescuer, and healer, I put myself first.

I burst into tears. "Father, they gave us no choice."

Loki's head whipped around, his eyes wide.

"I had no idea about any of it until they arrived. Angrboda came to our door with her children and forced her way into my home. She was aggressive; she picked a fight with us. Loki insisted that they stay. We were in danger. I didn't think I was strong enough to face the two of them." I wiped the tears away, sniffing. "What could I do? I had to protect my sons."

Not a word of it was a lie. Let him save himself.

"You *bitch*." Angrboda struggled to move, but the einherjar were holding her down. "I knew you were no better than these pretenders. If I ever see you again—"

"It's true." Loki's expression slowly shifted away from shock. "She knew nothing. We forced her to take the children in. They had nothing to do with it, nothing we didn't make them do."

I had to believe that he understood. That he knew whatever it was they had in store for Angrboda's children couldn't happen to mine.

Odin huffed. "How am I supposed to believe that? You'd lie to protect her."

"Of course I would." Loki craned his neck up, catching Odin's eye. "But what was she before I came to Asgard and claimed her? Quiet. Docile. Obedient. She isn't capable of what you think she's done. Do you really think she had a choice in any of this? She's too *good*."

They bit, those words. There was some truth in them, but I would never again be 'too good.' Time and spite had made sure of that.

A throat cleared, drawing attention to one of the often-vacant seats. Hod.

"I think Sigyn has suffered enough." He toyed with the collar of his shirt. "Váli is an asset to the einherjar, and Narvi is a fine student under my watch. While I can't condone anything Loki has done, this family has caused no trouble and to punish them for this, for something clearly beyond their control, would be an injustice."

Odin scratched his beard. "It amazes me that you have allies after all this time. Very well. Let the shame be punishment enough. The people of the city will make sure you feel it." He got up and walked down to the cages that held Angrboda's children.

"Don't touch them." Angrboda strained against her captors, eager for blood.

"I won't need to. Someone will do that for me." Odin peeked down into the mesh cage that housed Jormungandr. He hissed and snapped at the steel. "The serpent will be taken to Midgard and tossed into the sea, where it will inevitably be eaten by something bigger."

"No." Loki shuffled forward and was dragged back. "You can't just leave their lives up to chance, please."

"Let it earn life if it can." Odin rattled the second cage, the one where Hel was sitting, her legs pulled up to her chest, still in Narvi's old clothes. "The girl will be sent to Helheim, as suits her namesake. You wanted her to be a goddess so badly? Let her die trying."

"She's just a child!" Narvi cried out. "You can't expect her to survive!"

Odin's gaze turned to him. "You'd best hold your tongue before I change my mind about you." He went to the last cage. "And the wolf. He and I have a personal vendetta, don't we? He'll be trained with the einherjar to become one of our own. A force for the good of the realms. A play against fate."

Tears were rolling down Loki's face. "Please. Don't do this. You took Sleipnir. Wasn't that enough?"

"You should have thought of that before, Liesmith. It's far too late to beg for mercy." Odin climbed the stairs and sat back down. "Let Sigyn and her sons go. Take the others back to the dungeon."

"Father!" Narvi tried to move towards Loki.

Váli cracked him in the side with his shoulder. "Shut up, you idiot." The rune tattoos on Váli's chest had begun to change shade, a clear sign he was angry. But the wards in the room would never allow him to shift form.

The einherjar pulled Loki and Angrboda to their feet. They fought, but it was no good.

"I love you!" Loki screamed as they pulled him toward the doors. "I will find you, I swear it! I love you!"

But the three children couldn't answer.

The doors slammed shut. Fresh tears welled up. I didn't know how to help any of them. And even though they weren't mine, even though their existence was a kind of betrayal… I wanted to save them.

"As for the rest of you," Odin said, leaning forward to peer down at us, "you keep getting lucky. Don't find yourself in this position again."

"So we should just ignore the prophecy then?" I snapped. "The one where you murder and imprison us?"

A smirk rose beneath Odin's beard. "I have no idea what you're talking about. If that were a prophecy, we'd all know it, wouldn't you think?"

He looked to Frigg, then to Thor. They shook their heads.

Bastard.

"If you won't admit it, let us go." I had no hands to wipe the tears away, so they dripped down my neck, underneath the collar of my dress.

"Fine. Uncuff them." He waited as we were each let go and pulled to our feet. "And don't forget to say your farewells to your husband's brood."

It was a test. To see if I'd betray myself. I urged Váli and Narvi forward, towards the door, and when I was sure Odin had looked away, I looked back and caught Hel's eyes. They pleaded with me to stay, to find a way to help. But I couldn't. In a room full of gods, I was nothing at all.

CHAPTER FIFTY-SEVEN

*"The monsters have been taken care of. The choices we have
made today will abate Ragnarok and ensure the safety of the
nine realms for the foreseeable future."*

—Odin - Public Notice

O ur hall was ghostly when we returned. The remnants of the battle were strewn
across the floor; chairs knocked over and shattered, makeshift weapons
discarded, boot prints coating the floor. A pool of blood where I'd been cut.
The smear of red as I'd dragged myself away, trying to protect Hel.

And now they were gone. No more Angrboda to curse my name and all my naive
habits. No more shed snakeskin or puppy howls or dancing shadows. All that odd
fellowship, the common ground, gone. And our lives were once again in tatters.

Narvi slid his hand into mine. "It's going to be okay."

It had to be, didn't it? How much worse could things get than they were? Every
decent moment had continuously been snatched away from me. When were things
going to change?

Váli grumbled as he picked up a chair and put it back. The leg was bent. It wobbled
and fell over again. He screamed and launched it at the wall, shattering it into pieces that
clattered to the floor. He stood there, huffing and puffing, the blanket around his waist,
his tattoos changing colour, and neither of us was going to get in the way of whatever he
did next. Wolfhides were nothing to trifle with when they were angry.

"Narvi," I whispered. "Get your brother some trousers."

The moment Narvi left the room, the front door burst open. I had the wildfire in
my hands in a breath, but it was Hreidulfr. He slammed the door shut and raced past

310

me, bumping me and snuffing out the flame.

"Yggdrasil above." He took Váli's face in his large hands and stared down at him. "I thought you were dead."

"I'm not." The rage in his face cooled at the sight of him. Váli's hand covered Hreidulfr's, and he bent his neck up to kiss him. "I'd never die on you."

I blushed and turned away to give them some privacy. Narvi had come back with the trousers and put them on a chair instead.

Narvi looked at me. "What now?"

"Now," I sighed, "we have a drink."

I went to the cupboards and pulled out a few bottles of spiced mead, the kind Loki liked, then took them to the long hearth in the middle of the room. Narvi followed, four cups in his arms. A moment later, Váli came with furs and Hreidulfr with cushions.

There's a silent knowing to mourning. A sadness that falls into place like a mist, and it's so thick that the only way to see through it is to sit close and stay together. So we started a fire, curled up on the floor around it, and told Hreidulfr what had happened.

Váli reached up to touch Hreidulfr's cheek, his head on his lover's knee, lying next to the hearth. "It's all ridiculous. Loki's a bastard, that's easy. But what kind of asshole do you have to be to throw away kids like that?"

Hreidulfr kept staring into the fire. "I don't know."

I let the silence sit for a moment, but I could see the war raging in Hreidulfr's mind. "Is there something you need to say to us? Do you regret being here?"

"That's not an easy question, ma'am." Hreidulfr didn't look at me. "If it wasn't for Váli, I'd probably turn tail and run. It's not a nice thing to say, I know. When I was growing up, Ma told us to do the right thing, no matter what. And I don't know what the right thing is. If those kids of Loki's kill the gods, that's definitely not the right thing. But neither is tearing children from their parents and sending them off to kill or be killed. I mean, won't something like that just make them hate us more?" Finally, his eyes met mine. "I died in service of my gods, but the longer I'm here, the more I see that the gods are just as broken as the rest of us. I don't want to be on the side of anyone who'd do what Odin did."

I let out a breath. "Whatever you decide, I understand. This isn't what we planned for ourselves either."

Hreidulfr looked down. Váli was staring up at him with worry in his eyes. "I want to be where you are. You can be my compass."

Váli smirked. "No pressure then."

Narvi leaned over, resting his cheek on my shoulder. "Do you think they'll be okay?"

"I don't know." I stroked his brown hair, long and beautiful like his fathers'. "I hope so. Jormungandr is smarter than anything in the sea. And Hel, she's powerful. She won't go down without a fight."

"And Fenrir is here," Váli said. "I might be able to keep an eye on him if they train him with the rest of us."

"You'd do that?" I asked.

Váli pursed his lips, searching his mind. "I guess. It's hard to hate him. None of this is his fault. We share a shitty father, so I feel like I owe him."

"What about Father?" Narvi looked up at me. "What will they do to him?"

I drew in a long breath, blinking back tears. "Nothing good."

The next morning, after a fitful sleep, Narvi and I went to Valaskjálf to find answers. Váli had training and it was more important than ever for him to appear obedient. So we went alone.

But there was chaos when we arrived at the entrance of the dungeons. A pair of einherjar were being screamed at by a burly, hairy man in full armour.

"You morons. And she just, what, got away?" He slapped one of them in the side of the head. "What in the nine am I going to tell the Allfather, hmm? I should take your heads right here, put you out of commission until sunrise."

I approached cautiously. "Has something happened?"

The man in charge gave me a sideways glance, realized who I was, and then rolled his eyes. "You. Just great. You should be in there with them, but instead you're pestering me."

I raised my eyebrows. "You know, I'm getting tired of all this attitude people keep giving me. Perhaps you'd like to test me, see how quickly I can light your mouldy beard on fire." I let him consider it for a moment. "What happened?"

He sighed and turned to face me. "There was an incident in the night. The wild woman and that weasel of yours got into a fight. She beat him good, nearly tore him to shreds with just her teeth. These two absolute shit stains—" he pointed behind him—"went to pull her off and let her escape."

"We didn't let her do nothing," the smaller of the two barked, his face a mess of blood and dirt. "She smashed my head into the wall until I blacked out. She's an animal!"

"She's just gone?" I asked. "They haven't found her?"

"Not yet. They will. She can't hide from Odin." The bloodied einherji rubbed at the side of his face.

"And my father?" Narvi's face had gone pale. "Is he alright?"

"I had the men take him to the infirmary a while ago. He got what he deserved, but not enough, if you ask me."

The Goddess of Nothing At All

"No one asked." I turned, dragging Narvi with me. When we were safely out of earshot, I pulled him to my side. "He's fine. He's stronger than that."

There were tears in Narvi's eyes, but he had that look he got when he was thinking, brow furrowed, eyes narrowed. "Why would Angrboda hurt him? It doesn't make any sense. There's no way she could blame him for this."

"I don't know." I lowered my voice, whispering into Narvi's hair. "But I'm going to make him tell us exactly what happened, and then we're going to figure out how to get him out of this mess. Again."

Except he wasn't at the infirmary either. One of the apprentices told us that Loki had seemed unconscious when he'd been brought in, but when they'd turned their backs to get healing supplies, he disappeared. They'd searched the entire building and found nothing. Not so much as a trail of blood. He was just gone.

"So he planned this whole thing, didn't he?" Váli leaned over the fence, his head close to mine and Narvi's. The clatter of battle sounded from behind him, the training session still in full swing. His face was a mess of fresh bruises, but he'd already refused to talk about it.

"He didn't come here?" I asked.

Váli scoffed. "Why would he? We aren't exactly best friends."

I pointed behind him, and Váli looked. Fenrir was chained to a post, howling and yipping at any of the einherjar that came close. The poor thing seemed anxious now that he was away from everything he knew. "I thought he'd come for Fenrir first. Can't we do something?"

"No." Váli shook his head. "If I get too close, they'll know I'm up to something. Everyone knows what Loki did, and they know I fought back." He gestured to his face. "I need them to trust me. Maybe if I'm patient, I can be more involved in his training. I think that's my best bet. But if Loki's planning to steal him away, good luck to him. There are tens of thousands of warriors in and out of here everyday, and they keep the pup under warded lock and key. It won't be easy."

I sighed. Between the lack of sleep, the exhaustion of the previous day, and simply…the acceptance that these things were inevitable and commonplace for us, I had no willpower left. "Let's go home. Maybe he went there. I don't want him bleeding out on my floor." I gave Váli a quick caress on the cheek. "I'll have something hot for supper for you and your *friend* when you get home."

Váli blushed a bit, a thin smile on his lips. "Thanks, Mum. Now leave before you get me in trouble."

"Loki?" I closed the front door behind me. He wasn't in the kitchen, but that would be an awfully obvious place to hide. I signalled to Narvi to start checking the rooms on the right side, and I went to the left. My bedroom door was ajar. And as I peeked in, a tiny mewling came from the far corner, behind the bed.

As I rounded the mattress, a full-grown forest cat was lying in the darkest corner of the room. It was thin, unhealthy. Its fur was old and grey, and its emerald eyes peered back at me, tired.

I put my hands on my hips and let out an exasperated breath. I was no longer the young woman who sprang to his aid out of unbridled love, and this routine was getting old.

And yet...

I knelt down in front of the cat and held out my hands. "Come on, Loki. It's just us."

The cat let its head fall again, making no effort to get up. So I pulled it into my arms as gently as I could.

"Narvi! Bring the healing kit." I laid the cat on the bed as Narvi rustled through cupboards in the kitchen. "I can't help you if you don't change back. You're safe."

And he did, after a moment. He still wore yesterday's clothes, dirty and covered in blood. A piece of the flesh of his shoulder was torn away, the markings jagged like teeth. He was bruised and the skin on his cheek was broken over the bone.

"All this to escape?"

Loki didn't so much as smile. "We had to try. They took everything, Sig."

"It's not over. You still have us, and we can try to fix this."

"How?" He stared into the corner, listless. "Hel and Jormungandr are already gone. They made sure we knew. I don't even know where to start looking for them."

Even after everything, I still hated to see him cry.

Narvi came in, rune ink and poultice bottles tucked under one arm, a bowl of clean water in the other hand. He knew what he was doing, so I let him clean Loki's wounds.

"We know exactly where Hel is going. If we just—"

"What?" Loki spat. "*Ride* to Helheim? How? It's closed off to everything. Only Odin's been there, and he's not exactly going to divulge those secrets to us."

"If you just listen—"

"I'm tired of listening!" Loki was trying to sit up, but Narvi pushed him back down, still attempting to clear the dirt from his shoulder. He looked ready to push the boy away but thought better of it. "They're going to take all of you. You saw the prophecy and you *know*. We can't just let them do this. We've tried to follow the rules, tried to do what they said. They stole from us anyway. Four of my children, Sigyn.

Four. It's time I steal something from them."

"Father, please don't do anything rash." Narvi rinsed the bloody rag and opened the bottle of rune ink. "You're going to make things worse."

"How can it be any worse than this?" Loki looked at Narvi like he'd lost his mind.

Narvi stopped, brush and ink in hand. "You could die. We could die."

It was enough to give Loki pause, but he shook his head. "You're the only one who's going to survive. The rest of us are doomed."

"Awfully sure of yourself for someone who doesn't believe in fate." I took the brush from Narvi and started to paint runes near the bite in Loki's shoulder.

Loki slapped the brush from my hand. "Why are you helping me if you think I'm such an idiot?"

I looked at the brush on the floor, the ink splattered across the wall and the sheets, then back to him. "Apparently because I'm also an idiot. Forget the ink; just heal him."

Loki shut his mouth long enough for us to work together, closing up the wounds. When it was done, he looked more or less intact. It was his eyes that looked empty.

He got out of bed and left the room, forcing us to follow him to his own bedroom. Rummaging through his wardrobe, he began to change into fresh clothes.

"Where are you going?" I leaned against the doorframe.

Narvi was trying to get into his line of sight, make him look at him. "You should sleep."

"I can't. I have to do something." Loki stopped to look at me. "They're my children. You have to understand."

"When are you coming back?" Narvi's eyes were glistening.

Loki tipped his head back, drawing a breath. He pulled Narvi into his arms, and I caught sight of the tear that disappeared into the top of Narvi's hair. "When I can. They'll be looking for me. I love you, son. Always."

Narvi pushed back, his face red. "Then why can't you just stay? Why do you love them more than us?"

"I don't." Loki stumbled over the words, trying to draw Narvi back into his arms, but the boy wouldn't have it. "It's just that you're safe. You have your mother to protect you. You don't need me like they do."

"Of course I need you!" Narvi backed away, hugging himself. "You think I'm naive, but I'm not. Someday you're going to do something stupid, and you're going to die. And if you die, I'm not going to forgive you, because you could've been safe with us, but you left anyway. You always leave."

"Narvi, please—"

"No! I'm not watching you go this time." Narvi turned and stormed out. A door slammed a moment later.

"*Skít.*" Loki dragged his hand across his face.

"He's right." I stared at him as he looked up, his face twisted in distress. "Ever since you cut off Sif's hair all those years ago, you've been looking for new ways to get yourself into trouble. You always choose trouble, even when you're screaming from the rafters about how little trouble you want to be in. Someday, you won't come home. And I'm not sure what's worse: that, or that I expected it."

I left Loki alone to dress. To make his choice. And he did. From my seat in the study, pretending to read, I heard the front door open and close. Everything fell silent. Not a creak of wood or a breath of wind against the hall. Quiet, except for the pained weeping coming from the crack under Narvi's bedroom door.

CHAPTER FIFTY-EIGHT

"Weaving is one of the ancient arts of seidr, and when one
of the völur sit down at a loom, she's paying tribute to the
Nornir. They weave each of our fates with such care, how
could we feel anything but awe?"

—The Practice and Application of Seidr

Weeks passed, and Loki didn't come back.

Váli and Hreidulfr became our primary sources of information since they were around swaths of people everyday, and people loved to gossip. Angrboda had somehow slipped out of Odin's grasp, and no one had found her. There were rumours that Loki had run off with her, and yet more rumours that she had forced him into servitude in some dank cave somewhere, the two of them giving birth to more unimaginable beasts.

It grew more and more dangerous for us to be seen outside now that news of what Loki had done had spread. Narvi left for his lessons at the archives long before sun-up, to avoid being seen. He travelled in a different cloak each day, took different routes. Our last sources for food and materials closed their doors in my face. Hreidulfr did the shopping for us and hunted with Váli when time allowed. He was always careful, coming and going. It wouldn't do us any good for him to be caught associated with the Family of Lies.

Váli was the only one who seemed to be doing better than before. He'd taken a lot of beatings in the beginning, but he was vocal about his distrust of his father. He started calling himself Váli Sigynjarson to whoever brought it up. He'd already been on track for a promotion, and it wasn't long before his loud opposition of Loki and his tireless efforts had him training other einherjar, and, as he'd planned, Fenrir.

But it was Narvi who brought home the newest, strangest rumour.

"I overheard Hod talking with Frigg today. She was there looking for something. A book in the locked part of the archives. She's getting ready to leave."

"Leave for where?" I scooped out a bowl of stew and set it in front of him.

"Everywhere, I think." He blew on the first spoonful, far too hot to eat. "Uncle Baldur's been having nightmares that he's going to die. She thinks the dreams are true."

I looked across the table. Váli looked up from cleaning his knife, and his eyes locked on mine. "You don't think…"

I put a bowl down for him as well. "You can't blame your father for every little thing. It's just a nightmare, and even if it's prophetic, your father's never done something like that. I don't think he's going to start now."

"No?" Váli put the half-clean knife down on the table, the cloth stained old-blood-brown from years of use. "They take his kids away, and you don't think he's capable of just about anything?"

He was right. Loki had talked about stealing something of theirs when he'd left. A life could be stolen, technically speaking.

"It makes a horrible kind of sense, doesn't it?" Narvi's voice was quiet. "Uncle Baldur is Odin's favourite son."

Váli shrugged. "I always thought that was Thor, but Thor's a lot harder to kill."

"How does Frigg plan on stopping it?" I leaned my weight on the table.

Narvi swallowed. "I heard her talking about asking everything in the realms to swear an oath. She wants them to swear not to hurt Uncle Baldur."

I whistled. "That's some very old seidr. Leave it to her to dig up something like that."

"How does it work?" Narvi asked.

"I'm not exactly sure." I tapped my fingers on the table. "It's something I learned existed but nothing we'd ever be allowed to try. She has to be perfectly in tune with nature in order to communicate with it. She could ask anything – wood, iron, animals, flowers. Do it right and you couldn't so much as poison him because the flower would have promised not to. It would make someone undefeatable. That's why the runes for it have been locked away for centuries; it's too powerful."

"Well…" Narvi looked from Váli to me. "What do we do?"

"What do you mean 'we'? This has nothing to do with us." Váli shovelled back more of his stew.

"Baldur is our uncle, and if our father wants to kill him, he could die too." Narvi pushed his bowl back, only half finished. "We can't just let it happen."

"I can," Váli said. "He's your father, not mine."

The Goddess of Nothing At All

Narvi threw his spoon at his brother. "You're his son whether you like it or not. I don't want to be responsible for anyone's death when we knew and we could've *done* something. We have a moral obligation to save Baldur's life, even if you don't care about Father, which you *should*—"

"Please, stop fighting," I begged, massaging my suddenly aching temple. "I hate that you picked up all this morality somewhere because I'm very tempted to let Asgard devour itself, and you're making that very difficult for me." I took a deep breath, trying to regain my patience. "If I can confirm that the dreams are portents, we'll try to help your uncle, alright? And maybe your father while we're at it."

"How do you plan to do that?" Váli asked, wiping the stew from his tunic. "It's not like we can just *ask* someone. No one trusts us."

"There's still someone who might tell me."

He scoffed. "As if. Who are you going to ask? The Nornir themselves?"

I walked quietly, listening to the calm of the forest. Birds chirped and animals rustled in the bushes. The breeze blew on my bare arms and shook the leaves. I'd missed the calm of it all. I hadn't set foot near Yggdrasil in years, not since Idunn. It would never feel like home again, but the peace still enveloped everything.

I'd tried. Tried talking to her. But on the rare chance we were even in the same room together, she turned away at the first sight of me. I'd smiled at her once, and her face had blanched like she was going to be sick.

It wasn't just the betrayal. Whatever had happened to her in Jotunheim, it changed her. And I couldn't bear to know.

As I stepped into the clearing, I pulled my hood up over my head, moving quickly. Guilt reared itself in my chest. I shouldn't be here. It wasn't my place; it wasn't for my eyes anymore. But it was what stood between me and the answers I needed. If I could just avoid being seen—

Idunn was on the scaffolding at the base of Yggdrasil, perched on the highest rung of the ladder. She was reaching, grasping for an apple that grew just too far away. One foot was already off the rung, trying to give more leeway to her grasp. It was careless, putting herself off balance like that. What if she fell?

Without a second thought, I held my hand out and whispered a rune, pushing downward with my fingers. The branch dipped, and the apple set itself in her palm. Idunn snapped the apple from its branch and looked around. Her eyes settled on mine, and we stood for a moment, staring.

The branch straightened itself back into place. I didn't smile, didn't wave. She wouldn't want that. Instead, I kept walking, my head down. Past the scaffolding and around to the other side of the tree.

I didn't have the heart to look back at my past. There was too much in the present that needed to be protected.

Rounding the extremely broad tree, I came upon the entrance of twisted, gnarled bark. Tiny roots had twisted together in the shape of patterned knots, making the door look almost god-made, though She had been that way before the gods had built the city around it. Inside was true, pitch darkness.

I summoned a lantern, and the space illuminated. The walls were made of the tree itself, Her jewel tones glimmering with the light I had cast. Every inch was knotted bark, and the smell of damp soil and moss was strong enough to drown out any other smell. Nine passages sloped out and downward. Above each passage was a series of runes that gave each a name.

Yggdrasil's nine roots, leading somewhere in the nine realms. The root I needed would take me to Urd's Well, the dwelling place of the Nornir.

The floor was slick under my boots. I held the narrow walls to keep my balance, letting the light guide my way. I'd tried to travel the roots without a lantern once in my youth. It had been like walking into a void. I'd fallen and gotten confused, so I followed the wall downward, but when I reached the end, I was back in Asgard. I'd been convinced in the dark that I'd been going the right way.

After a lengthy walk down, making careful work of the slope, light appeared in the distance. Cool air brushed against my face, refreshing after the warm, claustrophobic passageway. I smelled the saltwater before I could see, heard the crashing of waves. I blinked the darkness from my eyes and looked ahead into the bright ocean landscape. The root had let out onto lush green grass that grew to the edge of the beach. The ocean lapped at the land, leaving wet stains on the sand as the waves drew in and out.

I lifted my skirts and kicked off my shoes, the grass dewy between my toes, and headed away from the water.

The Nornir were sitting near a small fire, under the shade of a tree. Three women, one old, one young, and one middle-aged. Urd, Skuld, and Verdandi. Their fingers were covered in rune tattoos, their clothing simple and adorned with tiny details from nature. They were around a loom, weaving long threads through it. As I drew closer, whatever they were making remained shapeless. Just a strange tangle of coloured threads and no picture at all.

"Welcome, Sigyn," Skuld said without looking up. "Would you like tea? You'll need to take it yourself; our hands are a bit busy."

"What are you making?" I sat down on one of the log seats, far enough away not to be a disturbance.

The Goddess of Nothing At All

"A life." Urd reached for another colour of thread, fishing it from a basket beside her. The thread came with her, but I couldn't see the end. It just kept coming, unravelling from nowhere.

"A boy will be born. He needs a future. Many futures." Verdandi pointed to one incomplete area. "He might take over his father's farm." She pointed somewhere else, as equally incomprehensible. "Or he may die of illness when he's only 7. There are so many possibilities."

"And you do this for everyone?" I struggled to see anything that made sense to me, but there was nothing.

Skuld nodded. "There are many tapestries to weave, and the picture only becomes clear as a life makes a choice." She gestured to the bottom, sweeping her hand upward. "As he lives, we will see his actions clearly. Only when he dies will the whole image be known."

"But you know his future," I said. "You're the Nornir. You know what's coming."

"*I* know what's coming." Skuld put a hand to her chest. "But many things are coming. It isn't until we narrow the choices that anything becomes inevitable."

"Do you know why I'm here?"

"I do." She let her thread fall and stood up, brushing off her red skirts. "You want to know about Baldur."

"Is he really in danger?"

"Oh, that is very clear. By no choice of his own, Baldur is headed for a very dark future." She motioned for me to follow her.

Around the other side of Yggdrasil's root was a clear pool. It was pure, a crystal blue with nothing below the surface but darkness. Skuld sat down next to its edge, and I took a place beside her. She reached into the water past her elbow, and when her hand came back, it was with a rolled-up tapestry, bound in the middle with ribbon. It was perfectly dry and a tag hanging from it read 'Baldur Odinson.'

Unwinding the ribbon, Skuld laid the tapestry out in the grass. It was longer than the one they had just been making, much longer.

"The life of a god needs more space." Skuld pointed to the bottom, where the image of a new born was stitched. The child was bathed in light. Images wove their way up the tapestry: a broken ankle, a first kill, the day he met his wife. It was all there. Some things that I knew and many that I didn't. And at the edge of the wild, unintelligible colours was an image of Baldur asleep. His face was contorted as if he were having a horrible dream.

I ran my hand down the fabric. "This is beautiful, but it tells me nothing new. Nothing I can use."

321

"You already know what to ask." Skuld watched me curiously.

The words were stuck in my throat. I really didn't want to know.

"Show me Loki."

Skuld reached into the pool again. She fished around a little longer this time, giving me a smile. "Some lives are wilier than others. Loki doesn't like being seen."

Finally, she drew out another roll. It was battered around the edges like it had travelled a long way and had seen many things. She unfurled it on top of Baldur's.

It felt…intrusive. I was about to peer into Loki's past, into things he had or hadn't told me. Things that he might have kept secret for a reason. More than anything, I expected to find an unfamiliar life. One he had hidden because part of me suspected that everything he had ever told me was a lie.

But it was all there. A baby cradled in Laufey's arms. Learning seidr with his mother. Her slow death. Growing up under Odin's influence. Nights spent seducing Odin's marks. Sneaking into Freya's room. Fighting with Heimdall. His exile and the century of things that he had and hadn't mentioned to me.

A smile spread across my lips, and my eyes grew misty. The next section was more colourful, more vibrant. There was a large image of the two of us sitting at his fire the night we met.

Skuld pointed to the next picture, a nondescript instant of Idunn and I laughing. "This is important. This is exactly the moment he fell in love with you."

I blinked back the tears.

Nearly every image after had me in it. Our seidr lessons. Our first kiss. The first time we slept together. Times that we fought side by side. The births of Váli and Narvi and Sleipnir. Years of memories with our children.

Then Idunn. And our fight. Him leaving. A dark, lonely image of Loki, curled into himself, sobbing into his hands, alone in the woods. The colours faded into greys and greens and midnight blues. Angrboda. Pain. Seidr. And three children. There was one small moment of brightness, of him looking on both of his families together. And then the image of it all being torn apart.

At the top, next to the blankness of the future, was an image of Loki carving out a weapon, half his face distorted like he was becoming something else. Another shape.

I looked to Skuld. "Well, it's ominous, but it's vague. It doesn't necessarily have anything to do with Baldur. What else can you tell me?"

"Your father has already made arrangements to avenge your brother's death." Skuld rolled both the textiles up and put them back in the pool. "Frigg will try to stop it."

"Will she succeed?"

Skuld stared into the distance for a moment. "Maybe. But Loki is in pain, and pain is a good motivator. He'll find what he needs if he looks hard enough."

I slumped over. "I'm so tired of all this, Skuld. Should I even try to stop him?"

"You should. It's true to you and to who you are. It's…unlikely that you will. But not impossible. Trying will make the difference. Trying will set new things in motion." She reached for my hand. Her skin was cool, like there was no life in her. "Your path has never been easy, and there are many choices ahead. But there is always something after that, and after that, until we are dead. Your after might be bigger than all this. Don't give up."

I laughed. "I don't know if I want something bigger. This is already more than I want. I'd like to sleep. To rest. To stop struggling."

"And that's the trouble, dear. You're not ready." She stood up and pulled me with her. "You will be. You will hate it, but you will be."

Putting my other hand on top of hers, I gave her a tentative smile. "I wish you'd given me better news."

"Lies get us nowhere." She walked me back to the root, past her sisters who were still hard at work. Just before the entrance, she stopped me. "If all goes as planned, you'll find Loki in the gardens at Valhalla at midday, one week from now. It would be better for you if you found him before that. Changed his mind. I don't hold hope for it, but there are paths where you succeed. Good luck."

And I went back up to Asgard, my head reeling. One week.

We searched everywhere for Loki, as quietly as we could. Hreidulfr went to the public places we couldn't go, like pubs and markets, while the rest of us searched the places we knew he liked. Preferred hunting grounds, his old cabin, the homes of old allies. We were on our last day and still he was nowhere to be found.

I tried one last door.

It was late. I'd waited on purpose, until most people were inside and the candles were pouring out windows. And then I knocked.

The door opened. Lofn was there, a thick fur robe tied around her, covering her nightclothes. Her eyes went wide at the sight of me, and she pulled me inside, slamming the door.

"Are you crazy? Why did you come here?"

"I'm sorry. Something is happening, and I can't find Loki. I know what happens to people associated with us; that's not what I want for you. Just…have you seen him?"

"No." She crossed her arms over her chest. "Not since he took Idunn. He wanted to stay here, and I told him to never come back. Like you should have. I should never have gotten involved with you two, certainly never should have married you."

I rolled my eyes. "Do you think you're the only one who says these things? It's easy to say, from the outside."

She shook her head, clearly impatient. "He's not here. He'll never be here again."

"Worth a try." I turned the door handle, moving to leave, then stopped. "If it helps ease the guilt, the marriage was good while it lasted." Then I left.

CHAPTER FIFTY-NINE

"Baldur was plagued by these nightmares. He couldn't say
who or how, but he knew without a doubt that he was going
to die. If only we'd understood in time..."

—Asgard Historical Record, Volume 36

Narvi at home under threat
one of us slept. We knew what was coming.

I made Hreidulfr promise to keep Váli and Narvi at home under threat
of death. I couldn't have them getting in the way or becoming tied to
whatever happened next. I went to Valhalla alone.

The hall was nearly empty when I arrived, despite the tables being set with endless
platters of food. A roar sounded from the garden doors, where einherjar were pressing
out into the daylight, trying to shove their way through.

It was impossible to see past them into the garden. Many of them towered over
my head, craning their own necks to see past the throng. I pushed, forcing myself into
what little space there was between the soldiers. Something clanged in the distance, and
a cheer went up again.

It took forever to reach the front. But there he was, Baldur, God of Light, standing
just in front of the Valkyrie fountain. Thor stepped forward and swung his hammer at
his brother's face with all his might, but the hammer stopped short, lingering in mid-
air. Thor slipped and landed on his ass, the sudden loss of momentum making him
stumble. Another cheer.

Someone threw a rock. It stopped inches from Baldur's face and fell to the ground.
Someone else struck at him with a piece of lumber, which snapped in half rather than
strike him. It seemed like Frigg's plan had worked.

I looked around. All the gods were there, laughing and drinking and trying to kill Baldur. A large collection of items had built up at his feet, and he laughed at each attempt, clearly enjoying his new immortality.

They'd even managed to get Hod to join, though he didn't seem to be enjoying the spectacle as much as his sighted counterparts. Eyvindr wasn't with him, but there was an old, hunched woman keeping him company. That was something.

Loki, though, was nowhere to be found.

Skuld had been very specific about when, and obviously this was the right time and place. So where was he? My eyes flitted to the birds in the trees, then to a cat that was slinking through the crowd.

Yggdrasil shade me, he could be anyone.

As little as I wanted to do it, I walked along the edge of the circle, making my way to Frigg. She looked up as I got closer and gave me one of the falsest smiles I'd ever seen.

"Congratulations on such a great feat of seidr. I'm glad you've saved him." I crossed my hands over each other, head down, attempting to appear demure and submissive.

"It's a very good day." Frigg's gaze went back out to the scene in front of us as someone threw a tomato at the God of Light. It burst in mid-air, not a single drop landing on him. "Nothing can hurt my son now."

"Nothing? Can you really be sure that you've asked everything in the nine realms? It's an awfully long list."

"I'm certain. I spoke with everything worth asking." Frigg's gaze drifted for a moment, as if something invisible had caught her attention.

"What didn't you ask?"

She spoke faintly, distracted. "Useless things. Grass… mistletoe… cloudberries…" And then she stopped registering that I was there at all, her eyes glassy and distant.

Frigg hadn't been as thorough as she ought to have been. Skuld knew, and so would Loki, somehow. My eyes caught on the crone speaking to Hod. She had something in her hand. A small spear almost as long as an axe. It looked woven from smaller pieces, but I wasn't close enough to see what. She lifted her arm and said something that brought a smile to Hod's face. Then she flung the spear.

A shriek poured from Frigg's lips just before the spear pierced Baldur's chest.

There was a gurgle in his throat as Baldur tried to breathe, red trickling over his lip. He dropped to his knees, hands grasping at the thing protruding from him. Trying to pull it out. Then his body seized, and he fell, his limp body curled in the dirt. Unmoving.

Frigg was at his side before I could remind myself to breathe. She cradled him in her arms, blood staining her clothing. Ear pressed to his chest, she waited. There was nothing but the long, drawn out silence as she listened for his heartbeat. A wail escaping her that froze my blood, and she collapsed onto her son.

"Come back!" Tears streamed down her cheeks, fists clenched around the fabric of his tunic. "Please! I was supposed to keep you here; you can't go!"

But he was already gone.

Everything she had done had been for nothing. Her son had died anyway.

Then the garden came alive with cries of pain and vengeance. How had it happened? Who had done it? How was one of their gods dead?

I wiped at my cheeks, expecting tears. But they were dry. My brother was gone. But how many years had it been since we'd spoken? I loved him, had loved him. But I barely knew him.

It should hurt.

Trying to think through the shock, I grasped at facts. The old woman who'd thrown the spear…Who had she been? Hod was still there, but the woman was gone. And then the yelling pierced the fog that had fallen over me, drawing my attention back to the world.

"He threw it!"

"It was Hod!"

"Murderer!"

"Murderer?" Hod stepped back, stumbling into someone behind him. His face was a mess of confusion, his eyes wide. "Who's been killed? What's happened?"

Several of the einherjar stepped forward, each speaking out of turn that they'd seen Hod throw the spear, that he'd killed his own brother.

"I didn't kill anyone!" Hod was struggling to keep his balance with so many bodies jostling around him. "I can't *see*; how could I kill anyone?"

"No!" I pushed forward, trying to break through the people who were swarming closer to Baldur's body. "Hod didn't do it! It was the old woman!"

But they weren't hearing me.

"I saw it! It came from where he was standing!"

"His own brother!"

"No." Hod stepped back. "It wasn't me. I didn't throw anything!"

"Restrain him!" Odin cried out, pointing at Hod. A pair of einherjar took Hod by the arms and hauled him into the circle, forcing him to his knees next to Frigg and the body of Baldur. "We knew that someone was coming for Baldur, but we never could have imagined it would be you. I knew you were jealous of him; you always have been. Living in the light while you were stuck in the dark. But I never understood how desperate you were."

"What?" Hod was fighting against his captors, trying to push back. "When I was a child, yes, but it's been two centuries! I have my own life, my own things to love. I didn't want him dead—I don't want him dead…" Hod settled, grief washing over him.

"They say they saw you. Will you call all these people liars?" Odin crouched in front of his son.

"Yes, Father. They lie. I didn't kill him."

Odin shook his head. "A better man would face his death with dignity." Odin wiped a tear from his own cheek and stood. "A life for a life."

No.

I pushed through the crowd, trying to get to him before they could hurt him. I was nearly there when someone pulled me back by the wrist. A hand touched my cheek and a burst of warmth flowed into my skin, dropping me instantly into a half-sleep. My knees buckled, and the strength went out of me. An arm around my back to bear my weight, pulling me ahead, my feet stumbling, dragging me through the enraged crowd.

Away from Hod.

It was like being underwater. I swung my fist, trying to break free. I was so sluggish, so sleepy that it was barely a brush against their cloak. I couldn't see their face.

I made an attempt to fall forward, back into the crowd. It was just enough to see Vidar, that newest addition to Odin's brood, slide out from the throng and drive a sword into Hod's back.

Hod screamed. A blood-curdling, desperate sound. The cry that forced its way out of my throat ripped it raw.

I fell like a stone, hitting my knees on the ground.

He was dead.

I hadn't saved him.

The stranger in the cloak hauled me up, pulling me out of the garden through the mass of screaming einherjar. They were mourning. Two gods dead.

Hod was dead.

"Sigyn, get up. We have to go."

The world was a blur. I looked up, finally able to see inside the hood. Loki. He had dragged me all the way into Valhalla, hands under my arms, trying to pull me to my feet. "You."

I couldn't keep my feet under me. My body was as limp as a ragdoll. As he was dragging me out of Valhalla, Frigg's voice rose above the crowd. "Who will go to Helheim and bring Baldur back?"

What about Hod?

My legs stuck against the floor as Loki turned me into an alcove in Valaskjálf and used the wall to prop me up. "Snap out of it. We need to leave."

I looked up at him. His face was so close to mine. The hazy part of my mind remembered the tapestry, the moments we'd been this near to each other. How had it ever been that easy?

"You killed him."

"He deserved it," Loki snarled. "They took my *children*, and I'm supposed to leave them alone? They're taking *everything*. I can't just do nothing, Sig, I can't! They think they're above the rest of us and they can't get away with this, and Baldur—"

"You killed Hod."

The anger dropped from his face, replaced with something else. Something dark. "I didn't. I wouldn't."

"It was your fault." The tears were falling again, soaking into the collar of my dress.

He was struggling for words. "It wasn't—I saw Hod, and I just…it was good to see him. And I shouldn't have been there. I wasn't thinking about him, just what I needed to do. I killed Baldur, but Odin killed his own *son*."

"But he's dead, Loki. You wanted vengeance, and the price was *our friend. Again.*" I tried to move away, but my legs still wouldn't hold me. Loki grabbed me, keeping me from falling, and the two of us slid down to sit on the floor.

"It's not what I wanted." Loki pressed his forehead to mine, hiding us behind his cloak. I pulled in a rasping sob, guilt pouring over me. He wrapped his arms around me like there was anything he could do to console me. I shoved him, but he held tighter. "I'm sorry. I didn't mean for this to happen."

"Didn't mean it?" I pried his hands off me and forced him away. His face was slick with tears. "I was going to stop them, save him! And you paralyzed me and took me away instead!"

"You could've *died.*" He propped himself up on one hand and wiped his face. "I would save you a thousand times even if it meant killing everyone in the nine."

I stared at him, waiting for him to hear himself. "And that's exactly why Odin is afraid of you."

His brow furrowed, and he bit his lip, the weight of it sinking in.

Noise poured into the hall.

Loki was on his feet in a heartbeat, pulling me up so hard that it hurt my wrist. "I don't want to fucking hear it. It's time to go."

CHAPTER SIXTY

*"There will be no more mention of the previous master
archivist in these pages. He has died a murderer of the worst
order, and he will receive no immortality by our hands."*

—*Archives of Asgard, Daily Records*

Váli had Loki pinned against the door before he could finish his sentence. The blade of the knife bit into Loki's throat, a trickle of blood already sliding down the metal. Váli's teeth were set in a growl, every muscle in his body tensed with the force it took to keep his father trapped. "Every time I think you've hit rock bottom, you make it worse. You're a fucking monster."

Hreidulfr put his hand on Váli's shoulder. "Breathe, love. Put the knife down. Hurting him won't change anything."

"Oh, but it will," Váli hissed. "Killing him stops everything. No more tricks, no more pain. Just the end. Maybe killing him stops Ragnarok."

I stepped closer. "Does it? How can you know for sure?"

Narvi pulled in a laboured breath, curled up in his chair, his legs drawn up against his chest. His weeping was like choking, grief so strong it pushed the air out of him, the background noise to Loki's imminent death.

Váli whipped his head around, snarling at Narvi. The tattoos that peeked out from under his shirt had started to ocellate, and his eyes were wild. His voice turned gravely as he barked the order, "Shut him up!"

He wasn't paying attention and the blade dug into Loki's skin, drawing a hiss but nothing else. Too afraid to speak, Loki's eyes caught mine.

As much as the moment was cathartic, someone would get hurt if Váli couldn't

330

control his rage. I touched my hand to my son's shoulder, a rune on my breath. Except mine was stronger than Loki's had been, and Váli collapsed to the floor in a sleeping heap, the blade clattering down next to him.

Loki slumped against the door, hand pressed to the small wound on his neck. "I think I nearly pissed myself."

"Shut up," I snapped at him. "Hreidulfr, help me get Váli into bed."

Hreidulfr and I hoisted Váli up, each taking a shoulder. My son was all dead weight and muscle, and it took us a few minutes to haul him into his chaotic mess of a bedroom. Hreidulfr settled him onto the mattress and pulled the blankets up over his lover's chest, pressing a kiss against his temple.

I shut the door behind us. Loki had found a cloth to stem the bleeding, and the three of us sat down at the table. He knew better than to sit close to Narvi, who was still sobbing, and so Loki chose the furthest from all of us.

I put my arm around Narvi. "I'm so sorry, darling."

He pulled his wrist across his face, and it came away wet and sticky. "Hod can't be dead."

"I wish he wasn't. I tried to help…" But there was nothing I could say that was going to ease his grief, especially when both the boys blamed Loki. I pulled him against my side, blinking back my own tears. "But this, all of it—" I looked at Loki "—has to end here."

Loki's whole body tensed. "How can you say that? They took my children and—"

"With all respect, sir," Hreidulfr said, turning to Loki. "I'm the only one here who isn't acting on emotion. On Midgard, no one would question what you did. You'd have been within your rights to kill Baldur. I understand what you did and why. But you keep putting people in danger, and I can't let you do that to Váli. He told me what's supposed to happen to him, and I already have enough nightmares about his insides being used to shackle you down. I don't need you trying any harder to get him killed."

Loki's face paled at the accusation.

Hreidulfr turned to me. "So what now? How do we keep everyone alive?"

We fetched parchment and charcoal and went over the facts. The realms thought that Loki was gone, disappeared into thin air. He would stay missing, never leaving the house in his own shape. And no one could know what Loki had done. Váli had direct access to Fenrir, and he could act as eyes, ears, and messenger. Hreidulfr would continue to funnel supplies to us and would use his temporary postings around the city to bring us news. We drew out an escape plan in case things went badly. A place to meet on the border of Jotunheim, where we could seek refuge in exchange for information.

It was as good a plan as we were going to get.

I turned to Narvi. "What would you like to do?"

His eyes had dried halfway through the planning, but he hadn't said a word. "I don't know."

"Do you want to keep studying?"

Narvi was quiet for a moment. "It's the best way to honour him. He would want me to work harder."

"I think it's important you keep your routines, as much as you can." Hreidulfr tapped his hand on the table. "No one is coming for you, and you can't act like they are. It'll make them suspicious."

"I want a funeral for Hod." Narvi blinked back more tears.

"Of course." No one else would be celebrating the life of the man who had supposedly murdered the God of Light. It would be up to us.

Narvi stood up, composing himself. "I want to do it tonight, but there's something I have to do first. I'll be back soon."

My heart ached, worry flooding me. But what could I say? "Be careful, please."

We watched in silence as he pulled on his boots and left.

When he returned a while later, he had someone with him.

Eyvindr.

His eyes were bloodshot, his face pale and empty. He trembled, and if a stiff breeze came by, he might collapse under it.

"He should be there," Narvi said before anyone could ask. "No one should mourn alone."

I approached Eyvindr and took his hand. "I'm so sorry. I wish there was something I could say…"

Eyvindr sniffed. "There isn't. They're calling him a murderer." His breath hitched, and the next words came out as a wail. "They left his body for the crows!"

I pulled him against me, holding him as tightly as I could. Narvi started to cry again, and the room was silent, brimming with grief. Loki kept his eyes on his own lap.

When he'd gathered himself, Eyvindr took a look around. "Will we do it here?"

"No. We know a place that's better. Private." Narvi pulled his satchel onto his shoulder. "Somewhere we can speak honestly."

Eyvindr nodded, wiping his tears with his sleeve.

It took longer than I would've liked to walk out of Asgard and into the woods where Loki's cabin still sat. No one spoke. We pushed forward, two by two, with Loki and I bringing up the rear. He knew better than to look at me, and it was better that way. I

332

wasn't sure what I'd do if he spoke.

The cabin had seen better days; the roof was threatening to cave in, and the old benches around the firepit had turned decrepit with time. But we made ourselves as comfortable as we could, all of us tucked into furs, a cup of drink in our hand. We'd brought more than enough to last the night.

"Do you want to start?" I asked Eyvindr.

He shook his head.

"I will," Váli said. "When I was a kid, Hod caught me picking on Narvi. Mother had sent me to bring him home from his lessons, and he was so peaceful, just *reading*. So I started talking nonsense, trying to distract him. Narvi got so frustrated that he started to cry. And Hod, he came over, as patient as could be, and made me shelve all these books for him. Must have been hundreds. And he did that every day for a week until I could come into the archives without causing trouble. Smart bastard." He tipped his cup and poured a mouthful of mead onto the ground. "For Hod."

I held up my cup. "I was jealous of Hod for a long time. No one else ever was. He was smart and skilled but quiet. No one ever envies humble people. But I did. He somehow saw everything, even without his eyes. He knew everything. He got to spend his days with the books, and when I was growing up, that was all I wanted. To be him, listening to all these stories and making sure they were preserved for the future. No one ever paid him any attention unless they wanted something, but I thought he had it all. I was lucky that he loved me for as long as he did." I tipped my cup and let the whole thing pour out.

There was a silence, waiting to see who would go next. Loki cleared his throat. "Hod believed in me when I was too young and too angry to think I was worth anything. I had no parents, and Odin took everything I had, but Hod was just a friend. He wanted me to be better. While I was choking on Odin's influence, Hod was telling me to smarten up. Make better choices. Eventually, I listened. Never well enough." He poured out a drink and then gulped back the rest. His head dropped, eyes pinned on the ground.

Hreidulfr held up his cup. "I didn't know him. But he did good work for the realms, and he made your lives better, and that's enough for me. For Hod." And he poured a drink.

We looked at Narvi. He took a drink straight from the bottle and wiped the residue from his lips. "I always accepted that I was alone. That I didn't really have anyone the way other people did. They were always too afraid of us. But Hod saw me. Every time I thought something was interesting, he found me a book or a scroll so I could chase the idea. And I don't have friends or anything, but I had him and a whole future in front of me. And now he's gone, and it's like everything else is too. I always thought he'd be there for whatever came next. I don't know how to do it without him." He let half the bottle trickle out in a thin stream, puddling on the ground.

And there was no one left but Eyvindr.

He drew a long breath. "I have never told anyone this, and I will never tell anyone again. I loved Hod with all my heart. He was everything to me. We always thought you knew, but we were happy as we were, our love as our secret. There will never be anyone like him again, not if the realms live to be hundreds of thousands of years old. And all I can think is that I'd rather be dead than here without him." He looked up at the stars, sniffing. "You know, he liked to knit. He would make these long, awkwardly misshapen blankets out of wool yarn, because he could do it by touch alone, but it was more difficult for him to get the shape exactly right. He'd make them again and again. I have six of them because he wanted me to have something to keep my feet warm at night. But nothing is going to be warm again because he's not here."

The silence after enveloped everything. No one knew what to say.

Across the fire from me, Loki leaned back, his face shrouded in darkness, as if it could hide his guilt as he sobbed.

CHAPTER SIXTY-ONE

*"No one has ever said anything valuable to someone grieving,
and yet they keep trying."*

—Thodan Ironhammer, *Memoirs*

B y the next day, word had travelled. Odin had sent Hermod, one of his many
obscure sons, to Helheim. He'd been given Sleipnir and told to ride as fast and
as hard as he could. Bring Baldur home at any cost.

I didn't hold out much hope for that.

A funeral was held for Baldur, to burn his body. He would have a new body in
Helheim, and this one would only rot. I watched alone from the trees on the edge
of Asgard's harbour as the procession brought Baldur's body along. People from all
over the realms had gathered to watch, lined in the streets all through the city. The
procession laid him down in the ship that he had owned and put everything he'd need
for the afterlife inside in case things didn't go to plan. Gold, jewels, food, wine. They'd
even killed his horse. And when his wife saw him lying dead in that boat, she collapsed.
Dead. She was laid out next to him, and the whole thing was set alight, a fire as bright
and bold as befitting of a God of Light, and pushed out to sea.

No one spoke of Hod.

We did what Hreidulfr suggested. We laid low. For a month, we kept out of sight and
out of trouble. We waited for news of Hermod, because with it might come news of
Hel, and an idea of what would come next.

We bided our time.

CHAPTER SIXTY-TWO

"But the gods saw how the wolf grew every day and knew
that the prophecies foretold that it was destined to harm
them. Then the Aesir designed a plan..."

—*Gylfaginning*

"Are you sure?" We were moving as fast as we could without running, trying not to draw any attention as we made our way around to the backside of Asgard, toward the harbour.

"Positive. They told me the training wasn't working." Váli pointed to one of the einherjar's ships in the distance. "They're going to chain Fenrir up for good."

I stopped him in his tracks, and Narvi nearly ran us over trying to keep up. "Have you seen your father?"

Váli shook his head. "Nowhere. He never leaves the house as himself now. He could be anyone, and we can't wait."

"What did Fenrir do?" Narvi leaned in, voice low.

"Nothing. But I told you, he's been getting big. Real big. Loki wasn't joking when he said there's seidr in him. He talks. He's stronger than any of the men. They started testing him, tying him up to see how strong he was. Nothing could hold him, and Odin doesn't like it, not one bit. They went to the dwarves this time and commissioned something unbreakable."

My eyes darted around, trying to think. It was just us three against an army without even Loki's brute force to help. "Can you get us on board?"

"Come on." Váli led us forward, toward a ship brimming with battle-ready einherjar. And next to the ship was Fenrir.

"Ymir's breath, Váli."

"I know."

Fenrir was as big as a small house. Even sitting, he towered over the soldiers moving around him. Someone commanded him into the water, and he plodded in, paddling around next to the boats.

"Is he a threat?" I whispered as we approached the dock.

"Speak to him. You'll see." Váli led us onto the ship as they were packing on supplies; crates of bows, swords and spears were jammed between the seats of rowers. They were readying for war.

A woman stepped in front of us, blocking our way with her spear.

"They can't be here." She pointed to Narvi and I.

Váli grabbed the spear from her hand and threw it overboard. "Do I look like I'm negotiating with you? Sit down and remember your rank."

She hesitated, scowling at him. And then she sat.

There were another fifty warriors on board. On either side were another two ships, loaded with more einherjar. My gut curdled.

Váli led us to the side of the ship, leaning out over the water. Below, Fenrir paddled happily in the harbour, tongue hanging from between his teeth.

Váli called down to him. "Brother! Why are you down there?"

Fenrir looked up and caught sight of Váli. His tail started to wag, splashing water everywhere.

"I'm too big for ships now!" His voice was gruff, but he spoke like a child. Then he stood and put his front paws on the side of the wood. The entire boat swayed under the extra weight. His head still came up over the side, face to face with us. "Hello, Not Mother. Hello, Narvi."

I couldn't help but smile. "Hello Not Son. Your father sends his love."

Fenrir whimpered. "I miss him. He came three days ago as a mouse, but I don't speak mouse. Tell him to come again."

Váli stroked Fenrir on the nose. "I will; I promise."

That made him happy, and he began to pant, the hot breath all-encompassing. I blinked, trying not to be repelled by the smell of whatever he'd eaten for breakfast. "Darling, I need you to listen closely." I stepped up, as near to his ear as I could. It perked up as I whispered. "You should run. These people want to hurt you. We can distract them. Wherever you go, your father can find you, and you'll be safe."

The response didn't come right away. His ears twitched, and his nose snuffed, and finally he laughed. "You're funny, Not Mother. They can't hurt me. No one can. I'm stronger than everyone."

A horn sounded, and the paddles lowered into the water, making ready to set out. Fenrir hopped down from the ship's side, and it righted itself. With a bark and a paddle, the wolf was out in front, swimming his way towards the edge of the harbour ahead of the ships.

"What do we do now?" Narvi whispered.

Váli pushed the hair back from his face. "Nothing." He glanced behind himself at the small army on board with us. "We'll have to wait until we land."

The ship pulled up to a small dock on the island of Amsvartnir about an hour after we'd set sail. The three of us disembarked and followed the band of einherjar into the centre of the island. As we drew closer to where the others had gathered, I spotted warriors from other armies. Dozens had come from Sessrúmnir wearing Freya's colours. At least an entire Wing of Valkyrie stood at the ready. And in the centre of it all was Fenrir, tail wagging and oblivious.

The three of us pushed our way towards the wolf. At the front of the crowd was Tyr and his most trusted warriors. Váli was no oddity there, but Tyr noticed Narvi and I. He nodded our way, expecting an answer.

Váli leaned in, keeping his voice low. "There's no one in these realms who deserves justice more than my family. They should be here to see it carried out."

It was frightening how believable he sounded. A little bit too much like his father.

Tyr nodded again, giving his stoic approval. When the last of the armies had gathered and settled, he stepped forward.

Fenrir bowed down, his tail wagging as if he were winding up to spring into the air. "Are we going to play again?"

"Yes." Tyr bent to open a sack at his feet. "We have another test for you. If you're really the strongest in the realms, you'll be able to break this fetter. None of us can break it, but surely you can." He pulled a long cloth from the sack, as light and airy as Vanir gossamer. Tyr held it up for the wolf to see.

Fenrir's laugh was dark, judgmental. It seemed to echo off every surrounding surface, a howl that seeped under my skin and chilled me to my bones. And I knew. This was how it began. One small thing, and then another, and another. The strength, the laugh, the size of him. How each abnormality looked like malice until everyone around him was harbouring an uncontrollable fear of something they couldn't understand.

"You're joking! The last ones were steel." The toothy smile began to fade. Slowly, Fenrir sat on his haunches, watching Tyr with narrow eyes. He leaned forward, smelling the dainty ribbon, inspecting it. "Why would you bring me cloth?"

"Watch," Tyr said, tugging at the ribbon with all his strength. "You see that I can't break it, and neither can any other man here." He passed it to Váli, who pulled and ripped at it but couldn't tear it either. He passed it to another and another until Tyr felt he'd made his point. "We can't break it, but surely the strongest wolf in Asgard can." He held out the cloth for Fenrir to sniff again. "What do you say?"

In that moment, Fenrir looked at me. I tried to convey my fear without giving myself away. I didn't even dare to shake my head. And then the wolf turned back to the cloth. He sniffed it, and then each of the einherjar close enough to him. The mirth was gone. "You smell like you're afraid. If you're not lying, prove it. I'll let you tie me if one of you will put your hand in my mouth. If you're not afraid, if you're not lying, I won't hurt you."

Silence fell over the crowd. No one stepped forward.

My eyes went to Váli. His fingers twitched and stretched, his body rigid. We were running out of time, but what could we do against three small armies? Even if Loki were here, it wouldn't give us an edge against them.

"I agree to your terms," Tyr said, stepping forward. He reached out with his sword hand. Fenrir knelt down and opened his mouth only a sliver, enough to let Tyr slip his hand between his enormous teeth.

Váli turned to look at me, panic in his eyes. I tried to think. Was there a ward or a disenchantment that might help? I could set something on fire and give Fenrir time to run, but my boys would take the fall with me. I couldn't risk their lives, not for anyone.

The einherjar moved around us, taking the ribbon in hand. There was no time. I whispered, hoping a general disenchantment would break the binding from afar, but nothing happened. How much seidr had to be in that fetter to hold a giant wolf?

The einherjar wrapped the ribbon around Fenrir's legs. They tied his front paws together first, then the back, all four kept close by a tether in between. When they'd finished their work, I still had no answer. Each disenchantment I'd tried had failed.

The crowd moved back, waiting for the wolf to attempt breaking free. Váli grabbed my hand and squeezed so tightly that the blood stopped flowing to my fingers. He kept his face as cold and unfeeling as stone.

Fenrir tugged at the fetter, calmly pulling his back leg away from his body as if he expected it to break like a blade of grass. The cloth didn't budge. His eyes narrowed, and he tugged harder. Nothing. He began to thrash and tear, but it did no good. The fetter hadn't so much as popped a thread.

Huffing and panting, Fenrir stopped and stared into Tyr's eyes, his hand still between his teeth. The wolf clamped his mouth shut.

Tyr fell back, blood gushing from the stump of his arm. He writhed on the ground, clawing at his arm but refusing to scream. Fenrir threw his head back and swallowed the hand with a slick, sickening gulp.

Tyr's men pulled him back, out of the reach of the wolf, who had started howling long, mournful notes.

"Finish it!" Tyr commanded.

The three factions of warriors leapt into action, swarming the wolf. The Valkyrie took to the air, their swan wings springing forth from their backs. They flew above Fenrir, dodging around him as he snapped and lunged at them. Beneath, the other armies secured the wolf's fetter to a boulder, just one more thing to keep him in place. And Fenrir couldn't fight them all off.

A pair of Völur had already started to heal Tyr. There would be no bringing the hand back, but they would stem the bleeding, and he would live.

"Mother, please." Narvi pulled on my arm. "We have to help him."

"How?" I asked. And it was a true question. Trapped between all these weapons and warriors, I'd never felt so helpless.

A deep, anguished growl rose up. The job was finished. Fenrir couldn't move, not an inch. The more he struggled, the tighter it seemed to become.

"Brothers!" he cried. "Brothers, let me go. We have the same blood. Don't let them do this. Not Mother, Sigyn, please. Where is father? Father! Help me!" Fenrir begged, pressing his face into the dirt, his legs straining against the ties.

I bit into my lip, tears flooding my vision, trying to keep my mouth shut. It was the worst, most horrific choice. Us or him. But I would not lose my flesh and blood to save anyone.

Tyr was back on his feet, still holding the stump of his arm. "Get the blade. Do it right, no mistakes."

A pair of einherjar swept forward, one with an enormous, shimmering longsword in her hands. When Fenrir saw her coming, his despair turned to a snarl. "I'll kill you, I swear it. Bite your head off! Don't touch me. I'll kill you, I will!"

But she didn't care. She swung at Fenrir and when he opened his mouth to snap at her, she jammed the blade between his jaws, the tip of it digging into the roof of his mouth. The wolf's eyes went wide, not daring to move a muscle. And she wedged the pommel into the flesh of his tongue until it was stuck in place, keeping his mouth wide open. As soon as she let it go, the blade shimmered, and a pop reverberated through the air. It was some kind of seidr, though I couldn't tell what.

Left with only the chance to whimper, Fenrir slumped onto the ground, saliva dripping from between his teeth.

It was over. The warriors of all factions were talking amongst themselves. A cry went out, and the Valkyrie took wing, soaring back toward Asgard, a shining green flashing across the sky behind them. The rest started their way back to the ships. We didn't have much time.

I hurried to Fenrir, staying where he could see me. I rested a hand gently on his jaw, and he whimpered. "I'm sorry. I don't know how to free you, but we'll find a way. We'll get your father and get you out. I promise."

Narvi tucked his face into the wolf's fur, tears streaming down his face. "It's not your fault. You trusted them."

I looked back. Our affection was attracting attention. We needed to go before we were left to die on the island. "I'm sorry boys, but it's time." I looked up into Fenrir's enormous, tear-filled eyes. "He's coming for you."

We left him there, curled up in a ball, alone. Walking away cut a hole in me. I wanted to have saved him, wanted to have done the right thing. And in the end, I didn't. He'd ended up in shackles.

Was that going to be our family's legacy?

When the ships docked at the city, a messenger was waiting. He'd been sent to fetch Tyr and bring him to Gladsheim. Hermod had returned from Helheim. There would be news of Baldur—and of Hel.

CHAPTER SIXTY-THREE

"Despite the generosity of Asgard, the wolf had too much evil in it to be swayed. The gods deemed it too dangerous to remain, and it has been securely fettered, where it will remain for the rest of its days."

—*Public Notice*

Gladsheim was already full when we arrived. The gods had taken their seats, but they weren't alone. Anyone who commanded any influence in the city was present, from those in charge of the merchant and civilian quarters to the captains of every branch of Asgard's army.

As I scanned the crowd for familiar faces, I spotted Loki, though no one else would know it was him. He'd taken the shape of a woman, one of the faces he used for travelling the city. She was small and shy, plain and unassuming. The very opposite of Loki, which was the point.

We pushed through the mob, trying to reach him, but Odin held his hand up for silence. Beside him stood Hermod, dirty and road-worn. When the room settled, Hermod began to speak.

"I bring news from Helheim." He gathered himself, standing straighter, despite the circles under his eyes and the sag in his limbs. "I've been on the road a long time, and it wasn't an easy path. It took nine days to reach the bridge to the realm. It was guarded by a maiden. She asked me what business I had there, and I asked her if she'd seen Baldur riding past. She had.

"She told me to ride to the gates, but when I arrived, they refused to open. There was no way for me to pry them apart or to climb over, but with Sleipnir's speed, we

342

were able to leap over them. It's a dark realm. No sun to speak of, only torchlight and the glowing moss to see by. What I found on the other side...The girl, Hel..." He looked to Odin. "You sent her there to die or rule, and she's already taken command. She calls herself the Goddess of Death. She's put the dead to work, organized them. They're building a city there. They respect her.

"She agreed to speak with me. Asked me to stay in her hall. In the morning, I went to breakfast, and Baldur was there, his wife at his side. Hel asked why the Allfather had sent me, and I told her. She laughed at me. 'The realms weep for him,' I said, and she answered, 'I find that hard to believe.' When I swore it, she asked me to give my proof. And that is the deal. If we can prove that all things—living, dead, or never alive—weep for Baldur, he'll be returned to us. If even one thing refuses to weep for him, we lose him to Helheim forever." He sighed, staring out over the gathered crowd, his eyes dull. "I'm sorry; it's all I could do."

The crowd filled with murmurs, neighbour turning to neighbour as the weight of the task settled over them.

It was Freya who broke the din. "How can we prove that?"

Odin scratched his beard. "If Frigg can coax a promise from a rock, surely she can get a tear as well."

Frigg stood, her hands together in front of her. Her eyes were present, aware. "We'll do what must be done, as we always do. Who will help us? Who will ride into the realms and ask with us?"

The silence was broken immediately, the room filling with shouts and offers of fealty. The people were eager to prove their dedication. I put my hand up, though I didn't intend to help. We had enough to worry about.

"Good," Odin said, crossing his arms. "Prepare yourselves for the journey. Leave at first light. Ask everything in your path. Don't overlook anything and don't return until you've done everything in your power to make this right. Leave us."

The crowd broke, merchants and captains whispering to each other as they made their way toward the doors, offering each other supplies, horses, men. I turned to the boys. "There's something I need to do. Go home and stay inside. Don't let anyone in. I'll be there as soon as I can."

Váli gave me a suspicious look but pulled his brother along all the same. I turned and walked against the tide, trying to reach the place I'd last seen Loki, but when I arrived, she was gone. Following the crowd, I walked on my toes, trying to find her above all the heads. And finally, there she was.

I couldn't call out. It would draw too much attention. Instead, I pushed through the sea of people until I could reach out and tug on her arm.

Loki whipped around, surprised. But the shock quickly fell away. "Sig, you nearly gave me a heart attack."

I pulled Loki into a quiet hallway, dragging her further down until we were safely tucked in the shadows. The false shape fell away, and he was himself again, fire-haired and green-eyed.

A grin spread across his face. "Did you hear? Hel is alright! Such a spitfire, that one. Gods, if I could just get to her—"

"We need to talk." I looked around, not wanting to be overheard by eager ears.

"What's wrong?" There was already concern on his face.

I reached for his hand and took it. It was strange, touching him so casually, as if his skin didn't burn a hole in me. "Loki...something's happened. Fenrir's been chained up on the island of Amsvartnir. He needs you."

"Chained up?" He pulled his hand away, his lips curled back in a snarl. "How?"

"Odin gave the command. They were afraid of him, and they tied him with some kind of Dwarven cloth. He couldn't break free. There was nothing we could do."

There was a glisten in his eyes, each deep breath an exercise in constraint. "You were there?"

"I saw it. We tried to help him, but there was an army. I couldn't put the boys in danger. But Fenrir is alone now; you can get to him. You'll be able to help."

Loki pushed his hand through his hair, his eyes searching the hall as if there were answers there. Panic soaked his voice. "Why? Why this, why him? I thought they were going to train him?"

"I know. That's what they said." I cupped my hands over my mouth, trying to find the right words. "They got scared. He's so big and...he needs you. My disenchantments didn't work, and they put a sword in his mouth to keep it open. There's some kind of seidr on it—"

Disgust rippled over Loki's face. Rage began to spew from his lips. "A sword? A fucking sword in his mouth? How dare they touch him. Did they think something like this would just *stand*? That I wouldn't snap their fucking necks for this?" His voice was getting louder, more desperate. "I won't let them take him. They took so much already." A hitched breath. "All the years I tore myself apart for them. The scars, the nightmares, the things I've lost and now..." He was breathing in short, fast bursts. Loki's hands went to his face, and he let out a frustrated cry, so full of pain. "They're going to take everything, Sig."

I tried to steel myself against his pitiful display. "They're not."

"They will! They are!"

"You shut your fucking mouth."

Loki looked at me, startled.

I pushed him upright, pulled his hands away from his face. "Get yourself together. You can fall apart on your own time. Your children need you to be strong for them."

The look on his face was like a wounded animal. "But Sig, it's too much. Over and over again, I can't—"

"No. I don't care. I don't care how difficult this is for you or how overwhelmed you feel. This is what it is to be a parent, remember? Nothing is about us anymore. Odin strapped your son to a boulder, and he's bleeding and alone. No one can help him but you. And you're going to because that is the only fucking choice."

Loki nodded, an edge coming back to his face. A sharpness in his eyes. "Váli and Narvi are alright?"

"They're home." I nodded towards the window. "Go save your son."

Loki took a deep breath, his lips pursed like he was about to say something. But he didn't. The air distorted, and in a moment, he was gone. A hawk screeched and hopped onto an open windowsill. One stretch of its wings, and it was airborne, leaving me to sag against the wall and collapse into my own emotions.

CHAPTER SIXTY-FOUR

"Never get between a bear and her cubs."

—*Elven Proverb*

Loki didn't come home that night. I spent all night at the window, staring out into the darkness and waiting for footsteps. It was an odd thing, waiting up for him. Wishing he would come back and knowing things would be simpler if he didn't.

Morning came and there was still no Loki. Eventually there was a knock, but that was Hreidulfr. He brought pastries and we did our best to laugh as we ate. Laughter was easier to stomach than worry.

After breakfast, the four of us settled into my bed, Hreidulfr and Váli curled up together while Narvi jotted things down in a notebook. I faded in and out of consciousness, lying across the foot of the bed, too nervous to sleep and too tired to stay awake.

When the Gjallarhorn blew in the early afternoon, the rattle in my bones shocked me from my dozing. I pulled my head up and found Váli staring sleepily at me from the crook of Hreidulfr's arm.

"Get everyone up." I slapped him on the ankle. "It could be him."

Gladsheim was buzzing when we arrived. Some of the faces were familiar from the day before, the people who had offered to go out and help bring Baldur home. No one knew what was happening, but there was an apprehensive energy about the room. Frigg's seat was empty, and Odin's face was hard as stone.

Not long after our arrival, Odin called for silence.

"There's no reason to say this gently. Half of Asgard went out into the realms to save Baldur, and we failed. Someone refused to weep for him and now my son is lost."

"What?" Thor leapt from his seat, Mjolnir in hand. "Tell me who. I'll kill them, and we'll start again."

Odin shook his head. "One of the riding parties found an old woman on their ride. Jotun, they thought. She called herself Thokk, and when they asked her to shed a tear for Baldur, she refused and disappeared back into her cave. The riders searched for her inside, but she wasn't there. There was no other way out. One rider claims that they saw a hawk fly out of the cave after they went in."

"Has anyone heard of this woman?" Tyr asked.

"Never." Freya leaned on her elbows, head down.

"Do you know everyone in the nine?" Thor asked.

"Of course not. But I don't understand it. Everyone loved Baldur..." Odin tapped his fingers on his chair.

I bristled at that. I'd met plenty of people who didn't even *like* Baldur, let alone love him. What a deluded sentiment.

"What if it wasn't this woman at all?" Freya's head was still down, her voice low as she worked through the thought. "There's still someone out there with good reason to fuck up your life."

Odin looked at her. "You mean..."

Freya looked up. "Loki."

I wished it didn't but it made perfect sense.

"How can we be sure?" Thor's knuckles were white around his hammer's handle.

"Because most of us aren't idiots." Freya leaned back in her chair, staring at the ceiling. "I can have my völur divine it for confirmation, but he's been missing since he disappeared from the infirmary, and you just bound his son. I hate him as much as any of you, but if you thought he was going to let that slide, you were wrong."

"Hold your tongue," Odin snapped. "Has anyone seen him?"

No one could confirm that they had, and I certainly wasn't about to.

"We search for him. Starting tonight. Thor, go to Heimdall. Tell him to break protocol and join the search. We need to find Loki."

"Mother." Narvi tugged on my arm, breaking my focus.

My heart was slamming against the confines of my chest, and I tried to draw deep breaths to calm myself. We were sitting ducks in a room with a hundred souls that were going to want our heads as soon as they remembered us.

I took Narvi's hand and leaned to him. "Time to go."

The four of us kept our hoods up. One after the other, we slipped between the merchants and soldiers as they pressed toward the dais. The offers started, one person willing to give up their horses and carts to shuttle einherjar around the city, another offering their hunting dogs. Soon the whole room was calling out with some gift until the shouting dissolved into a collective cry for Loki's head.

I opened the front door to our hall and let the others go in before me. "Take only what's important and no more than you can carry. We leave tonight." I pulled the door closed and only then did I spot the shape in the hearthlight.

"Where have you been?" I approached Loki, ready to strangle him. "Do you have any idea what's happening out there?"

He smirked. "I imagine it's absolute chaos. Their poor darling, gone for good."

"So it *was* you." Váli stood next to me, arms crossed. "You are such a selfish bastard."

"Yes, well, that's the way of things sometimes, isn't it?" Loki stood up and put his palms on the table. "I'd have done the same for you. Pray I won't have to."

"Our fates are *linked*." Váli took a step towards him. "Whose fucking guts do you think they're going to tie you up with, hmm? What you did today might kill me. But you don't care, do you?"

"None of this matters." I turned to the three boys. "We can argue about it until they're on our doorstep, but it's done. We need to leave immediately."

"Agreed." Hreidulfr had already started opening cupboards, pulling out odds and ends.

"Hreidulfr." I waited as he turned to look at me. "You've been an important part of this family, but I can't ask you to come with us. We might not be coming back."

He kept working, putting his findings on the table. "Ma'am, if I were going to turn chicken, I'd have done it already. I swore to stay by him, and I meant it. Whatever this brings."

That was enough to draw a smile from me. "Alright. Do you need to get anything? We don't have much time."

"No ma'am. Everything that matters is here."

"Pack the rations then. Whatever will last and as much as your back can handle. Bring any golden apples you find. Boys, get your things."

The boys spread out across the house, the clatter and clamour of distress coming from every room.

"You're just leaving?" Loki glanced after Hreidulfr as he disappeared into the cellar.

"They're coming to hunt you down." I walked toward my bedroom, forcing him to follow. "We won't be here when they arrive."

"You can't just run from them. What good will that do?" Loki leaned himself against the doorframe, watching me pull my already packed travel sack from the chest at the end of the bed.

The Goddess of Nothing At All

"I'm protecting my family. Judge me all you like." I stopped and looked at him. "You could come with us. Not that long ago, you were the one asking me to run off with you. End this and be free with us."

"You don't understand, Sig." Loki came towards me, his hands held out. They were covered in bubbles, some popped and oozing red. "I couldn't get Fenrir free. The fetter is stronger than any of my seidr, and the blade is cursed. *This* is what happened when I touched it. My son is trapped there, and you're asking me to walk away."

"You know what? I am." I threw the bag on the bed. "I'm asking you to look at what's happened already. You wanted to burn everything, so you went off with the most hateful Jotun you could find and brought the *end of the realms* into existence. You're always lashing out, reacting to some harm someone does you without a second thought for which of us you might hurt, who you put at risk."

"Sigyn—"

"No, you listen to *me*. You told me you kept that book from us for a reason. So you could avoid the fate where Váli ends up dead and we spend an eternity locked up, yet you're driving us closer and closer to it. They can't kill him if they can't find him, so we're going. Come with us, because if you don't, his death will be your fault."

He didn't say anything. He just sat down on the bed and put his head in his hands.

I went back to work, pulling out my warmest traveling cloak and wrapped it around my shoulders. I didn't have time for him to pity himself.

I had everything packed and my hand on the doorknob before he said anything else. "Alright."

"Alright what?"

"I'll come with you." He stood up and took a deep breath. "After I do one last thing."

"Yggdrasil above," I turned away from him and went into the kitchen to throw my bag on the table. "It never stops with you."

"I mean it. Once I do this, I'll meet you. And then it'll be done forever. I promise."

I tapped my fingers on the table. "How am I supposed to trust that?"

"If you travel through the woods where my cabin is, not far from the other side is the border of Jotunheim. There's a lake and the mountains are beyond that. If you make camp on the far side of the lake, I'll find you. I swear it."

Váli had come out of his room with a stuffed bag and a bow over his shoulder. I shook my head. "The longer we stay still, the easier we'll be to find. I'm not waiting for you if it means getting caught."

"Four days from now. That's all I'll need." Loki put his hand on my shoulder. "It'll take at least a full day for you to get there. If I'm not there by noon on the fourth day, leave without me and go into Jotunheim. Find the first village and promise them information about Asgard in exchange for shelter. They won't turn you down."

Hreidulfr came up from the cellar with his arms full of food of all sorts. He dumped it onto the table and started to pack it into one of the spare bags.

"Four days is all you get." I stared daggers at Loki. "You're lucky you get anything at all."

"I know."

Hreidulfr drew attention to the two golden apples on the table. "This is it. What happens when they're gone?"

I packed them into the bag. "We'll figure that out when it's time. We need to get out alive first."

Narvi came out and the five of us looked at each other from around the table. "That's it then."

"That's it." I took a long look around the kitchen that I had lived in for so many decades. The books still piled on the table. The knife scratches in the wood. The herbs hanging from the walls that I'd never get the chance to use. "Say goodbye."

Narvi went to his father and wrapped his arms around him. Loki squeezed him so tight that it could've popped his head clean off.

"I love you. Be safe, son."

"I love you too. Don't make us wait."

Loki let him go, blinking back tears.

Hreidulfr stepped in and offered his hand. "May Yggdrasil guide you safely to us, sir."

Loki shook his hand, solemn. "It's been good to have you in the family. Look after my boy."

"Always."

And then it was Váli's turn. He didn't reach out, didn't move a muscle. Just stood with his bag and bow over his shoulder, cold as ice. "Don't fucking die. You'll break mother's heart."

Loki nodded. "Keep her safe until I get back."

I ushered the boys out the door, not waiting for a chance to say goodbye. I wasn't about to admit that he might never come for us. That this could be the last thing I said to him. It hurt too much. Instead, I stood in the doorway, the handle in my hand, and looked back.

"Do you remember," Loki said, coming closer, "we used to lie in bed and daydream about the future?"

"I do."

"I'm sorry for the things I couldn't give you."

No. I wasn't doing it. "Stop pitying yourself and be the force of nature you're supposed to be. Whatever you're about to do, there's no room for weakness. You got us into this, and you're going to get us out."

"Still. I'm sorry."

"Yggdrasil above, you idiot." I pulled him by the collar and pushed a rough kiss onto his lips. The shock of it had him nearly stumbling on top of me, his hand bracing the door frame for balance. His lips softened, and as he settled into the kiss, I drew away. "Don't fucking die."

Loki blinked, utterly confused. But when he stood, it was straighter. Like maybe something had put the wind back in his sails.

I left him in the doorway to decide what the kiss meant and fell into step behind the boys. The four of us headed to the gates of Asgard, keeping to the shadows, hiding under the cover of darkness.

CHAPTER SIXTY-FIVE

"I found that out when I sat in the reeds,
and waited for my best-loved girl:
body and soul was that wise lass to me,
and yet I couldn't have her."

—*Hávamál 96*

We made our way in relative silence out of Asgard, across the meadows, and into the woods where Loki had once lived. It was late when we arrived, stumbling through the forest in the pitch dark, not daring to light a lantern, but the tension kept us awake. The old cabin didn't seem sturdy enough to sleep in, so we started a fire and huddled around it, the quiet chirping of the woods enveloping us, each of us lost in our own thoughts.

I hadn't let myself think about it on the way there. I'd kept my mind on the plan: camp tonight, set out for the border in the morning. How rough the terrain would be, how much food we would need for the five—or maybe four—of us to make it into the mountains, how long it might take to find a village.

But staring into the lavender fire, it was hard to think of anything but the kiss. The reason had been simple enough; he'd been drowning in his own melancholy, and I'd done it to stir some kind of passion in him, some will to live. Like a bribe to keep going, whether I planned to fulfil the implicit promise or not. I hadn't expected it to feel...like nothing. An absence of hate. The touch of him had turned my stomach for so many years, and it was hard to put my finger on what exactly had changed.

There had been so many things. Meeting Loki's other children, learning to like them, then watching them suffer. Knowing the truth about the Seer's Prophecy and our fates. Expecting to be killed, or at the very least, not to truly live. Counting down the moments until I watched my children die.

All the anger I held for Loki didn't really matter anymore. It was there, but more imminent was the idea that this day might be the last. And if not today, maybe tomorrow.

Loki's actions had brought us here. Of course they had. But if Odin had heard the prophecy all those decades ago, my name doomed next to Loki's, and had done nothing...what else could it be but a betrayal? Odin had let my fate come for me.

It wasn't fair.

All the hate, all the effort of it suddenly felt like such an awful waste of time. If we were going to meet our end, I wasn't going to spend my last days filled with anger for the person who, for all his enormous flaws, had given me more of himself than anyone else.

When the end of everything came, my family would be all I had left.

Late the next morning, we rose, ate, and left. It was hard going, trudging through the forest. We intentionally kept away from anything that might look like a path, doing our best to skirt around the brush. The quiet still hung over us. Someone would bring something up, and we'd talk or laugh for a moment, and then the silence would descend again. There wasn't a lot of happiness to go around.

Váli held out a hand, signalling for us to stop. A stag was grazing in the distance. He was alone, his antlers bobbing as he ate, ears twitching for signs of danger. Váli passed his pack to Hreidulfr, making as little noise as he could. Then he notched an arrow into his bow and took aim.

The arrow snapped through the air and struck the deer in the flank. Its head reared back, and it cried out, but it wasn't giving up. It ran, darting between trees, making it impossible to hit a second time.

"*Skit*," Váli mumbled, borrowing his father's curse. He stripped off, tossing his clothes into a pile, and started to run through the trees, naked as the day he was born. And then he was changing, the tattoos that curved over his shoulder glowing. He fell to all fours, melting into the wolf, chasing after his prey.

Once he'd disappeared, I started to pick Váli's clothes off the ground and drape them over my arm. "At least we'll eat well tonight."

"If I could do that, I'd catch everything I hunted too." Hreidulfr chuckled, adjusting the pair of packs on his shoulders.

Narvi perked his head up. "Váli's caught the deer. He says we should follow."

I stared at Narvi. "What do you mean 'he says'?"

"Those runes I was working on with father to communicate with animals? We finished them last month. I can hear his thoughts when he's a wolf, but only at a short distance." Narvi blushed and started to walk away. "He's over here."

I caught up to him, stunned. "That's fantastic, Narvi! Why didn't you tell me?"

Narvi hesitated. "Things haven't exactly been good lately. It didn't seem like the right time."

Hreidulfr put his arm around Narvi's neck, absolutely colossal next to the lanky boy. "Never hold back good news, little brother. The realms need more of it."

That brought a smile back to Narvi's face, then something dawned on him. "I could teach you both. We should all know how to do it, just in case."

"Yes, you should." I squinted at the shape in the distance. A wolf was circling the carcass of a deer, splayed on the ground. "Among other things, it would be nice to know I'm approaching the right wolf."

"It's the eyes. Just like Loki." Hreidulfr said, pointing at his own. "Never saw a wolf with green eyes before."

A twig cracked under my foot and the wolf's head jumped up, ears perked. But once it saw us, it sat down next to its kill, tongue lolling out of its mouth. The arrow still sprouted from the deer's flank, but there were also a series of bite and claw marks along its body.

The wolf licked its lips.

I gave Váli a scratch behind the ears and set the clothes on the ground. "Nicely done. Get changed, and we'll start working."

Váli yipped, then took the pile of clothing gently between his teeth and padded into the forest for a bit of privacy.

The three of us went to work. Hreidulfr strung the deer from a tree and let it bleed out. Once that was done, he began at the head, and I started at the tail, cutting into the hide of the deer. As we worked our way around the carcass, Hreidulfr guiding my hand, Narvi built a compact fire. He came back again and again with rocks big enough to cook meat on, and as the fire warmed, we passed him cuts to cook. We wouldn't be able to use the whole deer, but we'd take as much as we could carry and leave the rest for the wild.

Váli came back halfway through and sat down next to the fire, using his knife to flip the meat. "Not bad for a day's work. Could you hear me after? When I went to change? I think I was further away than usual."

Narvi nodded, desperately uncomfortable. "You said you found a creek and that there were berries nearby. But, brother…I heard everything, even when your mind was wandering. Could you just…keep some thoughts to yourself?"

The Goddess of Nothing At All

I burst out laughing as Hreidulfr turned bright pink all the way to his ears. Váli put a hand over his mouth, trying not to laugh. "I am so sorry."

We ate the first cuts while we waited for the next round to cook. We passed a few hours that way, talking and wrapping freshly cooked meat into some of the already empty cloth Hreidulfr had packed the rations in. When we'd had our fill and stuffed our bags, we smothered the fire and kept moving.

"That must be it." Hreidulfr shielded his eyes from the sun, staring out at the massive body of water below. "The lake."

"That's it." I'd known the one Loki had meant when he said it. I'd passed it often enough on excursions into Jotunheim. Enormous and shimmering a soft blue-green, it was the product of glacial runoff from the mountains. It was hard to miss.

Trees dotted the grass around the lake, and as the terrain crept closer to the tall, snow-capped mountains, the ground grew steeper, rockier. Sparse and unforgiving. Once we crossed into the snow, things would get very, very uncomfortable.

But first we had to wait for Loki.

CHAPTER SIXTY-SIX

"We all think we can outrun fate."

—*Unknown*

Two days out in the wilderness with the cold wind sweeping out of Jotunheim had never been a fantasy of mine, so we found ourselves a place to camp between a spattering of spruce trees. One had fallen over, leaning against another, and we set to work covering it with brush and branches to make a canopy. And just in time, too, since the rain arrived not long after.

There wasn't a lot of room inside, not with a tiny fire to keep the heat. A hole was cut in the branches for the smoke, and we hung more branches for makeshift walls. It wasn't exactly comfortable, but it was warmer and dryer than outside at the very least.

Night fell, and we laid down to sleep. Hreidulfr and Váli curled up on one side of the fire while Narvi and I took the other. I dozed in and out of dreams, and once, in the early hours, woke to small whispers and the not-so-subtle sound of kissing. Young, reckless love. I remembered what it felt like. Who was I to ruin whatever comfort they could find in the middle of this desperation?

The third day came and went. No Loki.

I woke on the fourth day with a knot in my stomach. I didn't think he was dead; he wasn't capable of dying that quietly. But it didn't sit right with me. Looking across the fire, Váli was still asleep, Hreidulfr behind him. Narvi's warmth radiated inside the sleeping roll, his back against mine. By all accounts, everything was peaceful…so why was there a war raging in my heart?

Loki had until noon. Then we would leave, with or without him.

I had people to protect.

The Goddess of Nothing At All

The fire had died in the night, so I reached into the corner where we'd stacked small bits of wood. Trying not to wake anyone, I put them on top of the ashes, tucking twigs and brush in between. A rune for wildfire and the flame was burning lavender once more.

Narvi stirred as I pulled myself out of the sleeping roll and sat up, rustling through the bag of rations. I put the last of the meat near the fire to warm and broke off bits of the quickly staling bread. Cheese and nuts, a handful of the berries we'd found nearby. There wasn't as much left as I'd have liked.

"I'll go hunting." Váli was rubbing his eyes, his leg stretching out the furs. "Today will be better than yesterday."

"Have something to eat first." I passed him a cut of meat, and he propped his head up on his hand, chewing sleepily. Hreidulfr's arm tightened around Váli's waist, a subtle snore rising up, and Váli smiled as he ate.

I kept my voice low. "He really loves you. You know that, right?"

Embarrassment wasn't something Váli showed often, but his expression was wavering between that and the happiest I'd ever seen him. "I know." And I thought he'd leave it at that, but a moment later, he pulled the furs down from his bare chest, pointing to a curl in the runes that were tattooed there. The runes came together in the shape of a wolf head. "A week before we left, I got them to add these." And beneath his fingers was a scattering of runes that, when you knew it was there, read *Hreidulfr*.

A silly thing that only a young person would do, tattooing their partner's name on them like their love would be as permanent as the ink. But I smiled. I'd once been foolishly in love too.

Soon, everyone was awake, the sound of barely conscious conversation permeating the little space. We pulled the outer layers of our clothing back on and stepped out into the day. The ground was still damp, but the sky was clear. Good for moving on.

That was when we heard the hoof beats.

I whipped around, trying to determine where it was coming from. Váli and Hreidulfr had already pulled their weapons from inside the shelter, a sword for Váli and an axe for Hreidulfr. Narvi was channelling energy, his fists locked at his sides.

The same phrase repeated in my head.

It could be Loki. It could be Loki. It could be Loki.

But there were too many hoofbeats. I summoned up wildfire, a flame roaring in each palm.

When the horses came over the crest of the hill, there were seven riders – six einherjar, and Skadi leading the charge. Beside her ran two wolves, frost-white and fangs bared.

There was nowhere to run. We were too easy to find, the only shelter, the only living things in sight. There would be no hiding.

I waited until they were in earshot. "Turn around and leave! We've done nothing!"

Skadi pulled her horse to a halt a dozen paces away and whistled. Her wolves circled back to her, still coiled up and ready to attack. She laughed. "Now why would I do that?"

"Loki isn't here." Váli stepped forward, head high. "We don't know where he is."

That laugh again, icy and unwavering. "Of course he isn't here. We have him already. But Odin wants a full set."

She whistled, and the wolves sprang into motion, closing the distance at incredible speed, their teeth bared with dozens of tiny daggers.

The air shimmered, a thin blue tinge surrounding us. One of the wolves collided with the barrier Narvi had summoned, bouncing to the ground. It shook its head and was up again, moving just in time to avoid the tip of Váli's sword.

The second wolf rounded the barrier and leapt at me. I lobbed wildfire at it, but it was too fast. It pinned me to the ground and the air left my lungs. Its foul, meaty breath was only inches from my face, gnashing and snarling, my forearm against its neck the only thing keeping it from ripping me to shreds. It was too heavy to throw. I filled my other hand with wildfire and pressed my palm into its eye.

The wolf rolled off with a yelp and dragged its face against the dirt, whimpering. Hreidulfr struck it in the side with the axe, and it backed away, limping. But Odin's einherjar had dismounted and they were on us, coming from every side.

I reached out for the closet one, runes on my breath. I touched my fingertips to her face, and her body jolted with electricity. She writhed to the ground, the scent of urine filling my nose. She tried to get up, and I kicked her in the teeth instead.

"You're really going to kill me, Lofarr?" One of the einherjar had wrapped his arm around Váli's neck, a blade against his skin. "I taught you to use that thing. This is how you repay me?"

The einherji hesitated, and I punched him in the face. Váli hissed as the knife drew blood. Then he sunk his sword into Lofarr's stomach. "Fucking coward."

Four to go. And Skadi, but she was still on her horse, watching. Hreidulfr was keeping them away from Narvi as the boy continued to whisper runes for shields and wards. But he'd learned to heal and protect, not to fight.

Pain tore into my leg as a wolf sunk its teeth into my ankle. I pulled the knife from my belt and drove it into its burned eye socket. It let go, howling.

Hooves charged toward me. Skadi dove from her saddle and tackled me to the ground. My head hit the dirt, and the world blurred, the weight of her muscle crushing the breath from me.

"No one hurts my wolves, Wife of Lies. Especially not you." Skadi's lips were pulled back around her teeth, snarling. I tried to fight back, looking for a way to push her off, but she was twice my size, and I didn't stand a chance in a fair fight.

I managed to pull my dagger from my belt, swinging for her throat. In the time it took me to raise the blade, she drove her fist into my stomach. Nausea poured through me. I tried to stab her somewhere, anywhere. Then she had hold of my wrist. She twisted. Wrenching pain ran up to my shoulder, a scream ripping from me. The dagger dropped.

Somewhere nearby, the boys were fighting their own fight, steel and violence the only thing I could hear. I couldn't see. Couldn't see if they were alive or dead.

"Leave us. We aren't him. Just let us go!" I willed the wildfire back into my palms and pressed it against her chest. Her skin was searing; I could smell it. She just grinned, the pain fuelling the wild look in her eyes.

"Not yet." Her fist hit my jaw and the world went black.

CHAPTER SIXTY-SEVEN

"She saw a prisoner bound under the hot springs
A lover of evil, in the likeness of Loki
There sits Sigyn, alongside her husband
And she feels no joy, do you not see?"

—*Prophecy of the Seeress 35*

I came back to the world in increments. My head ached as it lolled back and forth with the rhythm of the moving ground. The light burned through my eyelids, and my blood pounded in my skull in a way I'd never felt before.

When I managed to open my eyes, I had no idea where I was. The camp was long gone. I didn't recognize anything, though it didn't look like we'd travelled that far. The world was still rocky with Jotunheim on one side and the fields and forests of Asgard on the other. I strained to find something familiar, but there was nothing.

It wasn't, in fact, the ground that was moving, but a horse. A rope chafed at my wrists, almost cutting off my circulation. I tried to move, but the rope was fastened around my waist, tying me to the saddle.

"Are you comfortable, Goddess?" Skadi's face was over my shoulder. "Don't bother struggling. We're almost there."

"Where are you taking me?" Two of the einherjar who'd come with Skadi were riding next to us, each with one of my captive sons. They'd clearly gone down fighting, their faces already bruising.

"To your destiny. We wouldn't want to be late for that."

I didn't bother asking for clarification. I knew precisely what destiny she meant. "Where is Hreidulfr?"

"What, your little companion? We left him there. We just need you."

The riders brought us through a forest and up to the side of a mountain. There was a narrow cave entrance, well hidden by the trees. The riding party halted and pulled the boys off their horses. Skadi yanked me down with a quick tug of the rope, and I tumbled to the ground. The pain in my head erupted, and it was all I could do to keep from heaving my breakfast into the grass.

"Get up," Skadi barked, tugging again on the rope. I crawled to my feet, my head spinning.

"Leave her alone!" Narvi fought against his restraints, but it was no good. His lips moved, whispers on his breath, and the air rippled in front of him. His captor flew backward, losing control of the ropes.

"You idiots, cover his mouth!" Skadi pushed me forward, and I tripped over myself, nearly landing on the ground again. She laughed as the einherji forced my son's jaw closed and held it that way.

"You're dead, you stupid bitch!" Váli thrashed against the arms holding him and when the grip didn't loosen, he bit down on the nearest piece of flesh, drawing blood. He was rewarded with a set of knuckles to the face.

"You know, your father told me the same thing. You'd better get in line." She pushed me forward again. "In you go."

The cave was a dry, sickly warm echo chamber. It was tall enough to stand in most places but not always. Skadi was too tall by far and was forced to stay bent over. A light burned in the distance, a torch in the cave's pitch-black darkness. I felt around with my feet, trying not to trip over the jagged, rocky surface. I couldn't see a damned thing, and with no hands to brace myself, I couldn't afford to tumble down the slope ahead.

The further we walked, the hotter it became. The air smelled sulfuric. I couldn't place it until the torch-lit cavern came into view. The rocky floor ended a few meters from us, surrounding the milky blue water that steamed and hissed up towards its edge. They'd brought us to an underground hot spring.

This was really it.

When Skadi pushed me into the chamber, all hope fell away. I dropped to my knees on the rocks, barely feeling the pain as they hit the stone. In front of me was Loki, kneeling next to a flat rock outcropping, bound and gagged at the feet of Odin. His tunic was torn, and dried blood scabbed around wounds on his face and arms. I tried to crawl to him, but Skadi dragged me back like a dog on a leash.

The air was too hot, too stifling. My chest was a knot, tightening further as the einherjar pushed Váli and Narvi onto their knees in front of me. I had to save them.

And maybe it was already too late.

"You're going to wish you'd already killed me," Váli growled. "There'll be nothing left of you when I'm done."

"Lovely children you've raised, Sigyn. So polite." Odin nodded his head, and the einherji punched Váli in the jaw, silencing him.

"Stop!" Tears streamed down my face. Loki struggled against his ropes, screaming something unintelligible through his gag. "Father, please, whatever you want, I'll do it. Leave my family alone."

"I wanted a peaceful future for my realms." Odin rubbed his temples with his fingers. "I wanted to find a way around the prophecies. I did everything I thought I needed to do. I agonized over it day and night for decades, but there was no avoiding this."

"What?" I searched for the words, baffled. "You knew full well what was going to happen, and you did nothing! You let me marry him, and you *knew* it would land me here." I tried to get up, but Skadi's boot hit my back, pushing me to the floor again. I stared up at him. "And if your plan was to bring him into the fold, you failed. You broke him at every juncture and expected him to, what, love you for it? You had choices, *Odin*."

"Did I?" Odin restrained Loki as he struggled toward me. "Do you think we're here, at this moment, of our own free will? It was written, and if there's anything I've learned, it's that fate is sealed. No matter what wives-tales they tell about creating your own stars, none of us can escape it." Odin looked almost nostalgic, speaking with his free hand. "I couldn't save your brother. I couldn't turn Fenrir to our cause. And Loki...I couldn't keep you away from him. Years of second-guessing our every move. Can she truly tame him? Will the hammer and the wall and the horse be worth what it costs to keep him? Which of our actions drive us closer to Ragnarok? It's enough to drive a man mad."

Odin motioned again, and the einherjar dragged the boys into the space between Loki and I. They struggled to even sit upright, their heads bobbing. Váli's clothing had been torn, and his chest was a mess of wolf scratches. He'd been bitten on the shoulder and blood rolled down his arm, dripping from his fingertips. Narvi was barely conscious, bracing himself against the floor with his bound hands.

"Please, leave them out of this." I begged. "They've done nothing. Whatever you're going to do, do it to me instead. I deserve it; I was complicit. They're just children."

"I know," Odin said, kneeling to look me in the eyes. "Children really are the most precious thing to a parent, aren't they? I've had decades to prepare for you to betray me. Decades to keep you at arms' length, to remove you from my heart so that this moment wouldn't hurt. It helped, I think. Knowing. I could prepare to lose you. You've had some time to prepare as well; I hope you're ready."

"I will destroy you," I snarled, reaching deep for a connection with the energy, something to channel into fire, into death. To end this before he ended us.

"Oh, you can try." He stood again. "It won't do you any good. This cave is warded against all runes except my own. You won't be able to raise enough energy to warm your hands, let alone kill anyone."

He wasn't bluffing. There was nothing. No connection to anything.

"Please," I whispered.

"It's rather poetic, really." Odin pulled on Loki's hair, forcing him to look at his children. "You've given life to all manner of monsters. How fitting that it's going to be a monster that tears your family apart."

Loki screamed behind his gag, fighting Odin's grip, but it was useless. Tears rolled down his face, the cloth choking him.

"Just do it," Váli spat, pushing forward against the ropes that held him. The tattoos under his shirt started to glow. "I'm not afraid of you, old man. At least I'll die with some fight in my soul, some honour that I lived well. You're just a coward with an army."

Odin simply smiled. "I'd planned this the other way, but perhaps that's too simple. You've been raised to die fighting. Why don't we take that honour from you?" He began to whisper, his lips moving in quick patterns, a chant.

Váli's body jerked back, an involuntary shudder that came from his core. The tattoos were burning bright. A second jerk shook him again, his head jolting back. He screamed, his body cracking and creaking, the sound of breaking bone and the wet slide of moving flesh. The scream became a howl as hair sprouted from his skin in patches, his clothes ripping away. He became the wolf, panting and enraged.

Narvi was awake now, his eyes wide as he knelt next to the wolf. "He's not in there. His voice. I can't hear him."

The wolf turned to face me. His emerald eyes crazed, hungry. Animal. Void of Váli.

"What have you done?" I screamed. "Turn him back!"

The wolf leapt at me. It gnashed its teeth in front of my face, but Odin snapped his fingers, and it looked back. At the wave of Odin's hand, the einherjar tossed Narvi forward, leaving him bound and helpless in front of his brother.

"Váli, you know me!" Narvi cried, trying to crawl away on his bound hands. "It's me, you know me. I love you!"

The wolf stalked closer.

"No. Váli, come here!" I whistled, trying to get its attention. "Váli! Take me, you have to take me!" Tears poured down my face, the ropes burning into my skin as I pulled. "Narvi lives! Kill me, please, Narvi *lives*!"

The wolf's teeth were in Narvi's throat before I could draw my next breath.

I fell forward, wailing and crawling toward them on my bound hands. Skadi hauled me back by my hair and forced my head up. She leaned in, her lips against my ear. "I want you to watch."

The wolf shook its head, pulling the wound in Narvi's throat wider. Blood pooled around his legs. He struggled under the wolf's weight—Váli's weight—trying to loosen its grip. Choking on his own blood.

Its jaws opened for a second, only to clamp down again on his arm, pulling the flesh from it in thick chunks until the bone-white showed.

"Váli." Narvi's words were a rasp, bubbles rising at the open wound in his throat. His hand rose and fell again, and he pulled in a long, hard breath. "It's okay. I forgive you."

Blood trickled from his lips.

And I watched. Watched his body stop twitching, his breathing slow.

I watched the light leave my baby's eyes.

The wolf tucked its snout under the cloth of Narvi's shirt and tore open his stomach, spilling entrails onto the ground. It pulled out an organ with its teeth and chewed it, blood sticking to the fur around its muzzle. And then it swallowed.

I threw up, vomit sloshing across the cave floor. Everything in me was screaming and numb and out of control, and I couldn't move couldn't breathe couldn't keep awake didn't—

Skadi's boot hit my back, and I flew forward, nearly face-first into my own mess. The shock brought me back to myself. I was closer to him, to my baby, to the wolf. I crawled forward, slapping at the air with my arm. "Get off him! Get off!"

The wolf startled and turned to snarl at me, but when our eyes connected, something in them flickered. A moment of fear, of consciousness. Then it shook its head and growled. The flicker again. It pushed its face into the stone floor, whimpering. It smacked its head against the ground and scrambled to its feet. Darting around us, the wolf was up and dashing out of the cavern before anyone could stop it.

Sobbing, I pulled myself over Narvi's body, the blood seeping into my clothing. I pressed my ear to his chest, but I already knew. His heart was silent. The pain wracked through me, escaping my raw throat in a cry. "What have you done?"

"Penance," Skadi said, hauling me back up.

"What did *they* do to you?" I couldn't fight her. There was nothing left to fight for.

She threw me on the ground next to flat outcropping of rocks. "It's not about you or your sons. It's about Loki. It's always been about him and what he'll do to us all."

The einherjar pulled Loki up from the floor. His eyes were vacant as if no one lived behind them anymore. They cut his hands free and pulled him on top of the stone, laying him out like it was some kind of sacrificial altar. He barely flinched as they held him down.

"Loki, fight them!" I screamed.

But there was no one there.

Skadi passed my leash to Odin. She bent low over Narvi's body and reached into his open stomach. When she withdrew her fist, it was dripping red and full of entrails, his intestines draped over her fingers, his stomach hanging aloft.

My stomach lurched again, but there was nothing left to spill. "What is *wrong* with you?"

"We're protecting the realms from you." Skadi tied the length of pink, wet intestine around Loki's leg. It was loose; too tight, and it would tear. She wrapped it around one leg and then the other, then wound it around the base of the stone slab. The length of it kept moving, inching out of Narvi's stomach like twine on a roll.

"Are you comfy, Trickster?" She ran her bloody hand from his navel to his neck, leaving a long, snaking red handprint in its wake.

Loki said nothing. He just stared blankly up at the ceiling.

Skadi stood straight and laughed. "I think we've broken him."

She continued her horrific work until his hands, legs, and torso were tied to the stone, his arms up above his head and tied at the wrists. The line went taut, and the last inch of the intestine ripped free of Narvi's gut. She pulled up the end of her makeshift fetter and tied it off around his ankles. "What a shame. I suppose that's good enough. Ah, wait." She untied the gag from his mouth and brushed her hands together like it was the final touch.

"Loki! Get up!" I sobbed, pulling against my own ropes. "That'll never hold him!"

"Of course it won't. Just a bit of drama, really. The prophecy insists." Odin held up his hand. Runes slipped from his lips, and with the snap of a finger, the entrails turned to iron, binding Loki to the stone slab. "These will do just fine, however."

"You can't do this. You can't keep him here."

"I plan to keep you both here. As punishment for your crimes against the gods and the nine realms, you'll stay here until Ragnarok itself. You'll exist beyond time, trapped in this cavern with runes I crafted myself. You'll never fade, never die, you'll simply suffer."

The words were too ugly to begin to register in my mind. "What kind of father does this to his own child? His grandchildren?"

"It's adorable that you think it's finished." Skadi was standing above Loki with a bowl in her hands. She opened the lid and dipped her hand in. When she drew it back out, her fingers were carefully poised around the head of a snake. "This is the Hyrrormir. He's a flame adder from the craters of Muspelheim. But they're not called flame adders because they breathe fire, no."

She held the snake aloft, cradling it like a precious thing. She reached up above

Loki's head where the roots of something had grown down into the roof of the cavern. The snake slithered onto the roots and settled itself. Skadi stroked its head, then forced a root into its mouth. The snake hissed and bit down, distracted while Skadi bound it where it was. "He's called a flame adder because his venom is so potent that it burns the flesh upon contact. Just watch."

It was difficult to see, but a tiny glistening bead was building up at the end of the snake's fangs. And then it fell, so small it was almost imperceptible. It hit Loki just below his right eye.

He woke from wherever he had been, thrashing and screaming, tearing against the metal that bound him. The iron cut against his skin, but he didn't stop. The venom burned more than the chains.

"Oh, it's perfect." Skadi crossed her arms, admiring her handiwork.

"It'll do nicely. I do hope that this satisfies our bargain."

Skadi grinned, her teeth like a wolf. "Oh, it does. Father would be proud."

Odin pointed to Narvi's body. "Remove this mess."

"No, leave him." I clawed my way back toward Narvi. "My baby…leave my baby."

They didn't listen. One man took him by the legs, the other by the arms. Some dark piece of flesh fell out of him as they carried the corpse out of the cave, blood trailing on the ground behind them.

Odin let go of the rope, and the sudden slack sent me sprawling onto my hands and knees. My ears rang again, another of Loki's screams shaking through me.

Skadi followed Odin towards the tunnel, then turned at the last minute. Like she was savouring it.

"So this is it?" I crawled towards them on my hands and knees. "This is what you raised me for? Why you never gave me a title? So you could kill my sons and abandon me in a cave without even a hint of guilt?"

Odin smirked under his beard. "I've known your title for a very long time. I couldn't give it to you before; it wouldn't have made sense. But it will today and every day after. You've stood by Loki all these years for better or for worse. Now you'll stay by him in this cave, locked inside for good. Everything you did will be rewritten. You'll be forgotten. When people speak the name Sigyn, it will be this and this alone that they remember. Loki's wife, the woman who stood by the enemy of the realms and bore his pain. Sigyn, Goddess of Fidelity." He turned his back on me. "See what good those loyalties do you now."

And they left. They just…left.

The second they stepped out, the air shimmered. I pushed my hand against the opening and came against something solid. A barrier. I clawed at it, helpless, screaming.

The Goddess of Nothing At All

This couldn't be it. It couldn't be.

It wasn't the fresh scream or the begging that brought me to the moment. It was the cavern stirring around me. I turned back to Loki, struggling against his bonds. It couldn't be, but it was. A new drop of poison hit him, and dust fell from the ceiling, the walls shaking. And the intensity was building.

I jumped to my feet and ran to his side. The venom rolled slowly down his cheek, toward his ear, leaving swollen lines of red flesh in their wake. My ears rang. Dirt clouded the air, invading my lungs.

The snake.

I climbed onto the stone, feet on either side of Loki's chest. I was nearly face to face with the flame adder, its beady eyes piercing and angry. I just needed to pull it down and dash it on the rocks. I reached out, and my hand came up against another barrier. Cursing, I felt around it, but there was no way in. It wouldn't budge.

Another drop of poison, and Loki screamed again.

There had to be something. We were going to be crushed.

My eyes fell on the wooden bowl that sat abandoned in the corner.

I jumped down and dove for it, fumbling it in my useless, bound hands. I struggled to grip the curved surface. Every scream and moan from Loki and every shake of the walls around me tore at my nerves. The bowl dropped back to the ground, clattering and rolling. I needed to free my hands.

I found a jagged rock and rubbed the rope against it, praying that the friction would be enough to fray the strands. One by one the fibres broke, painfully slow as Loki begged, howling my name like he was dying.

"I'm coming. I promise, I'm trying."

He couldn't hear me, my name repeating on his voice like an unholy chant. *Sigyn. Sig. Please, it hurts. Sigyn.*

Finally, the rope broke. I scrambled to free myself, ripping at the knot with my teeth. It fell away. In one swift movement, I scooped up the bowl and fell to my knees next to Loki's head, the bowl held out above his face. The venom splashed against the wood, a dull, powerless drip on a dry surface.

Not thinking, I wiped the venom from his cheek with my thumb and immediately understood. It seared my skin as if I'd stuck my hand in white hot flame. It drilled itself into my nerves and bones, spider webbing out into my palm. I tried to wipe it off on my dress, gritting my teeth against the burn.

"Sigyn," Loki whimpered, his voice weak. "Sigyn."

"I know." I cried with him, kissing his unscorched cheek over and over, careful to keep the bowl balanced above us. "I'm here. I'm with you."

It took time for the pain to subside. I sat with him in silence, listening only to the rhythmic drip of the venom. If I'd ever thought I'd seen him in pain, I knew now that I'd only seen the surface of it. At last, he spoke, his voice barely a whisper. "I'm so sorry."

I sighed, trying to blink back the tears, but they spilled over. "I know."

"Don't say that. Say anything else. Blame them, blame me, blame someone." His voice cracked, tears wiping the venom from his cheek. "They took them from us. They murdered our boys, and I let it happen."

The last string of my resolve fell away. I burst into sobs, leaning into Loki's neck. In my grief, I nearly let the bowl tip. I pulled myself up and tried to stem the tide of my broken heart.

I couldn't let the bowl fall.

CHAPTER SIXTY-EIGHT

"It's done. Tell them the truth but remember:
she was no daughter of mine."

—*Message to Master Archivist*

Things were so quiet in the solitude of the cave, and yet there was so much to hear. The low bubble of the hot springs. Loki's laboured breathing. The drip, drip, drip of the venom. The screams that played themselves over and over in my mind.

The only thing to pull me from my grief was the ache in my arms. Holding the bowl aloft made them tired, and after a while, the weariness turned to pain. I tried to rest one at a time, but it wasn't enough. Before long, both arms were stiff and cold, begging me to just give in.

A voice of reason spoke through the fog of my mind, that darkness I'd retreated to, and reminded me that I had legs. That I could stand. I held the bowl at my hips and the blood rushed back to my arms.

Unable to keep it down any longer, I spoke up. "If you'd have come sooner, we'd have been long gone by the time Skadi arrived. Why didn't you come? What did you do to them?"

He waited so long to answer that I thought he might not. When he did, his voice was barely more than a whisper. "I did what I wanted. I always do. And look what it cost me."

"You said you were going to finish it," I snapped at him. "Not make it worse."

He didn't look at me. "I wanted vengeance. I wanted to tear open the secrets they've been keeping and remind the gods of how ugly they are. And I did. I followed them to a

369

banquet, and I killed a servant and told all their secrets, everything I knew about them. Laughed in their faces. They were furious. I ran, but they caught up. And now..."

"And now they've taken everything that matters."

"Yes." Loki choked on the word, fighting back tears. "Maybe he's still out there. Váli could still be alive."

"And if he is? Is there anything left of him?" I sat down and leaned on my elbows, resting my head against the stone. "You saw it, his transformation. It wasn't like what he does or what you do, it was something else. Something permanent. He *ate* his brother, Loki. He's not in there."

He shook his head. "Everything can be reversed; we just need the right runes."

"It doesn't matter. He's out there, and we're trapped. There's nothing we can do." I sighed. "He always hated seidr. The only runes he knows are the ones tattooed on his chest."

Loki pulled in a slow breath. "He's always been stubborn."

"Only with you." I looked into Loki's weary eyes and tried to manage a smile.

The corners of his lips turned up, only slightly. "He always was your child, right from the beginning. Never mine. There was always a mountain between us."

"He wanted to be his own man. He wanted to be better than you were."

"I don't know why," Loki smirked, tears spilling over. The sarcasm just barely hid the crack in his voice. "I was a perfect role model." He sniffed, and when he spoke again, his voice was soft. "I know what I did. To him, to Narvi. To you. I know he never forgave me."

"He loved you more than he showed. He was too young to understand that life isn't black and white. I used to be like him, thinking there was good and bad and justice for all. He didn't live long enough to know better. We do the best we can with each moment and hope our choices will be enough. Mostly, they're not."

"If I never came back to Asgard, you would've been happy." His chest rose and shuddered, the sob still held prisoner in his chest.

I let the thought sit on my tongue a moment, to see how it tasted. "If you hadn't come, I'd still be waiting for you."

He shook his head, lips pursed in defiance. "I destroyed your life. I always made the wrong choices. You know I did. Just say it."

I wanted to say something comforting, I did. But..."You did. We used to be so in love, but you ruined everything. Why? Why are you like this?"

His jaw clenched, and he pulled at the shackles again like he could run from it. But there was nowhere to go. "What chance did I have to be anything else? Odin made me into a liar, a thief, and a whore, and I lived up to those expectations *gloriously*, and everyone hated me for it. I tried to be better for you, I did. But this is all I am, Sig. There is no better part of me. Everything led here anyway."

He was right. None of it mattered. We were trapped in this endless nothing together, and we'd always be trapped. Everything was gone. I wanted to be held, to be told that it was okay, that tomorrow I'd wake and it would all be a terrible, terrible nightmare. But no one was coming. There would be no one to hold me ever again. This kindness felt like the least I could do.

"I hate what you did. To say anything else would be a lie. But you gave me so much. I fell in love again because of you. I'm stronger than I was before you. You gave me children and love and time. I don't want to return all that in order to undo the rest."

Loki smiled, pushing down a sob. "It's a beautiful thing to say, Sig, but you don't mean it."

"I mean it today. Ask me again tomorrow."

CHAPTER SIXTY-NINE

*"And She Endures
And She Endures
And She Endures."*

—*Midgard Prayer*

D
ays passed like years. It must've been days by then, surely. There was no
light outside to tell us if it was day or night, only the flicker of the torches,
which never went out. Perhaps they were like us, barely living, as if time were
meaningless.

Every single second crawled by like cold honey dripping from a vat. There was
nothing to do but mourn. Mourn for the sons I'd seen murdered in front of my eyes.
For the husband I was being forced to watch disintegrate in front of me like salt into
the sea. All of it played back every time I closed my eyes. Sometimes I could convince
myself it wasn't real, but then I would look at the dried red on the stone. The blood
had pooled there and then had run into the bubbling hot spring, turning it pale pink at
first and then eventually fading away. Now it was nothing more than a violent stain.

"Loki," I whispered. "Loki, wake up." The rise and fall of his chest didn't waver. It
had taken him an eternity to fall asleep, but he'd gone eventually, too exhausted to do
anything else. "Loki, the bowl is too heavy. It's too full, wake up."

His eyes fluttered, threatening to close again. I wanted to shake him, but I needed
both hands to carry the weight.

"Loki!"

He snapped to attention, pulling against the fetters. "What happened?"

"I need to empty the bowl."

He stared upwards and his breath hitched, panic written on his face. "*Skit.* Be quick. Please."

The snake's wide mouth hung dangerously above, a single fat drop of venom threatening to fall. Slowly, it gathered mass. I watched and waited and when it hit the bowl, I moved, as quick as my disused legs could manage. I stepped carefully, trying to keep the bowl steady. The venom sloshed over the side, dripping down my fingers. Pain burst through me, burning every nerve in my hand, webbing through my fingers and up into my elbows. I cried out, determined not to drop the bowl and send the venom splashing over the rest of me.

"Sigyn! Are you—" A scream ripped through him. The first drop of venom.

I fought through the pain and stumbled to the edge of the cave, pouring the venom into a dip in the stone. Another drop, another scream. The floor moved just slightly beneath me, the warning before the quake. I turned back, and my leg gave way beneath me. The bowl slipped from my fingers and rolled toward the stone where Loki was bound. I wiped my hands on the dress, scrambling to pick up the bowl. The pain kept shooting through me until I was screaming along with him, but I still scooped up the bowl and dropped to my knees at his side, holding it over his face.

With the sleeve of my dress, I wiped the venom from his cheek, but the pink lines had already risen across his skin, dripping toward his ear. He shook with sobs, straining to be free, to escape the pain. There was nothing I could do against the burning in my veins but grip the bowl so tightly that it numbed the tips of my fingers. To let it live and die in me.

I had to be strong enough for the both of us.

CHAPTER SEVENTY

*"What little we know of her, we know this; Sigyn was
unwavering, at her husband's side for eternity.
Dutiful, patient, faithful."*

—*The last written entry about
Sigyn—redacted—dottir*

I
f Skadi herself had strode back into that cavern and offered me a hot meal and a
warm bath, I'd have happily cut off my own arm in trade.

There was nothing to eat, nothing to drink, and nothing to do besides sit and
while away eternity. My stomach howled for a scrap of bread. I was constantly thirsty,
and I smelled like a sack of mouldy onions in a ragged bloodstained dress. The hot
springs were so close. I tortured myself, scheming over the idea of scooping up just
one bowl of that water, just to have one fresh splash on my face. I could stomach the
sulphur if only for one mouthful to quench my thirst. But every moment spent at the
water was a moment condemning Loki to suffer, and I just couldn't do it.

There were moments I wanted to. In this endless, tedious span of time without
sleep or distraction or anything at all, we fought. There were moments when he blamed
me for being too lenient, too trusting. When he snapped at me for casting him out
after he'd helped kidnap Idunn. If *I* had done things differently, we wouldn't have been
stuck in that cavern, our sons wouldn't be gone.

And for every piece of blame he laid on me, I had another for him. I cursed his
dishonesty, his inability to let things go. If he had just been content with what we'd
had, if he'd stopped aggravating every god he came across, we might be in our own bed
right now. Happy.

We used our words to tear each other apart. And yes, at my most furious, I thought about dumping the whole bowl of venom onto his face just to shut him up.

There was no leaving the fight. No walking away, taking space to clear our heads. Just him and I, minute after minute, forever.

But we didn't always fight. More often we sat in silence with our thoughts. And sometimes we talked. Love or hate each other, we were all the company we had.

I stretched my arm, balancing the bowl overhead. "Do you remember the night Váli carried Narvi home drunk?"

Loki chuckled. "I do. That was Gersemi's fault, I think. She and Váli kept filling Narvi's cup every time he looked away. He was as sick as a dog the next day."

"I can't believe she went along with such a dirty trick," I laughed.

Loki stared away, replying in a whisper. "She would've made a wonderful addition to the family. She'd have been good for us."

We sat in silence for a moment. "I don't know if it was like that between them. Romantic. Freya never would've allowed it anyhow." I stifled a yawn and leaned against my arms.

"You should try to sleep," Loki whispered, pity in his voice.

"I'll try to get a moment or two, but if I start to drop the bowl, wake me."

He nodded. Already the venom had burned thick lines into his face, swollen up like wax dripping along the curves of his cheek and forehead. Some had come dangerously close to his eye. We'd been able to confine the damage only to the right side of his face, but it didn't make any difference to the pain.

I bent over the stone and laid my face in the crook of Loki's neck. I must've fallen asleep instantly.

I was standing in our kitchen. Narvi was sketching runes in a book at the table while his father leaned over him, his hand resting on the boy's shoulder. So proud of him. And across from them was Váli, cutting an apple with his hunting knife, teasing his brother while he ate slices from the tip of the blade. It was perfect, every simple moment of it.

When I woke, my face was wet with tears.

CHAPTER SEVENTY-ONE

*"I love you, Mother.
It's alright."*

—*Narvi - a dream*

S it. Wait. Drip. Empty. Scream. Shake. Sit. Wait. Drip. Empty. Scream. Shake.
Seconds and minutes and days and months passed outside our walls, but
I could only guess at how long it had really been. We were neither alive nor
dead. It had been years, I was sure of that much. Years in this insanity, this unending
nothingness.

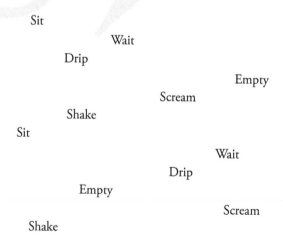

Loki had stopped reminiscing a long time ago. He didn't want to think about any of it. If I mentioned the boys or any of his children, he began planning. I listened to his long tirades about revenge, duty, and murder. How some of his children were still out there, how he would kill everyone who had harmed his family, how Hel and Fenrir would help him. If Odin wanted Ragnarok, he would give it to him. Each drop of venom that hit his face burned darkness into him. He spoke of gutting and flaying and castrating like it was poetry. His anger fuelled him, kept him alive.

The things he said frayed my seams. When he was quiet, my mind showed me the horrors again and again. Reminded me how alone I was, how entirely I had failed. I tried to remember happier things, but the moment I opened my eyes, I saw the room they had died in, the old stain on the rocks. I thought if I stared long enough, it might just bring them back. It never worked.

He wanted to destroy everything, but I only wished to die. To melt into my dreams and live there forever. At least when I dreamed, they were alive and happy, and if I could just join them…

Maybe if I wanted it long enough, wished for it hard enough, my heart would cease to beat and would carry me from this wretched place.

But I couldn't die. I knew that. Odin's runes wouldn't let me.

At least in Hel, I'd have a seat at the table.

CHAPTER SEVENTY-TWO

"Everyone must travel farthest with themselves."

—Midgard Proverb

I 'd had focus once. Thoughts.
Now I was never asleep.
Never awake.

Was I real? I knew I was real when the venom touched my skin. I could reach out and touch a drop. Remind myself. Add a scar to the tips of my fingers. My name. I was a goddess, I reminded myself. Not of Fidelity, no. I didn't want that. Of Nothing, of nothing. Sigyn, once. That was real. If I'd been given another name, would I still be real?

Loki saw things that weren't real, I knew that. The venom had taken his right eye, left it milky and white, and it stared into the distance, always. That was when he started talking to ghosts. He spoke to them, and they spoke to him. Angrboda. Fenrir. Narvi. Mother. Brother. Hel. He cried and screamed and fought with them. And I could do nothing but watch.

What had we become?

CHAPTER SEVENTY-THREE

"Please."

Please let it stop.

CHAPTER SEVENTY-FOUR

"It's been years since a new soul came to Asgard.
Midgard has changed, become something I don't recognize.
I…I am afraid."

—*Archives of Asgard, Daily Records*

The breeze was cool but the sun was warm, beating down on our skin like we were next to a fire. Lying in the grass, droplets of morning dew glistening onto our skin, it was the most peaceful I'd felt in an eternity.

I rolled onto my stomach so I could look at her more closely. Her straw-blonde hair draped over her bare shoulders, the porcelain of her skin, the cool grey of her eyes. She bit her lip and took a cherry from the picnic we'd brought. It dripped pink down her hand, and I plucked it from her fingers with my teeth, stopping to lick the juice from her skin. She shivered, gooseflesh running down her arms, her stomach quivering. I leaned in to kiss her, and the ground began to shake.

I blinked and the meadow faded away, another waking dream gone. All that was there was stone and sulphur and suffering. If the cave was shaking, then Loki—

But he was sleeping. Chest rising and falling, shallow breaths. And the room kept shaking. Humming, raising the hairs on my arms like standing too close to lightning.

I shook my head, but the noise didn't leave. It was growing, like a hive of bees stuck in my skull. I thought it might be madness finally sinking its claws deeper into me, but dirt was shaking loose from the ceiling, getting in my lungs. Coughing, I shook Loki with the hand I could spare.

"Wake up! Something's happening."

His eyes fluttered open, one emerald and one milky white. For just a moment, I

380

thought he would scold me, and then he saw it too. "What is it?"

"I don't know."

A thick, thunderous crack echoed through the cave. Whatever had broken was invisible, but it hit the floor and shattered like glass. A chill breeze rushed into the cavern, and the torches flickered in the wind.

A clatter of metal. The chains binding Loki had fallen to the ground, clanging against the stone and disintegrating. What clung to his limbs slowly cracked and fell apart, like a thousand years had passed in a moment.

We stared at each other for a long time, waiting for it to be a clever trick, some shared hallucination, but nothing else happened. Slowly, Loki pulled one of his hands downward, toward his face. His joints cracked and popped. How long had it been since he'd used them?

I kept my place above his head, holding the bowl until he could move away from the snake bound above him. "Are we...free?"

"There was only one way out." Loki moved in small, deliberate motions. Flexing each finger, each toe. He managed to bring his hands down from above his head, working out the stiffness of his limbs.

"It can't be..."

"Odin said we'd be free at Ragnarok, technically speaking. I wonder if he meant it that way..." He huffed. "For all the years of taking the blame for it, it looks like we're late to the party."

The green in his living eye glimmered, alight with something sinister that I didn't like. "You don't know what's out there. We need to be careful. We need to think."

He sat up slowly, reaching for my hand to help him. Odin's seidr had worked. We hadn't shrivelled and wasted away with time and neglect. Our bodies were weak, hungry, defeated, but whole. The only lasting things were the scars the venom had made on my fingers and Loki's face.

I put the bowl aside and helped him stand. We supported each other to stretch out, to awaken our limbs. Finally, I could move without being punished for it.

I took his hand and pulled him along with me. "Come here."

"I can't." He looked toward the tunnel to the surface. "There are things I have to do."

I hushed him. "It can wait a little longer. Sit with me." I helped him lower himself onto the stone ledge next to the hot spring. When we were settled, I dipped my hands in and pulled out a scoop of warm water. It was indescribable. The first tangible comfort I'd had since we'd set foot in the cave. My hands were bronze, glistening wet, while everything above the waterline was so thick with dirt that it made my skin grey. An eternity of filth.

I slipped my feet in, little by little, basking in the ecstasy of the water on my skin. My head tilted back, a sigh escaping my lips. It felt like the first day of spring after being shut away all winter. The warmth soothed the ache in my muscles and the screaming of my bones. I took a breath and slid all the way in, letting the water engulf me. I stayed there for a moment, the dull bubbling of the spring muffled.

When I surfaced, Loki was smiling. It was perhaps the only genuine smile he'd shown in a long time. I held my hands out. "Come in. The bottom is shallow here."

He painstakingly stretched his legs into the pool. The relief swept over his face as he sunk into the water.

Small blessings in desperate times.

I reached up and slid a thumb across his cheek. The grey streaked away, leaving a glimpse of the pale Jotun skin that lay underneath. "There you are," I whispered, continuing to wipe away the dirt. Bit by bit, the filth disappeared and before long, his face was clean. It would never be the same though. No amount of water could wash away the melted-wax scars that ran on his cheek or the milky white of his eye.

After I was finished, he did the same for me. His fingers sparked life into my skin. No one had touched me for all those years, and I was starved of it. His hands slid along my shoulders, my collar bone, my back. He scrubbed the sand from the tangles of my hair. He was thorough. Delicate.

"There." He cupped my face in his hands. "As beautiful as ever."

When he bent his neck to kiss me, I let him. If Ragnarok was coming, whatever was waiting outside would be harsh and destructive; there was no escaping that. I'd had enough pain. For one moment, I took the kindness.

"Thank you for everything." He touched his forehead to mine. "I can't ever repay this. But you know what I need to do."

I held his hands against my cheeks. "You don't have to do anything. We can just walk away. You and I can just sit back and watch everything burn. Loki, please. I have nothing left but you. Come with me."

He shook his head. "I have debts to pay. I promised them."

"Promised who?" I dropped his hands, my lip quivering. "There's been no one here but us. This whole time, it was me beside you. The only one. You're going to wager whatever you have left for some kind of vengeance, but *I'm* the only thing left, and you won't come back this time. None of us will. You're going to leave me to die alone."

"You could come too." One hand lingered on my face while the other travelled to the back of my neck. "We could do this together, for our sons. You and I. You could be my queen again. Together, like we were always supposed to be."

"I'm not going to burn the realms with you." I put my hands on his stomach. "I just want to rest. Please."

"I'll find you when it's done." He sunk his head down again, another kiss, and I fell into it. If I gave him everything I had, maybe it would be enough. Maybe I could make him stay. Maybe he would feel it and change his mind. I would be enough.

But I wasn't. Even with my body pressed against his, my arms around his neck, he still pulled away in the end. He pried off my fingers and waded past me.

I scrambled to pull him back, grasping for what was left of his shirt and missing. He pulled himself out of the hot spring. He turned back for a moment, wringing the water from the flame of his hair. "I'm doing this for us, Sig. Wait for me." And then his words fell silent, his lips moving in rhythmic patterns.

"Loki, no—"

The air shimmered and distorted, forcing me to look away. A bird shrieked, that familiar hawk screech. I caught a glimpse of it as it flew into the tunnel, out toward the world.

"Damn you, Loki!" I crawled out of the water and ran on my wobbling knees toward the exit. I tore one of the torches from the wall and stumbled up the jagged tunnel after him, into the dim light above.

It was dusk but still bright enough to burn my eyes. I shielded them and looked up to the horizon. The shadow of a bird flew toward the sunset. I screamed after him for all the good it would do. And then I started to shiver. The ground was covered in snow, the trees blanketed in white. How many winters had passed? What time had I emerged into?

Another shiver, this one deeper in my core. The water on my skin was turning cold. It would soon become ice and what little remained of my tattered dress would freeze to my skin. I'd die of exposure before morning, without a doubt. I held myself, bringing the torch as close to my skin as I dared. My breath rose like smoke in the air. I needed to find warmth.

I turned back to look into the cavern.

I couldn't step foot in there, not again. Not for one more second. I'd rather die free than spend one more moment in that prison.

The trees around the cavern were bare. I stepped carefully, snow seeping into my broken leather shoes, and I picked up whatever branches were small enough to carry. I could make a fire. Dry off. Survive.

The thought surprised me. I'd spent so much time wishing I were dead that the will to live seemed foreign. But still, it was there, burning like the smallest ember.

My stomach rumbled, begging me for something to eat, but I could only solve one life-threatening problem at time. With enough wood in my hands for a tiny fire, I knelt over the base of a tree stump and started to brush away the snow. The cold pierced my skin, and I wondered if anything I was doing would work. My mind felt dull. From the cold or from the captivity? Both.

As I was pulling together enough focus to summon wildfire, a rustle caught my attention. The bushes next to me were moving. I held out the torch, hoping it would be enough to deter whatever lay on the other side. A squirrel or a hare, maybe a—

The bushes burst open. A hulking grey blur leapt out from the leaves and tackled me to the ground. The weight of it bore down on me. Snarling white teeth, rancid breath, dripping spittle. It barked, so close to my face that my ears rang. I scrambled for the torch that had fallen just out of my reach. There was no time. I began to whisper runes, praying the wildfire would come to me quickly.

Hot slobber dragged across my cheek. I cringed, waiting for the teeth to bite down and tear me open, but they never came. The wolf yipped and bounced off, its tail wagging as it jumped in circles. When I didn't get up, it laid down beside me, its playful emerald eyes glittering in the torch light.

Those eyes.

It was impossible, but the name slipped off my tongue before I could stop myself from hoping. "Váli?"

The wolf barked, springing up like an excited child. It stopped and nuzzled its snout into my side, whining and barking.

I grabbed him around the middle and tackled him into the snow. "I thought I'd never see you again!" I pushed my face into his fur and sobbed, each pull of breath a desperate cry. He kept nuzzling against me until I could smell nothing but the wild, musty scent of his fur, his body warm against my skin.

We stayed there until I started to shudder from the cold. When I drew my hands away, the tips of my fingers were turning purple. The sun was gone, leaving us to the long dark of the night ahead. "Is there somewhere we can go? Somewhere warm?"

Váli squirmed out of my arms and waited for me to stand, wiggling his hind quarters. I struggled to my feet and followed him as he plodded into the trees. I tried to distract myself from the numbness in my fingers, the burning in my feet. "Have you been here the whole time? Waiting?"

He started yapping, a series of unintelligible growls and barks. He clearly had a lot to say, but there wasn't a word of it that I understood. "Darling, I don't speak wolf. Your brother was going to teach us—" Narvi's body flashed into my vision, Váli ripping out his innards—No. Not now. "Give me one bark for yes, two for no."

He gave me a soft bark, just one.

"Are you alright?" One bark.

"Can you turn back into yourself?" Two barks.

"How are you not dead?" An annoyed whine.

"Is it Odin's seidr?" A hesitant bark.

"Are you alone?" A pause. One bark.

I ducked under a tree branch. Váli was leading me deep into the forest. In the distance, long, flowing shadows moved between the trees like wraiths. The sight chilled my bones, but Váli kept on. As we drew closer, I saw them for what they were: furs, harvested with jagged teeth and left to cure in the branches.

"Did you do this?" One bark.

I reached out to touch a thick reindeer hide, feeling the inside. It was still quite fresh, still wet. Nowhere near ready for use. I moved to the next, a steely grey wolf pelt. It'd been there much longer. The inside was rough, the old meat gnawed and clawed away as raggedly as could be expected from a wolf with no tools. There were small holes where he'd torn too far.

Váli leapt up and took the pelt in his teeth, pulling it down. He looked up at me expectantly.

"For me?" One muffled bark.

I took it from him. It smelled like old, sour meat and some pungent musk, but that didn't matter. The warmth did. I couldn't feel anything anymore.

Váli trotted along ahead, pulling down fur after fur, selecting them on some hidden criteria I couldn't discern. He must've been working on the pelts for a very long time.

Ahead were a collection of bushy fir trees. They grew closely together but at their base was a shallow hole between the branches. Váli hunched down and crawled beneath them. With no other choice, I got on my hands and knees and crawled through, dragging my new collection of furs behind me.

Inside, the cold lessened. The air was still and dark. I fumbled with runes until at last I was able to summon a small flicker of wildfire in my palm to light the space. The trees we sat between had grown so closely together that they blocked out most of the wind. The inside branches had been torn away, leaving enough room for a wolf to live comfortably, though it was a bit cramped for the two of us.

I sat and wrapped the furs around my shoulders and over my legs. Váli busied himself digging a small hole in the dry dirt and filled it with twigs. When he was finished, he nudged it with his nose and whined.

I reached forward and let the fire roll off my palm and into the sticks. It crackled and flickered, and before long, the tiny fire was warming the space as best it could. I drew Váli close, pressing my face into his fur. "You can't know how much I've missed you. I love you so much."

He turned his face up to me, his teeth bared in a wolfish smile, and I jumped. Those teeth chewing Narvi's flesh. Swallowing it. Blood on his muzzle.

Váli whimpered, pressing his head against my skin.

"I know. There's a lot that needs to be said. And I'm afraid, I am. But I also know the real you would never...I'll try, I will. I love you." I scratched behind his ear and held him to me. "We'll figure it out, promise."

The plan was ridiculous, but there was nothing else to do.

After a fitful sleep pressed into Váli's fur, I spent the early hours fashioning fur into clothing, as best I could. He brought me fresh meat to cook and rabbit pelts for the insides of my shoes, to block the holes. We needed to get to Asgard, and I needed to do it without losing my toes. We fashioned a crude skirt and cloak with the bigger pelts and a collection of metal treasures Váli had hidden away in his den.

Afterward, Váli led me into the woods. The walking was difficult. Snow and cold found its way into every corner of the pelts, but we couldn't afford to slow down. The longer I was exposed to the elements, the worse things would get for me.

To distract myself, I told Váli what had happened in the cavern. He graced my tales with an appropriate growl or whimper, but it was a one-sided conversation. There were so many things I needed to know. What had happened to him? How much time had passed? How had he survived?

Then the answer came to me. Narvi was dead, but he had always written everything down. He had piles of journals in his room with meticulous notes. If we could get home, if everything was still there, I could learn. I could have one of my sons back.

I explained it to Váli. "If Ragnarok is coming, I'm not going to die in this silence."

Váli stopped short and whined, pushing at his muzzle as if he were trying to slough off his own skin.

"I don't know the runes, Váli. If we can find something, maybe I can change you back, but this is a start, isn't it? We might need to force it out of Odin, and I swear I'll find a way, but this is what I can give you right now." I ruffled the fur between his ears and moved on, working my way up the next hill.

Váli ran ahead, up over the top of the hill, and disappeared. I kept climbing, stepping carefully, trying not to slide back down. From the other side, he started to bark. Nervous about what that might mean, I picked up the pace and found him dancing around at the top of the hill, wagging his tail.

Just on the other side was a home. It was hard to say if anyone still lived there. There was no smoke coming from the chimney and no firelight to be seen from the outside. Snow had drifted up over the bottom of the front door, blocking it off. But it was four walls and some shelter, and I was happy to have it.

"Come on." I started my way down the hill, skidding on my boots when it got too steep. The top of the left boot cracked and opened, snow flooding it. I cursed and kept going. Váli was almost at the house when he stopped and started to sniff the ground. Whatever he smelled led him on a zigzagging path toward the front door. He barked and hopped toward the door, growling as he dug out the snow.

"What is it?" I pulled on the handle. It wouldn't move at first, but it came open when I threw my shoulder against it. The carnage was immediate. The old, frozen bodies of a man, woman, and three children sat huddled in the far corner. They'd been there a long time, if I had to guess, blue and frozen stiff. The cold had kept them from rotting.

The house had been ransacked. The table was tipped on its side, and the chairs were broken and scattered. There didn't seem to be much left worth anything. But we didn't need anything of value. Just a fire, a boiling pot, and some clothes.

I shut the door behind us and approached the pile of bodies. It was truly gruesome, and, in another time, it might have brought me to tears, made me leave. But the truth was that they'd been luckier than many. They had died together and gone to Helheim together. They hadn't lived to see Ragnarok and whatever came after. Their deaths had been quicker than the slow torture Loki and I had endured.

When other suffering was stacked next to ours, everyone was lucky.

Váli was sniffing the floorboards, exploring every corner of the little house. Memories pushed themselves to the front of my mind, making my hands tremble. Narvi's scream as Váli tore out his throat. He hadn't hesitated, not for a second. He was Váli the wolf. The wild beast. The murderer.

His head perked up when he noticed me staring at him. The tips of his ears twitched, his tail dropping between his legs.

I forced my face to loosen, the anger falling away. It wasn't him.

I closed the distance and dropped to my knees. A new sound escaped him, a low, mournful howl. I took his face in my hands and made him look at me. "What happened wasn't your fault, alright? It's everyone else's fault. Mine and your father's and your grandfather's. It's our fault that Narvi is dead—"

The howl deepened, desperate as he pawed at me, trying to get away from my hands. I hadn't said it before. And he knew, of course he did, but there was something so final about hearing it. I held him tight.

"Do you hear me? This guilt isn't for you to carry. This life has turned all of us into things we'd rather not be, but your brother is not your fault."

The howling abated, and he pawed at my knees. I drew him in, and we sat in that embrace for a while until the numbness was too much to bear. I sighed and let him go.

"Do you think you can catch us something to eat?"

Váli yipped once and padded toward the door. I held it open and let him go, watching for a moment as he went bounding across the open field.

While I waited for him to return, I picked up the broken pieces of the chairs and the table and piled them into the hearth. A little wildfire brought the wood to crackling, and gradually the heat spread through the room. I found the boiling pot tucked behind the table, toppled on its side. I stuffed it to the brim with fresh snow and set it over the fire to melt.

And then there was the problem of clothing. Feeling only mildly intrusive, I started to rummage through the family's belongings. The wife had been a sturdier woman than I. Her dresses hung low over my chest and drug on the ground when I walked. I dug around until I came across the husband's things. The trousers fit just fine, and I managed to find a tunic that was minimally stained from the labours of hard work.

By the time Váli started scratching at the door, I'd found myself a travelling cloak and had pried a pair of tightly fitting boots off the body of the mother. I opened the door and found Váli sitting proudly, the fresh carcass of a white fox at his side.

CHAPTER SEVENTY-FIVE

"First will come the Fimbulwinter, three long winters, one after the other. Kin will kill kin out of greed and survival, and the people will forsake the gods. And then the end is nigh."

—*Unnamed Scholar, Prophetic Musings*

Though I still had no idea where we'd been kept, we knew exactly where to find Asgard. The World Tree loomed in the distance, and we walked toward it at as steady a clip as we could manage. The new clothes made it easier, but the boots left blisters on my feet and eventually callouses. We reached it at sundown on the third day.

I'd expected to find the city empty. If the chains had broken and Ragnarok was coming, why was Asgard full of torches, candles, and citizens going about their daily business in the snow? Why hadn't they gone to war? Had no one told them?

We approached the gate in silence. It wouldn't do us any good to be seen. It was simplest to stay off the road, following the inside of the wall. Our path wasn't entirely accurate, and we found ourselves coming too close to busy taverns and well-lit kitchens that hadn't been there before. I pulled my hood up and kept my head down, Váli not straying from my side, staying on small streets until finally we came to Valaskjálf, the centre of everything. And next to it, our hall.

It was a shameful sight. A piece of the roof had fallen in toward the front. Bushes had sprung up wildly around it, and the walls were warped with age. They could've torn it down, but instead, a bind rune had been painted on the door, something to keep any evil inside. Our poor home. Forgotten, cursed, and left to rot.

The door squealed as I pushed it open. Váli ran into the dark, his nose to the ground. Snow was piled up in the kitchen where the roof had fallen in. There were no footsteps on the ground, nothing that seemed freshly moved or out of place. No one had been here in a long time, let alone Loki.

I held my palm out, letting a fresh spark of wildfire light my way to the bedroom. The door was still intact, still open. Inside, the bed was unmade. Had I left it that way the night we ran off? The furniture was covered in rune etchings, names carved by daring kids to prove they'd been inside. Crumpled next to the bed were a pair of lady's underthings that weren't mine.

I sighed. At least most of the roof still held, and the hearth was still piled with kindling and wood. I bent down and lit the fire, letting the warmth seep into my bones.

I sat there, waiting for Váli, but he didn't come back. Concerned, I went looking for him. He wasn't in the kitchen and a quick peek into the study found it filthy but empty. The door to his bedroom was open, and there was a rustling coming from inside. When I peeked in, I found Váli with his muzzle in a pile of old laundry.

"What are you doing?"

He startled and jumped back, that whine on his voice again. He squirmed for a moment, and it looked to me as if he might be considering his options. His bed had been stripped bare and his things were thrown around his room, so I cleared a spot on the moulding mattress and waited. Could a wolf look embarrassed?

After a moment, he sunk his head back into the pile of tunics and rustled through them until he found what he'd wanted. With a crumpled piece of clothing in his teeth, he jumped up onto the bed and set it down on my knee.

"What's this?" I held it up and stretched it out. It was a large tunic. "This isn't yours, is it?" Váli's ears sunk, and he laid his head on my lap. Of course it wasn't.

"You miss him, don't you?" He nodded his snout against my leg. I ran my hand down the fur on his neck. "Did you find him?" He let out two soft yips, a no. "Oh my darling, I'm sorry…You know, I used to think that love would be easy. That once you went through the excruciating pain of waiting and finding each other, everything else would be simple. And maybe that's true for someone, but not for us. We both loved so deeply that it burned, but it didn't help. But even if we don't get to keep the one we love, they brought us happiness, and maybe that needs to be enough."

Váli looked up at me, answering with an unimpressed groan.

"I know, I could hear the bullshit even as it came out of my mouth." I nudged him up. "Come, let's find those notes. I'm tired of talking to myself."

Váli hopped down and padded off to Narvi's room. The door stood ajar enough to push open with his nose. Breathing deeply, I followed. A sliver of moonlight lit the floor. I summoned up a lantern and tossed it in the air above my head.

His room was a mess; it always had been. For all Loki's tidiness and Váli's military precision, Narvi had never learned anything from them. His furs laid in a pile next to his bed, stray pieces of clothing hanging from the bedpost. The clay pots along the walls had once held Narvi's collection of healing herbs. There was nothing left but brittle, shrivelled twigs.

The writing desk sat directly under the window. A row of candles lined the top of the desk, melted to varying heights, wax pooling at their feet. Stray paper, books, and quills were strewn across the surface in a state of disorder only Narvi had been able to follow. He'd loved to sit there until the break of dawn, lost in his work.

He never would again.

I braced myself against the desk, anguish washing over me like the tide. It was one thing to sit trapped in that cavern, knowing he was gone, and another to see what the world looked like without him in it. All the vibrancy of his world and him missing from it, like a rip in reality. To touch the parchment he'd once touched, to enter a room that would never again have him in it. My little boy who was so brilliant and so free and was no more. Gone.

My tears were falling onto the pages on the desk, the faded ink running across the yellowed parchment. I wiped my cheeks and forced the grief back down. We couldn't afford to lose a single rune from Narvi's work. I gathered up each stray paper and piled them on the bed. While I cleared the desk, Váli padded around the room, picking up discarded notebooks gently in his teeth and dropping them next to my own pile. It was already more than I could carry at once.

We returned to the bedroom with everything I could fit in my arms. The fire had made the disused old room almost cosy. While I shook the dust from the musty bed sheets, Váli stoked the fire, one log at a time, tossing each in with a lack of precision that might've lit the house on fire if he kept at it. I rummaged through my old clothing until I found a nightdress and traded my trousers for comfort.

Váli hopped up into the bed next to me. For a moment, I felt content, sitting with my son who loved and protected me, warmed by a lavender fire, surrounded by books. But the further my mind wandered, the more I thought of death and Ragnarok. There was too much to be done to enjoy anything for long.

I pulled the stack toward me, scattering the notes across the bed. The loose papers were devoid of order, so I cracked the old leather cover of the most familiar notebook, a violet one Loki had given him for his 15th birthday.

My fingers caressed the browning pages. Each rune was written meticulously, all his efforts concentrated on one thing. I flipped through the pages, blinking away the tears. I'd always tried to look over his shoulder, to catch a glimpse of what he was doing, but he hated anyone watching. Only Loki had been allowed. Sketches of hares and moths filled one page while another labelled an intensely detailed drawing of Alflaug's Thistle, listing all its practical uses. Narvi's passion would've made him a blessing to the nine realms. If he'd lived.

There was a promising passage toward the back of the book:

> *My work is starting to pay off. Last month, I was able to communicate with a hare using only seidr and my thoughts, but I hadn't succeeded in replicating the process with other animals. Today, I was finally able to break into the mind of a crow. We've always assumed that crows are fickle and cruel, but this one told me a wonderful story about his mother and brothers. I need to begin compiling my work if I ever want to convince anyone else I can do it.*

I left the book open beside me and started to thumb through the loose pages. Sketches, jots, ramblings, home study from Hod. Nothing of use. I picked up the next notebook and found an older entry.

> *It finally worked! Father told me that animals have an intelligence we don't bother to account for, and he was right. His ability to speak with Sleipnir and nearly any other horse is because he was one for so long. He learned their language, but he also learned to hear them. I don't think even he understands the magnitude of that. And now I've done it as well. I sat in the stable with Sleipnir every day, and I've finally found the runes! Won't Mother be surprised!*

Below was a long list of runes, something significantly more complicated than any seidr I'd taught him. They were sketched out over and over in slightly different iterations. The last one was circled.

"Váli." I nudged him gently, rousing him from sleep. His ears perked up. "I think I've found it."

He hopped up and shook himself before thumping his paws into my lap, eager for his miracle. I took his face in my palms and pressed my forehead against his, breathing deep. It wouldn't do to get too excited; I couldn't handle that kind of heartbreak if it didn't work.

I whispered the runes against his fur, focusing on my heartbeat, on his breathing,

The Goddess of Nothing At All

on the heat flowing between us. Each rune was precise and necessary, and I whispered them in long, repeating chants, in desperate prayers. Let me hear his voice. Let me speak to my son.

A whisper rose in the back of my mind, like another consciousness within my own. *"...knew...much...missed you, even Loki. It was so hard, Mother. Please hear me."*

"I do! Váli, I'm so sorry!" I wrapped my arms around him, crushing him against my chest.

"You hear me!" His voice came to me in two parts; the one that barked and whimpered, and the words that came to me from the back of my mind, a thought separate from mine. *"I waited so long for you. I knew you couldn't be dead. You never came out, and I couldn't go in, but why would Odin lock you in if you were dead? I didn't know what to do, but I had to wait for you. Maybe Hreidulfr was dead, and I just couldn't... Mother, I had nowhere else to go."*

"I'm here now." I held him and listened, his fear and loneliness soaking through every single word.

CHAPTER SEVENTY-SIX

"I've lived a thousand years in this hall, eating and drinking and waiting. I'm ready to die."

—*Journal of Halla Einardottir, einherji*

Váli and I spent the next two days preparing for what we knew was coming. There had clearly been a flaw in Odin's seidr, but if Loki and I were free, Ragnarok was likely well on its way.

I dug through our old things until I found a dagger and one of Váli's short-handled axes. Váli critiqued me as I practised, hopping around under my feet. He criticized my sloppy form in close combat and corrected my axe use. I'd seen enough einherjar train for battle that I was certain I knew what I was doing, but my son vehemently disagreed.

I read through old texts, looking for passages on transmogrification, but there were thousands of books and a limited amount of time. I kept digging through the shelves, skimming glossaries and chapter headings. Some of the books were destroyed, bloated, or mouldy. Wherever Loki had learned his shapeshifting runes from, I wasn't finding them. And so, I kept looking.

While I read, Váli hunted. He always went out in the cover of night, avoiding any part of the city that was too busy or too bright. Each time he left, he came back with wild game between his jaws, but I knew that wasn't all he was out hunting for.

Váli and I were eating in front of the fire on the third night when something moved in the kitchen. Váli leapt to all fours, his body wound back, teeth bared and ready to pounce. I crawled to my feet, trying not to make any noise.

The kitchen floor creaked again. Between the firelight and the smell of cooking food and smoke, we'd already given ourselves away. But let it come. I'd kill whatever it was and not bat an eye.

Then Váli's ears perked. He sniffed the air. Confused, I watched his entire body react to whatever it was he was smelling. I mouthed the words at him, trying to ask him what it was, but he was hysterical, his thoughts an excited blur. As the steps got closer, he bounded toward the door and sat waiting, his tail thumping against the wooden floor.

The door opened to reveal a familiar man, broad as a bear, sword at the ready. My jaw dropped. "Hreidulfr?"

Like all the Midgardian dead, he hadn't aged a day, but he'd still changed. He'd grown his beard out, and there were rune beads braided into it. His hair was longer, tied back into a little tail. He was gruffer than I'd remembered. Worn.

"It can't be. Ma'am, is that really you?" Hreidulfr skirted past the wolf and pulled me into his arms. "You're supposed to be dead."

"Dead?" I slapped him on the back, laughing with relief. "Is that what Odin told everyone? If only he'd killed us; it would've been quicker."

Eager for Hreidulfr's attention, Váli jumped up and started pawing at the man's stomach.

Hreidulfr took his paws in his hands and stared at him, frowning. "Those eyes…"

I put my hand on his shoulder. "Hreidulfr, I'm going to need you to sit down."

He nodded and followed me to sit on the end of the bed. He left a respectable space between us, but Váli quickly hopped up, panting and wagging his tail, staring at Hreidulfr, who stared warily right back.

"Ma'am, I'm going to be straight with you." Hreidulfr pulled his gaze away from the wolf to look at me. "I know what I see, and I want to hope for it, but you've got to know. There's so much I haven't told anyone for so long. Odin told everyone that you'd all been killed, but I thought '*if he were dead, I'd know it.*' I looked for you. Bought a horse and spent a year travelling, just looking for any sign of your family. I had to try. But a man can only hold hope for so long, you know? It broke my heart, but I thought, if Váli's dead or not, he's not coming back. I tried to move on. Found someone once or twice, but nothing ever worked out." Tears slicked his cheeks. "I still miss him every day like someone took my arm clean off. I won't survive any more heartbreak."

I smiled. "You're right. When Odin trapped Loki and I, he sealed Váli in his wolf-hide. He's come home for you."

Hreidulfr choked in a breath and pulled Váli into his arms. He tried to speak, but nothing coherent came out.

Váli pawed at my leg with his back foot. *"Tell him that he snores like an ox when he sleeps on his stomach and that I used to pick him water lilies because he liked the smell."* I raised an eyebrow at him. *"Do it."*

And so I did.

"How do you know that? No one knows that." Hreidulfr looked between the two of us. "Did he tell you?" I explained the runes, and Hreidulfr laughed, holding Váli's face between his big hands. "No one's picked me water lilies since you left."

"I could teach you if you like. To talk to him. But first I have so many questions." Hreidulfr nodded. "Ask them."

I asked the thing I least wanted to know. "How long have we been gone?"

"Longer than I know, ma'am." He gave Váli's head a ruffle and sat up straight. "I lost track lifetimes ago. You wouldn't even recognize the realms. Midgard's lost its belief in the gods. We get a few new souls now and again that believe in the old ways, but Midgard is covered in buildings that reach the sky and electricity they've forced to do their bidding, things I can't understand. The half of them don't even know how to fight." He stared off into the fire, working his thumbs nervously into his calloused hands. "Everything's different."

It was too much to process. Lifetimes. I tried to give voice to the things that were solid, get away from this vague eternity. "Odin locked us away. Loki is missing. Narvi is dead."

"Sigyn, I am so sorry." Hreidulfr reached out and pulled me into his arms.

I let him hold me for a moment, my face pressed against his chest, and I wiped away a tear. "Why did you come here tonight?"

Hreidulfr looked down, his eyes red and glistening. "I came to say goodbye, ma'am. I went back to the einherjar eventually because there was nothing else to do with myself. Eternity is long. And tomorrow is the last day for us. We ride out for Ragnarok in the morning." He looked down at Váli. "You waited until the last damn minute, didn't you?"

"Has anyone seen Loki?"

"I've heard whispers, ma'am. They say that Heimdall saw the other army more than a day's ride from here. They're marching toward the fields of Vigrid. They also say that Loki's on one of the ships of the dead, right next to his daughter." He turned to stare at the floorboards. "I wish I had better news for you."

"Sweet boy, there's no good news left." I did my best to smile, though I knew it would hardly be reassuring. "If I have to be here, at the end of everything, I'm glad to have found you first."

"Ah, I know I can think of something you'll like. Give me a moment." Hreidulfr sat straighter and scratched his beard. He snapped his fingers. "That little girl that was so taken with Narvi, she pissed off her mother something fierce."

The Goddess of Nothing At All

"Gersemi?" I frowned. "How do you mean?"

He chuckled, a sly smile on his lips. "She went and married some young man that owns a bakery down in the middle of the city. Half of Asgard thinks she did it just to spite Freya." He laughed and shook his head. "You should've seen it. I stood guard for the wedding, and her mother was as drunk as a rat in a barrel of mead. Thor had to drag her out by her hair to keep her from burning the place to the ground."

I laughed and the looseness felt good. "You're right, I do like that."

Hreidulfr chuckled along for a moment, but it faded as Váli nuzzled himself into his side once more. "Ma'am, I hate to ask. You've got other things on your mind, I know. But I just...I want to hear his voice one more time before I die."

Váli's ears perked at that, and the whining started again.

I hushed him. "Yes, yes, I hear you. Hreidulfr, I don't suppose you know any seidr?"

He shook his head. "Not a bit. I stick to what I'm good at."

I moved to sit cross-legged on the bed. "Come on, sit across from me."

When he was settled in, I put my hands on his knees. He looked up at me, a strange mix of nervous and eager.

"I'm going to channel energy and push it into your body. It's going to feel strange, but you need to let it in." I put the notebook in his lap and pointed to Narvi's notes. "You'll need to say these runes over and over with your hands on Váli. You'll know when it's worked. Do you understand?"

He nodded. "I'm ready."

The feeling of energy under his skin startled him at first, but it was the runes that kept us awake into the small hours of the night. It wasn't simple to learn the curve and length of them, to feel the power of them around your tongue. He was a man who memorized strategy and movement, not words on a page. And so, we repeated them again and again, until at long last, he could chant them alone, steady and accurate.

There was no mistaking the moment that it worked. Hreidulfr's eyes shot wide, and he nearly collapsed onto Váli with his full weight, holding him with enough force to make the wolf howl.

Quietly, I stood and tiptoed from the room. I drew my borrowed cloak around my shoulders and stepped out into the cold of the ruined hall beyond the bedroom. The world was still dark, but morning would come soon enough. Let them have their moment.

I brushed the snow from the top of the kitchen table. A pile of my old books were still at the place I used to sit, a bear fur wrapped around the back of my chair. I shook the snow away and wrapped it around my shoulders, sitting down. Pulling my feet into the chair, my knees against my chest, I took it all in.

The shelves were crooked. Some of the bowls had fallen. The herb hooks were empty, and the cellar door was open. The hearth was piled with snow, cupboard doors hanging off their hinges.

Nothing here was mine anymore.

I hadn't had any waking dreams since I'd left the cave, but I could see it all so clearly, like I was watching my own life play out in front of me. Sitting by the fire with Loki when we'd come in from the rain. Fighting with him over chores and the children and Idunn. When he'd laid me out on the table and touched me until I melted. Early mornings. Crying babies. An eight-legged horse in a diaper. Reading until we couldn't keep our eyes open. A thousand, thousand memories under this roof, and all of it would be gone tomorrow, missing from these realms like none of us had ever lived.

I sat there until the chill seeped in through my boots and I could no longer stave off the cold. When I went back into the warmth of my bedroom, I found them curled up against the headboard, Hreidulfr scratching behind Váli's ear. They looked up when the door opened, happy, if only for the moment.

"You didn't have to stay out in the cold, ma'am." Hreidulfr scooted to the side to make room for me to sit.

"Nonsense. The fresh air was good for me." I set my cloak aside and sat next to him, an appropriate distance away. "But I need to ask you something."

He nodded. "Anything. It seems I owe you."

"You don't owe us anything." Váli chirped.

"He's right. You're your own man, and we don't hold debts." I pulled my hair loose and started to tuck it into a cleaner knot on the back of my head. "Nevertheless, I have to ask you a difficult question. We'll be riding to Vigrid as well. Loki doesn't know that Váli's alive. This entire thing has been a play for vengeance, and if Loki thinks he has something left to lose, maybe he can convince Fenrir and Hel, Jormungandr if he still lives—"

"He's alive," Hreidulfr cut in. "They found him in Midgard, in the ocean. In all of the oceans. They say he's so long, he can bite his own tail."

"Gods," I whispered, trying to imagine such a thing. "Maybe Loki can stop this. Maybe we get to keep living if he can just convince them."

Váli huffed. *"I wouldn't count on it."*

"No. Me either." I looked into the fire. "But I'd rather die trying than hiding here in the dark. Will you come with us?"

"Of course I'm coming with you. Do you really think I'd wait hundreds of years for the man I love to come back and then just let him *leave?*" Hreidulfr rolled his eyes. "With respect, ma'am, you can't keep me away."

The Goddess of Nothing At All

"You're sure?"

"If you ask me one more time, I'm going to take it as an insult." He sat up and put his hand on my shoulder. "You're my family. That's all there is to say."

I pursed my lips, blinking back the tears. "Well then. We'd best get to work."

We stayed up for a long time, getting the details in order. Hreidulfr stole a pair of war horses from the stables, fit with all the trimmings we'd need for riding. Váli went hunting and brought back enough for a good meal for the three of us. We sharpened blades, found mismatched armour, and talked about what plan made the most sense.

And at long last, there was nothing else to do but wait for first light. It was already the early hours of the morning, but my mind was racing. I made the boys lie down to rest and promised to keep watch until sunrise. There would be no sleep for me. My mind was too busy wondering what it would be like to die.

Would I see Narvi in Helheim?

Would I finally be allowed to rest?

CHAPTER SEVENTY-SEVEN

"The sun turns black, land sinks into the sea;
the bright stars scatter from the sky.
flame flickers up against the world-tree;
fire flies high against heaven itself."

—*Prophecy of the Seeress 57*

The bone-rattling jar of the Gjallarhorn woke me, jolting me upright. I ran to the window and peeked through the boards. There was light in the sky. I'd fallen asleep.

We'd missed our chance.

"Get up! We need to go!"

The horses were still saddled and loaded. Hreidulfr and I were out the door as quickly as we could manage, pulling on our boots and cloaks. Digging my heels into the horse's flanks, we rode out onto the path towards the gate, Váli racing along beside us.

A thunder of hooves filled the air, the einherjar pouring down the main street of Asgard, towards the gates. I pulled my hood up and slipped in beside the rest, letting us become part of the charge. I urged my horse faster, trying to get to the front. We needed to get there first.

But it was no use. There were too many horses. We were part of the pack, and as we thundered on with them, I tried to think of something else, some other way to stop this. We had time. Vigrid was still leagues away.

As we rode past Sessrúmnir, Freya's soldiers fell in beside the rest, doubling their numbers. The ground shook under the force of a hundred thousand feet, hooves throwing powdered snow into the air.

The Goddess of Nothing At All

The light in the sky dimmed and flickered. Our own shadows moved beneath us, stretching out like an entire day had passed in minutes. Heads craned up, the horses still surging forward. A shadow was racing along in the sky, chasing the sun. The shadow widened, engulfing the light and throwing the realm into darkness. I held my breath, waiting for the sun to come back.

It didn't.

Flames flickered to light across my vision, wildfire and lanterns and torches. A chill settled in, all the warmth missing. And still we pressed on, knowing that Sol and her sun were gone for good.

The crowd was getting too thick. We'd be boxed in soon, and Váli might be trampled. I nodded my head to Hreidulfr, signalling to move, and the two of us veered out towards open space.

Finally, without all the bobbing heads in my view, I could see Vigrid. The field was barren, covered in nothing but snow, and in the distance were the tallest mountains in Jotunheim. Something was behind them, a light obscured by the ice. It burned so bright I had to squint just to look at it.

An enormous, boney hand reached up from behind the mountain and took hold of its peak, pulling itself up and over. His body was fire, licking the air and melting the ice from everything he came near. And he was coming for us, gripping his red-hot longsword in one hand. Surtr, the flame giant from the prophecy.

Yggdrasil protect us, we were never going home.

We needed to run because there would be no fighting this. I looked around for an answer, and there, on the shores that met the edge of Vigrid, was a pack of ships, emptying their cargo out onto the snow. A sea of dead souls, wraiths, and beasts, some missing skin and clothes and limbs, all marching to their next deaths.

The closer we got, the more the sight of the ships turned my stomach. Morbid nannies had told me the stories as a child; one ship would be made from human skin, another from human hair, and the last, the largest of them all, was Naglfar, the ship of nightmares. The toe- and fingernails of the dead were wrought together like dragon scales to serve as the hull of the ship, warped and yellowed and disgusting, more horrible than anything I'd ever pictured.

"Do you see him?" I had to yell over the hard rhythm of the horse's hooves.

Váli barked, keeping in time with us as best he could, though his legs would never be as long and as steady as a horse. "*In the middle!*"

I looked toward the centre of the field. The opposing armies were rushing toward each other, blades drawn, eager to begin what they'd waited an eternity for. In the middle of it all, a burst of teal flame shot out and upward, knocking a dozen soldiers from their mounts. The damned fool had rushed headlong into the fray.

A massive wave hit the edge of the sea and spilt out onto the bank, far enough to reach us. The horses startled at the water underfoot and stumbled. I pulled the reins hard, trying to get it under control. A serpent burst forth from the sea, as big around as the trunk of Yggdrasil and just as tall. Its body sunk deep into the water and in the distance, curls of its seaweed-covered body twisted in and out of the water, beyond the horizon. There was no end in sight.

It bent its head down, and I knew him. The same colours, the same cool manner. But now Jormungandr was so big that every single scale was bigger than my hand. His mouth was a cavern, and his breath smelled like briny ocean water. We were barely a snack to him. My heart was trying to escape my chest as his eyes fell on us, his enormous teeth unsheathing for the kill.

"Wait!" I screamed. "You know me! When you were young, you stayed in my home with your father and your mother! You ate eggs and slept near my fire! You know us! We've come to protect Loki!"

Jormungandr crooked his head and came closer, tongue licking the air. Smell. That was how a serpent smelled things. We stayed very still, letting him make his way to each of us, waiting. Whatever he found must have passed the test. A gentle rattle echoed from his throat and he gently knocked the side of his cheek into me. "Ssssigyn."

A howl shook the air. I clapped my hands over my ears, trying to block it out. There was only one thing it could be, but I wasn't ready to believe it. Jormungandr's' head shot up, and he slithered out onto the battlefield, wrapping himself around the peaks of the mountains, the end of his tail never leaving the water.

"By the Norn, I nearly shit myself." Hreidulfr tried to catch his breath. "Never in all my years—"

Lights burst out along the black sky, green and purple, shimmering. The rhythmic beating of swan wings rose out above us, several hundred Valkyrie joining the fray. Each Wing passed at breakneck speed, tossing daggers below them like rain. Once they were clear, a flurry of arrows shot out across the sky.

"We're out of time." I pulled tight on my horse's reins. "New plan. We stay together. We go in, we get him, and we leave. This battle is not our concern. Agreed?"

"*Agreed.*"

The battle was raging, weapons and seidr flying in all directions. It was too thick to continue by horse. I jumped down and slapped the beast's bottom. It whinnied and ran, hopefully to safer pastures.

If anywhere was still safe.

Hreidulfr abandoned his horse as well, a pair of hand axes at the ready and

Váli on his heels.

I hadn't even reached for my weapon when the first of the dead charged at me. The damned thing was missing an eye and the gaping, rotten hole startled me. If Váli hadn't jumped onto it and tore out its throat, it might have been a very short battle for me.

"*Stop daydreaming!*" Váli fell onto his victim and bit down once more for good measure.

"Right." I pulled in my focus, giving my head a shake. I scanned the horizon for a moment and caught a glimpse of teal flame. He'd shifted east. "Follow me."

We ran together, trying to avoid fighting with either side, skirting around trolls and Jotun Jarls and battle maidens. Fighting would only slow us down, so we struck only when struck at, following Loki's ever-shifting location.

It was hard to run. The snow was being packed to ice beneath our feet, and where Surtr's flame came too close, it melted and turned to mud. By the time I caught a glimpse of Loki, we were covered in dirt and blood.

I heard his laugh somewhere on my left. It was him, but it was manic, unrestrained. A flash of light blinded me for a moment. When my vision cleared, I found half the crowd around him on the ground, charred and smoking.

"Loki!"

He didn't turn.

I didn't have that kind of time. I cast a sharp rune and pushed, summoning a current of air to cut a path towards him. Bodies flew, divided by the wind. The three of us ran before the warriors on either side could regain their senses and attack. "Loki!"

He turned. His hair was wild and tangled, and he was covered in filth and sweat. He grinned when he saw me, and it pushed the melted wax of his cheek up in a way that was unsettling. The milky white of his eye stared right through me. My Loki might not be in there at all.

"You came!" He pulled a sword from one of the lifeless bodies at his feet and turned to meet me, his arms open.

I held out a hand against his chest, keeping him at a distance. "Loki, this isn't the time. I—"

"Darling, this is the only time! We're nearly out of it." He wrapped his arms around me, and I submitted to him for a moment, watching over his shoulder for a stray axe. He planted a kiss above my ear and broke away, sweeping his hand out toward the scene before us. "Look what I've done for you. I brought them all here. Everyone already had their axes sharpened. They just needed someone to say the right words."

How could he stand in the middle of a battle and still be so long-winded? I needed to stall. I clasped my hands together, whispered a set of runes, and drew a dome over us with my fingertips. A moment later, the air around us shimmered, and the four of us were locked inside a barrier with a young Jotun, a long-dead wench, and a single einherji. Before I could make another move, the Jotun and the wench turned on the einherji, ripping him to shreds with their blades. Then they turned on us.

I pulled my daggers from my belt and readied myself, but it never came to that. Loki stopped the young Jotun's heart with a bolt of electricity while Váli and Hreidulfr ripped the dead wench limb from limb.

Loki took a moment to look closely at Hreidulfr. He squinted. "Do I know you?"

Hreidulfr wiped his hand on his trousers and reached out. "I suppose you do, sir, though it's been a while."

"Hreidulfr! I barely recognized you!" Loki pulled him in for a hug, slapping his back. He released Hreidulfr and pointed at his eye. "Though my vision isn't what it used to be. And look, you've got yourself a pet." Loki pursed his lips, a sadness settling over him. "Looks just like him, doesn't he?"

Váli snarled. "*Who are you calling a pet, you traitorous, conniving—*"

Hreidulfr bent down, stroking Váli's fur. "Come on now. He doesn't know better."

All around us, both sides of the battle were banging their fists on the barrier, trying to get inside. It wouldn't hold forever.

I turned to Loki and gave him a push. "I thought they were your army?"

"Oh, no, the prophecy is quite exaggerated. I knocked on a few doors, yes, called on a few favours, but these aren't my armies. Besides, they're not after me; they're after you." He stopped a moment and scratched at his chin. "Yes, that may be a bit inconvenient. Hel!"

I followed his gaze toward the sky. High above the chaos floated an impenetrable darkness, wispy and cascading, like smoke born from shadows. It turned at Loki's call, and I saw that it was a living thing. It crept toward us, the wisps churning around itself, around the core that bound it together. Hel. She'd grown into herself, tall and beautiful. She was made of sharp angles, still half living flesh and half dead. Darkness flowed around her like a gown, bits of her pallid blue skin peeking out as it crawled and stretched over her body. She was as horrible and breath-taking as death itself. I couldn't tear my eyes away.

"Isn't she something?" Loki put his arm around my back. "Goddess of Death, ruler of Helheim. You should see what she's done to the place." He chuckled, distant and frightening. "I guess we all will, soon."

"Loki, please." I took his face in my hands and turned his gaze to mine, hoping it would be enough to draw his full attention. "We have to get out of here."

But he wasn't listening. His gaze had travelled back to the sky. Hel had reached the barrier, sweeping down like a cloud. She lowered herself onto the dome and sat on its peak, staring at us. "Yes, Father?" Her voice was ethereal; dark, deep, and yet as sweet and seductive as honey.

Loki gestured to me. "Sweetheart, you remember Sigyn?"

"I do." Hel bowed her head. "You tried. I never forgot."

I blushed. It was hardly the time to get caught up in the past, but I did appreciate the sentiment.

"The family is having a bit of trouble with your army. Can you do something about that?" Loki waved towards the barrier, where the decrepit forces of her army were pressed up against the walls, attempting to rip through.

"Of course." She lowered herself through the barrier as if it were made of nothing and settled onto her bare feet beside me. She reached out and set a cold hand on my cheek. The cold flooded through me, sending gooseflesh down my spine. She looked into my eyes. "You can ask."

"Is he here?" The words slipped out before I could decide if I wanted to know, my pulse thudding in my veins.

"Narvi is safe." Her smile was kind. "He was angry that I wouldn't let him come, but it's too dangerous for him here. He is more precious a friend than I could ask for, and I need him for what comes next."

My hands went to my face, tears threatening to spill over. And for a moment I considered my options. I'd come here to save my family, but if Narvi was waiting, it would be so simple to join him. But it was too dangerous a thought to entertain. Instead, I looked at the family that needed me. "Please take care of him."

"Always."

She went to Hreidulfr next and touched his cheek. He jumped, but as she worked, the rattle against the barrier calmed just a little more.

Then it was Váli's turn. She knelt down in front of him. "I told you I didn't have him, Father."

"What are you talking about?" Loki bent over her shoulder, peering down at the wolf.

Hel reached up and touched her rotten hand to his temple, her other hand on Váli's muzzle. The recognition on Loki's face was immediate.

He dropped to his knees and pulled Váli in. "I thought you were dead."

"*You were never that smart.*" Váli's voice was timid, not his usual biting self.

Loki squeezed Váli until he barked a cough. "I don't care what you think I am. I wished for you back every day."

"*I*—" Váli broke off into a mournful howl and nuzzled into his father.

"Loki." I knelt down next to them. "It's not too late. We can take them and leave, all of us. You wanted to be a family. Let's go. Call off your children, and we can run to the ends of the nine and never look back. We can be happy, all of us."

Hel stood, the darkness falling around her ankles like a gown. "I won't. This battle is ours to win, and the gods have taken too much from me and my brothers. I speak for them when I say that we're ready to die for that."

I pointed to the battle. "They'll throw everything away for this."

"They have nothing to throw away. Our lives were taken from us when we were ripped from our parents and discarded. Everything after was the life they gave us, not the one we deserved." She rolled her shoulder, and the bones under her rotten flesh shifted. "When they die, they'll join me in Helheim like the rest. We give ourselves to rid the nine of these tyrants and begin again."

Hreidulfr stepped forward. "All respect, goddess, but you're not giving any of *us* a choice. Some of us want to live."

"And you're welcome to try. If you don't, you always have a place in my halls, all of you. What else is family for? But you won't change our minds." Hel's eyes fell on Loki. "You should take Father."

"What?" Loki's head shot up, and he sprang up from his embrace with Váli. "I'm not letting you do this without me."

Hel took him by the hands. "You've suffered enough for a hundred lifetimes. If you can find happiness, you should. You'll join us below someday, no matter when, but if Sigyn wants to take you, you should go. Be happy."

An explosion sounded from outside the barrier. The Aesir forces had been gathering around it, beating their axes on it, but whatever the blow had been, it rocked the barrier to its core. Fire illuminated the sky in the distance. A wyrm, The Nidhogg, had joined the battle, swooping down with enormous wings to shake the ground as it landed, crushing everything beneath it.

"Decide, Loki." I shook him. "The boys and I are going, with or without you. You wanted this family, and now it's time to choose them."

Loki rubbed his palm over his face, deliberating. I steeled myself for the words I expected, the firm denial. He'd always done what he wanted, and there was no reason for it to be different on the last day of the realms.

"Alright." He looked up at me, his emerald eye peeking out from between his fingers. "What?"

"You're right. I'd be a fool to walk away from you." He laughed too loudly, pushing back his mess of loose hair and braids. "Besides, isn't the grandest trick of all, to convince them to kill each other while we all live?"

I had to force my slack jaw closed. "Then you'll come?"

"Sigyn, you're acting as if *this* is the craziest thing I've ever done." He turned to look at the barrier. It wouldn't be long. It was starting to fray, holes opening big enough to reach into. Outside, the carnage continued. Lightning flashed down from the sky, illuminating Jormungandr overhead grappling with a broad shadow that held a familiar hammer. The hammer came down on the head of the serpent, and Loki flinched. Jormungandr hissed and snapped his jaw forward, attempting to snag the god in his teeth.

The life paled from Loki's face. He stared, unwavering, as his son fought off Thor's strength, snapping at the tiny god that ran across his scales. He spoke as a strained whisper. "What have I done?"

Hel put her hand on Loki's shoulder. "They chose this. Go."

Loki turned to her, eyes glistening, then pulled her into his arms. The darkness enveloped them both, sweeping around their bodies. When he pulled away, he pressed his hand to her cheek. "I love you. Tell Narvi I'm sorry."

"I will." She pried herself from his grip and beckoned me over. "I'll clear a path, but that's all I can do. I've been away from the battle too long already. Be well, family."

Hel rose into the air, the shadows swirling around her feet. She slid through the top of the barrier until she was high above us, then held up her arms. The darkness churned, and a stampede of her soldiers came pouring toward the barrier, pushing back the einherjar and Valkyrie poised outside it.

"Now!" I whispered a rune and the battered barrier fell. Loki and I barrelled forward, Hreidulfr and Váli on our heels.

A pair of einherjar lunged in front of us, blocking our path. One pushed us back, her round wooden shield held up, a sword darting out from around its edge. Loki pressed his hand against the wood and the shield burst into flame, throwing her off balance. Hreidulfr cut her down with two swift strokes of his axes, her body dropping into the mud. The betrayal in her eyes was evident.

"Traitor." Her hands grasped at his legs as she fell to the mud.

He stood motionless, staring down at her while Váli sprang past him toward the next warrior.

"*You remember she was nothing but a sour old hag, right?*" Váli barked.

"Yeah." Hreidulfr gave her a kick to the ribs and stepped over her, but the lost look was still in his eyes.

I followed them, leaping over body after body. The ground was filling up with corpses from all sides. The Jotnar lay entangled among Hel's armies and the einherjar, lying together in some grim version of peace.

My heart stopped. I called for the others to wait, pointing at what I was seeing. There, in the centre of a hoard of dead warriors, was Odin.

He'd ridden Sleipnir into battle. The two of them were covered in decadent gold and white armour, almost impossible to miss. And they seemed to be holding their own against the enemies surrounding them, though how long that could last was hard to say.

"Sig—"

"I know, Loki. We'll try." I waved them forward, dodging through the fight, towards Sleipnir. If we had the chance to bring him home, we couldn't waste it.

But Odin saw us before we could make any moves. His face soured. "You."

"Yes, us." Loki stabbed his dagger into the neck of someone in his way. "Give me back my son."

Odin laughed. "And what makes you think I'm going to do—"

He flew off Sleipnir's back as the horse bucked him off.

Sleipnir forced his way through the crowd, towards us, leaving Odin to pull himself off the ground.

Loki reached out for his son, letting him nuzzle into his chest. "I guess that settles that, doesn't it, *Grimnir*? Hard to have friends when you're always making enemies."

"You'll die today." Odin was breathing frantically, pushing his way towards us. "Every last one of you. And I'll bask in it, every moment—"

The ground shook. Again and again. Like running.

Odin turned. Behind him, closing in fast, was a wolf like a mountain, teeth bared and snarling.

Fenrir.

There was no time. No time to run, to fight back. We managed to brace ourselves against the quaking ground, and that was it. Fenrir bounded forward, his muzzle darted out, and it was done. Odin was lodged between his teeth, blood pouring to the ground below. Not a scream or a quip. Just dead.

The noise was horrific. The crunch of bone and armour, the slick sound of meat. Fenrir tossed his head back and swallowed the body whole.

Anything that had been fighting close to us turned and ran in the other direction, which was well enough. We were stunned silent, staring up at Fenrir's blood-slick mouth in equal parts awe and terror.

Something stirred in me, and I pried Loki's hand off my arm. Fenrir looked down as I stepped towards him, hand outstretched. He bent down until he was face to face with me, so enormous that I suddenly understood what it would be to stand next to a whale. But I pushed my fear down and ran my hand across the fur on his nose.

"Thank you. And I'm sorry."

"No." Fenrir's voice boomed around me, and noticing me cringe, he started to whisper. "You've been long forgiven. You're not the one to blame for the evils of gods."

I nodded and stepped away, letting Loki and Váli step forward. With no inclination to eavesdrop, I turned to the battle. Still raging away from us, away from the enormous danger of Fenrir. But something was wrong. Something I could feel under my skin.

With runes on my breath, I tried to summon up a flicker of wildfire. I was tired, yes, but I knew the feeling of trying to cast while tapped of my own energy. This wasn't it. All around the battlefield lanterns were flickering, flames and sparks dull and weak.

With so many völur taking from the ground and the air all at once, again and again, the energy was fading. The well was drying up. What I could manage to pull up was in spurts, a little at a time. The edge of the battlefield was in sight, but we needed to escape before we were left with only our hands to defend ourselves with.

A hand rested on my shoulder. "Are you alright, ma'am?"

"Hmm?" I looked up at Hreidulfr. A streak of mud ran across his cheek.

"Your father is dead." His face was set with deep concern.

"Oh. Yes. Honestly, he's been dead to me for a very long time. But thank you for asking." I showed him the sputtering spark in my palm. "It's time to go."

Fenrir had stood up and was already walking towards the centre of the battle, one careful paw in front of the other.

"Come on. We're leaving right now." I walked past the others, heading for the closest edge of the battle. "There's nothing left to pick up, this detour is over."

"I'm hurt that you'd forget about me."

I turned. There, sword at the ready, was Heimdall. He was covered head to toe in shining chainmail, a grin plastered on his face.

"Goddamnit! Leave us alone." I stepped forward, positively done with this whole thing. "If you want this fight, you fight all of us."

He shook his head. "I used to think you were smarter than this, sister."

"I suppose you never really knew me, did you?" My fists tightened around the hilt of my dagger. "We're leaving, but it doesn't have to be through you. Stand aside."

He stepped toward me, axe in hand. "I've spent too many years watching, sworn to silence, but not this time. You have an obsession with your own doom, keeping him next to you. I've watched him murder and pillage and betray us all, and I will not let him leave here alive. Not this time. I'm done standing by."

Loki stepped between us. "This won't end well for you."

"It ends with your death, and that's well enough for me." Heimdall's body tensed,

409

hunched over like a wolf before the kill.

"Should I tremble? Do you really think *you'll* be the one to kill me? You're just not that good, watchdog." Loki pulled the axe from his belt, staring him down. "Woof."

Heimdall laughed. "Did no one tell you? You die today. Your name is on the list."

"I know that prophecy inside and out. We've served our punishment; there's nothing else." I reached for sputters of energy, anything that could help us.

"Do you really think there's only been one prophecy after all this time? Allfather collected them for decades. You found one piece of the puzzle. It always comes down to you and I, Loki. This moment. You don't live."

Loki's knuckles whitened on his axe handle and his remark wasn't as quick as it might have been. "Only if you're fool enough to believe in fate. Let's see who's better, hmm?"

"If it's all the same to you sir," Hreidulfr stepped forward to stand beside Loki, his axes at the ready. "I don't think I'll give him a fair fight."

"Come, all of you. Horsie, too." Heimdall waved us forward, inviting us to join. "It won't make any difference. I win, no matter what."

I summoned up a weak burst of light, casting it directly into Heimdall's face. He shielded his eyes with his arm, which was enough of an opening for Hreidulfr. He charged at the god, one axe raised to strike him down. With incredible speed, Heimdall took Hreidulfr by the wrist and threw him backwards onto the ground as if the warrior were no more than a sack of grain.

Loki dove forward, trying to catch Heimdall before he could regroup. I focused, only to feel the energy fading from my fingers. Stripped of my own power, I pulled my dagger out and stepped closer. Hreidulfr was still pulling himself up from the ground.

The blade of Loki's axe screeched against Heimdall's sword as he blocked. Loki kicked, catching him in the chest and pushing him toward me. There weren't a lot of opportunities, but I stabbed at Heimdall anyways. The blade glinted off him, leaving my wrist vibrating.

Despite being caught between us, Heimdall seemed at ease. It was no wonder. Against Thor, he wouldn't have stood a chance. Against two völur stripped of their power, a wolf, a horse, and an einherji, he could be reasonably confident.

A blur of grey fur whipped around my ankles and sprung up beside me, onto Heimdall's back. Váli dug his teeth into Heimdall's iron helmet, trying to wrench it from his head. On the third pull, it fell away and clattered to the ground. Heimdall stumbled away from Loki, trying to grasp the wolf with his free hand. All the while, Váli snapped at him in an attempt to remove any finger that came too close.

Seeing my opportunity, I struck hard, swinging in a swift arch toward his neck.

410

The Goddess of Nothing At All

Heimdall moved, lurching as he tried to pull Váli off. I hit armour once again.

Heimdall reached over his shoulder and grabbed a fistful of wolf fur. He pulled Váli up and over his shoulder, tossing him to the ground. Váli landed with a yelp, his back paw bent in the wrong direction. Several of the einherjar had caught sight of the battle at hand and rushed toward Váli. Sleipnir sped towards them, barrelling several warriors on their backs as Hreidulfr raced to Váli's side.

With the odds stacked in his favour, Heimdall stepped toward us. His sword came down at me, and Loki intercepted, parrying the blow and pulling back to strike again. They swung at each other, trying to find an opening, trying to find that edge. A sharp, wolfish squeal sounded off from behind Heimdall. Loki faltered just long enough for Heimdall to crack him in the jaw with his empty fist. The strength of it nearly brought Loki to his knees, but he managed instead to drive the handle of his axe into Heimdall's cheek.

Heimdall fell to his hands next to Loki. Loki pulled back to kick him, but my brother was quicker. One swift motion of his sword severed the back of Loki's grounded foot. He screamed and crumbled into the mud, the tendon of his ankle split in two.

"Loki!" I ran forward and drove my boot into my brother's face. He fell onto his back, his teeth bleeding. I threw my weight onto him and swung my blade down. Heimdall caught my wrist mid-swing, the blade dangling above his face. One sharp twist was all it took to release my grip on the dagger. Screaming, I swung with my second hand, and he knocked the dagger from me as if I were a child, leaving me weaponless and restrained.

Writhing on the ground, Loki grasped at his ankle as Heimdall climbed to his feet, hauling me up with him. He turned me around, pressing my back against his chest like a shield. "Get up, Silvertongue. Don't you want to protect your precious bride?"

Loki hissed and swung himself up, putting all his weight on his one good leg. Blood leaked down his boot and into the mud under his feet. The unhinged smile was back on his face, his teeth stained red. He spat, bloody phlegm splattering across Heimdall's boot. "I should've killed you years ago."

"Finally, something we can agree on." My brother took hold of my hair and pulled my head back.

I'd had enough. I screamed and summoned up what trickle of energy I could find. I forced my palm onto his face. The sputtering wildfire in my hand licked his skin, setting his brows and hair ablaze. His grip loosened, and he fell back into the mud, trying to extinguish the flame.

"We have to go," I said, turning back to Loki. Blood seeped from his leg and his lips.

He shook his head. "He'll catch us. We finish this now." He limped forward and buried his axe in Heimdall's back. The scream that ripped from my brother pulled at my nerves.

The axe came back out with a splash of blood, the wet sound of it turning my stomach. Heimdall rolled to his side, still struggling to stand. Loki wound the axe back again, but Heimdall's foot connected with Loki's good leg, propelling him to the ground.

He was on him before I could move, driving a dagger deep into Loki's chest.

The world seemed to dim then, for just a moment. I tried to focus on pulling up enough energy to do something, anything, but I couldn't. The realms could burn for all I cared. Everything that had ever mattered lay bleeding out into the mud in front of me. My world shattered like glass dashed across the stones.

The sickening crack brought me back. Loki had driven his axe into Heimdall's skull. My brother's head nodded, his body swaying, trying to stay upright. His eyes rolled back into his head, and he fell, splayed out on his back, still as night.

I moved without really knowing it, hearing myself scream like I was underwater. Kicking Heimdall again and again, his limp body not reacting. The rage boiled under my skin, and I felt something crack in his chest. "You can't have him! You. Can't. Have. Him!"

Loki coughed, a sputtering laugh. "Sigyn, he's dead."

Shaking, I stopped, trying to catch my breath. Heimdall's eyes stared up at the sky, blank and cold. A pool of blood soaked into the mud, spreading out from his skull.

Hreidulfr came to my side. Váli was perched on his back like a child, front paws around his neck. Sleipnir sauntered up behind them.

"*The battle's over,*" Váli said.

We looked behind us. It was a massacre. The forces of either side had been cut in half, but the enemies of Asgard were running rampant. Hel's army ran side by side with the Jotun, cutting down swaths of warriors as if they were insects under their boots. Snow on the mountains cascaded down to the ground in wet, melting torrents. Flames ripped over everything that would catch, and the smell of charred bodies filled the air.

The realms were falling.

CHAPTER SEVENTY-EIGHT

*"This is it. The end has come. The sun is gone but the realm is
on fire. I can see them. I can smell the cooked flesh
and burning forests. They are coming,
and they will not be stopped.*

I'm sorry, Elena."

—*Final Record, Archives of Asgard*

"Can you stand?" I reached out to Loki. His face was paler than I'd ever seen it. He nodded and took my help. I pulled him up slowly, his arm over my shoulder. He reached for the dagger protruding from his chest, and I slapped his hand away. "If you pull that out, you'll bleed to death right here. Hreidulfr, make us a path." The edge of the battlefield wasn't far. We just needed to make it to the woods. I could heal him.

Hreidulfr nodded. Váli leapt down from his back and hobbled forward beside him, biting ankles and tearing flesh as Hreidulfr went blow for blow with the einherjar that stood in our way. A pair of Jotnar looked for a moment as if they might attack but changed their mind when Hreidulfr cut down another of Asgard's warriors.

I held Loki up, shouldering his weight as he hopped forward. We walked as quickly as we could over bodies and through the mud. His breathing was wet, laboured. We didn't get far; his mangled ankle slowed us at every step.

Sleipnir pushed his nose into my arm, then sidled up beside me so that his saddle was next to us.

"Yes, alright. Loki, can you climb up?"

Loki gave a weak nod. I held him stiffly as he hooked his good foot into the stirrup and struggled to swing himself up. But he managed.

"You hold onto him, you hear me?" I forced the reins into Loki's hands. I squeezed his hand. "I'll heal you. I just need you to be strong for a while longer." He tried to speak, but the words were a gargle, a choke. I cursed under my breath. "Go, Sleipnir. We don't have much time."

Sleipnir trotted ahead, careful of his speed. Too fast, and he'd jostle Loki off; Loki was already swaying more than I liked.

"Nearly there!" Hreidulfr yelled before taking a punch to the face. Váli ripped a hole in the shieldmaiden's leg in answer, another body in the path.

The danger was thinning. There were so few einherjar left. We just needed to get somewhere safe, somewhere that I could treat Loki without—

A spear flew through the air and hit Sleipnir in the flank.

Sleipnir's scream ripped through the noise of the battlefield. He stumbled, trying to catch his balance. But he couldn't. He fell to his side, the spear jutting out towards the sky, and Loki crashed to the ground.

I ran to him, sliding into the mud beside him. He'd landed on his side and rolled onto his back. His skin was cool to the touch. Every breath was laboured, his chest expanding and contracting in desperation. There was no time.

"Protect us!" I called over Sleipnir's screams.

Stretching out my hands, I placed them gently on Loki's chest, avoiding the dagger that was lodged there. I drew long breaths in and let them out, focusing on the runes I needed to bring him back from the brink. There was so little energy left. I felt around for some hidden depth to summon for my own. There was something there, deep in the roots. I pulled it up with all the strength I had. A vague warmth ran through my skin, into the tips of my fingers and into Loki's chest. It lasted for a moment and was gone again. I wouldn't get anything else.

Loki coughed. Blood spattered onto his lips. It wasn't enough. If I'd had a reed, poultice, disinfectant...but there was nothing. Everything I'd ever learned, and now the moment I needed it most, I was helpless.

Loki's hand grasped at the back of my neck, pulling me down toward him. His voice was a wet, gurgling rasp. "You need—to go."

"No, I won't leave you." My teeth ground together, fighting back the grief and anger. I touched my forehead to his, my tears dropping onto his cheeks. "I'm not going anywhere."

He coughed again, and I felt the warm spatter of his blood on my cheeks. He choked out the words. "I love you. Go."

I shook my head against his, clutching his hand in mine. Each deep breath brought a rattle in his chest, the bubble of the blood in his lungs. He was right. Without seidr, there was nothing I could do.

"I need you, Loki. Please stay."

He inhaled deeply, trying to find a bit of air, but there was none. He struggled to speak, to tell me something, but there was no breath for words.

I released his hand and pulled my wedding band from my finger, shaking like a leaf. I slipped it onto his smallest finger, the only place it would fit. I could barely speak through the tears. "You take this, and you wait for me. I'll meet you in Helheim, you hear me? I want it back."

Loki nodded, trying desperately to drag the air into his lungs. Each breath was quicker, shorter. He was drowning, and I couldn't save him. It would be slow, and I'd watched him suffer enough for one lifetime.

I took hold of the dagger's hilt. Everything in me screamed not to touch it, begged me to do anything else. He was shaking, his eyes alight with panic, his mouth opening and closing searching for air. With my empty hand, I cupped his cheek and said the only thing left to say.

"I love you too." And I pushed the blade deeper.

He seized. He sputtered, choking, his nails digging into my hands. Then he fell limp, the life gone from his eyes.

I collapsed onto him and screamed into my hands. All I could feel was the shaking of my body, the suffocating pressure pushing in on me. His solid, unmoving body under my hands. There were voices, Hreidulfr and Váli, but I didn't know what they were saying. Someone pulled at my shoulder, trying to bring me to my feet.

"Come on, ma'am. We have to get you out of here."

I pulled away, trying to stay with Loki, but Hreidulfr was stronger. He grabbed me by my arm and hauled me to my feet.

"No!" I reached for my husband, lying there in the mud. "Let me stay! I can't leave!"

Hreidulfr picked me up and threw me over his shoulder. I lashed out, slamming my fists into his back. "Ma'am, where he's gone, you can't help him. I'm not about to leave you to die." He started away from Loki, and my eyes caught on the shine of white and gold metal.

Sleipnir's eyes were open, lying completely still, not two feet from Loki.

It was too much to lose. I collapsed against Hreidulfr's back, sobbing into my hands.

"*We need to leave. We'll need horses.*" Váli's voice was as cold as ice. His father and his brother were dead and his mother a wreck and he was pushing on, because he would have to.

Hreidulfr tapped me on the back with his rough hand. "If I put you down, are you going to run off?"

I shook my head. "No."

He put me down next to Váli and pointed to a group of discarded horses lazing around the edge of what was left of the battle. "I'm getting us two horses and coming back, and Yggdrasil shade me, if you make me chase you, I'll knock you out when I catch you."

"I won't." I sniffed, wiping the wetness from my face. My hand came away sticky and red.

Hreidulfr walked away, treading carefully towards the horses.

Váli was sitting near me, licking his injured paw, as silent as the grave.

"Váli, I'm sorry—"

"*Don't.*"

I didn't.

I turned back, toward the carnage behind us. The fire had spread. Surtr and his sword were heading toward Vanaheim, his heavy footsteps shaking the ground. He dragged the tip of his sword on the ground behind him, lighting everything behind him as he passed.

There was a mass of grey fur lying in the centre of everything. Fenrir's carcass was splayed out over dozens and dozens of other bodies. His bottom jaw had been ripped from his face. A lake of blood was swelling up, swallowing everything that lay around him.

I hadn't even noticed that he'd died.

Those left standing moved from body to body, finishing off any ally of Asgard who might still be alive. Among the dead would be everyone I'd ever known. My brothers. My father. Those who I'd once called friends. Idunn, Freya, Alruna, Frigg. Anyone who could fight or heal or help would've died here today to defend their home, their people.

In the distance, Jormungandr was still wrapped around the mountains of Jotunheim, struggling against Thor. Lightning crackled around them. Thor ran, leaping along Jormungandr's back, toward his head. He brought the hammer down, and a sickening crack echoed. The serpent crashed to the ground and bounced, its weight pulling it back into the water. The destruction pulled the ground away at the edge of the sea, stirring up a wave that splashed back onto the battlefield, sweeping away swaths of bodies. Amid it all, Thor found his way to safe ground. He took a fumbling step forward and another. He hadn't walked ten paces when he stopped short and crumpled to the ground.

Hel rose above the battlefield, her darkness swirling around her. She turned toward Vanaheim on Surtr's heels, and the remnants of her army turned as well. How long would it take them to sweep across all the realms that offered resistance? What would be left when they were done?

The clomp of hooves caught my attention. Hreidulfr held a pair of horses by the reins, leading them back to us. He'd also managed to bring back a torch, torn from a burning bush and wrapped with cloth to keep it alight. "We'd best get going. That flood is heading right this way."

"But to where? There's nowhere to run."

I stared off into the distance, toward Asgard. Yggdrasil still stood in the distance, faintly illuminated by a realm on fire. Its branches hung over the empty city, awaiting an army that would never return. "We go to Yggdrasil."

Hreidulfr gave me the reins of one horse, and we both saddled up as quickly as we could manage. Váli couldn't keep pace with us, so Hreidulfr held him one-armed against his chest in the saddle. Waves licked at our heels as we rode, the sea swallowing up more land behind us, always coming closer but never catching up.

I tried to focus on the movement of the horses, the world around us, but I couldn't. I kept seeing Loki's eyes, the struggle of his breath. Kept feeling the crunch of the tissue under the knife in my hand.

At long last, the gates of Asgard came into view. As they did, the ground began to shake beneath us.

I turned back. Surtr was heading for Asgard, coming to burn it to the ground. I pressed my heels into my horse, challenging Hreidulfr to match my pace. If we didn't arrive before Surtr, our chance at safe passage would be destroyed.

We raced under the gates of the city. There were no lights burning, no one in the streets. In all the time I'd lived there, I'd never seen Asgard so utterly abandoned.

When we finally made it to the base of Yggdrasil, the clearing was empty, Idunn's cabin abandoned, its door wide open. The ground was shaking; Surtr was getting closer. Hreidulfr's horse spooked and threw the boys off. I jumped down to help them up, and my horse bolted as well. It didn't matter, though. The journey was over.

A light caught my eye above us. A leaf, smouldering bright with orange flame. The World Tree was on fire.

I turned at the sound of hooves, a horse bursting into the clearing, a Jotun on its back. White-haired, bloodied, and giant. Skadi.

I turned back to Hreidulfr. "Find the entrance to the tree. Take Váli to safety. Go."

He shook his head. "I can't do that, ma'am, I—"

"Go!" I screamed, and he did. Váli called out in protest, but Hreidulfr held him tight, racing toward the base of the tree.

Skadi stopped and dismounted, taking her time as if it hadn't just run out.

I stood my ground. "Why are you here?"

She grinned, almost feral in the firelight. "A rat will always lead you safely from a sinking ship."

I reached for the daggers on my belt. "So you're running away from a fight? Are you always so loyal?"

She laughed. "As if I ever gave two shits about Asgard. I'm Jotun, little goddess. I care about my own and having vengeance for what was taken from me."

I let a little smirk creep onto my lips. "Perhaps we're not so different in the end."

She pulled her sword from her belt. "You want revenge? Come and take it."

I stretched out my shoulders, letting all the grief and pain come to the surface. Everything I'd pushed down, everything I'd tried not to feel. I pictured the light leaving Narvi's eyes, Skadi's fingers pulling his entrails from him, Loki dying under my hands. When I opened my mouth, I heard Loki's laugh spill out, angry and unhinged. "I think I will."

Skadi charged at me and swung. She was twice as strong and twice as big as me. I'd never beat her in a fair fight. I dove, rolling to the side under her feet. I was close enough to touch her, so I slid my blade into her calf and rolled back out of the way. She shrieked and whipped around to find me no longer underfoot. I stood and waited for her to make a move, blades held out, one glistening with her blood.

"*Hóra!*" She lunged toward me and swung her arm, catching me in the chest. The force of the blow tossed me through the air. I crashed into a tree and crumbled to the ground, my body screaming.

"Is that all?" I wiped my lips, and my hand came away bloody.

She screamed again and brought her sword down from over her head. It lodged into the grass, narrowly missing me as I dove between her legs. The sword refused to come back out as easily as it went in, and I used the time to drive my dagger into her thigh. I pulled down, tearing the muscles in her leg. She fell to one knee, nearly pinning me beneath her. In the time it took me to roll out of the way, she had twisted around and grabbed me by the arm.

Hoisting me up and around, she held me in front of her, hanging by one hand. She couldn't hide her pain or the sweat on her brow, but she clearly thought the battle was finished. All around us, leaves were burning as they fell, curling up and turning to ash on the wind. Somewhere in the distance, a branch cracked and plummeted to the ground.

"Good try," she panted. "But this was never going to end any other way."

I laughed, flashing a grin at her. "You're a monster, Skadi, but you're not that bright." I pulled myself up and drove my dagger into the flesh of her hand. Reflexively, she pulled her hand back, letting me drop to the ground.

The Goddess of Nothing At All

I struggled to stand, the pain of the fall ringing in my knees. Skadi pulled the dagger from her hand and threw it aside. She hauled herself up, and I backed away, letting her come to me. She wore fury like an old mask, eyeing me up, waiting for my move. We were at a stalemate.

"Come now, Sigyn. Wouldn't it be easier to just die like your kid?" Her knuckles were white as she clenched her fists and stretched them again.

A shape moved behind her. I smiled, letting her see my teeth. "It would. But I still have things to do."

Skadi screamed. Váli, against everything I had said, had returned and leapt up onto her back. He drove his teeth into her neck, shaking his head and tearing the meat from her throat. He came away with a mouthful of tattooed white flesh.

Skadi fell to her knees once more, blood gushing down the front of her armour. I strode up to her and kicked her solidly in the stomach. She stammered as she fell back, staring up at the burning carcass of Yggdrasil.

"*We have to go.*" Váli licked his teeth and turned back to Yggdrasil.

"Not yet." I stepped over Skadi, watching the sheer terror in her eyes. I knelt, my face close to hers, the tip of the blade against the leather armour at her stomach. Her eyes protested, but she couldn't speak. I pushed the dagger through the leather and into her stomach, carving her open. Her body lurched.

"It's almost poetic, isn't it?" Recognition passed over her face as I echoed the familiar words back to her. She even whimpered. I dropped the dagger and shoved my fist into her stomach, grasping whatever entrails I could reach and pulled them out. I kept pulling, inch by inch, until her chest stopped rising and falling, until she was finally dead.

I stood still, looking down at the woman who had helped murder my boy and imprison me. I tried to calm my heart, tried to breathe. I wiped my wet hand on my trousers and laughed, nervous and desperate, terrified of myself.

Váli padded up to me, watching me with wary eyes. "*What in the nine... Mother, what the hel was that?*"

I stretched my neck and stepped over the corpse, toward the tree. "It was a long time coming, that's what it was."

A crack sounded from above. The tree was nearly entirely ablaze, and from the shake in the ground, Surtr was here. I'd wasted valuable time, but I wasn't sorry for it.

Váli ran as fast as he could manage with his battered leg, and I followed on his heels. We ran until we saw Hreidulfr standing in the entrance to the tree.

"You scared me half to death! I thought you'd both gone and died on me." He waved us down and pushed me inside.

419

Yggdrasil still smelled like decay, with a new scent of ash and smoke. The flame was working its way down to the base, lines of red visible above us. The pathways to the realms were still open. We could go to Jotunheim if the flood and the fire hadn't reached there as well. Midgard would be a wasteland. Vanaheim was gone. Our options were limited.

"In here." I ran forward, moving quickly down the slope. We had to move fast; falling was the least of our worries.

The root went on forever. The smoke became thicker, invading the air even as far down as we were. Behind me, Hreidulfr was whispering to himself like a prayer. "Yggdrasil protect us, shade us in our moment of need—"

At last, the light appeared at the end. I picked up my speed, afraid that the tunnel would collapse before we could reach safety. I bolted out of the root and into the blinding light.

The sound of the waves washed over me like a balm. My eyes adjusted slowly, and I looked out over the water. The swans were still there, floating lazily near the cliff. Standing above the water were three women, looking down at us as if they'd been waiting.

Hreidulfr shielded his eyes. Váli nuzzled his snout into Hreidulfr's chest to protect his own. "Where are we?"

"Those are the Nornir." I waved to them, and they began their descent from the cliffs. I walked towards them, forcing him to follow.

"By the nine realms," Hreidulfr breathed, his face turning pale. "I think this is about as much as I can handle today."

"Welcome." Skuld reached her hand out to take mine. "We thought you'd come."

EPILOGUE

"Finally, I might be allowed to tell my own story."

—*Sigyn Odindottir*

T he Nornir took us in. They fed us, warmed us, and healed our wounds. We
bathed, and they found us clothing, which I could only assume they'd woven
themselves. And when it was done, they sat with us as we mourned what we
had lost.

Váli kept his distance for days. I'd scared him, I think. And when he eventually did
make the effort, he refused to speak to me about his father. In a moment of confidence,
Hreidulfr told me that Váli didn't blame me. Not quite. But he had watched me push
in the knife.

Give him time, he'd said.

All that was left was time. Time in which I was alone with my thoughts and my
regrets. Everything I had ever done. My son and his love had solace in each other while
I had no one. Each day we spent below Yggdrasil festered in me like an open wound,
because even if Váli didn't blame me, I blamed myself.

We hoped to stay there for only a few days at first. I itched to go back above, to
see what was left. But the root had sealed itself off, full to the bottom with charcoal and
broken pieces of Yggdrasil. None of us knew if there was even a realm above to return
to. When we asked the Nornir, they refused to say. That was their way with most things.
We asked them why the sun still shone under Yggdrasil when it had been destroyed in
Asgard. I asked if Loki had found his way to Hel. We asked for the runes to return Váli to
his true form. It seemed like every answer was beyond their ability to give.

Our days turned into weeks and then months, and then eventually, I lost track of time. It never rained at Urd's Well. We slept in comfort under the stars, in a warm summer that never changed. We caught fish in the sea to compliment what food the Nornir gave us. They fed us all manner of vegetables and fruit, as well as some familiar golden apples, but where it all came from, they refused to say.

There was too much time, too much peace. I worked at my seidr, trying to find some energy left in the ground. It took a long time to find it, for it to replenish. When it did come back, it felt correct. Like a missing piece of me had returned. But I longed for someone to share it with. Someone to sit knee to knee with while I twisted the runes into new shapes that suited the blackness in my heart.

I was watching the water once more, sitting in my comfortable solitude. The swans bobbed in the corner of my vision, almost mesmerizing, but I wasn't really watching them. I was looking inward. I barely heard the footsteps as they approached.

"Would you mind a little company?" Skuld's voice was unmistakable.

I looked up at her and forced a smile. "Of course not. Join me."

She sat down next to me, her bare feet hanging over the edge. "I think you might stay like this for the rest of your days if I let you."

I didn't look at her. "I suppose that's true."

"I can't allow that. It's not your fate to waste away, little goddess. There is more out there. We would see you thrive."

I looked up, watching her face closely. "See me thrive? How can I be anything more than this bitter shell? I'm trapped in this paradise of horrific, endless quiet."

The young woman gave me a sly smile. "You always ask me about the past, Sigyn. What you could've done differently. What would have changed. But that direction gets you nowhere. I can tell you something about your future, though, if you want to know it." She held up a finger as I opened my mouth. "But be warned. Knowing means the end of this 'horrific quiet,' as you call it. There's no going back."

I looked up, watching the waves disappearing into the horizon that travelled to nowhere. Did the water fall off the edge there, as flat as a serving platter? "Tell me."

"If you go above, back through Yggdrasil, the realms are waiting."

I turned to her. "Really? Why didn't you say that before?"

"Because they needed time to return, to grow. It wasn't safe."

"And now it is?"

She bobbed her head, considering. "Safe enough."

"When can I go?"

Skuld smiled. "As soon as you can dig yourself out."

The tunnel was entirely blocked. The charcoal was piled deep, spilling out onto the grass. I summoned up a lantern and threw it inside. I'd managed to dig some of it out, my hands and arms charcoal-dust black. I hadn't even made a dent and some pieces were bigger than I could lift alone.

"*What are you doing?*" I turned to find Váli behind me, sitting on his haunches next to Hreidulfr.

I looked back at the mess in front of me. "I'm getting out."

"Ma'am, we don't even know what's up there. Could be the whole of the realms is under water." Hreidulfr scratched his beard, eyeing the debris.

"Skuld says it's not. I need to know."

He shook his head. "Ma'am, I gotta say—"

"Hreidulfr!" I turned in time to see the fear flash in his eyes. "If you call me ma'am one more time, I'm going to rip your tongue out."

Váli snapped his teeth. "*You don't speak to him like that.*"

I sighed and rubbed my palm across my face, surely leaving smudges. "I'm sorry. I just...I need to get out of here. You understand that, don't you? I can't be trapped for another eternity. There's nothing here for us."

"*Nothing but peace and relaxation?*" Váli gave me a sideways look. "*I can't believe you. We finally have a good life, and you want to drag us back into the mud.*"

"*You* have a good life, Váli. You two have each other. I have nothing but my regrets. I can't stay here knowing that this doesn't have to be the end of my story. That there may be something up there, waiting for me. I don't feel finished. Do you?"

I turned back to the pile and pulled a thick piece of charcoal from the top. I hefted it up and walked past them to throw it onto the grass. "Don't you want to find the runes to reverse what was done to you? Wouldn't you like to be a man again? If there's nothing there, we come back. If there is...we talk about it. Alright?"

The two shared a long look. Finally, Hreidulfr shrugged and moved to pick up a heavier piece of half burned wood. "Seems fair to me."

Váli sighed and fell into line, following us out with a thick branch in his teeth.

We dug for nearly a week. The first day was simple, but overnight, we woke to the sound of the top of the tunnel collapsing downward. We'd been lucky. Every day after, we hauled out wood in shifts. Once we reached three paces in, I cast a gust of wind upward to loosen the wood and send it tumbling down, safeguarding against the inevitability of a cave in.

The work was tiring, but it gave us something to do, something to busy my mind. On the fifth day, I cast a gust of wind upward and the avalanche lasted half the time it normally did. We cleared out another pile, and I cast the wind up again. It brought down a rain of twigs and nothing else. We'd reached the end.

The next morning, we fastened our long-abandoned weapons to our belts and went to the mouth of the root. The Nornir followed.

I turned to them. "We might be back nearly as soon as we've left, but I can't take the risk of not thanking you. You saved us all, and we could never repay you."

Urd waved the compliment away. "Hush, child. Go on up. See what awaits you."

I nodded. "We'll come back to bring word of what's happened and—"

Skuld crossed her arms, a playful smile on her face. "We already know what's happened. It's only for you to find out." She took my hand and turned it upward, placing a long scroll in my palm. It was one of their tapestries. "Open this when you're above."

Urd gave me a smile. "We'll see each other again when we're meant to, yes?"

I nodded. "Yes. Thank you." I gave her hand one last squeeze and turned toward the surface.

The climb up was treacherous. There were still branches and bits of coal along the floor that hadn't fallen. We used the lantern to guide us and stepped slowly, though the anticipation was threatening to kill me. I needed to know.

Of all the things I'd expected, I hadn't expected light. We were near the surface and somehow, the sun was shining through the debris of Yggdrasil.

The mouth of the root was blocked. We pushed, and the large block of charcoal fell to the ground in a puff of black dust. The door to the outside was still open, but Yggdrasil was gone, only fragments of Her trunk still standing. We walked out into the crisp autumn air.

We turned together to look up. The shade of Yggdrasil's branches was gone. Her trunk had been burned away, along with everything else. But there was something new. Wooden tendrils grew out of the ground around what was left of the trunk, circling upward. They bound together in the centre, some heading outward toward the sky. Tiny leaves sprouted from some of the branches, shimmering purple and blue and hanging among them were tiny, golden apples. The beginning of a new world tree.

Whatever had happened during our time below, the world was young again. There was a new sun being pulled across the sky. The forest that once surrounded Yggdrasil was long gone, and thousands of tiny saplings grew in its place. The wall around Asgard was clear as day without the forest to block the view, and it had crumbled to pieces, some sections barely standing at all.

The irony wasn't lost on me.

The boys followed without a word, all of us in awe of what we found. Idunn's home was gone as if it had never been there. We looked up, beyond the saplings, toward the hill where Valhalla stood. Had stood. The great halls of Odin and his sons were nothing but rubble.

We walked through what was left of the streets. Nature had taken much of it back. Only a handful of old homes and shops were still there. I didn't recognize the flowers or herbs that popped up from the ground between the stones. So many new things had learned to thrive there. Did they even have names?

It seemed to be nearly midday when we arrived at the top of the hill. No one said a word as we stepped through the rubble, looking for something that might be meaningful. I left Hreidulfr and Váli to their search and pressed on toward where the garden had once been.

I heard it before I saw it. I slowed my pace, stepping carefully. There was no possible way. A few of Valhalla's walls were still intact, more than enough to hide behind. The closer I walked, the louder the noise became. It was...familiar.

I leaned behind the old doorway to the garden and peeked around the edge. The garden was in ruins, but the grass had been cleared in places, giving proper room to frolic. And that's just what it was being used for.

There were five of them. Three ran around the grass, tossing a disk back and forth for fun. As they turned and ran and jumped, I saw each of their faces. Odin's son Vidar. Thor's sons, Magni and Modi. All of them grown up. They'd survived somehow. Had they been hidden away like us, a preservation of the bloodline for the days after?

At the edge of the grass stood two other familiar faces. Baldur and Hod were as fresh and alive as if they'd never died at all. They spoke quietly between each other, peaceful smiles on their lips.

However it had happened, the joy of seeing Hod wasn't enough to keep my blood from boiling.

A hand touched my shoulder and I jumped. Váli and Hreidulfr had caught up to me. They peered carefully around the corner, and when they'd seen what I had, they backed away. We stepped gingerly, avoiding any noise that might bring the men running. An alcove still stood in what was once Valaskjálf. We stepped in and pressed ourselves against the walls.

"*You knew, didn't you?*" Váli was unimpressed. "*This is why you wanted to come back.*"

I shook my head. "I didn't know, but it changes everything."

"What does it change?" Hreidulfr crossed his arms over his chest, worry etched across his face.

I pointed back toward the garden. "Look around you. The realms have a chance to begin again, to be better than what they were. Do you really think that the sons of Thor and Odin are going to allow that? They'll build Asgard back up in the image of themselves, of the Allfather, and all this will begin again. What are we worth if we allow that to happen?"

"I don't know…" Hreidulfr scratched at his beard, shuffling his feet in discomfort. "We could just walk away. We don't need to go back to war again, always looking over our shoulders. You told Loki that if he'd just walked away, he'd—"

"*Father was right.*"

I looked at Váli, shocked. Everything about those words seemed unnatural coming from his mouth.

Váli hopped up onto a fallen stone, closer to eye level with us, staring at Hreidulfr. "*You and I couldn't even walk together in public before out of fear of being caught. I thought if we just behaved and bided our time, something would change. What they made me do…*" He tripped on his words, tried to compose himself. "*They killed my brother, tortured my parents, and destroyed the siblings I'll never know. I'm starting to wonder if any of us were ever on the right side of things.*"

"What if we could build something better?" I leaned against one of the only solid walls. "What if instead of building the realms around death and war, we start with life? We could challenge the gods and create something fair. Something free."

"*What about that?*" Váli nodded at my hand. "*The Nornir had to have known. What does it say?*"

I'd nearly forgotten. The tapestry was crushed in my fist. Just thinking of opening it stole the breath from me. Maybe I didn't want to know what was inside.

I pulled the ribbon and unrolled it.

Inside was a record of my life, from the bottom upward. Playing as a child, years of learning, a lifetime with Loki and my children. But none of that was what stood out. Above Loki's death, above Ragnarok, above our time with the Nornir, was something that took up the entire rest of the tapestry.

It was a sprawling image of me staring out of the page, clothed in a flowing dress, flame in one hand and glowing light in the other. In the background, a shining city I'd never seen and the shapes of people I didn't know.

And on my head, a crown.

"*What's wrong?*"

I turned the scroll for them to see.

They looked in stunned silence.

426

The Goddess of Nothing At All

"I think that settles it then. Are we agreed?"

Váli nodded, his tail thumping against the stone. We looked to Hreidulfr and waited. He scratched at his beard and hugged his thick arms around himself in silence. When I was sure he might never speak again, he looked up. "I want to believe you. It sounds wonderful. But what can we do about any of this?"

I looked out past the crumbled stone, toward the vibrant, imperfect slate of land that had once been Asgard. We had lost everything except each other, and I knew that no matter what we did here, no matter how much we changed the realms and saved the future, it wouldn't erase the nightmares. That I'd still wake in a cold sweat and feel for a man who wasn't there. Still weep for the child I'd lost. No amount of good deeds would balance the scale. But we would do it anyways.

It wouldn't be easy, but I was ready.

"Hreidulfr, we're going to fix everything."

In Every End There is Also A Beginning.
There is More to This Story.

Book reviews are key to supporting the work of indie authors.
Please consider rating and reviewing The Goddess of Nothing At All.
Your honest reviews help books find their perfect audience.

If you want the latest news about upcoming books by Cat Rector,
join the mailing list at catrector.com

Thank you.

ACKNOWLEDGEMENTS

I never thought I would be typing out a thank-you page. I always said that people like me don't get chances like this. And if it weren't for the people below, I would still believe that.

First and foremost, I need to thank Erin Kinsella. When you think about the mundane events that lead you to your greatest moments, it's easy to believe in fate. When Erin stumbled on my call for beta readers, I had no idea it was going to spark a friendship and collaboration that would last years. This book was an incoherent mess that others had given up on, and if it wasn't for her, you wouldn't be reading it today. She's a beacon of light and support in the online writing community, and I am so very fortunate not only to get to work with her every day, but to call her one of my closest friends.

Long before I was taking writing seriously, Jessica Brown was reading my work. She spent countless hours writing ridiculous fanfiction with me when we were teens, and she was the first person to read this story when it was in its very first draft. Without her enthusiasm, I would've let the story die there. We've been through so much together, more than our share, and without her decades of friendship, I'd be lost.

To my partner Vincent Vanloo, who never once made fun of me for sitting in a corner obsessively reading books about Gods and myths and ancient magic. He listened to countless monologues about horse gestation, cauterization, and poisonous flowers. I even dragged him to a strange pagan festival and after all this, he somehow felt safe sleeping next to me at night. I couldn't have completed this project without his support and the blind acceptance that this was exactly what I needed to be doing.

I owe so much to the dozens of people who beta read my work and championed this story online. There are so many of you, more than I can name, and I am so very grateful for the time and love you've put into this project. Thank you to each of the members of the Discord groups The Write Life and Publishing Pals who were not just supportive, but who went above and beyond to show me kindness. Thank you to Lyra

Wolf and Genevieve Gornichec, who have been so welcoming and kind as I've dipped my toes into the Norse writing space. Thank you as well to the members of the Street Team, all the ARC readers, and to all the people who have been cheering me on for the last few years.

Thank you to my family. To my mother, who always did whatever it took to make sure we were safe and taken care of, and who taught me how to survive, no matter what. To my sister, who never gives up on anyone and has so much love to offer the world. To my father, who inspired me with his love of reading. None of us ever takes the easy road anywhere and it was through you that I learned the value of hard work, kind words, and doing the right thing.

To the reader, thank you. I don't know you, but you're here and I appreciate you being here. This book isn't a kind book, and it's not for everyone. It was born out of hardship and a need to explore what lurks in the shadows. If you're here because you connect to that somehow, because the shadows feel like home, welcome. I hope you've felt seen.

FURTHER READING

If Norse Mythology intrigues you but you're not sure where to go next, please check out some of these titles. There's also plenty of information online or at your local library. Some more expensive or rare texts might be in your local university catalogue.

Source Books:
The Prose Edda
The Poetic Edda
Gesta Danorum
The Sagas of Icelanders - Penguins Classics Deluxe Edition

Research:
The Norse Myths - Carolyne Larrington
Trickster Makes the World - Lewis Hyde
Vaesen - Johan Egerkrans
The Viking Way: Magic and Mind in Late Iron Age Scandinavia - Neil Price
Seidr: Het Noordse Pad - Linda Wormhoudt
Gods and Myths of Northern Europe - H.R. Ellis Davidson

Retellings:
Norse Mythology - Neil Gaiman
Tales of Norse Mythology (Leather Bound Edition) - Helen A. Guerber
Norse Myths: Tales of Odin, Thor and Loki - Kevin Crossley-Holland
Vikings: The Battle at the End of Time - Tony Allan

Fiction:
Please check out the blog on my website, CatRector.com, or my
Goodreads lists for recommendations

CONTRIBUTORS

Edited by Charlie Knight
cknightwrites.com
twitter.com/cknightwrites

Manuscript Critique by Erin Kinsella
erinkinsella.com/manuscript-critiques

Cover Art by Grace Zhu
gracezhuart.com
instagram.com/gracezhuart
twitter.com/gracezhuart

Character Art on Website/Socials by LilithSaur
instagram.com/lilith_saur
twitter.com/lilithsaur

Viking Era Ornaments by Jonas Lau Markussen
jonaslaumarkussen.com/graphics-sets/vikingornaments

Cover Text, Interior Formatting and Design by Cat Rector

GLOSSARY OF TERMS

This glossary is a general guide for readers who are unfamiliar with the terms used in this story, however, many of these terms have nuance and history that can't be expressed in a blurb. I encourage you to go search out your own information, either using the internet or with the reference page I've added.

Aesir: One of the two tribes of Gods, referring to those whose home was Asgard. See the Pantheon Tree for details.

Alfheim: One of the nine realms, home of the elves.

Asgard: One of the nine realms, home of the Aesir Gods, and the main location of our story.

Bifrost: The rainbow bridge that connects Asgard and Midgard.

Einherjar: The chosen warriors of Odin. It was believed that when someone died in battle, they might be chosen to Valhalla, where they would dine in Odin's halls and become a part of his army of Einherjar. They would train every day and their wounds would heal every night, and at Ragnarok, the end of the realms, they would fight against the enemies of Asgard.

Ergi/argr: Old Norse term. In the Viking Age, ergi was used to accuse someone of being unmanly or to insinuate effeminate behaviour. Being unmanly or cowardly was one of the worst things a man could be known for. Insults were taken very seriously in the Viking Age. Calling another man ergi was so insulting that it could result in a holmgang, or duel, in order for the accused to regain his honour.

435

Fathur-morthingr: Father-killer. Invented word, derived from Scandinavian languages for use as part of the Jotun language.

Fólkvangr: The name of the meadow where Freya's hall is built.

Ginnungagap: Before the existence of the realms, Ginnungagap was the void that sat between Musphelheim and Niflhiem. When the two realms drew close together, the fire and ice mixed to create the giant Ymir, whose body was used to create Midgard.

Gladsheim: One of Odin's halls. Used as a meeting hall, it contains thirteen seats for the Gods. In some texts, only the male Gods had seats in this hall, while in others it's nonspecific.

Gótha nótt: Good night. Taken from Icelandic, the closest modern relative to Old Norse, for use as part of the Jotun language.

Grimnir: One of the many names of Odin. Means 'hooded' or 'masked one.'

Hangi: One of the many names of Odin. Means 'hanged one.'

Helheim: One of the nine realms. Home of the dead who aren't placed in Freya's halls at Sessrúmnir or in Odin's halls in Valhalla. Sometimes believed to be the resting place of those who died dishonourable deaths of disease or old age, but this may be a view influenced by the introduction of Christianity.

Jotun: The term for the people of Jotunheim. Some sources refer to them as giants but this is technically false according to many sources. They were more likely just another tribe of people apart from the Aesir and Vanir.

Jotunheim: One of the nine realms. Home of the Jotun.

Midgard: Known to us simply as Earth, the land of humans.

Midsommarblot: A traditional celebration of the sun. Midsummer refers to the middle of summer, and in modern times usually indicates the summer solstice. The word blot can be simplified as 'sacrifice', but more literally it's a request towards the Gods, or a trade. Celebrations included enormous campfires, song, dance, drink and offerings made to the Gods. Is still celebrated in Scandinavian countries and by pagan/heathenistic/wiccan religions.

Musphelheim: One of the nine realms. A mostly uninhabitable land of fire and volcanoes. Home of the fire giant Surt.

Niflheim: One of the nine realms. A realm of ice and snow. Some sources consider Niflheim and Helheim to be the same realm, while others disagree.

Norns, the: Can refer to many female beings who alter fate, but in this story it refers to the three most well known. The fates are seen in many mythologies as three women of different age groups, and in Norse mythology, they are Urd (the past), Skuld (the future), and Verdandi (the present). They have control over the fates of Gods and men, and can be called on when looking for answers, as Odin often did.

Ofnir: One of Odin's many names. Means 'inciter'.

Ragnarok: The final battle prophesied at the end of Norse mythology. A series of events will herald a battle between the Gods and their enemies. At the end of the battle, the realms will fall, ending life as we know it. One version of Ragnarok ends in rebirth, while many skeptics think that this is due to the influence of Christianity and the presence of Jesus during the time of the oldest recorded source.

Seidr: Seiðr. One of the many words used to describe viking age magic. The practitioners believed, among other things, that seidr could be used to alter fate, effect the decisions of others, and bring good fortune. There are many books available on both modern and viking age magic which I highly encourage you to look into.

Sessrúmnir: The hall belonging to Freya.

Sigfodr: Sigfoðr. One of the many names of Odin. Broken down, Sig means victory and foðr means father. While there is no way to confirm and can be chalked up to pure coincidence, this is the only clue from the Eddas as to the possible parentage of Sigyn.

Skít: An Icelandic word meaning 'shit', which has been attributed as Jotun language in this story.

Svartalfheim: One of the nine realms. Translates roughly to 'black elf home' and is the home of the dwarves, which are sometimes called black elves in ancient texts.

Valaskjálf: One of Odin's halls. His high tower is a part of this hall, but not much else is known. For the purposes of this story, it's used to house guests, Gods without halls of their own, or Gods who just need a place to sleep for the night.

Valfodr: One of Odin's many names. Means 'Father of the Slain.'

Valhalla: One of Odin's halls and by far the most known. When someone was killed in battle during the Viking age, Valhalla was one of the places where the fallen dead could go for an afterlife.

Valkyrie: A powerful female warrior with swan wings on her back. She was able to take the shape of a swan and did so in several Germanic tales. They were said to attend battles on earth take the souls of the worthy dead up to Asgard. Their duties also included serving the Einherjar food and drink in Valhalla.

Vanaheim: One of the nine realms. Home of the Vanir.

Vanir: One of two tribes of Gods, referring to those whose home was Vanaheim. See the Pantheon Tree for details.

Völva/ Völur: One of the many names for a practitioner of seidr in the viking age. Usually women, they were said to have ability to see fate, contact the dead, or speak to the Gods, among other things. There are attestations of male völur, but it was less common, in part because it was looked down upon as an unmanly profession. For the purposes of this story, not all facts known about the völur on Midgard are applied to the people of the other nine realms.

Yggdrasil: The World Tree. This massive ash tree connects the nine realms by its roots and is home to a variety of animals. For the purposes of this story, Idunn's golden apples grow on its branches and it has nine roots instead of the three attested to in the Eddas.

Ymir: The giant that was created at the dawn of the realms, and from which all things descend.

ABOUT THE AUTHOR

Cat Rector grew up in a small Nova Scotian town and could often be found simultaneously reading a book and fighting off muskrats while walking home from school. She devours stories in all their forms, loves messy, morally grey characters, and writes about the horrors that we inflict on each other. Currently, she lives in Belgium with her spouse. When she's not writing, you can find her playing video games, spending time with loved ones, or staring at her To Be Read pile like it's going to read itself.

The Goddess of Nothing At All is her debut novel.

Find her on Twitter and Instagram at Cat_Rector
Or visit her website, CatRector.com

Lightning Source UK Ltd.
Milton Keynes UK
UKHW010930111121
393791UK00001B/170